Elusive Shadows

by

Tarn Young

Book Two of a Trilogy

Grosvenor House
Publishing Limited

All rights reserved
Copyright © Tarn Young, 2013

The right of Tarn Young to be identified as the author of this
work has been asserted by him in accordance with Section 78
of the Copyright, Designs and Patents Act 1988

The book cover picture is copyright to Tarn Young

This book is published by
Grosvenor House Publishing Ltd
28-30 High Street, Guildford, Surrey, GU1 3EL.
www.grosvenorhousepublishing.co.uk

This book is sold subject to the conditions that it shall not, by way of
trade or otherwise, be lent, resold, hired out or otherwise circulated
without the author's or publisher's prior consent in any form of binding or
cover other than that in which it is published and
without a similar condition including this condition being imposed
on the subsequent purchaser.

A CIP record for this book
is available from the British Library

ISBN 978-1-78148-665-8

*This book is dedicated to my mum, Joyce
With much love*

Personal Acknowledgements

My husband, Alan, whose editing skills,
patience, encouragement and nautical knowledge,
proved invaluable

My 'guinea pig' readers for their enthusiasm and support:
Mum, Joyce Hill, daughter, Joanne Lee,
daughter-in-law, Cathryn Young

My son, Stephen, brother Garry and nephew, Christopher Hill for
suggestions and help in the production of the book cover

My love and grateful thanks to you all

Acknowledgements

*'Google' search engine, a huge time-saver! For the
extensive research required to give this book
authenticity and credibility.
'Google' - Translate
Main web sites: Nottingham History – nottshistory.org.uk.
Wikipedia – enwikipedia.org.uk.
The Ships List – theshipslist.com.
gregormacgregor.com.
Encyclopedia Britannica – britannica.com
Victorian London – victorianlondon.org.
Middleton Guardian – menmedia.co.uk/middletonguardian.
Salford Hundred – Ancstros,
annals and history BBC –
bbc.co.uk. Jstor –
archives on line parish clerks
- lan-opc.org.uk'A
English Victorian Society - kspot.org/holmes/kelsey.htm
'Who discovered it?' - discovery.yukozimo.com/
who-discovered-polio*

Books
'The Writer's Guide to Everyday Life in Regency and
Victorian England from 1811-1901', Author - Kristine Hughes
'Nottingham - As it is Spoke' - Volume Four, Author - John Beeton
'Nicholls's Seamanship and Nautical Knowledge'
– Brown, Son & Ferguson, Ltd. Glasgow
'Everybody's Pocket Companion' (reference book)
A Mercer, M.R.S.C.
'Great Classic Sailing Ships' – Kenneth Giggal
(paintings by Cornelis de Vries)
'The Encyclopedia of Ships' – General Editor, Tony Gibbons

Author's Notes

The novel's time frame of 1855 (February to December) coincides with the 'Second Industrial Revolution' in the transition years between 1840 and 1870. Technological and economic progress gained increasing momentum, with the adoption of steam-powered boats, ships and railways, the large scale manufacture of machine tools and the use of steam powered factories. 'The Crimean War' (October 1853 – February 1856) was a conflict between the Russian Empire and an alliance of the French, British and Ottoman Empire and the Kingdom of Sardinia.

Information with respect to dates, times, specifications and descriptions are accurate. Actual historical events affect the lives of some of the fictional characters, both rich and poor, e.g. sinking of the 'William Brown' off Newfoundland; *'The Lightning'*, making its first voyage to Australia in just 77 days and returning in a record 64 days, a record still unbroken by a sailing ship and The Riots in Philadelphia - August 6th 1855. Riots broke out in the city, spawned out of an intense rivalry between the Democrats and the Know-Nothing party.

Letters were the prime method of communication (Penny Post 1840 - telegrams for more urgent messages). Train travel was still in its infancy, with only a few miles of track in use. Land and sea travel still relied on the astute use of a humble compass.

In some chapters, the dialogue has been conducted in the local Nottingham dialect. This is synonymous to an area named 'Narrow Marsh', where everyday living was a struggle for the unfortunate, but remarkably stoical and optimistic inhabitants. The dialogue has been spelt phonetically, to assist the reader.

Footnotes have been inserted to inform the readers of some interesting facts with respect to the period, including modernistic sounding words actually used during this time.

My fervent hope is that the reader will once again engage with the characters and events in the second book of the trilogy and let their imagination extend their enjoyment of a fascinating period of British History.

BOOK ONE, 'Silent Torment' is set in the mid-nineteenth century and follows the physical and psychological journey, of Lizzie Cameron, daughter of crofters Agnes and William Cameron in the Highlands of Scotland. The untimely death of Agnes in childbirth leaves William distraught. He shuns his newborn son, Robert and gives him away to his friends, Martha and Donald Stewart, to be brought up as their own child. Years later they are reunited.

William and Lizzie seek work in Glasgow. Their possessions are few, but include Lizzie's 'keeper' box, a present from her father. Josiah Monks, a local priest, accommodates and secures employment for them.

Lizzie becomes housemaid at Low Wood Hall and befriends Kate, extrovert daughter of the owners. Kate becomes pregnant and draws the reluctant Lizzie into a scheme to keep her baby, along with Aunt Jayne, Kate's co-conspirator.

Lizzie leaves with Kate's baby, without word to anyone, including her brother, Robert and first love, Daniel Lorimer. She boards a steamship to Liverpool. A brief encounter, with Marcus Van Der Duim, ends in a proposal and a promise to meet again, after Lizzie fulfils her pact with Kate.

Lizzie's plans go awry when she misses a Royal Mail Coach. Jack Garrett, an independent coachman, changes her route and, subsequently, her life. She arrives in Nottingham en-route to London and visits the Goose Fair, where stallholders, befriend her. In Nottingham she is knocked over by a runaway horse in thick fog and loses her memory. Narrow Marsh locals chance upon an unconscious Lizzie and the baby and take them in.

Lizzie assumes the name of Hannah Merchant and rears Rosalie as her own, but her memory remains locked away.

Jack Garrett, the coachman, leaves without Lizzie, but takes Molly his lover instead. The coach overturns and Jack is killed. Lizzie's luggage, including the 'keeper' box, containing important documents, are recovered by Molly, who survives, but Lizzie has the key. The box's secret will remain locked away for five years.

Meanwhile, Kate receives word that Lizzie has failed to reach her destination. This sparks a series of dramatic events at Low Wood Hall.

In Nottingham, Lizzie touches the lives of everyone whilst experiencing the trials and tribulations associated with the local community. Five years later, after a chance meeting with Daniel Lorimer, her memory partially returns and the 'keeper box' resurfaces. This leads to a number of startling revelations and the final piece of the jigsaw falling dramatically into place.

'...A thing of beauty is a joy forever:
Its loveliness increases...'
Endymion (1818)
JOHN KEATS, (1795-1821)

...'Two of these people would meet untimely deaths, but the re-acquaintance of the other two would bring *untold joy*...'

Prologue

The year is 1855 - Lizzie Cameron is thirty-five and Rosalie, thirteen. Lizzie and Marcus Van Der Duim live together in Littleborough, Lancashire. They have not been blessed with children, although Lizzie sees Rosalie as her own daughter. Marcus's first wife, Belle, his son, Jack and his ex-best friend, Andries, are missing, presumed dead, after their ship, 'The William Brown'[1] sank off Newfoundland.

Robert Cameron has discovered he is the father of Rosalie and is now actively seeking Kate Hemingway, Rosalie's birth mother. Lizzie's own emotional search for Kate, lies uneasily on her conscience. Their potential meeting could irrevocably change her own relationship with Rosalie, an integral element of the plot.

---

1 Under the command of Captain George Harris, the ship departed from Liverpool on March 18, 1841 for Philadelphia. At about 10 p.m. on the night of April 19, the *William Brown* struck an iceberg 250 miles (400 km) southeast of Cape Race, Newfoundland and sank, in similar circumstances to the 'Titanic' some 70 years later on April 14, 1912.

Chapter One

Anxious Times
February/March 1855

By 1855 most passenger ships on the New York/Liverpool route were commandeered for the Crimean war effort, with few available for the Atlantic run.

On a cold crisp February morning of that year, a passenger ship, the 'New World', docks at the port of Liverpool. Three seemingly unremarkable passengers disembark, before joining the paddle steamer, the 'Princess Royal', for their onward journey to Glasgow. Another traveller strides purposefully towards the ticket office, intent on booking a cabin for the return sailing to New York. They cross paths, totally oblivious of the others' existence, like elusive shadows manifested in the weak rays of a watery winter sun. Two will meet untimely deaths, but the re-acquaintance of the other two will bring untold joy.

༺◊༻

A week earlier, Lizzie Cameron and Marcus Van Der Duim, blissfully unaware of the events that lay ahead, breakfasted in the dining room of their home in Littleborough, Lancashire.

Marcus was reading a letter from his father. It conveyed the startling revelation that his first wife, Belle and son,

Jack, may have survived the sinking of the 'William Brown' in April 1841. His furrowed brow clearly betrayed his total astonishment. 'Elizabeth, this really is extraordinary news. My father has word from a business associate in Philadelphia that Belle and Jack may not have perished after all. They may be living in Philadelphia apparently.'

Lizzie smiled encouragingly as the news seemed extremely promising. 'Marcus, that's absolutely wonderful. What does your father say exactly?'

Marcus scanned the three-page letter and focussed on the all-important paragraph. 'He says his business associate visited a gentlemen's club a month ago and spoke to a new member who was discussing the tragedy of the 'William Brown'. It transpired that a friend of the new member was the skipper on the fishing boat that picked up survivors, before ferrying them to the port of Philadelphia. Father says he cannot be certain that Belle and Jack were among the several women and children rescued, but there is a definite possibility.'

Lizzie begged Marcus to continue. 'Does he say where they are now?'

Marcus frowned as he read the remaining content eagerly. 'No...no, he says that the survivors were taken to the Philadelphia General Hospital. Apparently, some died from the effects of exposure, but some survived and made new lives for themselves in America.'

Lizzie, inspired by the letter's content, spoke from her heart. 'Marcus, this could lead to you being reunited with your son. You have to go and find him, although Rosie and I will miss you terribly.'

Marcus's previous excitement abated as a frown creased his troubled brow and his eyes momentarily lost their sparkle. 'They could be anywhere Elizabeth, Philadelphia is a very big place, I wouldn't know where to start and, in addition, I would have to ensure the factory manager would be happy to take full control of the business while I am away.'

Lizzie, however, would not allow his concerns to prevent him leaving. 'Listen Marcus, Matthew Hargreaves is perfectly able to look after the business for a few months and there is every chance you will find them. Contact the friend of your father's and see if you can track down the fisherman who picked up the survivors. Do you think you would recognise Jack again. He will be sixteen now?'

Marcus's eyes crinkled at the corners and a smile played around his lips. *She is the most unselfish person I know.* 'Oh Elizabeth, I feel sure I would recognise him, as he is the absolute image of his mother. You always give hope to everyone and are such an inspiration, but I cannot leave you and Rosie and sail halfway across the world. It might be several months before I can return. How will you manage alone?'

Lizzie raised her eyebrows and looked intently at Marcus. 'I will manage, because I've coped with so much more, but know that I love you and will miss you very much. We thought we would never be parted again, but this quest is important Marcus...it is probably your one and only chance to find your son. This news gives hope of their survival...You cannot miss this opportunity and we will make this sacrifice if it means you will see your son again.'

Marcus held Lizzie's hand and looked deep into her eyes. 'Elizabeth Cameron, how would I manage without you?'

Lizzie lowered her eyes, then looked up and with a meaningful smile said. 'And you I Marcus, but you have to go.'

Marcus conceded reluctantly, before adding a suggestion of his own. 'Elizabeth, do think seriously about making that visit to Glasgow in my absence. I know how important you feel it is to find Rosie's birth mother and time will pass more quickly if you do.'

Lizzie sparkled in anticipation. 'I think I will Marcus and I might ask Robert to accompany me. The private detective we employed isn't any nearer to finding Kate. I worry that she is also engaged on a frantic search, although our paths haven't crossed. It is important that Rosie meets her birth mother, even if we lose her and I know it is the right thing to do. Anyway, when you arrive safely in Philadelphia, please write to me as often as you can. I will look forward to hearing that you have found them both alive and well.'

Their conversation was interrupted when Rosie sauntered into the dining room in her dressing gown. She still dragged her battered teddy bear along the floor behind her, even at thirteen.

Lizzie stifled a laugh as she observed the unfortunate treatment metered out to her much-loved bear. 'Good morning Rosie, come and have some breakfast. I'll get cook to make you boiled egg and soldiers if you like?'

Rosie's persuasive and mischievous smile appeared, as she contemplated her next request. 'That'ull be nice mam. Can I have a chocolate muffin as well?'

Lizzie and Marcus exchanged subtle glances. They never failed to be amazed at the amount and variety of foods Rosie enjoyed at breakfast.

'Well, see how you go with the boiled egg, then maybe you can have a muffin,' Lizzie proffered.

Rosie appeared completely satisfied that once again her mother had given in to her persuasive demands. 'Ok[2] mam,

---

2 The term 'ok' was first used figuratively in the mid nineteenth century, finding its way into British writing in the form 'okay' in the 1860s.

I'll just put the muffin here at the side of my plate in case I finish my egg.'

Lizzie sighed inwardly in the realisation that Rosie was indeed very much like her birth mother.

※

On that cold mid-February morning, Lizzie, Rosie and Marcus jostled amid the throngs of passengers embarking on the s.s. 'New World' for New York. Trunks, valises and other items of portmanteaux were already piled high on the dock awaiting stowage. The quayside bustled with excited travellers, while others were already aboard. Some were delaying their departure as long as possible, in an attempt to prolong their goodbyes with loved ones. Purveyors manoeuvred to gain the best site to pitch their wares from the many cane baskets brimming over with fish, flowers, and handicrafts. Potential customers bargained with sellers to procure a meaningful parting gift.

Lizzie stood close to Marcus, quietly contemplating the inevitability of their parting. The emptiness she would undoubtedly feel when the ship sailed, taking him to a destination far away. She had coped, until now, but the reality of the situation was overwhelming her.

Rosie's thoughts, on the other hand, were concentrated on the sheer size of the ship. She marvelled at the grandeur of the occasion. Elegant ladies with large hats, embellished with fur to keep out the chill, chatted amiably with friends and families. Women passengers wore warm winter coats with bustles and skirts that skimmed the ground. Rosie wished she was a passenger waiting to board...Perhaps one day she would sail off to some far away land with Jimmy. However, she did have difficulty picturing him wearing such magnificent attire. Would he ever aspire to any lofty principles of sartorial elegance, like Marcus, who justifiably blended perfectly with many other well-dressed gentlemen wearing top hats, woollen overcoats and fine merino scarves? Her train of thought was interrupted by Marcus as he bent to kiss her cheek. 'Now Rosie, look after your mother and try not to get into too many scrapes while I am away. I will miss you terribly, but in no time at all, you will be standing here waiting for me when the ship docks on its return.'

Rosie frowned, realising that Marcus had become a really important person in her life. He was always there when she needed to confide in someone other than her parents. His advice was always sound and, occasionally, he covered for her misdemeanours, much to Lizzie's obvious chagrin. Now he was going away for quite a long time. She would miss him. 'Yes Marcus...I will look after mam. I will miss you too, so hurry up and find your family, then come home as soon as possible.'

Her sincerity struck a chord with Marcus, who, until now, had not realised just how important his role was to Rosie. 'I will do my very best to find them. My son is very important to me, but so are you and your mam and I will think about you often.' Marcus's eyes misted imperceptibly, but he put on a brave smile before turning his attention to Lizzie. He encircled her in his arms and pulled her close. 'Well my darling, it is time for me to leave. I hope I won't be away for too long. I will write often. Please keep safe and know that I love you Elizabeth.' He kissed her softly on the lips before reluctantly releasing his hold.

Lizzie gazed into his eyes and for a moment, they existed only for each other. 'I love you too Marcus and I will be waiting here on your return. Have a safe journey and come back safe and well. Good luck and give my best wishes to your father.'

Marcus hugged them briefly once more, before boarding the ship.

To Lizzie, the quayside suddenly seemed very bleak and hostile. She would need to summon all her strength to keep smiling as Marcus waved goodbye.

The flower sellers had dispersed and the purveyors of other goods were packing their unsold wares on to carts before heading off to the markets. Relations and friends on the quay were scanning the passengers leaning on the guardrail of the ship, who in turn were waving scarves and handkerchiefs to loved ones left behind. *Where is Marcus?* she thought, as a sea of unfamiliar faces clouded her vision, when Rosie abruptly tugged at her sleeve. 'There's Marcus mam...he's standing by the couple holding a young child near the front of the ship.'

Lizzie focused. 'Oh yes...yes,' she exclaimed, excitedly waving her handkerchief at the distinctive figure. 'I will miss him so much Rosie, but we must keep smiling. He doesn't want us to be sad.'

Rosie put on a brave face. 'Ok mam, but I do realise just how much I will miss him too.'

The ropes were released from the bollards and hauled aboard, before the ship manoeuvred slowly and surely away from the quay. They watched it pass the breakwater into the open sea, continuing their vigil, until she eventually disappeared over the horizon, both wishing silently for Marcus's safe and early return.

⁂

Lizzie corresponded regularly with various friends and relatives and wrote once a month to her cousin, Morag. Her husband, Angus, fished for cod from Berriedale on the east coast of Caithness.

Rather disturbingly, she had not heard from her old friend and cook at Low Wood, Clara Meredith, for over a year. It was Clara who had informed Lizzie of Georgina Hemingway's untimely death, following an accident when she fell down stairs. This incident apparently triggered the family's move away from Low Wood, although the servants were kept in the dark and no one had an inkling where they went. The sale of the property was finalised very speedily and all the staff, except Dottie the maid, Clara and her husband, George were found alternative employment.

The couple were unable to get over the death of their mistress and reluctantly accepted a sum of money from Howard Hemingway for their years of devoted service. They were also allowed to stay rent free in a small cottage owned by the Hemingway's just outside Glasgow. However, all communication was via a third party and even they were not privy to the actual whereabouts of the family. When George died, a sad Clara remained at the cottage and continued to correspond with Lizzie.

Clara Milligan, Lizzie's adoptive mother in Nottingham, was her favourite correspondent. She'd received a letter from her only a few days ago, when she relayed the news of the death of the local street woman, Aggie Fisher. Aggie had succumbed to the cholera. Apparently, the outbreak was beginning to gain momentum and it was feared it might turn out to be another epidemic.

Clara was helping Aggie with food and brought water from the standpipe in the street, to which she added small amounts of baking soda. Some said it was the best way to beat the disease. Unfortunately, when Clara sought Aggie out a day after she appeared to rally, she found her lying dead in the street, predictably with a bottle of gin by her side. Apparently, the alcohol contributed to her dehydrated state and subsequent death.

Lizzie's eyebrows arched when she received another letter that morning bearing a Nottingham postmark. The handwriting on the envelope was obviously not Clara's, it was well written and the envelope exuded quality.

She scanned the single sheet of paper and was surprised and delighted to recognise the elegant signature of Rachael Phillips, who had employed her as a tutor in Nottingham.

However, she grimaced as she read the content; Clara had become ill, following her close association with Aggie Fisher.

Tillie, Clara's eldest daughter, was housekeeper to Mrs Sarah Askew, a friend of Rachael Phillips. Tillie told Sarah that her mother was ill, even though she was under strict instructions from Clara that news of her illness should not reach Lizzie. So, when Sarah told Rachael, the 'cat was out of the bag', which resulted in the hastily written letter that Lizzie now let slip to the floor.

Lizzie rang the bell for her housemaid, Elspeth but left the library immediately, not waiting for her to appear. She ran up the stairs to her bedroom and pulled out a case into which she flung several items of clothing. Panic set in...*what if she has cholera?...what if she is seriously ill and I don't make it down there in time?*

On hearing the bell, Elspeth hurried to the now empty library. She noticed the letter lying on the floor and spontaneously read the content. Sighing to herself, she climbed the stairs to her mistress's room, where Lizzie was in a state of high anxiety, with tears in her eyes.

'Elspeth, Clara is ill. I am not sure how bad she is, but I have to go to Nottingham immediately.'

This news came exactly a week after she said goodbye to Marcus, when the 'New World' sailed for New York.

Elspeth took charge. 'Why don't I finish this ma'am and you can go over to your brother's to make arrangements for Rosie to stay with them while you are away?'

Lizzie viewed her maid's suggestion with alarm. 'Oh no Elspeth...if Rosie knew I was going to Nottingham, she would want to come with me...Perhaps it would be possible, if Robert agrees; but, this is cholera...so I am not sure he will allow it, although Rachael Phillips would be happy for Rosie to stay with her. That may persuade Robert that it will be safe for her to go.

※

Robert was indeed sceptical about Lizzie's proposed visit. He pursed his lips and frowned as he listened to her proposal.

'...so you see Robert, Rosie will be well looked after, staying with Rachael. The Phillips' have a large property, some distance from the Marsh and Rosie will enjoy the company of Laura, Rachel's daughter, who is of a similar age. You know I would never put Rosie in danger. Please give me your consent Robert.'

Robert capitulated. She could always persuade him to agree to most things and he knew that what she said was true - *she would never put Rosie at risk*. 'All right, Lizzie, I will agree, but promise me you will take all necessary precautions. If Clara does have cholera, there's nothing to say you would not catch it yourself.'

Lizzie smiled gratefully at her brother whom she loved dearly. 'Thank you Robert and don't worry, I will be very careful, I promise.'

Robert wagged his finger. 'Well...make sure you do. Now when do you expect to travel?'

Lizzie kissed Robert lightly on the cheek. 'Why immediately, of course! just as soon as I can arrange a cab[3] to take me to the coach station.'

Robert shook his head, but understood his sister's urgency on this occasion. He went to inform Rosie in the garden room, where she and Harriett had been amusing themselves with the box of dressing up clothes. Rosie appeared at the door bedecked with a cardboard crown decorated with coloured stones, worn at a jaunty angle. Harriett's mother's red-heeled shoes and an old cloak completed the ensemble, which trailed along the floor. Harriett walked behind her in procession, obviously playing a menial role.

Robert grinned, he knew exactly who she was pretending to be, so he put on his serious face. 'The Queen of England, is it? Well, your majesty, your coach will be leaving shortly, so if you could disrobe and dismiss your lady in waiting, you will need to get a move on, as you are off to Nottingham.'

Rosie didn't need a second invitation, but tripped over in an attempt to rid herself of her 'glorious' robe, then Lizzie appeared in the doorway, obviously disturbed. 'Is it true mam? Are we going to Nottingham?'

Lizzie's eyes misted with sadness. 'Yes, it's true Rosie, but, unfortunately, it isn't in the best of circumstances. Grandma Clara isn't well. She is in bed and I need to go and look after her for a while.'

Rosie's smiling face collapsed into a frown. 'Is she very ill mam? Are we going to stay with her until she is well again?'

Lizzie played down the possible severity of Clara's illness. 'She isn't too well Rosie, but she will be all right once she has

---

3 The hansom cab was a kind of horse-drawn carriage designed and patented in 1834 by Joseph Hansom, an architect from York. The vehicle was developed and tested by Hansom in Hinckley, Leicestershire, England.

the right medicine. I will stay with her, but I am arranging for you to stay with Mrs Phillips. Are you all right with that?'

'Mrs Phillips? On St James Street?' A disappointed Rosie appealed to her mother. 'Oh, I thought I would be staying with you and grandma, then I could go and visit Jimmy.'

Lizzie sensed her daughter's keenness to visit her best friend. Since their move to Littleborough, Rosie had stayed with Clara on several occasions, so that she could meet up with Jimmy. In turn, he had been up to Littleborough a few times. Their relationship was still strong and Lizzie knew she would not be able to prevent Rosie seeing Jimmy, at least once while they were in Nottingham. However, Robert was not too keen and emphasized his wish for her to stay away from the Marsh. 'Rosie, I have only agreed for you to accompany your mother to Nottingham provided you stay with Mrs Phillips. If you cannot agree to that, then I am afraid you must stay here until your mother returns.'

Rosie looked from one to the other, but could see that the battle was lost before it began. 'Ok, daddy, I agree,' she said with her fingers crossed behind her back.

Robert ruffled his daughter's hair fondly and it wasn't long before Lizzie and Rosie embarked on the hastily summoned coach for their journey to Nottingham.

❦

When they arrived, Lizzie went straight to Rachael Phillips' home in St James Street, where her former employer gave them a warm welcome. Within the hour, Lizzie reached number fourteen Knotted Alley. She gave a gentle knock on the door.

Arthur Milligan feigned surprise at seeing Lizzie on the front step holding a suitcase. He hoped that the hints made to Tillie had not fallen on deaf ears. Luckily, his prayers had been answered and his well-intentioned bluff had succeeded. 'Well, me duck, I suppose yer must 'ave heard abaht our Clara and am really pleased ter see yer. Come in, come on in. 'Ave bin telling 'er wi should let yer know, but she wun't 'ear on it...said yer shun't be bothered, as she'd be on 'er feet in no time.' Arthur sighed, his pinched cheeks showed his anxiety. 'But she in't on 'er feet Lizzie and am aht of me mind wi worry. Mabel and Sam's gel caught it last week, but she's on the road ta recovery, thank the Lord. Our Clara's a different matter though, she's tired Lizzie and she's losing the will yer see.'

Lizzie put on a brave face and placed her hand on Arthur's arm. 'Well, I'm here now and I'll be getting the doctor to have a look at her. I'll stay with her Arthur, while you go round to Dr Robertson and ask him to make an urgent visit. If you tell him Mrs Van Der Duim will take care of the bill, he will come after his regular surgery finishes.'

Arthur's face was contorted with worry and a deep frown creased his forehead. His eyes were red and sore. It was indeed an effort looking after Clara whilst continuing with his shifts. 'I am ever ser grateful ter yer Lizzie. A knew if yer fount aht she were ill, yu'd be straight dahn, but as a said, she wun't hear on it.' He paused before asking the question he was certain he already knew the answer to. 'Who did let yer know anyrode?'

'Well Arthur, it was Rachael Phillips...and I am very glad she did. I know exactly what Clara is like, never one to make a fuss about her own problems, but I understand your position Arthur,' said Lizzie.

Arthur shamefaced, avoided direct eye contact, as he explained the truth of the matter. 'Am glad yer understand Lizzie. A did mi best ter let yer know through ah Tillie. A knew she would tell Mrs Askew and a just 'oped it 'ud get passed on ter the right person and luckily it did. Am not much fer writing letters Lizzie, as yer know.'

Lizzie felt sad for Arthur, finding himself between a rock and a hard place. She knew he had difficulty writing, due to his lack of an education. Clara was always the one to put pen to paper and ever anxious to show off the skills she had acquired, in which Lizzie had been instrumental. He stood there feeling hopelessly inadequate, before Lizzie placed her hand on his arm and tried to lift his spirits. 'The thing is Arthur, I *am* here now, so you must try not to worry anymore.'

Arthur nodded. 'Aye, yer right o' course Lizzie. Da yer want ter ga up and see 'er now? Despite her protests, she'll be pleased as 'Punch' ter see yer smiling face.'

'All right Arthur, you get off and I'll find my own way. Don't forget to impress on Dr Robertson the importance of his visit. See you later.'

'Tarrar me duck, I'll see yer.' Arthur's shoulders slumped and he retreated, closing the kitchen door behind him.

Lizzie crept quietly up the stairs, but could not avoid the creaks, which always occurred on the three middle steps, where the boards were well worn. The bedroom door had been left ajar and Lizzie poked her head through the gap to make sure Clara was awake. She was shocked to see how much weight Clara had lost and how weak and drawn she looked.

Clara's eyes moved to see who was standing in the shadows of the doorway, but her head remained motionless on the pillow. In her half asleep condition, she imagined she saw Lizzie, but closed her eyes as the impossible thought quickly vanished.

Lizzie crept silently to the bed and took hold of Clara's clammy hand, putting it to her lips. Once more Clara opened her eyes, delighted it was really Lizzie before managing a weak smile. 'It is yo Lizzie,' she paused, 'a toad him not ter fetch yer. Yer've got yer own family ter look after, never mind coming all this way ter see me.' Despite her annoyance, Clara's cheeks glowed through her pallor and her eyes brightened at the pleasure she felt in the presence of the woman she looked on as her own. 'Mind yo, yer a sight fer sore eyes, a can tell yer.'

Lizzie smiled at her friend, hiding her own thoughts, as she gently admonished her. 'I am cross Clara, that you didn't see the need for me to be here with you, to nurse you and help you get well again. You are like a second mother to me and if I can't be at your side when you need me most, it's a poor thing,' she paused as she looked around the room. 'Is there anything I can get you right now, before the doctor arrives? I have sent Arthur to fetch him.'

Clara was aghast. 'Oh, my Lord, a don't need a quack looking at me. A toad Arthur, if a cun just keep restin, I'll be back on me feet before 'e knows it.'

Lizzie frowned in determination. 'Well whether that's the case or not, I want the doctor to look you over and I need to know what is to be done to make you well again, so he *will* be coming and the best thing you can do is to stop worrying. Leave everything to those who are best able to help you right now. I've brought a warm bed jacket to put around your shoulders, but for now, try to get some sleep and I'll see what needs doing downstairs. I know how fussy you are when visitors are expected.'

Lizzie kissed Clara lightly on the cheek. Her eyes were already drooping, but now there was a faint smile on her lips. Lizzie observed her friend once more, before quietly closing the door behind her.

In the hour before the doctor arrived, Lizzie cleaned up the scullery and living room. Arthur's vain attempts at keeping abreast of the household chores, maintaining a job and looking after Clara hadn't been too successful.

Dr Robertson arrived and acknowledged Lizzie, before alighting the stairs to examine his patient. Twenty minutes passed before he returned to the living room with his verdict. Lizzie and Arthur watched expectantly as he opened his bag and took out two small bottles of medicine and a note for Lizzie to obtain some powders from the chemist.

He placed both his hands on the table and addressed the worried pair. 'Well now...I have examined Mrs Milligan thoroughly and whoever has been looking after her so far has done a good job under the circumstances. What we need now is a concerted effort to rehydrate her. Plenty of clean, boiled water with a few drops of Indian Brandee[4], as often as she will take it. Mrs Van Der Duim I need you to obtain some glucose salt packets from the Apothecary, which you can mix with plain boiled water. It is most important that you follow a strict hygiene rule and it would be prudent for only one person to enter the room, to cut down the risk of contamination. I would also recommend that a bowl of clean water, with a small amount of chlorine, be kept outside the door. Use this to cleanse your hands and make sure you wipe them dry on a clean cloth. Now, if I can avail myself of the washing facilities, I will take my leave, but I will call again in two days to see if the patient is improving.'

---

4 Indian Brandee is a herbal remedy for digestive disorders.

Lizzie and Arthur spoke in unison. 'Thank you doctor, we are very grateful.'

Lizzie needed to speak to the doctor alone and quickly followed him into the street. She approached him tentatively. 'Does this mean that she will get better doctor?'

The doctor appeared sombre, which made her tremble inside. 'Well now...Mrs Van Der Duim...Mrs Milligan is not out of the woods by any means, but there is hope that she will recover if she is lucky. You must realise that she is not a young woman and she will need round the clock nursing. If you are prepared for that, then there is a good chance. The next twenty-four hours will be critical.'

Lizzie affirmed her determination. 'Clara is very important to us, so I will be taking very great care of her. Thank you again. Please let me have your bill, which I will settle immediately.'

Lizzie observed the familiar terrace before returning inside, hoping fervently that Clara would be pushing her milk cart around Narrow Marsh again very soon.

The following day, Rosie was to be found in the playroom with Laura, who was almost six months older but more interested in dolls than climbing trees. Rosie was bored with feeding, washing and changing the doll that Laura had given to her, so informed her that her mother had given her permission to visit her friend Jimmy in the Marsh.

Rosie checked with Nanny Augusta, in charge for the day, before leaving. Rachael Phillips was visiting her elder married daughters who lived in The Park, a short distance away. Nanny Augusta, a happy go lucky woman, had looked after the girls since they were babies. Unfortunately, Rosie's ability to tell fibs completely overwhelmed the poor woman.

Rosie was at her most persuasive. 'Nanny Augusta, you know my mam is down at grandma Clara's who isn't well? She said while she was there, I could go over to see my friend Jimmy and call in to see her later. Is that all right?' Rosie expected a refusal, but considered her scheming and plausible subterfuge would seal the deal.

Nanny Augusta, however, was uncertain about Rosie's request and so replied. 'Are you sure your mother is happy for you to go there Rosie? I understand that Clara Milligan is quite ill and I wouldn't have thought it was a good idea?'

Rosie reflected on her position and considered her next approach. 'Mmm...perhaps I should just visit Jimmy instead? I promise to come back before Mrs Phillips is home.'

Nanny Augusta felt this a better proposition. 'All right Rosie you may go, provided that you are back by three thirty. Mrs Phillips will be home around four.'

Rosie smiled to herself, satisfied that she had achieved her goal. 'Thank you so much Nanny Augusta. I promise I will be back before then.'

***

Rosie's luck held as Jimmy Mitchell had the day off. His eyes lit up as he spotted her walking towards him.

At seventeen, Jimmy had already been working at the drift mine for seven years. He hated every second spent there and was seriously thinking about moving away, possibly Liverpool, to sign on a merchant ship. The only reason he stayed was that he couldn't contemplate not seeing Rosie for even longer periods, but she was here now, smiling and linking her arm in his as they walked up the street.

'What brings yo down the Marsh Rosie?' queried Jimmy in his own inimitable way.

Rosie grinned as she looked around furtively, half expecting her mother to put in an appearance. 'I've come to see you Jimmy Mitchell, what else?'

He was inordinately pleased with her response and his mood lifted temporarily. 'I was hoping you would say that Rosie. Does yer mam know yer 'ere?'

Rosie pouted and shrugged her shoulders. 'Not exactly Jimmy, but I just had to see you. Probably be best if we are not seen though. Lets take a walk by the river.'

They reached the River Leen and sat down by the riverbank on a wooden bench under an old Willow Tree.

'What yer bin up ta then Rosie? I heard yer were staying wi Mrs Phillips on St James Street. How did yer get away?'

Rosie winked and laughed, causing dimples to appear in her cheeks. 'I used my trickery on Nanny Augusta. Told her me mam said I could come to see you. I agreed to be back around three thirty, so she let me go. If you sound convincing enough Jimmy, you can usually get away with it.'

Despite the effect Rosie had on Jimmy's mood, she noticed he still wasn't quite his usual cheerful self and wondered if there was anything more serious troubling him. 'What's the matter Jimmy? Aren't you pleased to see me?'

Jimmy broke into a grin, fetched an apple out of his pocket, cut it in half with his penknife and presented it to her. 'Course I am Rosie, I was just thinking about yer. It's not that...am just fed up that's all. Fed up wi working at the mine, but mostly fed up wi me dad. He's nothing but a bully Rosie. One of these days, I will fight back. The only thing stopping me is me mam, she'd pay forrit if a said sa much as a word aht uv line.'

Rosie frowned. She could not imagine how Jimmy must feel, as she hadn't known any kind of violence in her life. She made another attempt to cheer him. 'Thanks for the apple Jimmy. Yer know, one day, yer won't have to put up with yer dad. When we are married, we can move away from here and you'll never have to suffer his beatings ever again.'

Instead of cheering up, Jimmy became more morose, as he knew it would be a good few years yet before he could even consider marrying Rosie. He also doubted her new family would be happy with that plan, now she had moved up in the world. 'I can't wait Rosie, but it's too far in the future, if indeed we 'ave a future. You are still only thirteen. It would be another two or three years before we could be wed and I doubt yer dad 'ud give us permission anyway,' he paused. 'No Rosie, I'm thinking of leaving now. Going away somewhere, perhaps ta sea. Somewhere so far away, I'll never set eyes on him agen. A could do it Rosie. A could try and join a merchantman. Then when I've made enough money, I could come back fer yer.'

Rosie's eyes darkened, as she assimilated her thoughts. *Why was he talking like this? Was it really so bad that he needed to go far away. Could she persuade him to stay? What would she do without him to confide in and plan adventures?*

They did not see each other very often now, but they had an understanding that when she was old enough they would be together. Now he was shunning her for a life at sea and planned only to return when he had made enough money. She did not care about money, only that they be together. She noticed Jimmy's eyes were dull, without their usual sparkle and his mouth turned down, despondently. Even her positivity failed to raise his mood. 'Well Jimmy, we've only another couple of hours and it's quite cold now. Is there anybody in at your house? If not, we could sit in your kitchen and have some hot milk.'

Jimmy suddenly brightened, as he remembered his mother had gone shopping and his father would be at the Loggerheads propping up the bar. 'No Rosie, no one's 'omm at the moment. Come on, let's hurry. We can get warmed up by the fire and help ourselves to two of me mam's scones which she baked this morning.'

They arrived at Jimmy's house and located the key under the mat, where his mother always left it, in case there was no one home and he needed to let himself in. They were soon enjoying mugs of hot milk and buttered scones. Rosie bathed in a warm glow as she imagined their future together...baking scones and sitting by the fire in their own cosy parlour—

Her idyllic vision was rudely interrupted as the front door suddenly flew wide open. Jimmy's mother was pushed unceremoniously through the gap, followed by his father. Rosie and Jimmy leapt up and Rosie dropped her mug as she rushed to hide behind the well-worn armchair.

Jimmy's father eyeballed the guilty looking pair and quickly jumped to the wrong conclusion. He momentarily forgot why he was manhandling his wife and turned his anger on Jimmy, as he unfastened the large leather belt, which was holding up his beer soaked trousers. 'Nah then, what's all this? What da yer think yer on wi boy? Al 'ave none of that malarkey in this ahse.'

Jimmy retreated behind the chair to protect Rosie and himself from the threatening figure of his father. 'There's noat going on dad. Rosie and me just came in ta get warm. 'Er mam is dahn in Nottingham looking after Mrs Milligan.'

Bill Mitchell wasn't listening. He considered Jimmy to be a blatant liar and immediately raised his belt to his son.

Suddenly, as if her life depended on it, Ida Mitchell sprang forward and jumped on her husband's back, cursing him loudly for his bullying ways. 'Leave him alone Bill, they've done noat wrong. Rosie's a good gel and she's only thirteen, just a kid. They're friends, that's all.'

Bill Mitchell was not used to his wife contradicting him. His face took on a purple hue and his eyes flashed murderously as he lifted his wife clean off the floor with one hand and flung her unceremoniously across the scullery. 'Don't yo interfere woman. It's noat ter do wi yo.'

Jimmy Mitchell was aghast as he observed his mother's frail figure lying on the floor. Bile rose in his throat and full of anger at his father's actions, he let fly with his fist, landing a punch squarely on his father's jaw. Rosie was frozen to the spot and hardly recognised her own voice as she shouted at the two men. 'Stop it, stop it both of you. Someone will get badly hurt...please stop.' But it was too late, Jimmy had suffered enough and this was the final straw. He quickly followed up his first punch with several more before his father staggered backwards, crashing into the cast iron stove. Bill hit his head hard on the oven door as he slumped down on to the floor. There was a sickening silence as Jimmy gazed stupefied at the tell tale trickle of blood flowing from the back of his father's head.

Ida went over to where her husband lay, seemingly unconscious. She looked down on his inert body with loathing, and then turned to face her son. The tone of her voice portrayed a certain urgency, but was without blame. 'Jimmy...now lissen to me son. You have ter go...right now... if 'e comes round and you're still here, he'll kill ya fer sure. You've just time to grab yer coat and a warm jumper, then teck the money from the tin on the top shelf and go.'

A flummoxed Jimmy cast his eyes wildly round the room. He picked up his jacket and jumper from the back of the chair and pocketed the money contained in the tin, then spoke softly to his mam. 'Yer know mam, a don't want ta leave yer like this, but a know he'd kill me if a stayed. Will yer be all right mam? Am sorry fer what 'ave done, but 'e pushed me too far this time.'

Ida smiled, but the sadness showed clearly in eyes, which lacked any spark of emotion. She needed to be brave. She would not let her son down in his hour of need and hugged him close to her. Fighting back tears she whispered the words Jimmy wanted to hear. 'Course a will. A can 'andle 'im. Don't worry. But get yersen far away son and you Rosie me duck, get back 'omm and don't say a word to anybody abaht this, or Jimmy 'ull be in trouble...Now go lad and don't look back,' she advised, pushing them both towards the door. As Jimmy exited, a broken hearted Ida held him one last time, before letting him go. 'A love yer Jimmy. Teck care of yersen and stay aht o' trouble. Tarrar.'

After Rosie and Jimmy left, Ida eyed her husband vindictively and cursed the day she ever set eyes on him.

※

Rosie and Jimmy ran from the terraced back-to-back houses and took refuge in one of the abandoned caves that littered this part of the city. Their hearts were beating wildly as they sat recovering on a rock, out of sight of any passers by. It was Jimmy who broke the silence as he took hold of Rosie's hand and looked earnestly into her eyes. 'Lissen Rosie, am going ta 'ave ta leave yer, just like a left me mam, but I'll be back one day.'

Tears rolled down Rosie's cheeks, as she, like Ida, had to let him go. 'Where yer going to go Jimmy?' she asked, fearful of his reply.

Jimmy responded with less conviction than he felt. 'Am goan ta meck me way ta a sea port Rosie and try and join a ship. But mark me words, as I told yer before, I'll be back. Will yer wait fer me Rosie?'

Rosie smiled sadly, but responded positively. 'Course a will Jimmy. Yer know that, only please don't stay away too long, a don't know what I'll do without yer.'

Jimmy took her in his arms and kissed her softly on the mouth. 'That'ull seal it Rosie. Don't ferget me. Am going now. Get yersen 'omm before yer get inta trouble. I'll see yer again Rosie. Bye.'

Rosie fought hard to hold back her tears. 'Bye, Jimmy, I'll see yer.'

Jimmy pulled his jacket collar up high, then stuffed his hands into his pockets and walked out of the cave. Rosie watched the retreating figure and wondered if she would ever see him again.

Nanny Augusta waited on the doorstep of number 64, obviously relieved to see her young charge hurrying into St James' Street from Beast Market Hill. Rosie arrived breathless, but smiled weakly at the nanny, who lightly admonished her for cutting it so fine. 'Rosie Cameron, you better get yourself inside quickly, before Mrs Phillips arrives back home.'

Rosie had not recovered from the trauma of the last few hours, so scuttled past Nanny Augusta, before she could get a better look at her tear stained face.

Lizzie was totally unaware of her daughter's most recent escapade and when Ida Mitchell came knocking loudly on her door, she was somewhat surprised. 'Why, hello Ida, Come on in.'

Ida, in a state of shock, mumbled her thanks as she stepped into the scullery. She appealed to Lizzie in a barely audible voice. 'A need yer 'elp Lizzie. It's Bill, 'e's 'ad an accident. Can yer come ovver ta mine?'

Lizzie recognised the urgency in Ida's voice and immediately called to Arthur, who was polishing his boots in the living room. 'I'm just going round to Ida's, Arthur. Clara is sleeping at present, so she'll be all right for a while.'

'Aye, ok me duck,' he acknowledged as he spat onto his boots and vigorously attacked the leather.

Lizzie arrived in Foundry Yard, went straight to the scullery and immediately spotted the inert figure of Bill Mitchell lying in a pool of fast congealing blood, which seeped from a deep head wound at the base of his skull.

Despite Lizzie's loathing of this bully of a man, she knew she needed to assist Ida and bent down to check his pulse. A brief moment elapsed before she looked grimly at Ida and shook her head. 'I am so sorry Ida, but I cannot feel a pulse...I think Bill is dead.'

Ida's hand went involuntary to her mouth, as her worst fears became a reality. 'Oh my God, Lizzie, what'ull happen to him?...what'ull become of him?'

Lizzie comforted Ida and helped her to the armchair, unsure that her friend had fully understood the enormity of the situation. 'Listen Ida, you mustn't worry, I will see to everything.'

Ida's eyebrows knitted into a frown. 'No Lizzie, not Bill...Jimmy, what'ull become of Jimmy?'

Lizzie suddenly remembered Jimmy's absence. 'Oh I see Ida, do you want me to break the news to him? Where is Jimmy?'

Ida did not speak, but stared open mouthed at the expired body of her husband.

Lizzie placed her hand gently on Ida's arm. 'Is he on a shift Ida?' she asked, as she observed the shocked, pale face of her friend.

Ida rallied and with a supreme effort, gathered her thoughts. Unsure how much to disclose, she looked at Lizzie then back to Bill, before making a decision. 'Er...no, Jimmy's not on a shift, he wah here when Bill had his accident,' she paused momentarily lapsing into silence, while she conjured up a likely explanation for the 'incident'. 'They...they had a disagreement...yes, that wah it, Bill came home drunk and... and picked an argument wi Jimmy. He...' Ida looked wildly round for inspiration. 'He took off his belt, lunged forward and tripped ovver the poker, but Jimmy dodged out of the way and fled, just as Bill fell,' she paused again. 'Yes...he fell and banged his 'ead on the stove. Jimmy wah out the door before Bill hit the floor. He...he want goan ta wait around ta gerra beating...oooh Lizzie, what'ull happen? A dunno where he's gone. What if he comes back and–'

Lizzie cut Ida short. 'Ida, don't worry, Jimmy will be all right. He is probably staying away to give Bill time to calm down, although the tragedy is that he's dead now and Jimmy doesn't know. Anyway, there is nothing we can do for Bill, so I will make a cup of tea and then contact the authorities.'

On hearing the word 'authorities' Ida jumped up from the chair, terrified of official intervention. 'No, Lizzie, no... yer can't da that...what if they think it want an accident?... what if–'

A concerned Lizzie seated Ida back in the chair. 'They won't think that Ida. They will realise Bill's demise was due to an accidental fall, sustaining a fatal blow to his head in the process. Don't worry, I will explain everything.'

Almost a week later, Lizzie called on Rachael Phillips to see how she was coping with Rosie and to impart the dreadful news of Bill Mitchell's death. After this unenviable task, she made her way to the playroom and poked her head around the half closed door. Her daughter was pretending to be a school mistress and admonishing Laura, who she said, was not up to scratch with her times table. She spent the next couple of minutes listening in amusement to their play.

Rosie spoke with authority. 'Laura Phillips, eight times seven is not fifty four, it's fifty six, so we will have to recite the table over again. Let us begin, one eight is eight...'

Laura began chanting rhythmically, as Lizzie entered the room. '...seven eights are fifty six.'

Rosie turned and acknowledged her mother's presence with a smile. 'Hello mam, I'm really pleased to see you.' Then by way of explanation, 'Laura and me are playing schools.'

Lizzie grinned and walked over to her daughter. 'Well Rosie, you seem to be enjoying yourself. Perhaps you won't want to come over with me to see grandma Clara?'

Rosie beamed, her face lighting up like the brightest moon. 'Really mam, is she better then?'

'Yes Rosie she is much better and would love to see you.'

'Ok mam, are we going straight away?' she paused, deciding she should play dumb about the incident at the Mitchells, 'and can we go and see Jimmy?' She peered closely at her mother to judge her reaction, which was not one she expected.

Lizzie's face clouded as she struggled with an answer to an impossible question. 'Well Rosie, I have something to tell you, but it must wait until we are at grandma Clara's, but we can't see Jimmy, as he is away at the moment.'

Rosie was confused and subdued. It was unclear how much her mother knew of the situation. 'Erm, well, er...have you seen Mrs Mitchell recently mam?'

Lizzie was unusually guarded in her reply. 'Not since earlier last week, when Ida came round to ask for my help with something. I didn't see Jimmy though, apparently he was out. Anyway Rosie, I thought as grandma Clara is on the mend and over the worst, you could pay her a visit as she is no longer infectious. Mind, she still needs to stay in bed, until she fully recovers.'

'Oh that's really good news mam,' responded Rosie, who was thankful that her mother appeared unaware of her visit to the Marsh. 'I'd love to go and see her. Did Mrs Mitchell say where Jimmy was?'

Lizzie shook her head. 'No, no she didn't say. Apparently he wasn't on a shift, so I expect he was out for a walk or something,' explained Lizzie, making light of the situation.

'Ok mam, I'll just grab my coat and say goodbye to Mrs Phillips, then we can go.'

<hr />

Rosie bounded up the Milligan's stairs and charged into Clara's bedroom before Lizzie could stop her. Fortunately, Clara was more than happy to hear some cheerful banter and a bit of noise, as the house had been like a morgue these last few weeks...as far as she could remember. 'Nah then ah Rosie, come and sit wi me. Pull that chair up a bit closer and let mi gerra good look at yer. Well, me duck, yer shooting up. Yu'll be taller than granddad soon and yer filling aht nicely. Yer must be 'aving plenty o' fresh fruit and veg in yer new place. Yer look a proper young gel. Yer mam'ull 'ave ter keep an eye on yer, cause the lads 'ull be queuing up to teck yer aht.'

Rosie felt very gratified at Clara's encouraging words and touched her hand, which lay on the eiderdown. 'Can a hold yer hand grandma. Is it alright to do that, or will I catch it?'

A warm smile lit up Clara's face. 'Yer al'right Rosie, am ovver the worse and a 'eard the quack saying ter yer mam yestdee that it in't catching no more, so yer can oad me 'and all right.'

Rosie grinned and spoke convincingly. 'By the way grandma, I'll not be walking out with any lads, because I am waiting fer Jimmy to come home—' she paused momentarily when she realised too late what she had said, but immediately corrected the admission by adding, 'home from work that is grandma. Jimmy's the only lad for me.'

Fortunately for Rosie, Clara did not pick up on the slip and they continued 'chit chatting', until her mother called her. 'Rosie, I think grandma needs to sleep now. Come on down and I'll make you some warm milk. We can have some lunch and you can take some soup to her later.'

Rosie knew she had to be careful not to 'let the cat out of the bag' and bent down to kiss her grandma on the cheek, before releasing her hand.

Lizzie watched in trepidation as Rosie drank her milk before explaining the reason for Jimmy's absence. 'Last week Mrs Mitchell called round to ask for my help, as her husband had tripped in the scullery and banged his head. Apparently he had an argument with Jimmy, who left the house in quite a hurry. He might be away for some time, Rosie and Ida isn't sure where he is. Unfortunately, Mr Mitchell didn't recover and Jimmy will be unaware that his father is dead.'

Rosie displayed a look of utter amazement and shock as she struggled incomprehensibly to evaluate her mother's statement. *Jimmy's father was dead? He couldn't be, he didn't look dead*, although, she had to admit, she hadn't actually seen a dead person before and consequently decided to remain silent, until she figured out the implications. The one certainty was that Jimmy could no longer return.

Lizzie acknowledged her daughter's disbelief and sadness, unaware of the real reason for her reaction and her heart went out to her. 'Don't worry Rosie, Jimmy will be all right; he will probably return in a few days. He will certainly be shocked that his father has died, although he bullied him mercilessly, but he *was* his father and it will take time to come to terms with the tragedy.'

Rosie mulled over whether she should tell her mother the truth, but what would it achieve? She would be furious that she had visited Jimmy without permission. Ida Mitchell's distraught face flashed into her mind. Should she tell her that her son would not be coming back any time soon? That he was probably halfway to Liverpool or London by now. She decided to think about it and make a decision tomorrow.

Lizzie broke the silence. 'Are you all right Rosie? I know it must be a shock for you, but I promise everything will be all right.'

Rosie sucked in her cheeks and tried to keep her feelings in check as she replied. 'I am shocked mam, but Jimmy's dad was always taking the belt to him. It's not surprising he left. I am really sad, especially as he might not come back, but perhaps it is for the best and I know Jimmy can look after himself.'

Lizzie considered Rosie's behaviour lacked her usual passion, which gave her cause for concern, as she pondered the reason. Several months later, she would reach an understanding.

Chapter Two

The Walking Cane March 1855

Kate Renwick travelled from Boar's Hill, Oxford to London to meet Aunt Jayne in anticipation of positive news to discover the whereabouts of her daughter.

In over thirteen years of searching, success had eluded them. They were no closer to solving the mystery of Rosie's disappearance than when they began.

Jayne Munroe greeted her niece enthusiastically, as they'd last met several months ago. She'd secured the corner table in Brown's Tea Rooms on Albemarle Street, Mayfair for their meeting. 'Kate darling, how lovely to see you again. Do sit down. I booked this table specifically as it really is quite private. I have ordered tea and sandwiches…I hope that meets with your approval?'

Kate kissed her aunt lightly on the cheek, confirming her pleasure at seeing her again. 'That's lovely Aunt Jayne. I cannot remember coming here before. Is it a favourite of yours?'

Aunt Jayne shrugged in reply. 'Actually, no, it was recommended by a friend. I was told that the food is really quite delicious and if one booked in advance, one could secure this table, close to the fire, actually quite fortuitous as it is cool out today.'

Kate took off her cloak and bonnet and sat at the table. The waiter brought an array of sandwiches and a pot of tea, leaving before they began discussing Rosie's disappearance.

Kate waited nervously for Jayne to begin. Were there any new developments? Their meetings were ritualistic; Kate always asked the same question and Aunt Jayne always gave the same answer. It was disappointing for Kate, but Aunt Jayne always exuded encouragement.

'Do you have anything new to report Aunt Jayne?'

Aunt Jayne smiled as she poured their teas, then took a folded map out of her bag and placed it to one side of the table.

Kate cocked an inquisitive eye as her curiosity was aroused, but waited patiently for an explanation.

Jayne's eyes twinkled as she outlined her proposals. 'Well Kate, I do have a new idea for you. You remember we advertised in the Liverpool Mercury and the Manchester Times in an attempt to ascertain Lizzie's whereabouts? Well, I did receive a letter from a Mrs Amy Brandreth, concerning a possible sighting of Lizzie and Rosalie boarding a train in Liverpool. It appears that the Brandreth's encountered a Lizzie Cameron on board the 'Royal George'[5], the day after she disappeared. She believes she saw her again some years' later in Liverpool, possibly in the December of 1846. The only problem was that she couldn't be sure it was the same woman. She was, of course, surprised to see her, because when she first encountered her, Lizzie mentioned

---

5 The Royal George joined her sister ship, The Royal Sovereign on the Liverpool station on August 24th 1839, and was equally well fitted, having her saloon furnished in rosewood and crimson. She remained in service until about 1847. She sailed from Glasgow's Broomielaw on the River Clyde. The site where thousands of Glaswegians boarded paddle-steamers to Liverpool.

she was travelling to London. If she boarded a train at Liverpool, she could have travelled to any part of the country, so it wouldn't really have helped us. I did not inform you at the time, for fear of raising your hopes and it would probably have been a 'wild goose chase' anyway. However, with little progress achieved so far, I rethought the problem. I am fairly certain that Lizzie reached Liverpool or possibly as far as Manchester. Indeed, Mrs Brandreth's letter confirms my assumption. The rest of her journey is unclear but I have considered another avenue, which we should pursue.'

Kate immediately became more attentive, as her aunt continued. 'We previously concentrated our endeavours on following the route we believed Lizzie may have taken. So far, it has been fruitless and has brought much heartache. There have been times when our hopes were raised, only to be dashed. We assumed her journey from Manchester would take in Derby, Great Brington and Dunstable. Unfortunately, over the years, your father and ourselves have completely exhausted all the avenues connected with those towns and I feel there is nothing more to gain from pursuing them further, hence my new plan.' Aunt Jayne took a sip of her tea and smiled encouragingly at Kate, whose eyes took on their old sparkle, in anticipation of a new idea.

~~~

It had been many years since her niece showed enthusiasm for anything. The tragic loss of Kate's mother, immediately after the disappearance of her daughter, left Kate morose and disinterested in almost everything, including the male of the species. This was in complete contrast to all her previous enthusiastic encounters with the opposite sex.

Even her unexpected marriage to James Renwick did not appear to excite her. Jayne put that down to the fact Kate was not in love with him and only considered it a safe option.

The loss of her first love, of which the family knew nothing, including Aunt Jayne, left Kate dismissive of marrying for love, so she married for security instead. James Renwick was more than capable of supplying the latter commodity, although, to be fair, Kate knew he worshipped her totally. James was also devastated to learn the truth of the disappearance of her daughter and the part Kate played in the accidental death of her mother. However, he managed to put all that to one side and begged her to marry him, even though he knew she did not return his love.

Over the years, Kate had become very fond of James and financially, she wanted for nothing. After her marriage, the family moved to a recently built eight bedroom Victorian property in Boar's Hill, Oxford. Her father occupied one wing and Kate, James and their only daughter, eleven year old Beatrice, occupied the rest of the property. There were complications with Beatrice's birth, so more children were out of the question. This was an extreme disappointment to James, who longed for a son and heir. Even so, it was James who actively encouraged Kate to continue her quest to find her daughter, because he hoped she would again become the young fun loving girl he used to know, if Rosalie could be found.

***

A flush of anticipation graced Kate's cheeks, as Aunt Jayne outlined her plan. 'Subject to your agreement, we will travel to Manchester and speak to the coach drivers again. Your father has already spoken with them, but I think we should dig a little deeper and two women might elicit more favourable responses. My theory is that Lizzie may not necessarily have taken the planned route we've concentrated on so far. If I'm correct, she may have gone via Leicester and then through Northamptonshire, according to my interpretation of this map.' Jane turned the map to Kate and amusingly used the sugar tongs to point out the route.

Kate was ecstatic. 'That sounds extremely plausible. When can we go?'

Aunt Jayne laughed at Kate's new-found drive. 'Well Kate, I suppose, subject to confirming that Aubrey is ok with me disappearing for, maybe a week and you making arrangements for Beatrice to be cared for, we could travel this weekend. I know a lovely little Inn just north of Manchester and the landlord's wife, Mary, is most welcoming, so it would be lovely to meet up with her again and we could travel into town each day.'

Kate finished her tea and poured them both another cup. 'That's settled then. Gosh, I feel there may be something in what you say. We always assumed the route was Manchester, Derby, Great Brington, Dunstable and never considered that she may have, for whatever reason, travelled via Leicester. Oh Aunt Jayne, I feel really uplifted and can't wait to go.'

Jayne nodded her satisfaction. 'That's lovely dear. Now let's finish off these delicious looking sandwiches and order some cakes to celebrate.'

Kate hadn't felt this positive for several years and her mind was working overtime. She had almost given up hope and thought Lizzie and Rosalie were lost to her forever, until Aunt Jayne's plan refuelled her optimism.

Fate determined that they would not be the only ones visiting the Old Boar's Head. Nine years had passed since Lizzie and her brother, sat at the Inn's roaring fire on New Year's Eve, in 1846. They discussed Rosie's future and pondered as to why Kate entrusted her daughter to Lizzie, but had failed to inform Robert that he was the father.

It was now late March 1855 and Robert revisited the Inn on his way to a business meeting in Liverpool. He sat alone in an alcove by the fire, reading the papers. He discarded them several minutes later, then stared into the fire, watching the flames flicker before disappearing up the chimney. He clearly remembered when he and Kate had been in love, meeting in the disused cottage in Lorimer's field. They were exciting times, ones he would never forget, despite the fact that he was married with one daughter and another daughter, Rosie living with Lizzie, his sister.

His reminiscences were cut short by the realisation that he must leave if he was to make the connection with the Manchester to Liverpool train. He checked his watch. His life had been hectic recently and the business associate he was to meet in Liverpool was a stickler for punctuality. He would not appreciate a late appearance. He left hurriedly but tipped his hat to a middle-aged lady seemingly eager to occupy his cosy table by the fire, muttering a comment about the cold weather as he walked towards the exit. Almost immediately, Jayne Munroe noticed his abandoned monogrammed walking cane and hurried after him. 'Excuse me young man, but I do believe this glorious item, belongs to you.'

Robert gratefully accepted the cane from Jayne. 'Thank you so much. The cane is very precious to me, a gift from my sister last Christmas. I would hate to lose it. Thank you again.'

Jayne beamed with pleasure and settled herself into the seat vacated by the gentleman whose face seemed uncannily familiar, but couldn't quite place.

She picked up the local paper left by the man but abandoned the article she was reading, when Kate approached. 'Hello Kate, I just ordered coffee. Do come and sit close to the fire, as it is quite cold today. It's possible we will see a heavy fall of snow this week, if the temperature is anything to go by.

Kate pulled the chair closer to the embracing heat of the burning logs. England was certainly experiencing a cold snap and the north always seemed a degree or so colder than the south. Prior to Kate's arrival, Jayne's inherited paper reported that the first few months of 1855 were the fourth coldest ever recorded, but she cared little, sat in the cosy seat by the fire and eager to press on with her plan. She turned to Kate, who was also enjoying the ambiance of their surroundings. 'You are probably anxious to make a start. Mary has ordered a cab for 2 o'clock, which gives us time for a hot drink, before we depart for Manchester centre, where we can question the Royal Mail coach drivers.'

Kate's face reflected her excitement and anticipation. She was eager to ascertain if there was indeed a possibility that Lizzie took a different route thirteen years ago.

Aunt Jayne gently took hold of Kate's hand. She was very fond of her niece and they had become even closer over the last few years. Their determination to find Lizzie and Rosalie never waned. Kate's father had also been tireless in his efforts to find his granddaughter, but his recent poor health and the onset of old age had sadly defeated him.

Jayne encouraged Kate, but was careful not to raise her hopes unduly. 'I really do believe we may be on the right track, but we must remain resolute and not get too excited, as there is still a long way to go.'

Kate felt uplifted, especially as they were now in Manchester, where they might gain some valuable information. 'I am trying not to get too excited Aunt Jayne, because, we have known failure before; however, I have a good feeling about your latest theory.'

※

Robert stepped down from his coach to discover that his train to Liverpool had been delayed for two hours. This was unfortunate, but the problem on the line, gave him the opportunity to have a late lunch at the Royal Hotel on Moston Street, from where the Royal Mail Coaches departed.

During lunch, his thoughts turned to why Kate had kept the knowledge of her pregnancy from him, it was an unfathomable mystery, and it troubled him greatly.

Granted the need to find Kate was paramount, but both Lizzie and he still feared Rosie could be taken away. However, they knew in their hearts that it was the right thing to do. Their advertisements in the Glasgow Echo and a national had proved negative, so they took the desperate measure of hiring a private detective to inject new life into the search. To date, he was still no closer to tracing her, so they were also considering other options. Lizzie suggested they visit Low Wood Hall, Kate's family home, to uncover something that might help them, so it was decided they visit Glasgow as soon as practicable.

His thoughts still in turmoil, but centred on his new plan, Robert realised it was time to leave. He pulled his coat collar up close and retrieved his hat from the stand, fixing the brim over his brow to keep out the cold. Absently and for the second time that day, he neglected to pick up his walking cane. His musings were still on what might have been, as he proceeded out into the cold March afternoon.

Robert was passing the Royal Mail coach park when he noticed the middle aged lady from the Olde Boar's Head and once again tipped his hat in her direction, smiling an acknowledgement of their previous brief meeting. She smiled in response and watched as he continued on towards the station. *What a pleasant young man*, she thought as she tried again to remember who he reminded her of, but no one immediately came to mind.

At the time, Kate was unaware of her aunt's second chance meeting as she talked in earnest to one of the more senior looking coach drivers.

⁂

The afternoon was quite busy. People arrived from the train station, eager to secure a place on the reduced number of Royal Mail coaches, which no longer made the hazardous journeys to London. Robert Cameron boarded the train to Liverpool.

Ten minutes into the journey he realised to his horror that he had mislaid his walking cane again and he knew he would be unable to return before the morning to the only place he could have left it. He berated himself. How could he have been so distracted?

He determined to send a telegraph to the hotel immediately on arrival in Liverpool and ask 'lost property' to retain it until he returned. Furthermore, he was annoyed that Kate Hemingway was still having such a dramatic impact on his life and consequently wished more than anything that there could be an end to this drama. He hoped quite fervently that he could move forward with the business of living, without this persistent black cloud following his every footstep.

⁂

Nine years had passed since Kate's father, Howard, journeyed from their home in Dorset to speak to the coach drivers and ask if Lizzie had been a passenger on any of their coaches. He repeated the same journey five years later, but much to his consternation and disappointment, no one remembered on either occasion.

This time, however, Kate approached the problem differently from a perspective not previously explored. She courteously addressed one driver. 'Excuse me sir, but do you always take the same route down to London, or have there been times when you have taken a different route?'

The coach driver cocked an eyebrow questioningly, but his answer was not one she wanted to hear. 'Well miss, we no longer travel to London. The last Royal Mail Coaches ran in 1846...the railways you see...they've taken over. We always stuck to the same route, although some coach drivers did deviate. They were the privateers', but there aren't many of those left these days. They were easy targets for highwaymen you see and most people were terrified of being robbed on their journey. The Royal Mail coaches employed a driver *and* a heavily armed guard with a blunderbuss and two pistols...not so easy for would be robbers. If you want to question the independent drivers, they tether a little further up the road, but I doubt you'll get any more information from them...sorry miss.'

Kate was disappointed but thanked him and went in search of Aunt Jayne, who had wandered away from the rank, engrossed in her own thoughts. Kate tapped her on the shoulder and Jayne turned to acknowledge a somewhat deflated Kate. She placed her hand on Kate's arm, sensing she had not discovered anything useful. 'Sorry I wandered off Kate, but I reasoned you wouldn't need my assistance. I know full well that you can be very persuasive with the opposite sex, which brings me to my next point; I've just seen a gentleman whom I saw earlier at the Inn, such a polite and handsome young man...he reminded me of someone, but I can't think who...my memory isn't what it was.'

Kate stared glumly at her aunt, totally disinterested in her memory loss, before imparting the meagre information gleaned earlier. '...so you see Aunt Jayne, it was only the privateers' who deviated from the route.'

Aunt Jayne was intrigued at the mention of privateers, so in an effort to lift her niece's mood, she made a suggestion. 'Well Kate, I know it doesn't seem very likely, but just supposing, for whatever reason, Lizzie travelled with an independent driver. Perhaps we *should* talk with them.'

Kate's face brightened again. 'You could have a point Aunt Jayne. Lizzie wasn't very worldly wise and may not have considered that travelling with an independent wouldn't be as safe as travelling with the Royal Mail coaches; although, undoubtedly, your instructions to travel with the Royal Mail were explicit.'

Aunt Jayne smiled benignly, as a new idea began to formulate. 'Mmm...I did emphasise that particular point, but supposing she was delayed...the coaches may have already departed. She would only have two choices, take an independent coach or stay over in an hotel until the following day. My guess is Lizzie would worry that she would not be able to meet me on time and would, in her innocence, take an independent coach.'

Kate became animated with her aunt's reasoning and, hopeful of gaining some positive information, walked determinedly towards the two independent coaches parked at the end of the road. The younger of the two coachmen approached Kate and cheekily tipped his hat. 'Good day miss, do you wish to travel this afternoon?'

Kate shook her head. 'No not today, but I am hoping you can help me with something.'

The coachman's grin was roguish as he nodded his head, not wanting to pass up the opportunity to help such an attractive woman. 'Of course...of course...and how can I be of assistance to you miss?'

Kate's smile was disarming. 'I wondered if you could remember the route the independent drivers took to London. I realise it was some years ago, so you may not have been a coachman at that time.'

The man stated he had only been coaching for four years, but confirmed he always took the same route as the Royal Mail coaches. However, old Seth, a coachman of considerable experience and years in the trade, might be able to assist. He beckoned to the older man. 'Hoy Seth, come here a moment. This young lady's asking about the route we used to take down to London. I said you might be able to help her.'

Seth ambled over to the young woman and was quick to notice she looked quite well to do. 'Why do you need to know that miss?'

Kate replied cagily, although she was anxious to get the man on her side. 'A friend of mine travelled down to London around thirteen years ago and we've lost touch.

I am anxious to renew our friendship and hope to try and trace her.'

The old boy with a leathery lined face grinned, displaying a row of yellowing teeth. He had spotted an opportunity to make some money and pretended to think hard, knowing full well that all but a couple of drivers took the same route as the Royal Mail coaches. 'Well now miss, me memory's not so good these days.'

Kate was well aware the man was angling for a reward, so took a shilling out of her purse. 'Perhaps,' she smiled, 'this will help you recover your memory.'

The man hesitated, then took the shiny coin offered to him by Kate and feigned humble surprise at the offer of payment. 'Oh, there was no need to pay me, but it's kind of yer all the same. As it happens, I do remember now…it was the same route as the Royal Mail.'

Kate was disappointed but tried to press him for more information. 'How many independents were there thirteen years ago?'

Again Seth seemed to have trouble with his memory. Kate sighed. 'I will give you another shilling if you can try harder for me.'

Greedy now, Seth miraculously recovered from his memory lapse. 'Well now, let me see. Beside myself, there was only Jacob, Will and one other, Jack. Will died a couple of years ago and Jack was killed In an accident on the Dunstable to London Road. I believe Jacob and Jack sometimes took a different route…Jacob went via Leicester where his aunt lived and I believe Jack went through Nottingham. Jacob could have told you more, but he gave up coaching a few years ago…works in a cotton mill now I believe.'

Really excited at this promising lead, Kate asked one more question. 'What were Jacob and Jack's surnames?'

Wily Seth sensed her desperation so tried to extract a little more than a shilling for the extra information. 'I couldn't disclose their names miss...it wouldn't be right would it? Supposing you sought Jacob out. He might not be too pleased to answer your questions. He quit[6] as a driver under dubious circumstances and wouldn't want anyone sniffing around at his place of work now would he?'

Kate felt that the answers were within her grasp, so determined to extract the drivers' names, she dipped into her purse again. She held her hand out flat and showed the man a silver half crown. 'I assure you, I can be very discreet and you can trust me not to disclose my source, should I find this man, Jacob. Will this half crown assist you with your decision?'

Seth sniggered to himself. This was the easiest money he'd earned in a long time and he secretly did not have any qualms about telling the woman the only name he could genuinely remember. 'Well, as long as you don't mention my name and because you seem a decent person, I'll tell you. Jacob's name was Brown, but I don't know which cotton mill he went to work in. There's a good few around here, but he may have left the Manchester area altogether. I don't honestly remember Jack's name, but as he's dead, he'll not be able to help you will he?'

Kate was satisfied with his answer and handed over the half crown. She thanked him, but accompanied the thanks with a look of disdain at his greediness.

Aunt Jayne stood a little way off but overheard the conversation. 'Oh Kate, I am so glad you talked to the man. This information could be really valuable. Now, I suggest we

---

6 'to quit' meaning specifically 'to leave, resign or withdraw' from a job, line of work, committee, etc., dates to the early 17th century.

go over to the Royal Hotel for some refreshment. Today has been very successful...very successful indeed.'

※

The two women enjoyed the ambience of the small tearoom in the Royal Hotel and discussed the *expensive* information they had elicited from the coachman.

'Well Aunt Jayne, what do you have in mind for our next move?'

Aunt Jayne pursed her lips. 'I think Kate, we need to find Mr Jacob Brown, although, as the coachman said, there are many cotton factories in and around Manchester and *Brown* is a very common name. He may, of course, have moved further afield.'

Kate nodded in agreement. 'I think that is exactly what we should do.'

Kate and Jane speculated on the significance of the latest information, until they exhausted all possibilities, before hungrily devouring the tea and cakes. Kate was elated. It had been such a long time since she had seen her daughter, a baby of only a few weeks old. She could never have envisaged that thirteen years later, she still awaited a reunion.

Now, a decision had to be made whether to stay on at the Old Boar's Inn, or go back home and arrange a further extended visit later. Kate was eager to stay, but Aunt Jayne had business commitments at the beginning of the following week. They needed to spend time locating Jacob Brown, but if they cut their visit short now, they could come to Manchester again at the end of the week following Jayne's business meetings.

Kate moved to put on her coat, but as she placed her hand on the arm of the chair, her attention was drawn to a gentleman's cane, which clattered to the floor. She retrieved it and looked closely at the monogrammed handle, which immediately took her breath away. She steadied herself, staring incredulously at the elaborately engraved initials, *RWC*, which were irrevocably burned into her brain. Their close physical relationship had ensured that this would always be so. *Surely, it couldn't be his?* She almost laughed, but dejectedly dismissed the idea as ludicrous. However, a small doubt embedded itself in her subconscious. *A farmer wouldn't own such a cane...would he?*

Aunt Jayne eyed her niece curiously as Kate studied the monogrammed handle. 'Are you all right Kate, you have gone quite pale?'

Kate became emotional as the initials transported her back to happier times, but she quickly recovered. 'Yes, yes, it's nothing really. The initials on this cane reminded me of someone...someone from my past. I am all right now, but I think we should hand this to the proprietor. Whoever owns this cane will be very upset to have lost it.'

'Yes you are right dear.' Aunt Jayne paused as she glanced again at the cane. 'It does look familiar, can I take a closer look?' Her furrowed brow indicated her mind was searching back to a recent incident and then she remembered. 'How extraordinary...I have seen this cane once before today...a gentleman in the Olde Boar's Head...' Jayne remained pensive, recollecting her meeting with the man.

Her aunt's demeanour surprised Kate. She wondered where her aunt had made the mysterious man's acquaintance. 'I don't remember you meeting anyone at the Inn. Where was I?'

Aunt Jayne smiled. 'Well Kate, you were upstairs unpacking your case and he left before you joined me for refreshments. I did actually mention it to you when we were at the coach stage. That's when I saw him again, making his way to the station, but sometimes you are so embroiled in your own thoughts that you choose to ignore what others are saying and you sweep it away...sorry darling, but it's one of your few faults.'

Kate expressed surprise. 'Really...do I do that? I am sorry Aunt Jayne, that's not really a very good trait is it?'

Aunt Jayne grinned knowingly at her niece. 'No dear, perhaps not, but you have so many good qualities that people tend to overlook the bad ones.'

Amusement showed clearly on Kate's face, as she grinned wryly. 'Oh well that's all right then. I will try to listen more carefully in future. So...about this gentleman...what did he look like, out of interest?'

Jayne cocked her head and gave Kate a look that spoke volumes. 'Oh Kate, that's the first time in years that I have known you to take an interest in someone of the opposite sex. You're not getting bored with James are you?'

Kate blushed. 'No...no of course not. I am just curious as to who would own such a unique cane. It really looks quite an expensive item, individually made. See this intricate pattern of inlaid silver stars on the shaft? I bet it holds some significance to the owner. It just makes me wonder what that might be?'

Aunt Jayne took a closer look and noticed a small letter 'm' on one of the stars. She recognised the pattern and imparted her knowledge to her niece. 'Well Kate, if I am not mistaken, I think the stars represent the Seven Sisters.'

Kate was suitably impressed, but in her usual manner, dismissed it immediately. 'I see. How very impressive. Anyway, what *did* he look like?'

Aunt Jayne smiled as she shook her head, *so much for Kate's determination to listen more carefully.* 'He was tall and I think he had light coloured hair; although his hat was pulled down over his forehead, so it was difficult to see. What I did notice were his eyes, which I think were blue...they looked thoughtful and almost sombre, but when he smiled, they lit up...as I say, quite a handsome man and very friendly.'

Kate frowned. She had already dismissed the idea that the stranger could be Robert Cameron, but the small doubt resurfaced, so she pressed her aunt for more details. 'Anything else you remember Aunt Jayne? Was he alone?'

Aunt Jayne grinned. 'Oh yes, he was completely alone, but he did mention something when I returned his cane. He thanked me profusely and was obviously relieved to have been reunited with it...he said his sister had bought it for him last Christmas and that it was very precious to him.'

Kate paled, her heart began beating faster and she felt rather faint. Her Aunt's description had been very like Robert and the mention of a sister sent her mind whirling. Anxiously, but quietly, she sat back in the chair. 'Oh Aunt Jayne, I feel a little unwell. Please order me a glass of water. I need to sit here a while to recover.'

Aunt Jayne did as she was asked, but worried about her niece's present state, questioned her sudden change of mood. 'Kate what on earth has upset you so badly? You don't know this man do you?'

Kate coloured slightly, she wasn't sure, if it was indeed Robert, should she deny him yet again? She replied hesitantly. 'No...I don't know him,' she paused before continuing, 'no, how could I?'

Aunt Jayne studied her niece's expression and came to the conclusion that she may not be telling the whole truth. She placed her hand on her arm and spoke soothingly. 'Kate, dear Kate, you know you can tell me anything...anything at all. You mean the world to me and we have become so close since...since Rosalie's birth. What is it darling? Don't be afraid. He isn't a bad man is he? *Do* you know him Kate?'

Kate looked uncertainly at her aunt, unsure whether the possibility existed that this man could be whom she thought he was and, supposing by some miracle he was...she had never told anyone about him. She remained silent and sipped the glass of water brought by the waiter.

Aunt Jayne also remained silent, giving her niece time to recover from whatever it was that had upset her so much. This would allow Kate to decide whether she wished to share her thoughts or not.

Kate sat quietly looking into the fire and had to admit that the time had come to finally reveal her secret. 'I do have something to tell you Aunt Jayne. I've never spoken about it before because it was too painful, but I now realise that disclosure may lead me to find my precious daughter.' Kate took a deep breath before continuing. 'There is the distinct possibility that the man with whom you were briefly acquainted was Rosalie's father, Robert Cameron.'

Aunt Jayne's expression changed. She looked mystified and stunned by this dramatic admission, until everything suddenly fell into place. *Why yes...he...he reminded me of... of...Lizzie Cameron.*

Jayne took hold of Kate's hand and assured her that everything would be all right. 'Oh Kate, now I understand. I do believe you are right. At the time I couldn't remember, only that it was someone from my past and that was it...his sister, Lizzie. I'm quite definite, although there's a difference in hair colour; their features are the same. Oh my dear, this is good news...very good news indeed.'

CHAPTER THREE

Secrets Revealed
April 1855

A few days after Lizzie and Rosie returned from Nottingham, a letter arrived, bearing a Scottish postmark. In line with Lizzie's plans, it revealed an invitation to join her cousin, Morag, for a holiday in Caithness. Her cousin, Annabella, would be there, despite the fact that she was recovering after her husband's recent death.

There was an air of excitement at the prospect of being together again, despite the sad circumstances. Annabella's son, John, would not be present during their stay, as he was beginning a new term at Hull Trinity House Marine School. This was unfortunate, as John would have been company for Rosie and an additional incentive for her to make the journey.

Berriedale was a very small place and Lizzie pondered the fact that adults would probably be Rosie's only company. Extra encouragement and persuasion from Lizzie would be necessary to cajole Rosie into accompanying her. She had a distinct feeling that her daughter would be less than eager and prefer to stay with Harriett, with whom she had formed a close bond.

Lizzie was now more determined to visit Morag. Rosie had a week's break from school in April, which could be extended and they needed some quality time together.

She placed the letter on the hall table and went in search of her daughter, but as she crossed the hallway, there was a knock on the door. It was Robert who greeted her enthusiastically. 'Hello Robert, how lovely to see you, I wasn't expecting you until later this evening.'

He followed her to the living room and gratefully tumbled on to an ancient, but inviting sofa. 'So, how is my favourite sister?'

Lizzie grinned. 'You are a fool Robert, but it is, as always, wonderful to see you.'

Robert, pleased at her comment, explained his early arrival. 'I'm convinced we should go to Glasgow next weekend. I know it's short notice, but I have already written to the new owners of Low Wood, asking if they will receive us. I explained why we wanted to meet them and I can't see them refusing such a request. Cover is organised at the factory and Amy tells me it is about time we achieved something positive in our quest to find Kate.'

Lizzie brightened. 'I agree with Amy. The private detective isn't producing results, so we need a change of direction. I'll ring for refreshments and we can discuss the implications. Coincidentally, I have received an invitation to holiday with my cousin in Caithness. This should complement your plans if I'm not mistaken. Rosie and Harriett are presently upstairs with Elspeth and will be busy playing, so we won't be disturbed.'

'Ok, that's perfect. I have come straight from the factory and Amy is shopping, so I'm at your disposal. By the way, did I tell you about the incident with my cane?'

Lizzie frowned in exasperation. 'You haven't lost it have you?'

Robert grimaced then began somewhat sheepishly. 'The train was delayed before I made the journey to Liverpool on Saturday, so I took a late lunch at the Manchester Royal and placed the cane at the side of my chair. Unfortunately, my mind was on Kate, and I left without it. It wasn't until after the train left Manchester that I realised. I tell you Lizzie, I was absolutely mortified. You know how much I cherish it. Consequently, when I arrived in Liverpool, I sent a telegraph to the hotel to look out for it, but apparently it had already been handed in...which reminds me, I must write and thank the lady who found it. She left her name and address with the manager. I think I have it in my pocket...yes here we are, *Mrs Jane Montague, six Carlton House Terrace, Off Pall Mall, London*. Very posh! I am sure she would not be in need of a reward, but I will write to her nonetheless.'

The address seemed vaguely familiar to Lizzie, but she was unable to recollect why, being more concerned with Robert's apparent forgetfulness. 'Does Kate still have such an influence on your life?'

Robert frowned, but responded truthfully. 'Yes Lizzie, I am afraid she does. I wish she didn't, but there it is. You know I adore Amy, but sometimes I wonder what life would have been like if I'd married Kate. Above all else, I really want to know what was behind her decision to give our baby to you and keep me in the dark. After all, I was Rosie's father. Is that so wrong? Don't you ever wonder what might have been if you had married Daniel Lorimer?'

Lizzie's far away look betrayed her thoughts. 'I did wonder when we met again after all that time. I even wanted Rosie to be the product of our love, but that was before my memory returned and I was reunited with Marcus. Now I am at one with myself and we are very much in love. Of course, I'll always be very fond of Daniel, but my life has moved on now.'

Robert was relieved. *She always had a knack of putting things into perspective.* 'I hope I will feel the same way when I discover her reason for silence. I feel more hurt than anything...because she left without an explanation.'

Lizzie placed her arm around her brother's shoulder. 'Unfortunately, I cannot help you with the answers, as that part of my memory eludes me. I sometimes wonder if it will become clear. Hopefully, our visit to Low Wood and its surroundings, might trigger a memory. I believe Dottie, the housemaid, is still working at the Hall and it will be nice to make her acquaintance again; although I doubt she will know anything more. If anyone was aware of Kate's actions, it would have been Clara or her husband, George. You remember he was their coachman...but they left Low Wood when the Hemingway's moved and Clara informed me that he died without revealing anything useful. It was fortunate that the new owners sent my first letter on to her, otherwise we would have lost touch altogether. As far as I'm aware, she never returned, because both were devastated by Georgina's untimely death.'

'How is Clara? You mentioned that she wasn't too well the last time she wrote. Have you heard anything recently?'

'Nothing, absolutely nothing, not even from her friend, Mabel Drummond, who wrote on her behalf last year, after she became crippled with arthritis. When I first wrote, Clara could not throw any light on my disappearance and George remained tight lipped, although he probably knew more than he let on. As their driver, he must have been aware of movements to and from the house. Clara told me George was the soul of discretion and would take any entrusted secret to the grave, which, as it turns out, he did. If Clara had inadvertently discovered something, she would not have revealed it before George died. She did write to tell me that prior to his passing, he became delirious with fever and rambled, but not much made sense. The only thing of any relevance concerned him driving me to an hotel on the Monday I went missing. I understand it was 'The Buchanan', close to the docks, but he never mentioned Rosie and most of what he said was incoherent, but at least it is a starting point.'

Robert interjected. 'That's really odd, don't you think? If he was rambling, you would have thought he might have mentioned Rosie, after all, she must have accompanied you...'

Lizzie nodded in quizzical agreement. 'Mmm...yes, it's all very strange. I never thought about that. I must have stayed somewhere immediately before I sailed on the 'Royal George', so if he drove me there, he must have been aware of all the arrangements concerning Rosie. I am convinced he knew much more than he let on, but true to form, other than his ramblings, he remained silent when Clara pressed him, advising her that 'things' were better left in the past. We could visit her when we are in Glasgow, assuming, of course, she is well enough to receive visitors. I did ask Mabel to keep me informed, but so far, as said, there hasn't been any news one way or the other.'

Robert listened attentively whilst pinching his lips together. 'Mmm...I guess George was right about one thing, that certain life events are best forgotten. I think I'm possibly looking at my time with Kate with rose coloured spectacles[7]. If we meet again, I expect I will wonder what all the fuss was about.'

'I am sure you will Robert. All this speculation and intrigue will disappear once we establish contact with Kate again.

---

[7] Used figuratively in the 1850s, finding its way into print in 1861.

Now about our plans to visit Low Wood, Rosie has been doing so well at school that it would not hurt her to have an extra week or two off at the end of the Easter Break. I can easily tutor her myself while we are away and I'm sure the governor will be agreeable. I also know that Martha Langley, another teacher, will be happy to step into my shoes during that time, so I don't see a problem.'

Robert nodded sagely. 'I have every faith in your ability, but can you convince Rosie to stay still for more than a minute?'

Lizzie laughed. 'Yes, that is a problem. Her tutor has told me she has the brains, but sometimes lacks concentration. Anyway, after our visit to Low Wood, Rosie and I will continue to Berriedale. How would that suit you?'

'That's absolutely fine with me,' agreed Robert. 'We will leave early on Friday, the 6 April and book into an hotel for the weekend. That should give us ample time to visit Low Wood and Clara, before I see you off to Berriedale.'

'Ok Robert, that's splendid, although I think I may have to work hard persuading Rosie to accompany us.'

Lizzie set about organising the trip to Glasgow. Robert was to purchase the train tickets and she was to choose a place to stay. She had a very good idea what place that would be.

⁂

Lizzie broached the subject again before tea, but she was disappointed, although not surprised with Rosie's lack of enthusiasm.

An incalcitrant Rosie declared grown-ups boring and there wasn't anyone with whom she could have some fun.

The devastating consequences of Bill Mitchell's death, including Jimmy's part in it had affected Rosie deeply. When she wasn't in Harriett's company, she spent hours walking around the garden quietly contemplating the loss of her best friend. *Where he was now and what he was doing...?* Oh, she did miss him, even Harriett did not compensate for his absence.

༺⊱⊰༻

A day before their intended departure, Rosie was meditating on a bench under the old oak tree, in a secluded part of the garden. She lazily watched two horses canter around an adjoining field and mentally wandered back to the last time she saw Jimmy. Suddenly, an object landed close to her foot! She was startled but looked to see where it had come from, scanning the wooded area over to the right. Someone was calling her name urgently and trying to attract her attention!

'Pssst, Rosie, it's me, Jimmy.'

Foregoing her modesty, Rosie quickly vaulted the low hedge and rushed to her friend on the edge of the wood. 'Gosh Jimmy, what on earth are you doing here?' gasped an ecstatic and overjoyed, if somewhat surprised Rosie.

Jimmy hugged and kissed her enthusiastically before explaining. 'Well Rosie, I might not 'ave long. I've met up wi someone who 'as bin waiting fer his ship ta dock. He told me it would be mecking a return journey to Australia quite soon. If a can sign on, I'll be away fer at least eight months.'

Rosie was shocked initially at the length of the proposed voyage, but then smiled whilst holding her nose in jest as she released herself from Jimmy's hold. 'Oh Jimmy you are in need of a bath and look at your clothes. Where've you been?'

Jimmy considered his dishevelled appearance, right down to his muddy boots, then laughed. 'Mmm..sorry Rosie, I've bin sleeping aht doors and this is the result I'm afraid. Anyrode, will yer be around tamorra, 'cause if yer are wi could meet up, before I 'ave ta leave.'

Rosie was disappointed. 'Oh Jimmy, I am supposed to be travelling with me mam tomorrow. We are taking a holiday and staying with her cousins in the Highlands. That's why I am off school today, so that we can pack. I don't want to go, but I don't want ter hurt her feelings.'

Jimmy felt downcast and his face clouded over, but he tried to remain positive. 'Well, praps we could meet up when a come 'omm again?' Jimmy ventured, sticking his hands into his pockets, just as Lizzie called out to Rosie.

Ignoring the call she stared longingly at Jimmy and contemplated her next move. 'That's not for another eight months,' she paused. 'No wait, leave it with me Jimmy, I will meet you here tomorrow...I have something important to tell you. I'll find a way, but I've got to go now.'

A rejuvenated Jimmy perked up when he realised Rosie might be planning something. 'A'right, I'll see yer tamorra, same time, same place. Tarrar.'

With a twinkle in her eyes, she gave Jimmy a quick kiss on the cheek. 'Right Jimmy, Tarrar.'

Jimmy watched intently as she ran through the garden before disappearing into the house.

Lizzie was serving lunch but smiled when she noticed Rosie's improved demeanour. *Perhaps she is looking forward to our holiday more than I imagined*; although that thought was dispelled minutes later, when Rosie conjured up her most persuasive voice. 'Mam...this holiday...would you be *very* disappointed if I didn't come with you?'

Lizzie was dumbfounded but responded positively. 'Well Rosie, I *was* hoping we could spend some time together and you would have an extra two weeks holiday following the Easter break. Why don't you want to come?'

Rosie cocked her head and smiled persuasively. 'It's not that I don't want to be with you mam...the fact is there won't be anyone my age to have some fun with.'

Lizzie knew this to be a bone of contention and understood her daughter's reasoning. Her reply, therefore, indicated a certain disappointment and resignation. 'Oh Rosie, Rosie, I do understand your ambivalence. I suppose you could stay here with Harriett and return to school in time for the start of the new term. We could possibly have a holiday together later in the year when Marcus returns. How would that suit?'

Rosie's expression betrayed her feelings. She was ecstatic as she threw her arms around her mother's neck in gratitude. 'Oh mam, yes, I would like that. Thank you...you are really the best mother ever.'

Lizzie grinned appreciatively, realising that Rosie hadn't lost any of her persuasive powers, despite her age. Her character traits were becoming more and more reminiscent of Kate, by the hour.

Robert and Lizzie arrived in Glasgow mid morning on Friday and booked into the Buchanan Hotel off the High Street. It was over thirteen years since Lizzie had stayed there, on her planned journey south. Most of her memory had returned, but the period prior to and immediately after she left Low Wood remained locked away. Why she had been given Rosie to look after was still a mystery, but one she hoped would be solved during their stay in Glasgow.

Lizzie entered the restaurant and joined Robert at his table. 'Well Lizzie, how do you feel now we are here?'

Lizzie's response lacked its usual enthusiasm because memories had not resurfaced and she was subdued and disappointed. 'Unfortunately Robert, nothing appears familiar.'

An optimistic Robert placed his hand on his sister's arm. 'Don't worry, we have only just arrived and it will undoubtedly take a while for things to slot back into place. There's no need to feel despondent, as we have three days to spend in the area. Your visit to Low Wood and Clara might just be the trigger needed.'

Lizzie was grateful for the encouragement. 'Yes, you are right. Clara lives in a little cottage on Byres Road, just outside Glasgow by the way, but first things first, we should arrange our visit to Low Wood.

⁂

A rejuvenated Lizzie recollected many happy memories as the carriage approached the large estate of Low Wood Hall. It stopped outside the main entrance and Robert pulled the brass bell on the wall. The butler's orders were to show the expected guests to the sitting room to be received by the mistress of the house. Moments later Mrs Gwendoline Masters swept into the large room beaming at Lizzie as she took her by the hand. 'Hello Elizabeth, I am so pleased to make your acquaintance.'

Looking beyond Lizzie to Robert she was immediately impressed by the tall, good-looking man who stepped forward to greet her. 'You must be Robert, please do take a seat.'

Robert lifted Gwendoline's hand to his lips and made a small bow. 'Thank you Mrs Masters'. It is very good of you to receive us.'

Gwendoline's husband, Henry, was not blessed with either height or good looks and was ten years' her senior, so she was extremely flattered that this handsome man paid her such close attention. 'Do call me Gwendoline. I am very pleased to welcome you here. How was your journey?'

Robert gave her his most disarming smile. 'The journey was good and the hotel is most comfortable thank you.'

Gwendoline nodded agreeably. 'Do you both take coffee? I was just about to order refreshments?'

Robert took the lead, hoping to charm Gwendoline. 'Yes we do, that will be lovely.'

Gwendoline requested coffee and cakes, which was brought by Dottie, the senior housemaid, who, as she entered the sitting room, was clearly shocked to see her old friend Lizzie, seated as 'bold as brass'[8] on her mistress's sofa. She expressed her surprise with total disregard to her position. 'Lizzie, what on earth are you doing here? I thought...I thought perhaps you might be living in London...I...'

Gwendoline Masters shot Dottie a look of disapproval. 'Dorothy, you forget yourself. Elizabeth and Robert are guests of mine and, as such, I would appreciate you keeping your comments to yourself...please place the tray on the table and return to your duties.'

A suitably chastised Dottie exited the room with an embarrassed apology.

---

8 The first known use of *'bold as brass'* is in George Parker's book *'Life's Painter of Variegated Characters in Public and Private Life* of 1789'

Gwendoline smiled sweetly at Lizzie. 'I do apologise Elizabeth. Staff these days sometimes forget their place.'

Ignoring Gwendoline's chastisement, an astonished Lizzie considered how on earth Dottie could possibly be aware of her supposed destination? and shot a meaningful look at her brother.

Robert equally surprised, quickly composed himself, anxious to restore the equilibrium. 'Don't worry Gwendoline, I think it was the unexpected surprise at seeing Elizabeth again after all these years.' He paused before continuing... 'These cakes look awfully good.'

Lizzie purposefully held back her questions and allowed her brother to take control. 'I must say Gwendoline, this room is a credit to your excellent taste. The furnishings and decorations are a delight. Did you employ a designer?' asked Robert with interest.

Gwendoline blushed and smiled demurely as she soaked up Robert's compliments. 'Well no actually, I designed this room myself. I am so glad you like it,' she paused. 'Now, how can I be of assistance?'

Robert was now supremely confident in moving the conversation forward. 'Well Gwendoline, Elizabeth and I hoped you might allow us to view your beautiful home. The familiar surroundings may trigger a memory.'

'Oh Robert, nothing would give me greater pleasure. Where would you like to begin?'

Robert glanced at his sister, sensing her approval. 'Possibly the best place to start would be in Elizabeth's old bedroom.'

Gwendoline nodded. 'Well Elizabeth, I do believe that very little has changed, although the servants' quarters were re-painted shortly after our arrival. However, the furniture and soft furnishings were in such good condition that they did not require replacement. Please follow me and I will take you there myself.'

Robert slipped his hand under Gwendoline's elbow in a gesture of support, turning to wink at his sister who eagerly followed.

Lizzie entered the room and instantly felt very familiar with her surroundings. Her eyes alighted on the pegged rug and colourful counterpane, both made by her dear mother. 'Oh, Robert, it is just as I remember it.' She crossed to the window and smiled joyously as she espied the small vegetable garden, which in turn reminded her of their croft in Strathy. Excitedly she addressed Gwendoline. 'I wonder if you would mind leaving Robert and myself alone for a while, my memories are already flooding back.'

Gwendoline acquiesced graciously. 'Why, of course, Elizabeth, I will ask Dorothy to bring a fresh pot of coffee. When you are ready to see the rest of the house, let her know and I will return to escort you.'

Moments later Dottie knocked lightly on the bedroom door, which was quickly opened by Lizzie. 'Do come in Dottie. It is really nice to see you again.'

Dottie grinned enthusiastically. 'It is good to see you too Lizzie, but I am really quite shocked that you are here. I never thought I would see you again after...after—' Dottie broke off, unsure how to explain her thoughts.

Lizzie smiled and put her arms around the maid, who was obviously distressed, which contradicted her earlier emotions. 'I tell you what Dottie, we have so much to catch up on, so please fetch another cup from the kitchen and you can join us for coffee.'

'Oh Lizzie, I dare not do that. If Mrs Masters caught me she would be very cross.'

Lizzie grinned, remembering the many occasions she had sneaked cups of cocoa up to her room to share with Kate. 'Well Dottie, when this was my room, I used to use the back stairs and ran quickly along the corridor. Don't worry, Mrs Masters is probably safely ensconced in the sitting room. If she asks why you have been up here so long, I will cover for you.'

Dottie duly disappeared down the back stairs and Lizzie's excitement grew as memories of her time at Low Wood flooded back. When Dorothy returned, she actively included her in their conversation. 'I hope you enjoy living in this room. It has a lovely view doesn't it?'

Dottie relaxed in their presence and became more animated. 'Yes, it does. I feel very comfortable here', she responded. 'It is pretty much as you left it and I even kept the two little dresses in the back of the wardrobe, in case you came back one day. I remember you once telling me that you could not bear to part with them, because your mother made them for you. Mrs Masters doesn't allow us to have personal items, not like Mrs Hemingway, who, despite her strict ways, did allow us some personal possessions. I would rather work for Mrs Hemingway any day, but I needed the job and did get a promotion after you left, so I am reasonably content with my lot.' She paused, as she collected her thoughts, knowing very soon she might have to disclose the secret she had kept for thirteen years. Swiftly regaining her composure, she tentatively broached the subject. 'We...we were all very shocked when you left so unexpectedly and we did miss you.'

Lizzie held Dottie's hand to reassure her. 'Thank you Dottie, I remember our little talks and I missed you too.'

Lizzie felt anxious. She needed to tread carefully if she was to coax Dottie into revealing the truth. 'Do you remember my last weeks here Dottie?'

Dottie now relaxed appreciably and eager to unburden herself, began her tale. 'Why yes I do. You were very sad during those last two weeks...troubled and tearful,' she paused before continuing. 'I did see *something* unusual that occurred, which I kept to myself...You took a journey with George in the trap, but I noticed you left by the rear exit, instead of the main gate. When you returned, you were extremely upset and the rest of that week you hardly spoke. I thought at the time you were in some kind of trouble and then...on the day you left, George took your trunk out the back entrance and loaded it on to the trap. I realised, of course, that you must be leaving, but because your reasons were obviously private, I never spoke about it to anyone, until now. I hope I did the right thing Lizzie and didn't add to your troubles.'

Lizzie smiled gratefully at Dottie. 'Oh Dottie, no, I am sure it wasn't detrimental, but it has helped me now, helped me a lot. Did I...did I have a baby with me?'

Dottie lowered her lids in anguish. Soon she would have to reveal everything. 'No...no you left quite alone.'

Lizzie was puzzled and realised there was a lot more to this than she first thought. 'What happened after I left Dottie?'

A nervous Dottie fiddled with her apron. Lizzie realised the experience was obviously very painful and did not want to pressure her friend. 'Listen Dottie, if you don't want to tell me, it is all right, please do not distress yourself.'

Dottie met Lizzie's gaze and knew she must help her friend. 'No...no...I must tell you. I have kept this secret for more than thirteen years and it is a burden that I must finally let go.'

Lizzie took her hand once more and waited patiently. 'All right Dottie, I understand, just take your time.'

Dottie began. 'After you left, Mrs Hemingway became most annoyed and determined to employ a new senior maid, but Mr Hemingway suggested that I take on your role instead. I was given time to familiarise myself with my new duties and, as Mrs Hemingway was involved in interviewing a new maid to replace me, I was left pretty much to my own devices. I did notice Miss Kate becoming more and more withdrawn after she returned from holiday. She stayed in her room most of the time and took all her meals there. When she did come out, she looked very pale and was obviously troubled. A week later, I think it was, a letter arrived for her, which I placed on the hall table. That's when everything came to a head. She took it up to her room and later sought out Mrs Hemingway, who was in the library...I know I should not have listened at the door Lizzie, but there was such a commotion going on that I was expecting the servants' bell to ring anyway. I've never heard Mrs Hemingway take on so. I was shocked to hear Miss Kate talking about...her...her baby that was to be adopted. However, seemingly, she could not go through with it and told her mother she had given the baby to you to take to London. She said she intended joining you later, after she became twenty-one. Shockingly, she then admitted that you had not reached your destination. Apparently, you had disappeared and she had no idea what had happened to you. Mrs Hemingway exploded and the next thing, the door burst open, but neither noticed me standing there. Kate was screaming at her mother who held her firmly by the arm. Mrs Hemingway was pushing her towards the stairs. I thought it best to go back to the kitchen, as the shouting continued. Horrifyingly, when I returned to the hall, Mrs Hemingway lay at the bottom of the stairs with Kate cradling her head in her arms. It was awful, just awful.' Dottie broke off, drained her cup of coffee in quick gulps and looked tremulously at Lizzie.

Lizzie and Robert stared wide-eyed. Everything was falling into place. Dottie continued. 'I saw George attending to Mrs Hemingway, as Clara took Miss Kate to the sitting room. Shortly after, Mr Hemingway arrived and the doctor was sent for. Later, the butler called the servants in to the kitchen and we were instructed to keep quiet about the whole incident and several days later, the house was put up for sale. The Hemingways' left very soon after. Clara and George also left and I have never seen nor spoken to either of them since.' Dottie sat back in her chair exhausted, but satisfied that she had unburdened herself at last.

Lizzie broke the silence. 'Oh Dottie this must have weighed so heavily on your mind. I think you could use some time away from here. When are you next off duty?'

'Tomorrow Lizzie, I have a day off tomorrow.'

'Well Dottie, I am going to ask Mrs Masters if we can pick you up and take you out for the day. Would you like that? We intend to visit Clara.'

Dottie's face broke into a grin. 'Oh Lizzie, could I? I would love to see old Clara again. Do you think Mrs Masters will agree?'

'Don't you worry about Mrs Masters, just be ready tomorrow morning at nine o'clock and we will wait for you at the main gate. Meanwhile, I suggest you escort us to the sitting room, so that we can finish our tour.'

It was early afternoon when Lizzie and Robert finally managed to find time for lunch, which they took at the hotel. The morning's events were the main topic of conversation.

'Oh Robert, what a stroke of luck that Dottie was on duty, if we had gone tomorrow, it would have been her day off.'

Robert mused. 'Mmm...I thought Mrs Masters would have apoplexy when I asked her if Dottie could accompany us for the day. I don't think she was overly appreciative of her staff fraternizing with her guests.'

Lizzie grinned. 'No, she wasn't, but I see you managed to work your charms on her. Really Robert, you are such a flirt. The more I get to know you, the more I see a mischievous side to you. My congratulations on winning Mrs Masters over completely. Seriously though, what a revelation, I think we can forgive Kate for keeping the whole baby thing a secret. Georgina would never have allowed her to keep it and it would have been impossible for you and her to marry. We now know that the intention was for me to travel to London, to be joined at a later date by Kate. She must have been out of her mind with worry when she did not hear anything from me. How she envisaged I would manage such an epic journey, I cannot imagine.'

Robert was pensive. 'I don't think she could have orchestrated the whole thing herself. Kate was always good at planning, but she must have trusted someone enough to help her carry out such a scheme. Can you think of anyone?'

Lizzie lapsed into deep thought and then suddenly remembered something. 'Well, although my last year at Low Wood is still sketchy, I do remember Kate's Aunt Jayne making a visit some time during the year. Jayne was Georgina's sister, but they did not always see eye to eye. Kate and her were very close, so maybe she had a hand in the plan. She must have given birth in a nursing home, where the adoption would have ostensibly taken place.'

'You could have something there Lizzie. I must say, we've gleaned a considerable amount of information during our stay here. What we have learnt so far gives me confidence that we will bring this nightmare to a successful conclusion. However, you must still take the planned holiday with your cousins. While you are away, I will continue the investigation. Maybe Clara knows Jayne's address, if so, I will travel to London and ascertain if this Aunt Jayne still lives there.'

'That's a good idea Robert. I wish in a way I had not agreed to go to Berriedale, but I cannot let my cousins down now, so I am relying on you to move things forward.'

❦

The following morning they picked up Dottie at Low Wood and proceeded to Clara's. On arrival, Lizzie and Robert were dismayed at the rundown state of the cottage. They knocked on the gnarled oak door, without response. No one appeared to be at home, so Robert went around the back and peered in through the window. He could see a small figure huddled by the fire, so called to Lizzie to join him. Lizzie knocked purposefully on the window. A few moments passed, then Clara opened her eyes to see her old friend outside. She shouted in glee. 'Why Lizzie what a surprise, come on in my dear, the back door is open. I can't get up myself.'

Robert, Lizzie and Dottie entered the rear parlour and Lizzie threw her arms around the old lady. 'Clara, oh Clara, are you here alone? How are you?'

Clara smiled weakly. 'At the moment I am, but Mabel Drummond calls in every morning and evening to see that I am all right. I do struggle to get around these days. How lovely to see you Lizzie...you've not changed a bit, well perhaps more beautiful than ever and you too Dottie, but who is this good looking young man?'

Lizzie made the introductions. 'This Clara, is my brother, Robert.'

Robert bent down and kissed the old lady on the cheek. 'I am very pleased to meet you Clara. I have heard a lot about you.'

Clara giggled, thoroughly uplifted by their visit. 'I bet you have. Now, what's Lizzie been saying?'

'Oh nothing untoward, I can assure you. Lizzie has only kind words to say about you and your late husband, George.'

'Ah George, yes...my George was a good man. I do miss him so much Lizzie. Well, sit yourselves down and perhaps Dottie, you wouldn't mind making us all a cuppa. You'll find everything you need in the kitchen deary...Now Lizzie what brings you here?'

Lizzie smiled benevolently at her friend, still shocked at how old and frail she looked. 'Do you mean apart from seeing you? Well, I am on my way up to Berriedale to holiday with my cousins, so I thought it the ideal opportunity to look in on you. It has been such a long time since we were together at Low Wood Clara...too long, but as you know, I lost my memory for five years and still parts of my past are a complete mystery. However, what I do remember is the kindness shown to me by George and yourself.'

Clara suddenly became alert, despite her frailty. The days had been long and lonely since George died, but now she brimmed with excitement. The visit from old friends gave her a real boost and Dottie's 'tea' reminded her of the times spent together at Low Wood, before the death of Georgina changed everything.

Robert surveyed the room and noticed the dying embers in the grate. 'Can I fetch some logs Clara? This room is quite cool and you need to keep yourself warm.'

Clara nodded. 'Why, of course, Robert, you will find wood in the store outside.'

While Robert toiled, the conversation turned inevitably to the good times enjoyed at Low Wood and Lizzie's search for Kate.

Clara was eager for gossip and wasted no time in getting directly to the point. 'Well Lizzie, I was surprised when you wrote a few years ago explaining the situation with your brother and Kate. Mind, Kate was always drawn to good-looking men and your brother is certainly that. What a ta'do. Can't say I blame her. James was always a bit of a fop[9]...Are you any nearer finding her Lizzie? I do wish I could be of more help. Don't suppose you heard anything after I left, did you Dottie?'

Lizzie glanced sideways at Dottie, who appeared eager to recount her story. Finally, despite looking sheepish, she sought approval for her actions. '...I know I should not have been listening Clara, but it was such a commotion.'

Clara nodded. 'I can understand why you did Dottie but, as it turns out, it was a good thing, because now Lizzie and Robert have a lead to finding Kate.'

Lizzie interjected. 'Clara, do you know Jayne Munroe's address? We feel we should contact her, to ascertain her involvement in all of this.'

Clara stared thoughtfully at the old oak cabinet, which was bedecked with items of china and other knick-knacks, lovingly collected over the years. Their lively conversation had awakened many memories to good effect, as suddenly she remembered. 'Look in the dresser drawer Lizzie, where you will find George's address book. George was always the one for recording addresses.'

---

9 'Fop' was widely used as a derogatory epithet for a broad range of people by the early years of the 18th century

Lizzie was sorting through the various items in the drawer, when Robert re-entered the room with his arms full of logs. He was banking up the fire when Lizzie retrieved the all-important book. 'Is this the book Clara?'

Clara took the well-worn, red leather covered book and began scanning the pages. She quickly found the address she was looking for. 'Yes, here it is Lizzie, Mrs J Munroe, six... or is it five? Carlton House Terrace, Off Pall Mall, London.'

There was a stony silence, as Lizzie and Robert exchanged glances, clearly shocked at this revelation.

Robert was the first to speak. 'It can't be that address Clara, are you sure it's correct?'

Clara, oblivious to their reaction, peered once again at George's handwriting. 'Well, it isn't very clear I must admit, I am not sure whether it is a six or a five. Could you read it for me Lizzie?'

Lizzie stared at the address in the book; she could not decipher the number, but the rest of the address was clearly correct - *Carlton House Terrace, Off Pall Mall.* She looked quizzically at Robert. 'It is correct Robert...that cannot be a coincidence can it?'

Robert's eyes opened wide in amazement. 'No...no I cannot imagine it is, but surely the woman who found my cane cannot be the same person. She gave her name as Montague, not Munroe. What do you think this means Lizzie?'

Suddenly the significance dawned. 'Good Lord Robert, I do remember where I've heard that address before, Daisy Pickering mentioned it at the Nottingham Goose Fair, as my intended destination. That was the day Daniel found me and we were re-united, so it is very significant, as it confirms Jayne's involvement in Kate's plan. She may have used a false name to protect her identity. If Kate was with her, she could have surmised from the initials that there was a possibility the cane may have belonged to you, although there must have been other factors that led her to that conclusion. Perhaps they deliberately left Jayne's address with the proprietor, hoping you would contact her, without alerting you to their suspicions,' she paused, 'I *do* believe it *was* Jayne Munroe who found your cane!'

Robert gave a wry smile. 'You could be right Lizzie, except, as far as I remember, the lady appeared to be alone.'

Clara looked from one to the other. 'What are you talking about, what has Jayne Munroe to do with a cane?'

Lizzie looked to her brother to explain.

'It is complicated Clara. You see, I left my walking cane in an hotel in Manchester and this lady handed it to the proprietor. She left her name and address with him, in case I wished to contact her and the address she gave was six Carlton House Terrace.'

Clara and Dottie, though mystified, were not totally shocked at the explanation. Clara commented. 'I wouldn't be surprised if it *was* Kate's Aunt Jayne. She was very close to Kate, who often sought her advice, much to her mother's annoyance. In fact, if I remember rightly, she came to Low Wood a short while before we were told Kate was to take an extended holiday. We all know now that it wasn't a holiday at all, but an excuse for her to go away to have the baby. Do you remember the dinner party Lizzie, on the Sunday before you left? Jayne Munroe was to be the guest of honour, but she left abruptly about a week before the event. Mrs Hemingway was furious, because the party had been arranged for some time. Perhaps she returned to London to be there when you arrived.'

Lizzie nodded. 'Yes, yes Clara, I do believe you are right. As Robert said, Kate could not have carried out her plan without an accomplice and that one trusted person would be her aunt. If true, Aunt Jayne and Kate must have been searching for Rosie for the last thirteen years. How she must have suffered and what a coincidence they were in Manchester at the same time as you Robert. This means we have the chance to reunite them. What do you think Robert?'

Robert was positive. 'I agree! and on my return to Manchester, I will make plans to visit Jayne Montague, or should I say Munroe. At long last it would seem the end is in sight, thanks to you both,' said Robert looking at Dottie and Clara, but the old lady had closed her eyes, the last hour, albeit exciting, had also being very exhausting.

Lizzie realised they may have overtaxed her friend, so proposed taking their leave, promising to come and see her again tomorrow.

Gently Robert carried Clara to the bed in the corner of the room and covered her over with an eiderdown.

'Lizzie, before we leave, I will make sure her gate is fixed and secure the lock on her door.'

'Good idea Robert, while you're doing that, I will take a look in the kitchen and see what groceries she needs for tomorrow.'

By the time they left, the house was warm and secure. They felt happy in the knowledge that Mabel would be calling in on her later. Lastly, Robert dampened down the fire before silently closing the door.

⁂

When Mabel Drummond returned that night to prepare her friend for bed, she was surprised to find that Clara had somehow managed the task herself. She did not wish to disturb her, so picked up her dressing gown from the chair, hung it on its hook and left. She intended to return bright and early the following morning.

Before Mabel arrived, Clara Meredith had drifted off into a very contented sleep and dreamt about her early life at Low Wood. The visit from her friends had sparked memories of the good old days. But now, she was alone, her husband had gone and she too was tired. She missed him terribly, as he had been her rock and her soul mate. For a short while and with her friends around, she had regained some of her enthusiasm for life and was contented...yes very contented, but she was ready to go now, ready to join George. She knew it wouldn't be long. Then as the dawn was breaking, she saw him standing at the foot of the bed, smiling and beckoning to her. She wondered what he was doing there, but held out her hand, wanting desperately to be with him again...'*I'm coming George, I'm coming,*' she mouthed, stretching out towards him...'*wait for me*'...and as they became as one, Clara Meredith slipped peacefully away in her sleep.

Robert was near the end of his journey to London as Lizzie boarded the steam ship that would take her from Fort William to Inverness on the penultimate leg of her journey to Berriedale. Both were reflecting on the ups and downs of their visit to Glasgow. Dottie's revelations and the discovery of Jayne Munroe's address, followed by the sudden death of Clara Meredith, had brought mixed emotions.

Robert needed to concentrate his efforts on locating number six Carlton House Terrace. He hoped it would bring an end to the nightmare he had suffered since discovering he was Rosie's father.

Aboard the steamship, Lizzie was mulling over the implications. If Kate were found, would she want Rosie's return? It was extremely complicated and disturbing and both her and Robert were exhausted by their hectic schedules and very mixed emotions. Just what would the future hold?

CHAPTER FOUR

Destinies
April 1855

The whitewashed cottage in Berriedale, stood proudly on the waterfront at Shore Cove. The original cottage had one bedroom, but now provided the luxury of two, because Angus bought the adjoining cottage and knocked through a few years ago. They would need the extra space if Morag, his wife, became pregnant, but sadly she hadn't conceived. At thirty-three, in all probability, the time had passed for her chance to have a child.

An utterly exhausted Lizzie finally knocked on the black painted front door. Her two cousins rushed to greet her amidst much excitement and cries of amazement because their last meeting had taken place a lifetime ago, when Annabella was five, Lizzie almost four and Morag, two.

Lizzie was surprised at the physical difference between the two sisters. They were similar in height, but Morag, though pretty, was slightly plump with short brown hair and plainly dressed. Annabella, on the other hand, looked much younger than her thirty-seven years and outshone her sister physically. She was slim and attractive. Her dark hair tumbled around her face, almost disguising the long dark lashes, which accentuated her penetrating blue eyes. Oddly, the clothes she was wearing were more suited to the city than the little fishing hamlet.

Morag clasped Lizzie's hands and welcomed her into the parlour, where she immediately felt at home. The plainly furnished room, despite the furniture being old and slightly worn, seemed particularly warm and comfortable.

Lizzie was to share with Annabella, who took her case and placed it on one of the single beds. The fairly large wardrobe had been partially cleared by Annabella to make room for Lizzie's clothes. Annabella turned excitedly to her cousin. 'I am so glad you decided to come Lizzie. I am afraid I neglected my family after I left home and I'm not much of a letter writer, so there will be a lot for us to talk about and catch up on.'

Lizzie smiled graciously. 'I am glad to be here. I was so sorry to hear of the sudden death of your husband, it must have been a very difficult time for you coping alone, without much in the way of close family around you.'

To Lizzie's surprise, Annabella replied matter-of-factly. 'Yes...yes well, it did leave me in a difficult position. We'd recently returned to Oliver's mother's house in Glasgow, following our time abroad. We don't get along too well. Consequently, I need to make a decision whether to return or look for a property for John and I. Morag suggested I come to stay with her for a while to think things over. I am really glad she did actually because being here has given me a new lease of life.'

Lizzie was somewhat shocked that Annabella did not appear to be upset about the untimely death of her husband. What appeared to bother her most was the inconvenience of the living arrangements, which Lizzie considered less significant, compared to her husband's death, but she continued sympathetically. 'Yes, I think it will do you good. You will need time away to decide on your future.'

Annabella's mood changed again as she began sorting through her clothes, more than anxious to decide what to wear for the evening meal. 'Do you like this dress Lizzie? It is rather fetching, perhaps I will wear it tonight for supper.'

Lizzie, still shocked at Annabella's indifference to her husband's death, was even more surprised at her cousin's desire to dress for supper at the cottage, where no one would be there to see or really care about what she wore. Perhaps Oliver's death had more of an impact on her state of mind than she imagined. 'It is very pretty Annabella, but you don't need to impress anyone. The idea is that we spend our time here relaxing, without the need to dress for dinner. Indeed, I only brought simple clothes to wear.'

Annabella ignored her cousin and continued spinning around the bedroom in her rather lavish dress. 'Do you think this colour suits me Lizzie? I love red...red is definitely my colour.'

Lizzie was at a loss for words, but did not wish to dampen her cousin's enthusiasm. 'Yes, I think red definitely suits you Annabella,' she paused and looked towards the kitchen where Morag was struggling with a large pot of stew. 'Excuse me a moment, while I see if Morag needs help with supper.'

Morag was busy laying the table and cutting slices from a loaf of bread. 'Can I do anything Morag? The table looks a treat and that stew smells delicious.'

Morag felt cheered by her cousin's offer of help. 'Why thank you Lizzie, however, you must be very tired from your journey, but do sit down, as we will have time for a chat before I serve supper. I'm actually rather tired myself, as there has been so much to do this last week and Annabella isn't very domesticated.' She lowered her voice as she expressed anxiety about her sister. 'It's really strange Lizzie, but she has been acting peculiarly since her arrival. She's always washing her hair and putting on the most inappropriate clothing. I think she is in total denial about Oliver's death, perhaps even blasé about the whole matter. Do you think it is her way of coping?'

Lizzie raised her eyebrows. 'Well I know what you mean. Just now in the bedroom, she was sorting out a special dress to wear this evening, as if either of us would even notice what she wore. Maybe you are right and it's the only way she can accept his death.'

'Mmm, she was always looking in mirrors when we were young and was frequently too busy to help mother with the housework. I found myself doing her chores as well as my own, but right now, I could do with some help. I am expecting Angus back on Sunday morning, weather permitting, consequently, I have been extra busy with the washing and ironing.'

Lizzie noticed the dark circles around Morag's eyes. 'Well Morag, I'll tell you what, I could help tomorrow with some of the ironing and if you need any baking doing—'

Lizzie was interrupted by Annabella, who breezed in and slumped down on the sofa in front of the fire. 'Is supper ready? What are you two gossiping about...domestic matters no doubt?'

Morag gave her elder sister a withering look, but was determined not to have their first evening together spoiled by petty arguments. 'Well yes, we were, but I suggest that after supper we all relax and catch up on the last thirty odd years of our lives. I am sure you two will have many fascinating escapades to recount.'

After supper, Annabella insisted they leave the dishes and not waste any more time on mundane tasks. Morag agreed, because she was more interested in Lizzie's life, especially with relation to Marcus. They had corresponded regularly, but not everything was included in their letters, so for the first hour, Lizzie relived her exploits, especially those spent in Narrow Marsh before her long delayed reunion with Marcus.

Morag was obviously in awe of Lizzie's adventures, which seemed in complete contrast to her own, relatively uneventful, if not mundane existence. Annabella, on the other hand, became strangely quiet, a trifle moody and rather circumspect, until both Lizzie and Morag encouraged her to talk about her life.

Annabella instantly perked up and resumed her normal exuberant self. She was pleased that she both shocked and surprised them with her outrageous exploits, although obviously full of exaggeration and fantasy. The evening wore on and the girls continued to express pleasure at being together again. They complimented each other on milestones achieved and even managed to stay up until gone midnight before all were exhausted, when they reluctantly agreed to retire. Lizzie, however, still had difficulty sleeping, because she was trying to work out why Annabella was acting so strangely.

The following morning, Morag rose early to tend to the fire well before, first Lizzie and then Annabella, surfaced. The latter in a vibrant mood, watched her sister struggling with a large pot of porridge. 'Come on Morag, leave that and come for a walk with us. Sometimes you act like a real old woman. You need some fun in your life, so grab your coat and scarf and let's go.'

The three walked briskly along the shore at Annabella's insistence. The wind rushed through their hair and the sand was soft beneath their bare feet, which gave Morag's visitors a great sense of freedom. Morag was less enthusiastic because her husband's return always made her feel a little anxious. The Atlantic was notoriously rough at this time of year and the North Westerly wind had increased steadily over the last few days. The waves were whipping up and crashing hard against the rocks, sending white spray high into the air. Lizzie sensed her cousin's worry. 'Are you fretting about Angus, Morag?'

Her concerned smile said it all. 'Yes...yes, I am always anxious until he is safely home, especially at this time of year. Look you can see how rough it is out there on this coast.'

'Mmm...yes, it is quite rough, but Angus is an experienced fisherman and I've no doubt he will come back safely,' suggested Lizzie soothingly.

Morag didn't feel so sure this time. A premonition two nights ago hadn't helped. She'd seen him calling out from his boat, which was being thrown about in huge waves. One moment she could see him clearly from the shoreline and then both he and his boat disappeared. Her heart was beating fast as she awoke with a start and a terrible sense of foreboding engulfed her. She knew he always came back safely, but nevertheless, it still played on her mind.

'Of course, you *are* right Lizzie. It is stupid of me to imagine misfortune will prevail. I should be more confident in his abilities, but the sea can be very cruel and even experienced fishermen sometimes struggle with their small boats when faced with the unforgiving nature of the Atlantic.'

'Maybe so, but try not to worry, hopefully the wind will have lost its strength by Sunday,' said Lizzie. Then she looked around and noticed Annabella was not with them. 'Where is Annabella?'

While the two were discussing Angus's return, Annabella had strode off down the beach. Lizzie saw her first, standing some fifty feet away on an outcrop of rocks close to the water's edge, seemingly oblivious to the dangers of the waves that were crashing ashore all around her. She was looking wistfully at the horizon.

Anxiously, Lizzie called out. 'Annabella...Annabella, move back from the edge. Come on, we should return to the cottage anyway, breakfast is beckoning.' The wind whipped the words from her lips, as Annabella continued to stare out to sea, so she gestured for Morag to follow and picked her way towards the large rock upon which Annabella was precariously perched. Lizzie approached cautiously, until awareness dawned and she came to her senses turning around to see Lizzie reaching for her. 'Annabella, what on earth are you doing? Come back here where it is safe. You are soaking wet. Didn't you notice the waves pouring over the rock where you were standing?'

Annabella stared at the rock she had just vacated and was shocked to see the giant waves crashing over it. 'Oh...why yes, I didn't realise. The sea is mesmerising, don't you think?'

An anxious Morag joined them. 'Annabella, you frightened me to death. You need to stay clear of the rocks, especially when the tide is coming in. You could easily have been swept away and there wouldn't have been anything we could have done. Come on...let's go home, I think we need a hot drink and some breakfast.'

At the cottage, Annabella became quiet and reflective once again. She stared vacantly at Morag and Lizzie, who were enjoying a steaming bowl of porridge. Her sunny disposition had once again deserted her.

'Are you all right Annabella? You seem lost in thought. Is there something bothering you?' asked a concerned Morag.

Annabella peered at her sister. 'No...it's nothing really. I'm in a reflective mood that's all. I was thinking how sometimes, life works out in funny ways.'

Lizzie was by now seriously perplexed and had difficulty in adjusting to the constant ups and downs of her cousin's mood swings, but persevered. 'Are you thinking about Oliver, Annabella?'

Annabella stared at her cousin and thought how little Lizzie knew her; how little either of them *really* knew her. Both were cocooned in their own little world; Morag, barren, without a hope of conceiving and living a desperately hard life, as she keeps the home fires burning and Lizzie...the beautiful Lizzie Cameron - what did she know? So smug and happy, but totally naive when it comes to what actually happens in the big bad world. Besotted with a man she barely knew at the time, then embarking on a mission to find her daughter's birth mother. Didn't they long for adventure... real adventure that heightened the senses and made the heart beat faster?

In actual fact, *she* felt oppressed married to Oliver, oppressed and restless. She always wanted something exciting to happen, which it never did. Every day was the same - working, cooking, cleaning, nurturing. She wanted more...wanted to meet someone...have a wild, passionate affair, someone to make her feel alive again.

Oliver made her feel like that at first, before the boring repetition of a day-to-day existence and his controlling mother, Fennella Jamieson, invaded her life. Back then, he wanted to travel and craved the excitement of foreign lands. Shortly after their marriage, he was offered a job as a banker in Toronto. It came with a large house and servants. It was everything Annabella had envisaged for herself and for many years they were happy and content.

After twelve years of living the dream, Oliver became ill and his mother pressured him to return to Glasgow. She promised that they could have the whole of the West wing in her large country mansion. She advised Annabella that she would engage servants to administer the household tasks and Oliver's nursing requirements would be met when his health deteriorated, as it inevitably would.

He refused to return at first, mainly to keep Annabella happy, but as he struggled to cope with his illness and the pressures of his job, he eventually succumbed to his mother's wishes. A year later, they returned home. Within days, their lives became unrecognisable. Fennella criticised Annabella's abilities, complaining that she did not give Oliver enough attention. Annabella, in turn, took a job just to get away, but this only led to Fennella taking complete control. Annabella almost felt a sense of relief when Oliver became too ill to make love to her anymore. What had happened to the exciting young man she first met?

Her first husband had been the same, promises of travel and excitement, only for him to become staid and boring. She wasn't going to let it happen a second time she promised herself, but it had been exactly the same.

Now though, she was free again, free to seek out someone who wanted more out of life than married domesticity and when she arrived in Berriedale, a miracle occurred, she believed she had found him. Time would tell, but for the moment, she needed to embrace the reality of feigning excitement at seeing her sister and cousin again.

She wouldn't have to pretend for too long. Soon she could leave this God forsaken place and go far away...away from the responsibility of her own son, John, about whose age she had lied, in order to enrol him at school a year earlier. She reconciled this with the fact that he had been able to go to Hull College a year before the usual acceptance age and now he was expected to join a Merchantman[10], following his final year. *She felt safe in the knowledge that his grandmamma would always be there for him, making sure he trod the right path. However, the path Fennella's own son, Oliver, had taken...the expected direction, that of a secure job, marriage and a child...was not what she visualized for John. If he lived with her, she would undoubtedly smother him with her overbearing sense of self-righteousness...better that he had a naval career and only used Fennella's home as a base. Yes, that idea was much more preferable she reasoned.*

Satisfied with her plan, Annabella grimaced as she observed the predictable naivety of Lizzie and Morag. She could see they were waiting for an answer and tried to look suitably contrite. In a way, she felt sorry for them; sorry for the uncompromising, boring existence they seemed happy to embrace. She attempted to explain. 'Well yes, it hasn't been long and I do miss him, but I need a man Lizzie, someone to pamper me and provide some excitement. Life must go on and I need to move forward.'

Lizzie thought how brave she was and that perhaps she and Morag had been right in their assumption that her attempts to appear unmoved by her husband's death were

---

10 *Nautical* - A cargo ship used in commerce. The title of the 'Merchant Navy' was bestowed by George V on the British merchant shipping fleets, following their service in the First World War.

a front. *Yes, of course, that was definitely it, everyone deals with the death of his or her loved one in different ways and this was her way.*

'Well Annabella, if ever you want to talk about it, we are here for you, aren't we Morag?'

'Yes, yes of course we are. Anything we can do Annabella, you only have to ask.'

Annabella smiled to herself, she knew she wouldn't have to ask, as shortly her sister would unknowingly be making a huge sacrifice. Her plan was already in place and she began to feel extremely optimistic about the future.

Her optimism lasted but a few minutes, before Morag shattered her dreams by dropping a bombshell that had the potential to rip her carefully thought out plans apart at the seams.

A radiance lit up Morag's face, as she coyly began her tale. 'There's something I want to tell you.' She looked excitedly at the pair, before continuing. 'I didn't want to tempt fate, so I kept it to myself, but I am so excited that I have decided to share it with you now we are all together.'

Lizzie and Annabella stared expectantly at Morag. Annabella spoke first. 'What is it Morag. What on earth are you so excited about?'

Morag was all smiles as she delivered her news. 'I'm going to have a baby.'

There was a moment's silence as the news provoked different reactions. Lizzie was as pleased as 'Punch' for her cousin, but Annabella was shocked and angry, angry that her sister could possibly be pregnant at her age. 'What?...are you sure? You are far too old to even consider a pregnancy. You must be mad. Does Angus know?'

Morag looked puzzled at her sister's outburst. 'Why aren't you pleased for me Annabella? We have waited so long for a child. I know I am quite old to be contemplating bringing a baby into the world, but I can do it...I will do it. The doctor says I am healthy and there isn't any reason why I shouldn't carry it to term. Angus is delighted and can't wait to become a father.'

It was Annabella's turn to look puzzled as she continued to question her sister. 'When...when did you tell him?'

Lizzie and Morag hadn't any idea why Annabella was acting so strangely, but Morag, sensing her sister was clearly anxious, replied. 'I told him just as he was leaving on his trip. I was going to wait until he returned, but I couldn't let him go without him knowing he was to become a father.'

Annabella became quiet, believing she had been the last person to see Angus when, at the request of Morag, she had taken his lunch down to the beach, just hours before he set sail. Not happy with Morag's reply, she continued to question her sister. 'So you saw him just before he sailed? I thought you were going to stay away, as you couldn't bear to wave him off. You said you had already said your goodbyes at home.'

Lizzie and Morag were more puzzled than ever and stared incomprehensibly at Annabella, completely taken aback by her behaviour. 'I decided to go down after all. When you returned, I went out for a walk and saw Angus making the last preparations to his boat and, as I said, I couldn't let him go without telling him the good news,' replied Morag.

Annabella stood up from the table and stormed off to her room, leaving the two women staring blankly after her. Lizzie was puzzled and exchanged glances with Morag. 'What is wrong with her? Why on earth did she react like that? I would have thought she would have been so happy for you and why would it matter to her that you were the last person to see Angus?'

Morag seemed at a loss. 'I...I don't know. As I explained to you, Annabella has been in a very strange mood ever since she arrived, but I put that down to circumstances. Clearly we were right in our assumption that she misses Oliver more than she lets on and *you* know Annabella, she much prefers the company of men. Angus has been so kind to her Lizzie, paying her attention and making her feel at home. She seems to relate more to him than me. She always craves attention and perhaps she thinks he won't have so much time for her when he returns, if he is fussing around me.'

Lizzie was pensive. 'Yes...perhaps that is it. Shall I go to her?'

'It might be an idea Lizzie. Try to find out what is bothering her.'

When Lizzie entered the bedroom, Annabella was staring out of the window, thinking she must get a grip on her emotions. She was foolish to make such a scene. Baby or no baby, nothing had changed. *He wants me, I know it. Nothing will stop us being together, I won't let it. In three days I will be gone from here and it will all be over.*

Annabella smiled and turned around to face her cousin, anxious to regain her trust. 'I'm sorry Lizzie. I just don't know what came over me. I think it is a reaction to my loss. Morag and Angus have been so good to me and I know it is selfish, but I have confided in him quite a lot and have got used to the attention. He has helped me to come to terms with Oliver's passing. If they are to have a baby, Angus will not have any time to spend with me. He will need to help Morag, which is understandable and I have no right to expect him to listen to me babbling on day after day. Do you think she will forgive me for behaving the way I did?'

Lizzie put her arms around her cousin. 'Of course, Annabella, I am sure she will understand, but you'd better make your peace with her.'

Morag made some tea and set three cups down on the table. Annabella apologised to her sister and the three women sat down to talk about their future, a future, which would be unforgiving.

On Friday morning, two days before Angus was due home, Morag cleaned out the grate. She carried a large basket of logs in from the log store, but as she stood up, a gripping pain seared through her abdomen and she doubled over, crying out to Lizzie. 'Lizzie, Lizzie can you come quickly?'

Lizzie rushed through to the sitting room on hearing her cousin's urgent cries for help. 'What's happening Morag? Are you all right?'

Morag, deathly pale, crumpled up in agony. 'Something's wrong Lizzie. I have this terrible pain in my stomach.'

Lizzie became increasingly concerned as she helped Morag to the armchair. 'Sit here Morag. Don't worry, I am sure it will be all right.'

'Oh God Lizzie, it is getting worse. I think it's the baby. Can you fetch Mrs O'Connor, she lives near the cut through on the edge of the village?'

'All right Morag, but I'll call Annabella, I cannot leave you here alone.' Lizzie entered the bedroom and spoke urgently to her cousin. 'Annabella, Annabella, wake up...it's Morag, she is not well. Can you sit with her while I fetch Mrs O'Connor. I think she is losing the baby.'

Three hours later, Morag lay quietly in her bed, distraught in the knowledge that her much longed for baby was no longer moving inside her. Lizzie held Morag's hand as sobs wracked through her body. 'Oh Lizzie, it's gone, my little baby has gone. I feel that was our opportunity and we'll never have another. Even if we try again, my age will prevent me conceiving. Angus will be devastated; he was so looking forward to being a father. Now he will never know that joy.'

Lizzie tried to be positive. 'Oh Morag, I'm sure that's not true. The doctor said you are healthy, so...after a while, I don't see why you cannot try again, but right now, you need to get yourself well again. I think you should stay in bed for the rest of today and tomorrow. Annabella and I will see to everything before Angus comes home. Don't worry Morag, your time will come again, I'm sure.'

Annabella listened outside the door, her mind in turmoil. Yes, she wished Morag had not become pregnant, but guilt made her very sorry that she had lost her baby. After all, it didn't really make any difference. She walked into the room looking very sombre, but was unable to convey any empathy, as she believed her sister too old to bring up a child. 'Oh Morag, I am so sorry about the baby, but maybe it is for the best. Perhaps it is nature's way of telling you that you are too old to become a mother.'

Lizzie threw Annabella a look of disgust and firmly admonished her cousin. How could she say such a thing to her sister? 'I don't think Morag is interested in your negative views at the moment Annabella. It would be better if you could make yourself useful and put some logs on the fire, before helping me cook breakfast.'

Annabella, suitably chastised, placed several logs on to the already prepared fire, complaining to herself that the cinders would play havoc with her polished nails.

By Saturday morning, the wind was almost at gale force. The window shutters at the cottage windows rattled in their frames and made Morag even more anxious for Angus's safety. She called to Lizzie, who had been up at five, ironing sheets and making sure everything was prepared for Angus's return. Annabella was still fast asleep in bed, after a restless night. 'Lizzie, could you come here a minute?'

Lizzie, who was lighting a fire, put down the scuttle and went through to the bedroom. She pulled back the curtains. 'Good morning Morag, are you feeling any better?'

Morag smiled. 'Yes, yes I do feel a little better and wonder if I should get dressed. I don't want Angus to come home to a wife who is not ready to welcome him back.'

'I agree that you should look your best when Angus arrives, but I think another hour or so in bed will do you the world of good.'

Morag lay back on the pillow, grateful that Lizzie was here. 'All right Lizzie, I will do as you suggest.'

'I will bring you a cup of tea around eight thirty and then you can have a leisurely day and an early night to be ready for Angus's arrival on Sunday morning.'

Morag closed her eyes as Lizzie retreated from the room, before quietly closing the door. Her next task was to oust miss lazy bones from her bed. A lot needed to be done today and she had no intention of doing it all herself.

She prodded her cousin gently in the back, which coerced her into rising. 'Come on sleepy head, we've lots to do before Angus arrives tomorrow.'

For once Annabella obeyed. 'Quite right Lizzie, I need to wash my hair today, as I won't have time in the morning. My red dress needs ironing too, as we all need to look our best for Angus's arrival.'

Lizzie was dismayed at her cousin's perverse priorities, so left the room to continue with the chores alone.

By late afternoon, the wind was howling and blowing everything about on the beach. The wooden troughs, which the fishermen's wives used to gut and pack the fish, had been abandoned. It had become too dangerous for them to work in such conditions. Several lobster pots were scattered and broken.

Old Josh called on Morag to warn her that the fishing boats would almost certainly be anchoring off-shore in the lee of the land until around five thirty on Sunday evening. They wouldn't chance the early morning tide, as the gale was not expected to abate until late afternoon. The lantern procession, he said, would take place at dusk to guide the small boats safely into the inlet. He assured her that the community had dealt with worse conditions before and she was not to worry. However, he made it clear that she must not contemplate encouraging the boats to catch the earlier tide, under any circumstances, as she had done once before, in the very early days of their marriage.

Later, Morag explained to Annabella and Lizzie about the procession and mentioned the time she disobeyed the rules. 'Once, I went down by myself, hoping to guide Angus ashore on an early tide, as I was desperate to have him home. He was furious that I had put the fleet at risk and I have never repeated my error. Now, I join the rest of the procession to guide the fishing boats back into the inlet, past the rocks. Mind, I fear I may not be well enough to take part on this occasion.'

Lizzie offered encouragement. 'Don't worry Morag, if you are unable to join them, Annabella or I will go down to the shoreline to welcome Angus home.'

Morag looked unsure. 'No...no, Lizzie, I cannot let you do that, it is still quite dangerous and you are not used to the rough seas down there. It is easy to slip and get carried away by the sea. There will be others who are used to it; they will bring the boats safely ashore.'

༺༻

Annabella, however, had other ideas. She intended to rendezvous with Angus, just as she had promised herself, the day he'd left, following their torrid encounter on the beach. She had taken his lunch down to the boat and suggested a walk along the shoreline, to the next bay, conveniently out of sight of the other fishermen.

Angus thought Annabella had something urgent and private to discuss with him, so agreed.

They sat on the rocks in front of a small cave and there she began her objective, the deliberate seduction of Angus McCrea, with no thought as to the heartache and devastation it would cause her sister.

She hitched her skirts up above her knees, exposing the tops of her thighs and licked her lips suggestively, smiling at Angus. Transfixed and clearly shocked by such behaviour, he was, nevertheless fascinated by her actions.

Annabella spoke softly and looked unwaveringly into his eyes. 'Do you like what you see Angus? Would you like to see more?' She didn't wait for a reply, but instead, pulled her skirts up to her waist, displaying the fact that she was not wearing knickers.

Partly through shock and partly through excitement, Angus continued to stare at Annabella's exposed flesh. She reached out for his hand and placed it between her legs. Unable to resist such an invitation, Angus followed her lead, when she suggested they move into the cave where they would not be disturbed.

Quite why he allowed himself to go along with her wishes, he had no idea, but it was something he would soon come to regret. He meekly followed Annabella into the cave, where, quite expertly, she undid the buttons of his trousers. Soon she was moving her hands sensuously over his body and moments later they lay naked on the sand. His surprise was complete when she pushed his head down between her legs. She moaned and arched her back for him. His excitement was mounting, but she teased him further then pulled his face towards her, kissing him softly on the mouth, while she explored his body with her hands.

They had gone too far now for him to stop and as he entered her, his body shook at the sheer pleasure he felt. Never before had he made love to a woman who was so abandoned and giving of herself. He knew what he was doing was wrong, very wrong, but he felt powerless to stop himself.

Later as they lay together, he felt guilty. What if Morag found out? It would be the end of his marriage. What on earth was he thinking, allowing his wife's sister to seduce him so easily? How had it come to this? True he had become close to Annabella over the last few weeks, even finding her attention flattering, but he loved his wife...didn't he? They had been married for sixteen years and although she didn't always make the best of herself, she worked hard and provided him with sustenance and a comfortable home. Why then? What was it about Annabella? Was it the excitement of her seducing him, which his wife never did? He reflected on recent times. Morag required a lot of encouragement and was mostly too tired after a day's work to make love, but it was understandable. He was happy and they shared a closeness only those really in love could share. Anyway, there was more to marriage than the physical side...Oh God, she would never forgive him. How could he face her after this? He was troubled as he watched Annabella, who smiled knowingly at him, pleased with her achievements. 'Did you enjoy that Angus? Do you want me again?' she asked, moving over on top of him.

Angus pushed her away, disgusted with himself for betraying his wife so readily. How could they have done this to her? She did not deserve it. He pleaded with Annabella. 'Please don't tell anyone Annabella. We should not have done this. It is unforgivable and must never happen again.'

Annabella was unrepentant and had no intention of letting go of her man now. 'Why Angus? Why shouldn't we do it again? I know you enjoyed it and I know you would make love to me again in an instant, given the opportunity. Morag will never know. I will never tell her.'

Angus stood up and tucking his shirt into his trousers, gave Annabella a warning. 'Listen to me Annabella. This was a mistake. I love Morag and I don't love you. For both our sakes you need to keep quiet about this...forget it ever happened. It meant nothing to me.'

Annabella, angered by the rebuff, put another suggestion to him. 'Angus...Angus, I could make you very happy. We could make love like this every night. Let us go away together, we could go away from here and never come back.'

Angus was appalled. He realised the woman he had just lain with was very dangerous indeed. 'Are you mad? I don't intend going anywhere with you. When I do return, we will both try our best to make it up to Morag. Do you understand? She is your sister and my wife, for God's sake. Have you no shame?'

Annabella, subdued, but extremely aware, spoke persuasively. 'She might be your wife Angus, but she couldn't make love to you the way I do. Admit it, you want to do it again. You know you won't be able to resist me.'

Angus began walking out of the cave, but as he reached the exit, Annabella, not about to let him off the hook that easily, made an unveiled threat. 'I want you Angus and I *will* have you. If you do not agree to take me away from here, I promise you I will tell Morag everything. How you forced yourself on me; how vulnerable and powerless I was to stop you.'

Angus swung round, deciding to call her bluff, but seeing the determination on her face, changed his mind, deciding once more to plead for her silence. 'Please Annabella, don't do this to us. I could never love you like I love Morag. You will find someone to give you the attention you crave, but that someone is not me. I am going now and you should go back home and forget this ever happened.'

Angus turned rapidly and without looking back, headed along the coast to the jetty where his boat was moored. Annabella stood alone on the shore, looked out to sea and thought over her next move. 'I *will* get you to love me Angus McCrea,' she shouted determinedly. 'You *will* take me away to start a new life together. I *will* find a way to have you for myself when you return.'

❧

The wind had not abated by dawn and most of the community were still sleeping. It was expected the boats would be anchored off until the Sunday early evening tide. Consequently, Annabella's opportunity to be with her man again was paramount, along with her means of escaping from *'this God forsaken place'*.

She got up and dressed quickly, although at 5 a.m. it was still dark. She closed the bedroom door quietly and made her way to the kitchen. The boats could make the early tide, especially so if they were supported and guided by a light from the shore. A process she now knew had been employed by Morag on a previous occasion. True Angus might be angry at first, but he would soon see this as a perfect start for them to be together.

Annabella put on her warm cloak, drew the hood closely around her head and pulled on Morag's boots. They were a size too big, but with her thick stockings, they would be better than lightweight shoes for scrambling over rocks. She collected the lantern, conveniently located at the front door and moved silently out of the house, safe in the knowledge that she would be alone at the cove.

Annabella made her way toward the grassy bank close to the waters' edge, as a light mist descended. The light from the lantern cast an eerie glow on her surroundings, as she moved gingerly over the rocks, eventually arriving in front of the cave. She peered out to sea, where tiny specs of light were visible on the fishing boats, rising and falling on the waves, far out on the horizon.

Her mind was totally focussed. She would persuade him to leave, with no question of him returning to his wife.

Angus and his crew of three were stowing ropes and the fishing nets on deck, when he sensed a dim light flickering on the headland. His practiced eyes indicated a lantern's light swinging to and fro from the direction of the cove. The other fishermen anchored outside the bay, had already decided to lay-off until the second tide, predicted for five thirty that evening. The storm should have abated sufficiently by then for them to make landfall.

However, Angus was confused...*why only one light? Who could be signalling the small flotilla of boats?* He felt sure the lantern procession should not be on the beach before dusk, until after the flood tide had commenced.

He remained concerned, supposing it was Morag. If there was a problem with the pregnancy, she would have gone alone to the cove, hoping he would see her single lantern. She had attracted his attention that way once before when she was eager to guide him home safely, but that almost ended in disaster. Until now she had never since attempted it...maybe she desperately needed him home. Oh God, he hoped she was all right.

He shouted to his crew, above the howling wind, informing them he was going to try for the early tide, because his wife might be in trouble. They in turn warned him that it was madness and he should wait, but Angus ignored their advice and before anyone could stop him, he weighed anchor, then turned his boat in the direction of the light.

Morag advised Annabella previously that the procession of lanterns took place on the other side of Shore Cove, to guide the fishing boats into the narrow inlet and away from the rocks. Despite this knowledge, Annabella seemed blissfully unaware of the consequences of guiding a boat from this stretch of beach, where strong currents besieged the coast.

Annabella swung the lantern back and forth...back and forth. An age seem to pass before she spied the small fishing smack heading towards her through the gloom. It came closer and she could see a familiar figure in the stern. She hoisted the lamp high and swung it more robustly to guide the boat straight toward the beach and waved excitedly...*I knew he would come...I knew he would come for me.*

Too late, Angus realised he was on the wrong side of the cove, where the currents were strongest. How could he have been so stupid?

What on earth was she doing? She should be on the other side, close to the inlet. He was struggling to bring his beleaguered craft under control, when simultaneously, a huge wave and a strong gust of wind caught the boat broadside, throwing two of the crew members, including Angus, into the icy cold water. One crew member managed to grab the gunwale and was quickly hauled aboard by the remaining fisherman, but Angus was pulled away from the craft by the strong currents. He called out frantically to the figure on the shoreline, believing it to be Morag. 'I love you my darling, but I'm not going to make it...Please take care of our child for me. Please...'

Annabella watched horrified as Angus slipped under the waves, momentarily resurfacing, before vanishing into the murky waters. In her panic, she dropped the lantern and ran along the water's edge, peering into the blackness. For a fleeting second, she imagined that Angus's desperate figure had broken the surface once more, but she was mistaken. It must have been a trick of the light, a cruel jibe and instantaneously her chance of a new life tragically ended.

Terrified, she picked up her skirts and stumbled over boulders wet with spray from the waves buffeting the shore. One boot came off as she negotiated the jagged rocks and immediately, an intense pain seared through her ankle as sharp edges jabbed at her flesh. She fell awkwardly and lay there groaning in agony, as the waves washed over her. Her cries went unheeded. No one knew she was there and only seconds passed before she was caught by the undertow.

The strong currents finished the job, pulling her down into the cold blackness of the unforgiving coastal waters. Her lungs filled before she completely lost consciousness, sinking deep beneath the waves.

It was eerily quiet on the shore, apart from the monotonous surge of the waves, as the sea claimed its victim. The tidal rush had covered the sandy beach with foam and seaweed, completely obliterating any sign she once stood there. It would be several hours before her body would be found on the beach, near the secluded cave, where a few short weeks earlier, her actions had determined her fate...

⁂

The loud ringing of the bell down by the shore woke Lizzie and Morag. They were out of their beds in seconds, bumping into each other in the darkness, as they hurriedly entered the sitting room. Lizzie questioned her cousin. 'Why is the bell ringing Morag?'

Morag hastily pulled on a skirt and jumper stumbling as she struggled into her shoes. *Where are my boots?* she thought. 'It signifies danger Lizzie, an emergency. Have you seen my boots?'

Lizzie was perplexed. 'No...no, sorry, I thought you took them off in the kitchen, but they aren't there now. Are you going down to the beach?'

Morag was halfway out of the door as she shouted to Lizzie. 'Yes...yes, something is definitely amiss. I just hope one of the boats hasn't been forced on to the rocks. Wake Annabella and meet me down there.'

Lizzie dressed quickly and went to wake her cousin, but was surprised to see the bed was empty. She called her name, wondering if she had already woken and gone out for a walk, as she was nowhere to be seen.

Mystified, but anxious to join Morag, she pulled on her own boots and hurried down to the shore. It was still dark, but she could see several people already there and old Josh pointing to some wreckage that had floated to the beach. Morag was looking beyond the headland, toward the silhouettes of the fishing boats, which could be seen through the grey mist, although too far away to be clearly identified.

Morag counted them and realised one was missing. She prayed it wasn't Angus's boat. Lizzie saw her talking animatedly to Josh, but by the time she joined her, Morag was practically hysterical. Lizzie hesitated, but still asked the question. 'Is it Angus, Morag?'

Morag threw her arms around her cousin, sobbing loudly. 'I think so Lizzie...there is shattered wood reaching the beach and only one boat missing...I cannot see him. Josh says it could be any one of them, as most boats are alike, so we won't know for certain until they all return, or...or until bodies are found.'

Lizzie hugged her cousin tightly. 'If his boat has foundered, isn't there any chance he and his crew could have been rescued by another boat?'

Morag was distraught with a terrible sense of foreboding. 'We don't know yet for sure, but it looks as if a boat sank or was dashed against the rocks. No one could last more than a few minutes in those waters. Oh Lizzie, what on earth will I do? I love him so much.'

Lizzie was lost for words and unable to comfort Morag, she felt hopeless. It wasn't fair. Morag didn't deserve this. She'd just lost her baby and now possibly the man whom she described as her soul mate...Life was very cruel.

Josh decided to walk along the beach to the other side of the cove where he might find more evidence of a wrecked boat, or some other identification of the craft. He advised Morag against accompanying him. 'Lissen lassie, it's best if you go back home. If it is Angus and he and his crew have been picked up, he will have caught a chill, so get a fire going and put some broth on. It would be an idea to warm the bed as well.'

Morag was reticent to leave, but Lizzie persuaded her and escorted her up the grassy bank to the cottage. Once inside, Lizzie called again to Annabella, but to her surprise there still wasn't a response. 'Where is Annabella? Did you see her down at the beach Morag?'

Morag had not seen her sister since the previous night. 'No Lizzie, I thought she would have followed us down to the beach when the bell started ringing, but I did not see her there.'

'That's very odd, because after I dressed, I went back into the bedroom, but she wasn't there. I thought she might have gone out too. Do you think she might have returned after we left, then called in next door to find out where we were?'

Morag was puzzled. 'Why no Lizzie, Annabella hasn't made the effort to introduce herself to anyone at all. I just don't understand it.'

Lizzie pondered the question whilst she made tea. 'Here Morag, drink this. It has two spoons of sugar. Perhaps she's out walking, but it does seem strange.'

Morag cupped her hands around the mug of tea and drank the sweet brew gratefully. 'Oh Lizzie, I am praying Angus has been picked up. Do you think it likely?'

'Well Morag, he is fit and strong and if anyone can survive out there, then Angus will. We must try and stay positive. I will put some logs on the fire and get started on some broth.'

An hour later Annabella was still missing, but Josh had returned from the cove and was banging loudly on the cottage door. A startled Morag eyed it with fear and dread. 'Oh no Lizzie, they must have found him, will you answer it for me?'

Lizzie squeezed her cousin's hand and cautiously opened the door. Josh greeted her solemnly. 'Hello Lizzie, can I come in?'

Lizzie equally solemn replied. 'Yes Josh, of course...come through.'

Josh sat down on the sofa and held Morag's hand. He spoke softly. 'Morag, lassie, I don't bring good news—' He didn't get any further because Morag stood up wringing her hands. 'He's dead isn't he? You've found him?'

Josh took hold of Morag and seated her back on the sofa. 'Listen Morag, a body has been found, but it isn't Angus,' he paused. 'I am afraid it is your sister, Annabella.'

Morag's shoulders slumped, her face white with shock. 'Annabella? It can't be Annabella. Are you sure? She hardly ever went down to the beach.'

Lizzie's hand went involuntary to her mouth as she too took in the awful news. 'Why...why would she be there? It doesn't make any sense.'

Josh contemplated the two shocked women. 'Do you keep brandy in the house Morag? I think Lizzie and yourself could use one.'

Morag could barely speak, but directed Josh to the dresser. 'It's in the middle compartment Josh.'

Josh poured out two glasses and handed the women one each. 'I know you won't want to do this right now, but later, someone will have to make an identification. I am so very sorry Morag...Lizzie, but we are certain it is her. Everyone knows everyone else in Berriedale and one of your neighbours was with me looking for debris. It was she who discovered the body. She says she recognised her from a few weeks ago. Just hours before the men set sail, she saw her handing what looked like a lunch packet to Angus. Then apparently they walked off down the beach together.'

Morag remained motionless, unable to assimilate the information. It was Lizzie who suggested she immediately identify the body. 'Look Josh, I will go with you and make arrangements to bring her back home.'

'Don't worry, Lizzie,' said Josh, 'it's not necessary. I will make arrangements to have her brought back for you.' He looked from one to the other, but they both remained silent.

~~~

Annabella's body was brought up to the cottage and Morag was surprised. 'Oh Lizzie she's wearing one of my boots. The other must have come off, but I still don't understand what she was doing down there and where is Angus, why hasn't his body been washed ashore?'

Lizzie gazed sadly at the lifeless figure of her cousin and gently moved some seaweed and a wisp of hair covering her face. 'I don't know Morag...she must have had her reasons, but what they were we may never know. Josh apparently found your other boot and the remains of a lantern, which also washed ashore. For whatever reason, she was down there trying to attract the attention of the fishermen. Maybe she hoped that Angus would be able to land his boat there, but, of course, it would have been almost impossible.'

Morag looked puzzled. 'Why though?...why would she risk going down there, over those rocks? Why didn't she wait close to the inlet where the boats always come in?'

Lizzie was unsure and thought it best that they accept the fact that it was an accident and that she must have fallen into the sea. 'We both need to come to terms with this terrible tragedy Morag. Don't worry, I will make all the necessary arrangements. You have to keep strong, ready to meet the boats at five thirty this evening. Do you still intend to join the procession of lanterns?'

Morag nodded. 'Yes Lizzie, I will be going down there to join the others, but I fear that he will not be among the returning men.'

Lizzie reproached her cousin. 'You must not think like that Morag. Stay positive! His body has not been washed ashore on the early tide so there is every chance he has been picked up.'

Later, ten or more people gathered on Shore Cove, including Morag and Lizzie. Five thirty drew closer and the procession gathered momentum, each person hoisted their lantern high and swung it to and fro, as the lights from the boats twinkled like stars in an ink blue sky. The storm had abated significantly and now only a moderate breeze prevailed.

Cheers of joy greeted each boat as it sailed into the inlet and Angus McCrea jumped from the third boat, along with his beleaguered crew. Astonishingly, all were miraculously rescued after their boat was dashed on the rocks. He rushed up the beach to gather his wife into his arms. 'Oh Morag...

Morag, I thought you had perished. What were you doing over by the cave? Were you hoping I could land on that stretch of the beach? and why? You are all right aren't you? The baby is okay isn't it?' Questions flooded out without any answers being given, but both were so happy to be reunited again.

Morag could hardly catch breath as the relief of seeing her husband engulfed her completely. 'Angus...Oh Angus my love. I am all right. I will explain everything to you when we get back home. Are *you* all right? What happened to your boat?'

Angus smiled with relief at his wife, so pleased that she was standing there before him. 'I am fine, but we have a lot to talk about my love. Let's go home.'

Morag and Angus walked back to the cottage hand in hand, but Lizzie decided to stay with Josh for the rest of the evening to enable them to enjoy Angus's long hoped for return.

The homecoming, however, was tinged with sadness. Angus was clearly shocked that Annabella had lost her life to the sea, whilst apparently trying to attract the attention of the fishermen. Morag questioned Angus accordingly. 'Why Angus?...why do you suppose she was down there by herself?'

Angus, fell silent. While he was away, he had given a lot of thought about what had happened between himself and Annabella and had decided when he returned home that he would reveal all to Morag about his indiscretion. How it had meant nothing to him and that it had been something he had instantly regretted.

Now though, with her death, everything had changed and he immediately realised what she was doing down on that part of the beach. He remembered the threat she had made to him and maybe she had meant to carry it through. He thought it best that Morag knew nothing of his betrayal, although they had both been guilty. Better for her to remember her sister with fondness and concentrate on Annabella's good qualities. He didn't see any benefit in revealing what was to him nothing more than a moment of madness. He put his arms around his wife in comfort. 'I am so sorry that she died Morag. Just like you, I cannot understand what she was doing down there and maybe we may never know her reasons. You will get through this. I will help you all I can.'

Morag looked sadly at her husband, knowing she was about to break his heart. 'Angus, there is something I need to tell you. Let's sit down by the fire and I will get us both a brandy.'

Angus eyed Morag quizzically and wondered what on earth she was about to reveal. 'You are making me feel anxious Morag. You are all right aren't you?'

Morag handed him the glass of golden liquid. 'Yes...yes Angus, I am ok now, but I do have some more bad news...I've lost our baby, Angus. I miscarried a couple of days ago.'

Angus stood up and went over to comfort his wife. 'Oh Morag, I am so sorry. You have had so much to worry about. Why...why did that happen?' he asked with an overriding sense of guilt.

Morag took hold of her husband's hand and looked unwaveringly into his sad brown eyes. 'I...I believe it was God's will Angus. It wasn't meant to be, although Lizzie was saying that I am healthy enough and...and we could perhaps try again in the future. What do you think?'

Angus clasped her arm. 'Of course we can try again.' Then holding her close, he whispered in her ear. 'Try and stop me. I intend to give you plenty of loving while I am home, so I hope you won't mind.'

'Oh Angus, of course not...I do love you so. I want to make you happy. I am so glad we are both safe and together again, despite all the trauma of the last few days. We will be here for each other and we must include Lizzie in our happiness, she has been such a tower of strength since she arrived. She has promised to make the arrangements for Annabella's funeral and I am very grateful to her.'

The funeral was held the following week and on the Sunday, Lizzie talked to Morag and Angus about Annabella's son, John. He had arrived with his grandmamma from Glasgow for the funeral, but had returned to the Naval College shortly afterwards. 'What did you make of John, Morag? You looked as shocked as me at his physical appearance. He was the image of Annabella! The same dark hair and penetrating blue eyes, even that persuasive smile, but that is where the similarity ended. Personality wise, they could not have been more different. I thought he seemed a nice young man, although his grandmamma was really protective, almost overbearing. I got the impression he didn't particularly get on with her. I believe he will be leaving college shortly, so he may have already decided on his future.'

Morag agreed. 'Yes...I didn't mention the striking resemblance, but there was definitely no mistaking his parentage. I couldn't see him staying in Berriedale with Angus and me. It wouldn't be the place for him...nothing happening to excite a young man. What do you say Angus?'

'Well Morag, you're right, there is nothing much for him to do here, so I think we shall have to wait and see how things work out. You have his grandmamma's address and she has ours and Lizzie's, so we can keep in touch with her about his progress. I do know that a life at sea would be a wonderful opportunity for him to broaden his horizons and travel the world. Who knows what adventures might lie ahead for him?'

CHAPTER FIVE

Letting Go
April 1855

'Jimmy, Jimmy, are you there?' Rosie had succeeded in sneaking away from her aunt's house after school and now stood in the field close to the copse, peering intently at the natural camouflage provided by the deciduous trees. No answer! so she called a little louder. 'Jimmmeeeee...Jim–'

Her calling was cut short as Jimmy's arms came around her waist from behind. 'Shhh Rosie, you will break me cover.'

A surprised Rosie turned round to face her friend. 'Jimmy Mitchell, you frightened me to death. Where've you been hiding?'

Jimmy grinned mischievously, whilst taking in the shopping bag clutched in her hand. 'What yer got there Rosie?'

She opened the bag. 'It's some food I took from Aunty Amy's kitchen. There's a meat pie, some crusty bread, a wedge of cheese, some butter...oh yes and a slice of Madeira. You must be really hungry by now.'

Jimmy stuffed the pie into his mouth...nothing had ever tasted so good. 'Thanks Rosie, I've been living on rabbit for weeks.'

Rosie eyed Jimmy's dirty, ragged and torn clothes. The boots he wore sported a hole in the sole and the laces were long gone, but she had a plan to remedy these shortcomings. 'Listen Jimmy, I have the key to our house. Mam left it with Aunty Amy and I found it in the hall table drawer. Come on...we only have a couple of hours, before I must get back.'

They entered the house and Rosie attempted to light a fire with wood gathered the previous day. 'Jimmy you need a bath. We'll try boiling a pan or two, if I can get this fire going.'

Jimmy laughed at Rosie's efforts to kindle a flame in the kitchen grate. 'Let me do that Rosie, you will be there all day.'

Rosie reluctantly gave in and instead concentrated on filling two large pans with water. It wasn't long before their combined efforts paid off and Jimmy could relax in his much-needed bath, with Rosie occasionally topping up with a pan of hot water. Once out and now remarkably clean, Jimmy attempted drying his hair by placing his head close to the fire, but only succeeded in producing a 'head of steam'. He soon gave it up as a bad job and instead, wrapped a large towel around his waist before sitting with Rosie on the sofa. 'This is really cosy. I 'ant seen such a good fire in a long time. The nights can get proper coad out there, but it's not too bad if a can bed dahn in a barn, although there in't many of 'em round 'ere.'

Rosie was more than amused at Jimmy's attempts to flatten his hair before it dried. It stuck out in big spikes, so she teased him unmercifully. 'If you'd got any closer to those flames Jimmy, your hair would have caught alight. Oh, by the way, I've got some clean clothes for you to wear. They belonged to me dad and you can't be far off his size now. Here, put this shirt and jumper on.'

Jimmy accepted the clothes gratefully. 'How did you manage to get hold of these Rosie?'

Rosie winked. 'Because Jimmy, I use my head. Me dad's gone off to London for a few days, so it was easy to sneak them out of his wardrobe. I got these as well,' she said, holding up a pair of thick trousers and several pairs of socks. 'Unfortunately, I don't think any of his boots will fit you, so you'd better try on a pair of Marcus's instead.'

Jimmy looked unsure. 'What will you say to Marcus when he finds 'em missing?'

Rosie cocked her head, raised her eyebrows and placed her hands on her hips in exasperation. 'Jimmy, Marcus won't suspect *I* took his boots will he? He'll think they are at the cobblers or something. Anyway, we don't need to worry about that. He has lots of pairs of boots...probably won't even miss them.'

'Okay, but only if you're sure. They are a bit big, but if I put a couple of pairs of these socks on, they will be just grand.'

Rosie smiled, pleased with her ingenuity. 'Well, you look proper dandy in those. Tell you what, Marcus has an old hunting jacket that he keeps in the shed for pottering around the garden. That'ull keep you warm as toast.'

Jimmy was extremely grateful to his friend. *I'll always love her*, he thought, *she really is the best*. 'Aw Rosie, thanks alot. At least I'll look half decent when I join me ship.'

Rosie's face crumpled as she contemplated the big hole Jimmy would leave in her life. 'About that Jimmy, there is something you need to know,' she said, her face displaying the seriousness of the news she was about to impart. 'You will be shocked!'

Jimmy's face darkened and his brow furrowed, as he studied Rosie's sombre face. 'What is it Rosie? Has something happened?'

Rosie squeezed Jimmy's hand. 'It's yer dad Jimmy...he's dead. He never came round from the fall. Me mam sez the bang on his head killed him. I'm very sorry!'

Jimmy's face became ashen as he continued to stare blankly at Rosie. 'Are yer sure? He din't look dead. A thought he'd just bin knocked out.'

Rosie grimaced. 'He *is* dead Jimmy. Me and mam went ter the funeral the following week.'

Jimmy sat in silence and contemplated his part in the demise of his father. He couldn't go back now...in fact he would probably never go back. It was a cruel blow...although he wanted to see his mother again, it wasn't how it was supposed to be. He did not feel remorse for his father's death, in actual fact, he didn't feel anything. After all, he hadn't killed him...it was an accident, but his mother...how would she manage...what would happen to her?

A troubled Jimmy turned forlornly to Rosie for inspiration. 'What about me mam Rosie? What's she goan ter do?'

'Well Jimmy, she's being looked after by her sister in Derby, yer aunty Nancy. She went there straight after the funeral, but I know she misses you Jimmy and would want to know that you are all right. I couldn't tell her your plans, because I didn't know meself where you were going.'

Jimmy was sad. 'Me mam din't talk much abaht me Aunt Nancy. I just knew she wah me mam's sister. She's crippled yer know...got something with a long name like poliomy... something or other[11] when she wah young. I never met 'er.

---

11 Jakob Heine, a German orthopedist, is renowned for his study of poliomyelitis in 1840. His findings was the first medical account on polio and was granted acknowledgment as a clinical entity. He was largely acknowledged for explaining the disease as 'infantile paralysis'.

None ov me relatives ever came to see us Rosie. They din't agree wi me mam marrying me dad in the first place. The rest on the family went agenst me mam after that,' he paused. 'A think when a leave, yu'd berra tell yer mam. See if she cun gerra message to mine...tell her am alright and one day...one day I'll see 'er agen. Will yer da that fer me Rosie?'

Rosie considered his request. 'Okay Jimmy, I'll da that,' she smiled encouragingly, easily slipping back into the Nottingham dialect. 'But I will miss yer so much. It will be ages before we can meet up again...we can meet up again can't we Jimmy? It won't change anything, will it?'

'No, of course not Rosie, I'll find a way, *nothing* will stop me. I just canna ga back ter Nottingham. I will miss you too Rosie, but when I return, I will have enough money to ask yer dad if a can walk out wi yer. Praps I could even rent a place somewhere close and yer could come ovver fer tea. What da yer say Rosie?'

Rosie agreed enthusiastically. There was nothing she could do to prevent him pursuing his dreams and did she really want to? The day would come for them to be together. Even if he was away for months or years, he would come back to her and look after her as his wife. 'I can't wait for those times Jimmy. Now come here and give me a kiss. I am nearly fourteen you know, so I want a proper one that I can remember you by.'

Jimmy wasn't sure he could control his growing feelings for Rosie and didn't trust himself to be so close, but he could see that she would be disappointed if he didn't respond. 'Ok Rosie, close your eyes and prepare yourself for a very special kiss before I go. Yer have ta be back at yer aunt's and I have ta find me way ta Liverpool. That could teck me quite a while, but at least I'll be warm at night, thanks ta you.'

Rosie Cameron closed her eyes and pursed her lips, waiting for Jimmy to give her a proper first kiss. It didn't disappoint, until reluctantly, he pulled away and put on his cap before saying goodbye. He left Rosie to dream of the future they would one day share together.

Chapter Six

Reunited
April 1855

Robert Cameron surveyed the fine row of Regency Houses, which formed Carlton House Terrace. A Portico, topped by an ornate wrought iron balcony, framed the double oak doors of number six. He stepped up to the front door, pulled the small brass bell and waited nervously for someone to answer.

Several thoughts entered his mind as he observed the rays of the early morning sunshine. *What are my feelings for this woman who brought both fulfilment and sadness to my life? Will I recognise her?...Indeed, will she recognise me? Whatever happens, very shortly, my search for Kate will have ended.*

He pulled the bell once more, before stepping back to look again at the upper floor windows for a sign that someone was at home. Disappointingly, there were none. Five minutes elapsed and it became obvious that no one was at home, something he hadn't considered. *Were they out shopping?* Of course, there was nothing to suggest Kate Hemingway lived here with her aunt, but it would have been a start. His intention was to immediately explain the reason for his visit. After all, they both wanted the same thing, so what should he do now? Best write her a note and tell her that he would call again later this evening, but for that, he needed to go back to the hotel for paper and an envelope and then return again.

At the hotel, he found it much more difficult to compose an appropriate form of words than he had anticipated. Should he come straight to the point, declare whom he was and demand that she see him? or should he say he was someone who had information about her daughter? Perhaps that would be better. He didn't want to shock her. He also considered he should address the note to Aunt Jayne, well...not Aunt Jayne as such...rather Jane Montague. He began writing:

Dear Mrs Montague,

I called today, but found that you were not at home. I was given your address by the landlord of the Royal Hotel on Moston Street, in Manchester. It transpired that you kindly handed my cane to him when I inadvertently left it at my table.

I subsequently made this journey explicitly to give you my grateful thanks and to inform you that I bear news of mutual benefit. My intention is to call again this evening at eight o'clock. I hope my visit will not inconvenience you and, therefore, meets with your approval.

I remain, yours sincerely,
RWC

He pondered his signature following the valediction. Did he really want to sign himself using his initials? He decided he would, after considering the options, mysterious though they may seem to the recipient and proceeded to fold the letter in half before securing it in the envelope.

Several well to do people strolled in the spring sunshine along the street fronting Carlton House Terrace, but none were the residents of number six. Robert carefully lifted the flap of the letterbox and posted the letter, hearing it land on the tiled floor. *No going back now*, he said to himself.

He was slowly walking away, when he encountered an elderly gentleman unlocking the door of number seven. He turned and observed Robert making his way through the small shared courtyard and felt obliged to comment on the absence of his neighbour.

He tipped his hat and smiled politely. 'Good day, sir, I couldn't help noticing you were trying, via a letter, to make contact with my neighbour. Can I help you at all?'

Robert replied cautiously. 'Good day to you sir. You are quite correct, I have posted a letter to the lady of the house, as it appears she is away from home.'

The gentleman nodded his head. 'I am afraid they are both away at the moment and won't be back until Friday week. Is it urgent?'

Robert considered his position. He did not wish to elaborate, but was anxious to find out a little more about the residents of number six. 'Not exactly, it is a thank you note for Jayne, although I was rather hoping to speak to her personally.'

The use of Jayne Munroe's Christian name, was, he felt, perhaps over familiar, but it would give the impression that they were at least acquainted with each other.

The man held out his hand in greeting. 'Well...Mr...' he paused and looked questioningly at the stranger.

Robert smiled boldly and without hesitation introduced himself. 'Mr Robert Carmichael. I am pleased to make your acquaintance.'

'Good, good. I am William Shacklock, friend and neighbour of Jayne Munroe and her husband Aubrey. Have you travelled far Mr Carmichael?'

Robert felt he had gained the man's trust and was hopeful that Mr Shacklock would furnish him with additional information. 'Yes, I have actually, I came down from Manchester this morning and am staying at Mivart's at Claridge's. It's a coach ride from here, but is very comfortable. I intended to surprise Jayne, but now feel rather foolish, arriving on the off-chance.'

William Shacklock smiled, knowingly, but questioned Robert further to verify his credentials. 'How long have you known the Munroe family?'

Robert was happy to impart information that confirmed genuineness. It wasn't exactly the truth, but he wasn't lying when he stated he knew the family. 'I have been a family friend some years now, in fact, since 1841, when Jayne visited Low Wood Hall, home of the Hemingways', so I know the family by association.'

Mr Shacklock was satisfied that Robert was who he purported to be, so became more forthcoming with regard to their whereabouts. 'It is a pity that you missed them, but rather a coincidence that they are holidaying in your home-town of Manchester. I'm sure they will be equally disappointed, as undoubtedly they will have dropped in to see you. Aubrey is not with them, of course, as he is presently in America on business. It's just the two of them, Jayne and her niece Kate Renwick.'

Robert was extremely shaken. Renwick, of course, she must have married James after all. He expected her name to be uttered sooner or later, by someone who knew of her whereabouts, but this confirmed beyond a shadow of a doubt, that Jayne and Kate were also searching for him.

He suddenly felt the need to leave. He required a stiff drink to give himself time to come to terms with Shacklock's information. Excusing himself he tipped his hat and thanked William before beating a retreat to the nearest coaching inn, where he decided to return home immediately. If his reasoning was correct, he had a good idea where the women would be staying.

※

The day before Robert Cameron arrived in Manchester, Kate and Jayne were embarking on their third day of visits to the cotton mills in Manchester. They were staying at The Olde Boar's Head, in Middleton. Kate joined her aunt in the cosy snug and ordered a pot of coffee and sandwiches. It was their intention to continue their search for Jacob Brown, at one of the largest mills in the country, Brunswick Mill, in Ancoats. Brunswick formed part of a group of mills built along the Ashton Canal.

Kate was disappointed that Robert had not contacted Jayne prior to their second visit, so for the moment, thoughts of an immediate reunion were set aside.

Aunt Jayne observed the somewhat deflated expression on the face of her niece, but hoped to improve her mood by injecting some enthusiasm into their mission. 'You know Kate, I still have a very good feeling about this trip. I know we haven't had much luck so far, but remember we *have* made big inroads into finding Robert Cameron. We know he was in Manchester last month and there is a strong possibility he lives in this area. As for Jacob Brown, who knows? Finding him could still lead us to Rosalie's whereabouts.'

Kate's mood brightened. She determined to remain positive. 'You are right, of course, Aunt Jayne. It's just so frustrating; the end seems so near and yet so far. I was hopeful that Robert would have contacted you and there would not have been a need to go in search of Jacob Brown, which is becoming rather like finding a needle in a haystack.'

Aunt Jayne laughed in exasperation, unable to keep up with Kate's mood swings, which were up and down like a bandalore.[12] 'Kate, oh Kate, I wish sometimes your mood would remain constant and you could be positive in your resolve. Maybe life wouldn't be so much fun though. Now, from Aubrey's list of cotton mills in Manchester, the Brunswick Mill is relatively new...I think he said it was built in 1840, so it just might be the place Jacob Brown sought employment. It would still be recruiting new mill workers' as it had only recently opened. I suggest we make our way there immediately after lunch. We will need to take a cab, as it fronts the canal in Ancoats.

'That suits me very well Aunt Jayne. The weather is much improved, if still quite cold and the sun is shining, but I rather think I will need to take a muff[13] with me today and you should do the same. Let's finish lunch and you can take a short nap. We can meet in the lobby at 2 p.m.'

'That's a good idea Kate. Why don't you make the arrangements for a coach to take us into Manchester.'

At 2.35 p.m. Jayne and Kate stood outside one of the largest mills in the country, totally unaware that they were only a

---

12 'Bandalore' - the 19th century term for 'yo-yo'.
13 A muff is a fashion accessory for outdoors usually made of a cylinder of fur or fabric with both ends open for keeping the hands warm. It was introduced to women's fashion in the 16th century.

stones throw away from a smaller one owned by Robert Cameron. Aunt Jayne stole a quiet word with Kate before they entered the building. 'Let me handle this Kate, as I have thought of a plan to elicit the information without raising suspicion. Are you happy that I do this?'

Kate trusted her aunt and was happy to let her take the lead. 'Yes, of course Aunt Jayne, I hadn't really thought about it, other than establishing if Jacob Brown is, or was, a worker here.'

'Mmm...yes, but I don't expect anyone would give us that information voluntarily, without establishing who we are and why we need to know. I imagine there are plenty of debt collectors asking about people who owe them money and the workers tend to stick together. We hardly look as if we are in need of a job and usually information has to be paid for, which you've found out yourself.'

'Yes, well you are right about that. Shall we go in then?'

Both felt ill at ease as they approached the glass fronted reception office on the ground floor, adjacent to the stairs, which led right to the top of the imposing seven-storey building.

Aunt Jayne tapped on the window to attract the clerk's attention. A greying, middle-aged gentleman raised his eyebrows and peered over his pinz-nez,[14] pleasantly surprised to see a lady of a certain age and obvious breeding, smiling coquettishly at him, as if he were a dashingly handsome young man. Kate, equally surprised at her aunt's modus operandi, thought she could possibly learn something from her approach. Even at her age, Jayne was not averse to using her womanly wiles to get what she wanted.

---

14 Pince-nez are a style of spectacles, popular in the 19th century, which are supported without earpieces, by pinching the bridge of the nose.

Kate looked on in awe as, unabashed, Aunt Jayne engaged the man in conversation. 'I am sorry to bother you young man, but I am wondering if you could help me find a long lost relative of ours. His name is Jacob Brown and he is my younger cousin.'

The clerk peered closely at Jayne, somewhat puzzled that she continued with her flirtatious gambit. 'Well now, madam, Jacob Brown you say? And what makes you think you will find him here?'

Aunt Jayne continued the charade. 'We lost touch when he moved from the factory of a great friend of my niece, Mr Robert Cameron. You may have heard of him in these parts?'

Kate was full of admiration at her aunt's ability to elicit as much information as possible with a plausible story. She really couldn't imagine Robert having any involvement with the cotton industry, but, it was a good ploy nonetheless.

The man was now very interested and slightly amused, surprising both women with his reply. 'As it happens, I have heard of Robert Cameron; at least the owner of one of the smaller mills goes by that name. If he is one and the same, you would have already realised that I know him. Most of the owners along the canal are familiar with one another and, as a fellow owner, Mr Cameron sometimes calls on my boss, Mr Scrimshaw.'

Jayne tried to disguise her surprise at what was a most unexpected piece of information. This negated the need to find Jacob Brown, but Aunt Jayne felt obliged to continue anyway. 'Of course, of course, Robert does own a somewhat smaller, but nonetheless successful mill, but I think Jacob had ideas above his station and felt he could enhance his prospects by working for a larger company.'

The man smothered a grin. He was enjoying the cat and mouse game he now found himself engaged in. 'Did he now? Well, as it happens, I might know the gentleman to whom you refer, but I am not sure that I am at liberty to confirm or deny his whereabouts, without providing proof that you are who you say you are. All sorts of unscrupulous folk come in here demanding to know if so and so works here, but usually they are after money.' He paused, as he did not wish to offend this delightful lady. He was eager to continue a conversation that could lead to a financial reward. 'Of course, I am not suggesting that is your objective, but debt collectors come in many guises, so you must forgive me.'

Kate was by now itching to leave the mill and Aunt Jayne was no longer interested in either unscrupulous debt collectors or indeed Jacob Brown and was thinking of a way to end their conversation. They needed to take their leave of this man quickly, as he was obviously out to extract money in return for information.

It was Aunt Jayne's turn to surprise the clerk with a dismissive goodbye. 'Well, I can see that you have a good sense of loyalty, which is to be admired and I feel I may have put you in a very difficult position, so please forgive me. It is probably best if we forget the whole thing, so I thank you for your time and wish you good-day.'

The perplexed clerk was left staggered, all hope of a reward disappearing, as they exited the building.

Out in the street the women were delighted to have inadvertently secured the information they needed, without recourse to a meeting with Jacob Brown. Kate insisted on visiting the other mills along the canal immediately, but Aunt Jayne was more cautious. 'Well now my dear, at last the end is in sight, but we need to tread carefully. After all, Robert Cameron failed to contact me before we left, although he may have subsequently made the effort. As far as we know, he has no idea who I am and certainly doesn't know how close we are to finding him, so we should return to the inn and renew our efforts tomorrow.'

At 7.30 a.m. on Tuesday morning, Robert Cameron walked into the snug of The Olde Boar's Head, confident that this would be the place where he would finally meet up with Jayne and Kate. The weather had become much cooler over the last few days and he was glad to be afforded the comfort of an armchair and the warmth of a blazing fire. He was satisfied that the two women would also take breakfast between now and 9 o'clock, so he ordered a round of hot toast, marmalade and a pot of coffee.

His calculated guess, that they were staying here at the Old Boar where he first encountered Jayne, was confirmed, when just after eight thirty, she appeared and sat down at a table some eight feet away from the one he occupied. He was careful to keep his back to her, anxious to maintain the element of surprise.

She had looked briefly in his direction, hoping no doubt that her preferred table would be free. An agonising fifteen minutes passed before Kate appeared. She entered the snug and also fleetingly glanced towards Robert, but then Aunt Jayne caught her eye and she seated herself at the table for two, which was already set for breakfast.

Robert's heart missed a beat, as he saw Kate again for the first time in fourteen years. There was no mistaking her lovely smile as she passed him by. She seemed even more beautiful than he remembered and for the first time since he began his search, he had serious doubts that he could follow through with his mission. He thought often how he would be affected, seeing her again and how he felt at this moment...was it relief? or trepidation? was it a fondness? or did she really excite him, just as she had done all those years ago? Whatever the feelings were, he knew he had to 'grasp the nettle' and impart the good news that both Rosie and Lizzie were well. If she wished, he would take her to see them. He quickly wrote an introduction then motioned to the waiter and asked him to deliver the message...*Would you please be so kind as to join the gentleman seated by the fire? He has some important information he needs to share with you.*

Kate had her back to him and he watched nervously as the waiter handed the note over. After reading it, surprised and curious, she turned around questioningly, but did not recognise the sender, as he quickly turned his face away from her view. Aunt Jayne, however, was quicker and registered a glimmer of recognition. She was anxious to know what the note contained. Kate obliged. 'It is from the gentleman sat by the fire in the alcove. He has requested that I join him, as he has some information for me, but I don't recognise him.'

Aunt Jayne studied Robert again and became even more convinced that she recognised him. She was positive that this was the man whose cane she had found a few weeks previously. If that was indeed correct, then it was none other than Robert Cameron who made the request. She kept that thought to herself, as she wasn't one hundred percent sure, but excitedly encouraged Kate to pursue the invitation with the prospect of gaining some positive important information.

Kate rose decisively from her seat and walked to Robert's table. He removed his coat and stood as she approached. She could hardly believe her eyes as she came face to face with her first love, who held out his hand, gesturing for her to be seated. He greeted her nervously, unsure of her reaction. 'Hello Kate, how lovely it is to see you again. You haven't changed a bit. I would have recognised you anywhere.'

Aunt Jayne looked on as Kate, numb with shock, sat down opposite Robert. Her voice trembled and she shook visibly as she returned his greeting. 'Robert, what a surprise to see you! How did you manage to find me?'

Robert smiled affectionately. 'It has been a long while Kate. I have been searching for you for many years, shortly after it was revealed to me that I was the father of Rosalie.' His voice faltered slightly as he acknowledged his daughter. He was still upset and disappointed that Kate had not told him, but there would be time to discuss that and now wasn't appropriate. He continued in a soothing, yet sincere voice. 'Rosalie and Lizzie are well by the way.'

Kate's heart was thumping with joy as she realised her search was over. 'Oh Robert, I am so overwhelmed...so utterly delighted that they are both well. Can I see them?'

Robert took Kate's hand, neither able to interpret the feelings they held for each other, such a long while after they had met and fallen in love. 'Of course Kate...of course you can. Rosie is at my home and Lizzie will be returning shortly from a holiday in the Highlands. She will be so excited to see you and I will arrange a meeting as soon as possible after she returns home.'

Kate could hardly contain her emotions and excitement. 'Yes Robert, of course, I can't wait to see them.' She paused, as feelings of regret surged through her body. She was reliving the pain and heartache since that awful day, but that didn't prevent her searching Robert's face for any sign of the love he once held for her. Strangely, his demeanour remained impassive, although it displayed a certain warmth, but nothing more...nothing that would give his feelings away all these years later. Kate continued 'I have been searching since Lizzie failed to meet with Aunt Jayne in Dunstable. I waited anxiously for word that she was safe and was devastated when Aunt Jayne wrote to me with the news that she had not arrived as planned. Oh Robert there is so much we need to discuss...Would you excuse me a moment while I speak to Aunt Jayne?'

He stood up. 'Of course...why don't you ask her to join us, after all, it would seem that she is as much a part of this as any of us.'

Kate was disappointed at Robert's suggestion, as she hoped to spend more time alone with him, but, in her head, she was already planning another meeting before Lizzie returned. Aunt Jayne, on the other hand, was delighted to join the pair. Introductions were made - 'Aunt Jayne, this is Robert Cameron, Rosalie's father.'

Robert took Jayne's hand and placed it to his lips. 'I am very pleased to meet you Mrs Munroe...or should I say Mrs Montague?'

Jayne Munroe blushed but flashed a smile. 'You knew then? You knew exactly who I was and my connection to Kate.'

Robert smiled. 'Not at first, no...it was later, after a certain piece of information came my way.' He addressed them both, as they appeared as anxious as he to share their many experiences. 'There is so much for us to talk about, so why don't I order some fresh coffee? It is quite private here and we can perhaps clear up some of the mysteries surrounding the missing years. We'll probably need to meet again prior to your reunion with Rosalie, as there are many aspects to discuss and potential pitfalls to avoid to ensure success.'

Kate acquiesced and smiled encouragingly. 'Yes Robert, that is the right thing to do. But would you agree to see me alone tomorrow? This has been such a shock and there are things I would like to talk to you about before we all meet.'

Robert thought for a moment and considered it wouldn't do any harm, so returned her smile. 'All right Kate, if that is what you want. I could stay another night and we could meet tomorrow for lunch. Aunt Jayne could join us for dinner...is that all right with you Jayne?'

Jayne nodded. 'Yes Robert, I will look forward to it. I do think Kate and you should meet alone and I will be happy to join you later.'

Kate was overjoyed that Robert had consented. 'Oh Robert, that would be lovely. We were due to return home on Friday, but this changes everything.'

※

Kate and Robert, each a little anxious, met at the same table in the small alcove. They were alone again for the first time since their last assignation at the cottage on the Lorimer estate, which was, of course, for a very different purpose.

Kate was probably the most nervous, as she had never really recovered from losing him. Robert, however, was unsure of his own feelings, but felt he had moved his life forward.

Robert opened the conversation. 'You look really well Kate, in fact, just as I remember you.'

Kate blushed. 'Oh Robert, I am so glad you agreed to meet with me today. The years apart have flown by but in one respect, it seems like only yesterday that we last met.'

Robert deliberated and proceeded cautiously. 'I do understand what you are saying, Kate, but, unfortunately, we cannot undo the past. At the time, I must admit to being devastated when you didn't show at the cottage. I went there a couple of times afterwards and was at a loss to comprehend your sudden cessation of our meetings. Now I know the reason, but I am still surprised that you placed such a burden on Lizzie.'

Kate was distraught. 'Yes Robert, I know, it was unforgiveable, but I was utterly desperate. I wanted more than anything for us to marry and bring up our daughter together. I didn't stop loving you, but it would never have worked out. If I went against my parents' wishes, you would have lost everything. My father would have made sure of that and I would probably have been thrown out. Until my mother died...accidentally, my father was unaware that I was pregnant, which would have destroyed him. Prior to that, mother agreed to an adoption, but once Rosalie was born, I knew I could never give her up.' Kate's voice trembled as she recalled the awful memories of that time. 'What else could I do Robert? The plan was practically foolproof and I honestly thought everything would turn out all right. Lizzie was like a sister to me and I would never have done anything to endanger her. I intended to contact you and Daniel again when I reached London. I thought we still might have a chance to be together some time in the future and Daniel and Lizzie could renew their friendship as equals,' she paused...'then, of course, it went horribly wrong.'

Robert softened. 'I do understand your dilemma, but why didn't you at least let me know? Even if we couldn't be together, I could have understood the reasons. As it was, I was tortured by thoughts of you finding someone else and falling out of love with me. For a long while, I was in the depths of despair.'

Kate reflected on Robert's sadness. Had she been wrong to cut him out of her life without an explanation? She hadn't considered his desperation at the time, as her own future and that of Rosalie was all consuming. Now there was no way back...they had new lives, but she would always love him. Even now she felt excited in his presence...time had not diminished her feelings for him. 'I am so sorry Robert, if I could turn back the clock, I would do so in an instant. We all suffered because of my actions, not least of all myself. I lost my best friend, my lover, my daughter and my mother and I know it was all my fault, but did I really deserve to lose everything?' Kate's eyes misted with tears as she looked intently at Robert.

Robert returned her gaze and ruminated on what might have been. Kate was right, there appeared to be little option and she did lose more than anyone else. His heart went out to her and he placed his hand over hers. 'Oh Kate, I do forgive you and I am sorry for your losses. Lizzie's suffering was unimaginable, after her accident in Nottingham. She lost her memory for five years but regained it when Daniel, by a stroke of good fortune, came across her. I learnt later that I was Rosalie's father and that's when we started our search for you. I know you might not want to hear this Kate, but Lizzie has been a wonderful mother to Rosalie and she is frightened Kate... frightened that you will take her away. I have told her that you would not, but you must understand she will have mixed emotions at meeting you again. Your own meeting with Rosalie will require sensitive handling. I suggest you come to Littleborough, as she will feel less threatened in her own home.'

Kate's voice wavered but she agreed. 'Robert, that's an excellent idea. I too feel nervous at meeting them again. What if she doesn't like me? I am frightened of losing her all over again.'

Robert grinned. 'How could she not like you Kate, you win everyone over in the end. She is very like you, not particularly in looks, because she has blond hair, but in temperament, she is definitely her mother's daughter!'

Kate relaxed. 'Is she Robert? I wonder how Lizzie copes with that. She always thought I lived life on the edge and she was so much more cautious than me.'

After a moment's silence Kate changed the subject. 'Are you happy Robert? I really hope you are, even though I know we would have been so happy together if things had turned out differently.'

'Yes Kate, I am happy. I am married to Amy who is a wonderful wife and mother and now I have both my daughters' in my life, I couldn't wish for anything more.'

A stunned Kate was unsure of her feelings as she uttered a confession. 'Well even though I did marry James, I have to admit that I wasn't in love with him...not like you and I. We muddle along well, but my marriage lacks passion Robert. Once you have known that kind of relationship, anything else is second best. I would be lying if I said I was totally happy, but perhaps our kind of love only comes once in a lifetime. I will always be eternally grateful to James for marrying me after my indiscretion. We do have a beautiful daughter, Beatrice, who we both adore, but, is it enough Robert? Should I just be grateful, but destined to remain unfulfilled?' Kate spoke from her heart. 'I missed you so much Robert and still do...that will never go away. I hoped that if I found you again, you would still feel the same way, but I can see that your life has moved on and I must do the same.'

A hesitant, yet sympathetic Robert looked directly into her eyes. 'Oh Kate, Kate...we cannot go back. No matter how we feel, we cannot destroy our families. Another time, another place, we would have been together, but not now Kate. You cannot cling to a pipe dream. If it makes you feel any better, it isn't easy for me either. I love Amy, but it is a different kind of love. I feel safe with her, she is so loyal and I in turn owe her my love and loyalty. Sometimes Kate, we cannot have everything we want, but should embrace what we do have. Do you understand?'

Kate responded half-heartedly. 'I understand Robert, but I cannot agree. There is this yearning deep inside me and if I am true to myself, I cannot be content, while it gnaws away at my heart. However, I do respect your sentiments and will do my best to engage with them.'

Robert was stirred and hesitated a few moments before regaining his composure. 'This is difficult all round, but we must remain resolute. Our priority is to reunite Rosalie with you, her birth mother and to look after her as best we can. It would be selfish of us to try and resurrect something that would bring devastation to those we love. You have to try Kate, it is the least you can do.'

Kate smiled graciously, but remained unconvinced. 'All right Robert, it won't be easy, but I promise to try. I suppose I should seek out Aunt Jayne. She will have returned by now and will want to hear what has transpired.'

Kate stood to leave. 'Can I ask you one more thing Robert?'

Robert seemed perplexed, but answered. 'Of course Kate, was is it?'

Kate moved closer to him and looked deep into his eyes. 'Would you hold me close Robert, just one more time, then I promise not to mention my true feelings ever again.'

Robert obliged. 'Oh Kate, dearest Kate. You will always be close to my heart, but we cannot be together...ever.'

Kate trembled at his touch. 'All right Robert, I understand, but if you ever change your mind, I will be waiting.'

Robert was left to grapple with his own mixed emotions as he watched her walk away.

CHAPTER SEVEN

Reflections
April 1855

Lizzie arrived home after an exhausting three-day journey from the Highlands, delighted to find a letter from Marcus. Putting tiredness aside, she discarded her coat and scarf and perched on the chaise longue in the hall. She opened the envelope excitedly and began reading the long awaited letter.

My Darling Elizabeth,

I arrived safe and sound in New York. The cabin was well appointed and definitely worth the twenty-two guineas. I only wish you and Rosie could have made the journey with me, but, of course, we had to think of her schooling and I accept that it would not have been practical. The ship made remarkably good time after leaving New York, taking just over nine hours on the passage.

I miss you already. It's only been a short while since my departure, but the nights are particularly lonely. I miss being close to you, to feel the softness of your skin and the passion of our love making...I hope you feel the same.

I was delighted to discover the handmade Birthday cards from you and Rosie. How clever of you to hide them in my suitcase. My birthday has since passed, but I keep the cards in my room at father's home. We celebrated the occasion with dinner at The Girard Hotel, which Appleton's guide[15] describes as 'one of the largest and most magnificent hotels in the country!' I had to agree. Father often dines there, so we were afforded very special attention by the maitre de. We were served complimentary pink champagne, 'Dom Pérignon Rosé'...Rosie would have loved it, but her first taste of champagne will not be for some years! When I return, I must take you for a special meal...perhaps Mivart's at Claridge's. We could stay the weekend. I understand the rooms are very spacious. Did you know Mivart's was sold last year to a Mr and Mrs Claridge? They owned a smaller hotel next door, hence the name?

It seems like a lifetime since we said goodbye on the quayside in Liverpool. Thank you for not being sad. Your lovely smile was all I needed as you and Rosie waved to me. I watched until you disappeared from view and I will keep you safe in my heart until I return. Remember to look into the evening sky and seek out Perseus - I will do the same my darling, it will bring us closer together.

I think about you constantly, Elizabeth and I know you will cope magnificently. Perhaps the time will go faster if you take that holiday with Rosie when she is away from school on the Easter Bank Holiday. I remember you telling me that your cousin in Berriedale was constantly reminding you to visit her

---

15 Guide book - Appleton (Daniel) - Publisher: Appleton, Philadelphia (1846) and New York

and her husband. I know it is a long journey, but if you stayed over in Glasgow for a couple of nights, you could also visit Low Wood and break the journey, it would help to pass the time. What do you think?

Anyway my darling, I will close now, as I am anxious to post this letter before the next steam packet sails for Liverpool. Look after Rosie and yourself and remember I'll always love you.

Marcus. xxx

A tear slid down Lizzie's cheek, as fleetingly, loneliness engulfed her. With Rosie staying at her father's, the house seemed very large and conspicuously empty, despite hearing Elspeth busy preparing the evening meal. She perused the paintings, which adorned the walls. They included an eclectic mix of seascapes, rugged highland landscapes and two paintings by her favourite artist, Alexander Nasmyth. The first, a portrait of the poet, Robert Burns, was a gift from Marcus for their first anniversary and the other, on which her eyes now rested, was a large oil painting entitled 'A Stormy Highland Scene'. It hung proudly just inside the hallway...A wonderful picture of contrasts, which she never ceased to admire. The clever use of light shining strikingly through dark clouds, contrasted the dim shadowy foreground. Stormy skies, invaded by pockets of blue sky, highlighted a castle silhouetted amidst the majestic misty mountains, in an all-embracing mystical foreshore of delight. There was mystery and danger, excitement and wildness, but also, conflictingly, a feeling of great peace. Lizzie perceived its meaning as one of hope - hope that the clouds would be blown away, to reveal a bright summer day. One with the sun dancing on the water, with shadowy figures coming to life and revelling on the shore.

Tragically, the clouds had not disappeared for Annabella on that fateful morning as she waited anxiously on the shore. Lizzie's emotions were, therefore, mixed - joy at receiving a letter from Marcus but also sadness at the terrible events in Berriedale. *What was the real reason for Annabella's visit to the shore so very early on that storm ravaged morning?* she wondered. Lizzie knew her cousin was quite a selfish person, but it was difficult for her to imagine that Annabella would have gone down to the shoreline and put herself in grave danger, incredibly, with the sole intention of guiding Angus's boat home. Didn't she remember the lantern procession would have brought the fisherman safely home later that evening—?

Her preoccupation was suddenly interrupted by the doorbell ringing, just above her head. She gathered her thoughts, smoothed down her dress and opened the door. Robert, smiling profusely, greeted her, before picking her up and swinging her round. He was laughing like a young schoolboy and in such a good mood.

'Oh, Lizzie, Lizzie, you're never going to believe it...I've found Kate...she's been looking for you ever since you disappeared. She—'

Lizzie interjected, clearly shocked at such unexpected news. 'How...how on earth did you find her Robert? Was she at the address in Pall Mall? Does she want to meet with us?' she asked in a somewhat subdued and strained tone.

Robert, sensing his sister's anxiety sought to reassure her. 'It's all right Lizzie, you don't need to worry. Yes she wants to meet, but she didn't give the impression of an intention to whisk Rosie away, never to be seen again.'

'How do you know Robert? What did she say? Does she want regular contact with Rosie or more than that?'

Anxious frowns creased her forehead, as she stared unwaveringly at Robert.

Robert sensed Lizzie's apprehension, so took her by the hand and led her to the sitting room. 'Before I tell you more, let's make ourselves comfortable and I will ask Elspeth to bring a pot of tea.'

Lizzie listened attentively to Robert's encounter with Kate, before passing comment. 'Well Robert, part of me is really pleased but I'm still sceptical. Do you plan to meet Kate again?'

'Yes, I have agreed, subject to your approval, that it would be best if she and Aunt Jayne came over for lunch next week. It will be more congenial than say, a formal dinner and Rosie would undoubtedly feel less threatened on her own territory. We could then dictate its duration and so avoid any unpleasantness or an atmosphere.'

Lizzie nodded her approval. 'Yes, you are right Robert. When should we broach the subject with Rosie?'

'Well, she is with Harriett just now, but I could bring her over later and we could tackle it together,' smiled Robert. 'Now tell me about your holiday.'

Lizzie reflected on the fact that now was not the time to enlighten him concerning the dreadful events at Berriedale, so adroitly diverted his question. 'Well, it was nice seeing my cousins again, but as there is so much to tell you, I will wait until this evening, when Rosie is in bed.'

Robert realised all was not well, but did not want to press his sister at such a sensitive time. Something was obviously upsetting her, but he let it go.

Later that afternoon Robert returned with Rosie. He was exceedingly nervous. The prospect of revealing the news to his daughter was frightening, but he considered that she would accept her birth mother, if Lizzie supported him unconditionally.

The door opened and a delighted Rosie rushed over to hug her mother after three weeks away. This isn't going to be easy, Lizzie thought, hugging her in return. 'I've missed you so much Rosie,' she said as she observed the worried face of her brother.

'I've missed you too mam. Did you have a good time with your cousins?' she enquired excitedly, anticipating a present in the offing.

'Well, yes I did Rosie, but I will tell you all about it later as I have cakes and lemonade waiting in the sitting room.'

Rosie eagerly followed her parents to the sitting room and immediately noticed a square box perched on the table, wrapped in red paper and tied up with ribbon. 'Is that for me mam?' she asked, not waiting for an answer, as she tore at the tissue to reveal a white box. 'Oh I am so excited, what can it be?'

'Well, if you don't finish opening it, you'll never know,' grinned Lizzie.

She removed the lid to reveal a lovely pair of black patent pumps with a small bow on the front; her first pair of 'grown-up' shoes. Rosie was ecstatic. 'Oh mam, they are lovely. Can I really wear them? Shall I try them on now?'

Lizzie and Robert were delighted that Rosie really liked the shoes. *Maybe, she is finally becoming a young lady*, Lizzie thought.

She paraded around the sitting room for several minutes, before finally sitting down. 'Can I keep them on mam?'

'Yes of course, Rosie. Right until bedtime if you want.'

'Thanks mam, you are just the best mam ever.'

Lizzie experienced another twinge of trepidation at Rosie's statement, but both she and Robert felt the time was right to broach the immediate subject of their concern. Tentatively Lizzie began. 'Rosie, you know how much Marcus and I love you and how much more love you have gained since learning that Robert was your father.'

Rosie raised her eyebrows quizzically. 'Of course, I do. Why...why are you telling me again?'

Nervous anxiety was fast becoming Lizzie's companion, but she continued stoically. 'Well, your father and I have something to tell you. It is really good news and we know it can only bring further happiness to your life.'

Rosie was now infinitely curious and anxious to know where the conversation was leading. 'Am I having another sister?' she asked, unsure whether she wanted to share her parents love with someone else, as sharing with Harriett was quite sufficient already.

Robert replied. 'Well yes and no Rosie, except it's not that, but it may be a surprise.'

Lizzie took hold of her daughter's hand. 'What you are about to hear, may come as a shock, but whatever you feel about it, your father and I are here to support you. Your father discovered recently that your birth mother has been searching for you ever since you were born, shortly after you were given to my care for the journey to London. Do you understand what I mean by birth mother Rosie?'

Rosie's face darkened. 'Yes, yes of course I do. It means the woman who gave birth to me, before you became my mam.'

Lizzie was surprised that Rosie had worked out that she had not actually given birth to her. She had spoken about the menses, of course, when Rosie, at thirteen, entered womanhood. She'd also touched briefly on the rudimentary mechanics of childbirth. In addition, she reiterated that she would always be her mother, although she had not actually conceived her. Lizzie did not appreciate at the time, that Rosie understood more than she let on, but continued. 'Anyway, in effect Rosie, your birth mother has finally been found and she would like very much to meet with you.'

Rosie considered this statement with all its implications and looked from one to the other. She was unsure of her innermost feelings, but responded matter-of-factly. 'Look mam, I am sure she is very nice and I feel a bit sad that she lost me and has been searching for years, but I already have a mam, so I don't really need another.'

Robert wrestled to grasp the initiative back to Rosie's apparent negative response. 'Well, you don't really *need* another, but just think how much you would gain by having two. There would be twice as many presents on your birthday and at Christmas. You could go on holiday with her and her daughter. Your mother's name is Kate, by the way and she has a young daughter, Beatrice, who you could get to know, just like you got to know Harriett.'

Rosie remained silent for what seemed an age, while she tried to evaluate the good and bad points of having two mothers. She was not sure the good outweighed the bad. 'I don't know mam. Would I have to share you and dad with her daughter as well?'

Lizzie placed her arms around Rosie's shoulders. 'Listen Rosie, no matter how many people join our family, we will always love you and Harriett the most. Beatrice already has a mam and dad who love her just the same, but you will find people always have enough love inside them to spread around.'

A thoughtful Rosie pondered the statement. 'Oh, I see. You mean like grandma Clara loves Tillie, Alice, David and granddad Arthur and then still has some left over for you and me, mam?'

'Yes, Rosie, that's exactly it,' said Lizzie, grateful they were making headway.

'I suppose I could meet her then, but I *am* staying here with you. I don't want to live with her. That won't happen will it?' Rosie shuffled uneasily in her new shoes, as the impact of her parents' news penetrated.

Lizzie glanced at Robert, who shrugged, but remained silent. 'No...no, not if you don't want to, but we think you should give her a chance and try to get to know her. She has tried so very hard to find you and she loves you so much. It was very sad for her missing out on seeing you as a baby and as a young child...and now you are practically grown up. What do you say?' Lizzie fervently hoped for a positive answer.

'Okay mam, when will we see her?'

'Next week Rosie, we thought she could come to tea and you could have Harriett over as well. We could have a party, although Beatrice will not be there on this occasion. How does that suit?' asked Robert.

'A party! what with cake, ice-cream and jelly you mean?' Rosie was quite excited at the thought of a party, other than for a birthday or for Christmas.

Lizzie grinned. 'Yes, we could even have some balloons[16] and you and Harriett could make a welcome banner.'

The worry lines on Robert's face disappeared as relief eased his misgivings. 'That's settled then. We will need to organise the food and I will write to Kate and Aunt Jayne.'

---

16 The rubber balloon was invented by Michael Faraday in 1824

Curiosity and intrigue crossed Rosie's brow. Her eyes widened and she cocked her head to one side. 'Who is Aunt Jayne dad?'

'Aunt Jayne is Kate's real aunt. You call my wife, Amy, 'aunt' but really, she is your stepmother. Some older female friends are called aunt, even though they are not related,' explained Robert, as he relaxed into his chair, now that the 'ordeal' was over.

'Gosh, daddy that's complicated. What do I call Kate?' queried Rosie, looking intently at Lizzie.

'I think perhaps you should agree that with her when you meet. She may have a special name for you to use,' said Lizzie, as she quietly contemplated what this meeting would mean for them all.

Chapter Eight

The Reunion
May 1855

Kate and Aunt Jayne alighted from the coach and walked briskly to the front door of 'The Beeches', home of Lizzie and Marcus.

'Gosh, Aunt Jayne, I am so excited. Do you think Rosie will like me?' Kate enquired, as she nervously adjusted her cream kidskin gloves. Her mixed feelings intensified her emotions at the thought of meeting her daughter for only the second time in her life.

'Of course, dear, why wouldn't she? You are her mother and from what Robert told us, she is very like you in lots of ways.'

'Oh dear, I'm petrified, but here goes.' Her hands trembled as she pulled the bell on the stonework at the side of the arched oak door.

Only seconds passed before Lizzie opened the door and faced her old friend. A multitude of memories flooded their consciousness, as they gazed at each other expectantly, until Kate dropped her valise and engulfed Lizzie in her arms, before kissing her on the cheek. 'Oh Lizzie, Lizzie, you look so well. I recognised you instantly and you have become even more beautiful. Marcus is so lucky to have you as his wife.'

Aunt Jayne smiled contentedly in the secure knowledge that their task had at long last been fulfilled. Elspeth took their valises into the hallway, before relieving Jayne of two beautifully wrapped boxes, tied with exquisite ribbons.

Lizzie guided Aunt Jayne and Kate along the hallway, suggesting they take refreshments with Robert in the sitting room.

Rosie and Harriett were secreted in the playroom, waiting patiently for Lizzie's call to be introduced. Robert, sensing the emotional tension, stepped forward and kissed both women on the cheek, before handing them a welcoming glass of fresh lemonade. The French doors were ajar and a warm breeze, heavy with the scent of rambling honeysuckle, infiltrated the room.

A nervous Kate gazed around, hardly able to contain her excitement and hoping, above all else, that her daughter would feel as she did. She turned to Lizzie. 'Oh Lizzie, you cannot know how relieved I was to learn that you were both safe and well. Robert told me how awful it had been for you, in losing your memory after the accident. I am so, so sorry and never meant anything like that to happen. I honestly believed you would reach the planned destination without mishap.'

Lizzie took hold of Kate's hands. 'I know you did Kate. You were my best friend and we always looked out for each other. It was my decision to take an independent coach, which is where everything went wrong, but we mustn't dwell on that now. Be happy Kate, we are all well and together again. I'll fetch Rosie, as she is dying to meet you.'

Kate's demeanour took on the persona of a scared deer as she focused tentatively on Robert to seek confirmation of Lizzie's assertion. 'Robert said she would be, but I'm really nervous. What if she doesn't like me? I am a stranger to her after all.'

Lizzie smiled encouragingly. 'Kate you really don't have anything to worry about. Rosie is very like you in lots of ways, as you will come to discover. Above all, she is loving and makes friends easily. Just be yourself. Trust me, she can't fail to warm to you, just as we all did.'

Moments later Rosie made a grand entrance, in her pretty green cotton dress and black patent pumps, while Harriett stood shyly in the doorway. Rosie surveyed the frozen tableau until her eyes rested on Kate, whose own eyes had filled with tears. Not able to hold back any longer, Kate swept her daughter into her arms and held her tight, pressing her lips to her hair and breathing in her scent. She remembered clearly the last time she had done that. 'Oh Rosalie, Rosalie, how grown up you are. How I have missed you.'

Rosie pulled gently away, a little embarrassed and unsure how she should react. *So, this* was her birth mother! The resemblance was clear, apart from the colour of the hair. Boldly, without hesitation, she addressed Kate. 'Well me mam was right, when she said we looked alike. You're very pretty. Do you like my shoes? Me mam and dad bought them for me from their holiday...Just to let you know, me name's Rosie.'

Kate was overwhelmed and anxious to make amends for the blunder she had made. 'Yes, yes I do like them. They are very pretty, just like you Rosie. I'm sorry, I forgot your name, your dad told me you were known as Rosie, it's just that I named you Rosalie. Until I met with your father again, you were always referred to as Rosalie by my family. You must forgive me, I will try and remember.'

Rosie relaxed and sat between Kate and Jayne on the sofa. 'It's all right, I expect you will get used to it.'

Kate wasn't surprised at Rosie's assured confidence, as it was so reminiscent of herself. She was used to getting her own way and it appeared her daughter shared the same trait. Her face broke into a grin. 'Oh, Rosie, I am sure I will,' she paused. 'This is Aunt Jayne, without her, you would have been taken away from me and placed for adoption, so we have much to thank her for.'

Aunt Jayne winked mischievously at Rosie. 'I am so happy that we've found you again and I am very pleased to meet you Rosie.'

Rosie felt an immediate affinity with Jayne and consequently kissed her lightly on the cheek. 'Thank you very much Aunt Jayne for finding me. You must be very clever.'

Jayne was amused at Rosie's summation, but slightly embarrassed nonetheless. 'I don't know about that Rosie. It didn't go entirely to plan, but I am so very pleased we have all been reunited. I hope you will come down to London and visit me one day.'

Rosie's eyes opened wide in response. 'I'd like to, but I'm not sure me mam will let me travel that far,' she smiled, as she pointedly and expectantly looked to Lizzie for a sign of approval.

Lizzie, however, focused on Jayne acknowledging her invitation. 'I'm sure we can work something out. I'd also like to add my thanks to you Jayne. Rosie has already enriched the lives of us all and this reunion would not have been possible without your help.'

Jayne blushed. It had taken a very long time to reunite this family, with much heartache along the way, but it had been, nevertheless, worthwhile. 'It's my pleasure Lizzie, but we all played our part, you more than anyone, so I'm really indebted to you.'

Robert, purposefully remained in the background, allowing the scene to unfold, but now he took the opportunity to introduce his other daughter and soon the room was full of chatter, laughter and reminiscences.

It wasn't long before Rosie spotted the large boxes tied with ribbon, which didn't go unnoticed by Kate. 'Rosie... Harriett, bring those boxes over here to me and we can open them together. They are presents from Aunt Jayne and myself, so we hope you like them.'

Rosie took her sister by the hand. 'You first Harriett,' she said, handing the box with Harriett's name written neatly on a matching tag. Harriett carefully removed the ribbon and opened the box. A pink satin dress appeared from amid the crisp tissue paper. She positioned the dress over the front of her own clothes and tiptoed around the room. She felt every inch a princess, her face aglow with excitement.

In complete contrast, Rosie tore excitedly at the paper covering her own present and opened the lid. The box revealed an exquisite blue silk dress and matching sash, with pink rosebuds scattered over the bodice and skirt. She pulled it out and held it to her, her eyes shining brightly as she twirled around with Harriett. 'Oh mam, isn't it lovely. Thank you very much Ka...Kate. Do I call you that, or do I call you something else?'

Kate felt a surge of pride. She was so lucky that this moment had arrived, but the uncertainty of the reaction to her next proposal worried her. 'Well Rosie, I hoped you might call me mamma, if you approve, of course?'

Rosie cocked her head on one side and pursed her lips before she fell silent, taking in the suggestion. She appealed to Lizzie for help. 'What do you think mam? Will it be all right with you?'

Lizzie, already resigned to Kate being addressed by some form of maternal name, nodded her approval. 'If you are happy with that Rosie, it's fine by me.'

Kate bestowed a silent 'thank you' in gratitude to her friend, as Rosie agreed. 'Okay then. I'll call you mamma. Now we'll both have a name to get used to. Can I try it on mam?' she asked, already half way towards the door.

Lizzie succumbed easily to her daughter's insistence. 'All right, Rosie, off you go.'

The two girls hurried away and Lizzie watched as Kate's eyes proudly followed her daughter until she disappeared from view, followed by an excited Harriett.

Kate took the opportunity to make a tentative enquiry. 'What do you think to Rosie visiting me in Oxford soon. I would like her to meet the rest of the family to keep the momentum going, now that the ice has been broken.'

Lizzie expecting such a request encouraged Kate to strengthen the newly formed bond, although she was apprehensive. 'Of course, Kate, she is your daughter and it is important that you continue to get to know her. You have missed out on so much already, so I cannot deny you this opportunity.'

Kate was extremely grateful. *It's just like old times,* she thought. *She really is the best friend anyone could wish for.* 'Thank you Lizzie. You must also come down and visit as soon as Marcus is home.'

Robert sensed the women would like some time alone together and made a suggestion. 'Would you care for a walk around the garden Jayne? The roses are just coming into bloom and there's an overwhelmingly beautiful walk through the arbour down to the summerhouse.'

Jayne was delighted at Robert's perceptiveness, because it would give Lizzie and Kate time to catch up on the thirteen years they had spent apart. This was a very special day indeed.

After the guests had left, Lizzie had one more task to perform. She took out a sheet of paper and penned a letter to Georgina and Daniel, after all, her chance encounter with Daniel culminated in this moment. She would always be grateful to him, although his feelings probably remained ones of desire, rather than gratitude.

Chapter Nine

The 'Lightning' May 1855

May entered its second week and Marcus planned to be home in another couple of months. The exact whereabouts of Belle and Jack were still unknown, but he was optimistic that he would find them by the end of July. Lizzie was preparing Rosie for her visit to Kate, but her bedroom, of course, presented a problem. Lizzie surveyed the scene apprehensively. It was littered with an array of dresses and shoes, which would inevitably need her organisational skills. The emergence of Rosie from 'Tomboy'[17] to woman had at first been a gradual process, but since Lizzie and Robert bought the patent pumps and Mamma Kate the lovely blue silk dress, Rosie had very quickly metamorphosed into quite a young lady.

Her various outfits complemented her newfound life, but were cast aside if they did not measure up to the particular engagement envisaged. Her first passionate kiss... an experience in itself, proved that being a young woman definitely had its advantages.

Lizzie was standing amidst the confusion of Rosie's bedroom when the doorbell rang. It was Elspeth's day off, so

---

17 In 1579 the word 'tomboy' was applied to a bold or immodest woman. By 1592 it was applied to a girl who acted like a spirited or boisterous boy and that's been its meaning ever since.

Lizzie answered the door to an upstanding, handsome young man in naval uniform. Lizzie perplexed, peered at the stranger curiously. 'Can I help you?' she asked.

'Aunty Lizzie, it's me, John...John Jamieson, your cousin Annabella's son.'

Recognition dawned as John removed his blue peaked cap. 'Oh gosh, John, I hardly recognised you in uniform. Do come in. What brings you to Manchester?'

John stepped inside and Lizzie took his coat and cap. 'Grandmamma gave me your address, so I thought I would pay you a visit, as my ship is berthed at Liverpool docks.'

Lizzie smiled. 'Oh I see. I didn't realise you'd joined a Merchantman.'

'I hadn't when you last saw me, but I signed on when I finished college. I was nearing the end of my last term when mamma died and I wanted to do something with my life, before grandmamma could change my mind, so I went ahead,' John grinned.

'Well good for you John. Come through to the sitting room, I expect you would like some refreshment. My daughter Rosie is upstairs and will certainly be intrigued to meet you.'

Rosie, however, had already pre-empted the meeting and Lizzie could already hear her footsteps approaching. She had been quick to put on the blue dress and pumps, brush her hair and make her entrance, after overhearing their conversation. 'Oh there you are Rosie. Come and meet my cousin's son, John, who has called to visit while his ship is docked at Liverpool.'

John took Rosie's hand, held it briefly to his lips and bowed. 'A pleasure to meet you Rosie. I was sorry we didn't meet in Berriedale, but I was due back at the naval college for my final term.'

Rosie blushed, smiling coyly. 'It's very nice to meet you too, but, as mam must have told you, I didn't go to Berriedale either, as I wanted to stay with my sister, before returning to school for the summer term.'

Lizzie hid a smirk, as Rosie had deliberately and convincingly dropped her Nottingham accent. This new grown up Rosie would take a while to get used to. Not quite fourteen and she was already beginning to emulate Kate when conversing with the opposite sex.

Lizzie continued. 'While you two get to know one another, I will arrange for sandwiches and coffee. Do make yourself at home John.'

John turned his attention to his young cousin. 'How old are you Rosie? I am almost seventeen and a half,' he declared, clearly surprised at Rosie's maturity and how she conducted herself.

'Oh, I'm nearly fifteen. My boyfriend, Jimmy Mitchell, is nearly eighteen and has also joined a ship,' offered Rosie, lying about both ages and sitting precariously close to John on the sofa.

Lizzie, had she heard, would have been surprised at Rosie's comment. She was not aware of her meeting Jimmy since he had left Nottingham. Rosie, of course, would have had an answer ready, should the question arise.

John was curious and asked. 'Has Jimmy joined a Merchantman or is he in the Royal Navy Rosie?'

For once, Rosie was unsure, but took an educated guess. 'Oh, he's joined a Merchantman, but only recently signed on.' She informed, pleased that she used the term Jimmy used about joining a ship.

'I have also joined a Merchantman. I didn't fancy the Royal, going to war and all that. Which ship is he on?'

Much to her relief, Lizzie reappeared with refreshments, which negated the need for Rosie to conjure up an answer.

'So, how are you getting along, John?' enquired Lizzie, but continued without waiting for an answer. 'Rosie is going to stay with her mamma in Oxford, so we have been busy sorting out which clothes she should take. Will you be in Manchester for a while, or are you expected back?'

John frowned at the mix of questions and statements, but answered agreeably anyway. 'I am only here for five days, then off to Port Melbourne, Australia on the 14th. I sail under Captain Forbes, on the 'Lightning'. We'll arrive around the end of July, which means I won't be back home until the end of October.'

Rosie made a mental note of the name of the ship. She fully intended to glean more information by questioning John when the opportunity arose. *Supposing,* she thought... *supposing Jimmy is joining the same ship...I wonder*.

Rosie quickly formulated a plan. 'Mam, why don't I show John the garden and the horses in the paddock?'

Lizzie, pleased that her daughter was showing an interest in someone other than Jimmy, encouraged her. 'What a good idea Rosie, we'll finish your packing later. It would be good for you cousins to get to know one another, if you have the time of course, John.'

John, pleased to make friends away from Glasgow was happy to acquaint himself with relatives. 'Yes Aunty Lizzie... should I call you that? I know we are first cousins, once removed,' he informed knowledgably, 'but it feels more respectful to call you aunt.'

Lizzie demurred. 'Yes, of course. I do feel more like an aunt, as the gap in our ages does make a significant difference.'

Rosie and John chatted amicably as they meandered around the extensive gardens. Eventually, Rosie broached the subject of the 'Lightning'. 'Is the ship you are joining in Liverpool the only one sailing to Australia?'

John responded authoritatively. 'Well, it's the only one leaving on that particular date. Actually, it has been in port three days now. The emigrants aren't allowed to board until the day before she sails, on the 14th, but the crew board earlier.'

Rosie pursued her subject. 'I see, so a sailor wanting to join a particular ship, like the 'Lightning', might have to wait around a while before she sailed?'

John seemed suspicious. 'Yes...yes I suppose so Rosie,' he paused; it had dawned on him why she might be asking the question. 'Were you wondering whether Jimmy might be joining the 'Lightning'?'

Rosie was taken aback. Here was someone as devious as she. 'Errm...I suppose so...' She fell silent debating whether to tell John the truth, before deciding she would. 'Can you keep a secret?' she pleaded in a persuasive voice.

John grinned, warming to his younger cousin. He felt she was someone who wasn't averse to taking risks. 'Of course, Rosie. If you mean, will I tell your mam, then the answer is no. I've kept a good many secrets in my life already.'

This pleased Rosie. 'Okay, well me mam doesn't know that I met up with Jimmy, before he left, which is after we visited Jimmy's home town of Nottingham. He managed to find me here and turned up a few weeks ago. When mam left for Glasgow, he returned and we spent the day here. He told me he wanted to join a ship bound for Australia, so I wondered if the ship was the 'Lightning'.'

John understood and offered his advice. 'He might well sign up...it is possible. Were you wanting to see him off?'

Rosie was thoughtful. 'Well...I suppose so, but my mam would not allow it, so it may not be possible,' she smiled persuasively, hoping she had sewn the seed for a positive response. Rosie was nothing if not resourceful and when John responded, it was exactly what she was hoping to hear.

John's eyes signalled a bright idea. 'What if you could go and see the ship without your mam knowing the real reason?'

Rosie feigned non-comprehension. 'I don't understand, how would that work?' she enquired, flashing a smile.

'Well, supposing I took you out for the day to Liverpool on the pretence that you wanted to tour the ship. Would your mam allow that?'

Rosie once again indicated a token surprise. 'Oh I see. I hadn't thought of that. I don't think she would object if you were to accompany me. Would you do that?'

'I could, but it would have to be early tomorrow morning. When are you travelling to Oxford?'

Rosie smiled deviously, her plan had succeeded. 'Not until Saturday.'

'Okay Rosie, you have yourself a visit. Come on let's go back inside and I'll see if I can persuade your mam.'

Lizzie was instantly agreeable to John's suggestion, but had a warning for Rosie. 'You must ensure you do everything John asks of you Rosie. Ships can be very dangerous places.'

'Yes mam, of course,' she agreed and flashed a look of gratitude to John.

'I will take great care of her and bring her back safely, Aunty Lizzie,' he assured her.

Lizzie was already confident in John's abilities so invited him to stay the night, as an early start the following morning was indicated.

Rosie was overawed with the 'Lightning', which loomed magnificently above the dock where they stood. 'My goodness, John, I never thought she would be so large.'

John grinned, pleased she was impressed. 'She's not that big Rosie, although I admit to having the same thoughts when I first saw her. Would you like to go aboard?'

Rosie's excitement mounted as she contemplated the thrill of looking down from such a height to the quayside, which bustled with people. 'Oh could we John, could we go now?'

John was amused at his younger cousin's enthusiasm. 'Wait here Rosie while I request we go aboard.'

Shortly afterward, Rosie was leaning over the handrail staring down at the stevedores and dock labourers, who resembled Lilliputians[18] moving purposefully around the quay. 'Where do you suppose Jimmy might be?' she asked anxiously.

John reflected. 'He may be somewhere on the dock, or he could be in an alehouse, celebrating his luck on joining the crew of this magnificent ship. What do *you* think he would be doing?' he asked, as tiny laugh lines appeared attractively around his mouth.

Rosie grinned. 'Probably in an alehouse, could we try and find him?'

'Well Rosie, that's the main purpose of our visit, but we should tour the ship first, before trying to locate him.'

She enjoyed the splendour of the 'Lightning', but uppermost in her mind was the priority of finding Jimmy.

---

18 Lilliput is one of two fictional island nations that appear in the first part of the 1726 novel Gulliver's Travels by Jonathan Swift. Lilliput is inhabited by tiny people (Lilliputians) who are about one-twelfth the height of ordinary human beings.

She scanned the crowds milling around the gangway and suddenly realised that their task was all but impossible. 'Oh dear, so many people. Where do you suggest we start?' Rosie smiled weakly.

'Oh Rosie, Rosie, you sound like you have given up before we've even begun. Most sailors will go from one inn to the next, in the dock area, for as long as their money lasts. Granted it is unlikely we will spot him among the crowds, but don't worry, if Jimmy is hereabouts, I am sure we will find him.'

At the 'Earl Grey' on Dale Street, John insisted Rosie remain outside, while he investigate. No luck there, so they moved on to the 'Pig and Whistle', where several sailors were gathered at the bar. John ascertained that a man answering Jimmy's description was seen drinking in the inn earlier that day, but where he was now was anyone's guess. Luck was with them when the buxom barmaid at the 'The Fox and Goose' positively identified him just fifteen minutes ago and suggested 'The Vine' in Islington. Hot on the trail, John entered 'The Vine' and immediately spotted a man resembling Jimmy's description who he approached at the bar. 'Hello there, would you be Jimmy...Jimmy Mitchell?'

Jimmy swung round, astonished that someone was addressing him by name. Oh God, he thought, could he be an officer of the law. He replied cautiously. 'Who's asking?'

John smiled reassuringly, convinced he was addressing the right man. 'Well, I am looking for Jimmy, because his girlfriend is here from Manchester to see him aboard his ship. Do you know him?'

Jimmy was even more astonished to discover Rosie had tracked him down to 'The Vine'. How on earth did she get here, he thought, but remained tight-lipped. 'I might do, but who are you anyway?' Jimmy questioned shrewdly.

'I'm John, Rosie's cousin, so do you know him or not?' John asked with an air of impatience.

Still unsure that this man was whom he purported to be, Jimmy remained cautious. 'As a matter of fact I do know him, but he has already left for his ship, so you are wasting your time,' he said, with every intention of following the stranger outside.

John, although perplexed and still believing the man to be Jimmy, shrugged and walked out of the bar to impart the news. Rosie, was waiting anxiously on the walkway. 'Did you have any luck?' she asked.

John was still convinced Jimmy was the man in 'The Vine', but unable to prove it, he made a suggestion to Rosie, without wishing to raise her hopes. 'A man in 'The Vine' said Jimmy had already left to board ship, but I got the impression that it wasn't the truth. There isn't much more we can do Rosie, so I suggest we walk back to the 'Lightning'. Hopefully, we might catch up with him there.'

Rosie's shoulders slumped with disappointment. 'All right John, perhaps we should.'

A few minutes later, Jimmy downed his pint and out of curiosity, but coupled with cautiousness, walked out onto the street. Rosie was immediately recognisable, even at a distance. He called after her, although still shocked at her presence. 'Rosie Cameron, what are ya doing 'ere?'

Rosie, ecstatic at hearing Jimmy's voice, turned quickly. Jimmy, with a smile on his face was hurrying towards her. 'Jimmy...Jimmy, I'm so glad to see you. Are you all right?'

'Oh Rosie, I am now. Come here and let me look at you.' Jimmy held Rosie at arms length and admired what he saw. 'I don't know what yerv done ta yersenn, but yer seem to have grown up. What 'ave yer done wi my Rosie? Why ya wearing them posh clothes?'

Rosie stared at Jimmy, she'd forgotten she was wearing the blue silk dress and patent pumps. 'I've not changed Jimmy. It's still me. I don't know what ya mean.'

Jimmy, still surprised but pleased she had sought him out, now looked beyond Rosie to the man he had spoken to in 'The Vine'. John was watching them a short distance away. 'Who's that Rosie? Yer never mentioned ya had a cousin.'

Rosie signalled to John. 'Come on John, come and meet Jimmy.'

They introduced themselves then proceeded to the 'Lightning', both men vying for Rosie's attention.

In an immediate game of 'one-upmanship' Jimmy and John fell over themselves in an attempt to out do each other. 'Have you two known one another other long?' Jimmy enquired.

John responded with a smirk. 'No...no not really, but we are getting on famously already.' He placed a protective arm around Rosie, who then came up with a comment herself.

'We were only introduced yesterday, but John has been very kind. If it hadn't been for him persuading me mam to take me to see the ship, I would never have got away with coming here.'

Jimmy looked slightly put out. 'Oh, I see. So you *are* cousins then?'

'Well, we are second cousins, but more like friends really,' smiled John.

Jimmy wasn't going to allow John the upper hand, so placed his own arm around her waist and kissed her on the cheek. 'Well Rosie, it's really great ta see you. I din't expect we would meet again for a long while, but 'ere yer are in the flesh.'

Rosie blushed. 'Yes, here I am. So what do you suggest we do before I have to return home?'

John released his arm from Rosie as he didn't really want to rub Jimmy up the wrong way and said. 'I have to check out a few things on board now, so I will come back later Rosie.' Then he spoke pointedly to Jimmy. 'I promised her mam I would take great care of her, so don't let me down.'

Jimmy's anger subsided as quickly as it had risen, because he realised John had bowed out. 'Of course I'll teck care of her. I've done that since she wah small.'

Rosie smiled gratefully at her cousin. 'Thanks a lot John. Thanks for bringing me and giving us some time alone before we return home.'

'That's ok Rosie, it's my pleasure.' Then turning to Jimmy said. 'I'll catch you later Jimmy. I expect we will see a lot more of each other when we sail.'

Jimmy nodded and conceded that perhaps the guy wasn't so bad after all. 'Yes, I expect we will. It's me first ship, so yer cun show me the ropes, I'll certainly need a hand.'

Rosie smiled knowingly. She hoped they would bond, as John could be a fellow conspirator in her determination to maintain communication with Jimmy. An able seaman's position would push Jimmy's resolve to the limit, but with an officer as a friend, Jimmy's life might be more bearable. If she could persuade John to write to her, she could monitor Jimmy's welfare. After John took his leave, the couple strolled hand in hand along the dockside. Rosie broke the silence first. 'You know Jimmy,' she said gazing lovingly into his eyes. 'John is a good person. He is only looking out for me and...and he isn't a threat...you do know that?'

Jimmy felt foolish. 'I know Rosie...it's just that, it's my place to watch ovver yer, not his. I suppose he wah keeping his promise ter yer mam and I don't really think he wants yer in that way, him being yer cousin annawl.'

Rosie released her hand teasingly. 'Oh really...so yer don't think he could possibly fancy me then Jimmy?' she scolded.

Jimmy looked abashed. Why was it he could never do right for doing wrong where Rosie was concerned? She always had to have the upper hand. Now, once again, he had dug himself a hole. 'No...no, I din't mean that. He probably does fancy yer, but he knows now that he's got no chance.'

Rosie was amused. 'No, of course not...not a chance,' she said, leaving the final words hanging in the air. It wouldn't hurt to keep Jimmy on his toes!

Chapter Ten

Independence
May 1855

Rosie eyed her mother across the breakfast table. She'd arrived back from Liverpool and decided to tell her about meeting Jimmy. Not the whole truth, but at least part of it, so that her mother would relay the all-important message to Ida. She'd rehearsed the speech and now was the time to deliver it. Her practised look of innocence enveloped her face, as she gained her mother's attention. 'You know that John showed me around the 'Lightning' mam, well, you'll never guess who we saw.' Rosie waited for Lizzie to react.

'No Rosie, I can't imagine. Who would that be?' asked Lizzie intrigued.

'Jimmy, mam, we saw Jimmy! Turns out he signed on the very same ship as John. We talked for a while and then he asked if I would take a message to his mam, to let her know he was all right. Of course, I wasn't sure if I'd be seeing her for some time, being as she lives in Derbyshire, but it was good to see him again mam. John said he would keep an eye out for him and that they'd write and let me know their news.'

Lizzie was surprised and somewhat concerned, as Jimmy was the last person she believed Rosie would encounter. 'Well, I am so pleased he is ok. Undoubtedly his mam will be relieved because I know she misses him greatly. Rather coincidentally, I received a letter from Clara this morning, to ask if I would visit Ida on my way to Nottingham, so I'm sure your news will be truly welcomed...Why didn't you mention seeing Jimmy last night?' Lizzie quizzed her daughter.

Rosie thought quickly in an attempt to divert her mother's curiosity. She replied simply. 'Err, I forgot mam. I was too busy deciding what to take to Mamma Kate's.'

Lizzie raised her eyebrows and scrutinised her daughter suspiciously, although she was more concerned with the journey Rosie was about to undertake alone. 'When the train nears the station, look out of the window for Kate. Don't go wandering off down the platform. Stand still and keep your eyes on your case.'

Rosie's eyes rolled comically. 'Mam, don't worry about me. I will be all right. Mamma said she'd be at the station early, just in case the train gets in before time.'

Lizzie observed her daughter. *She's growing up quickly and much more confident than I at the same age. At least she won't have to change trains, a great relief in itself.* 'All right Rosie, but remember, don't converse with anyone on the journey. Confine yourself to polite pleasantries only. I've packed sandwiches, a drink and a book to keep you amused, in your valise.'

Later that morning, Rosie was ready to undertake her first independent journey. She was excited, but Lizzie, apprehensive. She couldn't help but recall her first journey with the infant, Rosie, which had not gone to plan.

Once on the train, Rosie sat herself opposite two spinsterish ladies, which relaxed Lizzie somewhat; however, her anxiety hadn't gone unnoticed. The elder lady, who was wearing a plain grey dress and highly polished boots, sensed the atmosphere. 'Don't worry my dear, we will make sure she doesn't come to any harm. This is my sister Fanny and my name is Esther. We are travelling all the way to London and will keep an eye on her.'

An instantly relieved Lizzie was confident that the two ladies would keep their word. 'Thank you so much...Esther, that's very kind of you.'

Rosie's eyes rolled mischievously as another thought crossed her mind. *If mam knew the things I'd got up to, she wouldn't be worried about a little train journey*. However, when she saw her mother's anxious demeanour, she felt quite sorry and hastily reassured her. 'Right mam, you'd better go now, before the train pulls away. The ladies will look after me. I'll see you when I come back,' she said, ushering Lizzie on to the platform before shutting the train door with a satisfying clunk.

'All right Rosie. I'll miss you. Have a good time and give my love to Kate,' She waved enthusiastically before crossing the connecting bridge to another platform prior to catching the afternoon train to Derby.

Rosie's train entered the station and she scanned the platform as she hung her head out of the window for a glimpse of her mamma. She immediately spotted the unmistakable Kate, accompanied by a tall good-looking man and a girl who looked a few years younger than herself. She waved enthusiastically, as the train doors opened allowing the passengers to disembark.

Kate hurried to greet her daughter as she stepped down from the carriage. She hugged her tightly, whilst instructing James to carry Rosie's case. 'Have you had a good journey

Rosie? We have been so looking forward to your visit. Come and meet the family.'

Rosie peered over Kate's shoulder and noticed the glum countenance of her sister. *That's not a good start*, she thought *and she's definitely not looking forward to my visit. Oh well, perhaps she has been standing there a while and is just fed up waiting.* She gave Kate a hesitant kiss on the cheek. 'I am really excited to be here and Mam sends her love. She worries too much about me. Do you know, she waited until the train almost started moving, before getting off, so it's a wonder she isn't with us now.' Rosie grinned. The mental image of Lizzie getting stuck on the train and making the unscheduled journey to Oxford amused her greatly.

Kate brightened. *My goodness, Lizzie was correct. She is my daughter all right.* She felt contentment, as Rosie slipped her hand in her own. 'Well Rosie, now you realise just how precious your children are, so please forgive us for being overprotective.'

'Mmm...I suppose so. Would you write mam a quick note to let her know I arrived safely?'

Kate nodded. 'Of course. As soon as we get home, I will pen her a letter. Will she be at Clara's?'

'Yes...well, she will be by the time the letter arrives,' informed Rosie.

Kate made the introductions. 'James, this is my daughter, Rosie.'

James immediately warmed to her as she offered her hand. 'Hello Rosie, I am very pleased to meet you. This is our daughter, Beatrice, she has been really looking forward to your visit.'

Beatrice, retaining her glum persona, responded in a dispassionate monotone. 'Hello Rosie, I'm Beatrice. My mamma and papa have explained to me who you are.'

Rosie, determined to be cheerful, was undeterred and smiled convincingly, shaking Beatrice's extended hand. 'I'm really pleased to meet you. I am sure we will get along famously.' The word 'famously' had been included in her vocabulary after her meeting with John. She thought this an appropriate time to gauge the effect on her younger half sister.

Beatrice's mood did not go unnoticed by Kate, who had hoped her younger daughter would make more of an effort, so she cajoled her accordingly. 'Well you two, if the weather is fine tomorrow, we will visit the London zoo and stay overnight with Aunt Jayne. There's an aquarium full of exotic fish and animals such as hippopotamus, elephants, llama's, giraffes and even lions.' Kate was willing them to respond positively, but the result was only partially effective.

Rosie bubbled with excitement. 'Oh mamma, that would be wonderful. I've never been to a zoo before.'

Beatrice, however, was determined to put a dampener on the whole idea. 'You've never been to a zoo? It's a bit boring really. I've been quite a lot with mamma.'

Kate, slightly angry with her daughter, raised her eyebrows. 'Beatrice, that's enough. I want you to apologise to Rosie for your outburst. She is here to have a good time and I know you have been looking forward to her visit, so let's ensure she feels welcome.'

Beatrice shrugged in defiance at her admonishment, but prudently thought better of continuing in the same vein, after noting her mother's angry countenance. 'Sorry, Rosie. You'll enjoy it, if you've never been before,' said a contrite Beatrice.

'It's all right Beatrice, I'm sure we'll both have a good day.'

Kate ushered the girls into a waiting coach and soon they were standing inside the hallway of 'Highclere House'.

They removed their coats and hats, before Kate showed Rosie to her room, saying. 'Don't worry about Beatrice, she was up very early this morning and is probably tired. Tomorrow is another day; one, which I hope will be the start of everyone getting to know each other. I do hope you like your room?' she asked anxiously.

'It's lovely thank you,' replied an unusually subdued Rosie.

Kate was concerned, but she was confident all would be well eventually. 'I'll leave you to unpack. Come down to the sitting room when you've finished, where there's fresh lemonade and cakes,' smiled Kate. She dallied a few moments gazing proudly at her daughter, before leaving. *I've missed so much*, she thought, regretfully, *but I will make up for the lost years.*

Ten minutes later, Beatrice sidled up to the doorway of Rosie's room intent on mischief. 'Can I come in Rosie?' and without waiting for a reply, sat down at the window seat. She watched as her half sister unpacked the items from her valise.

Rosie, acutely aware of the atmosphere, cocked her head to one side and asked. 'You don't like me very much do you?'

Beatrice didn't mince her words. 'Not really. Oh I will pretend to mamma and papa that I do, but they are my parents, not yours. Mamma told me she only invited you here because she felt sorry for you.' Beatrice raised her eyebrows as she considered the effect of her statement.

Unfortunately, she was unaware of Rosie's feistiness and her ability to turn the tables. 'I don't believe you and I will ask mamma if it is true,' smiled Rosie sweetly, which left a shocked Beatrice to reflect on the consequences of her fabrication.

Rosie hung up her clothes without further comment to Beatrice, who, unused to her word being questioned, flounced out of the room, slamming the door behind her.

Rosie's face broke into a grin. She had her answer, without recourse to question her mother. Although disappointed that Beatrice had taken a dislike to her, at that point, she determined to change her opinion.

⁂

Later, Kate introduced Rosie to her grandfather, who was delighted to meet his granddaughter for the first time. 'Come in my dear, I have looked forward to this day for a very long time. Come and give me a hug.' Howard Hemingway smiled benevolently and extended his hands in a welcoming gesture, whilst rising unsteadily from the old comfortable toile de Jouy chintz covered sofa.

Rosie was instantly drawn to the old gentleman and without hesitation, put her arms around him and kissed him on the cheek. 'Hello grandfather, I am pleased to meet you. Mamma told me all about you and how you searched for me all those years ago. I am sorry you did not find me, but we are all together now,' grinned Rosie as she studied Howard's face. *He must have been quite a handsome man in his younger days,* she thought absently.

The indeterminably long wait was over and tears of joy misted his rheumy eyes. 'Stand back and let me take a good look at you,' he said, as he observed something in her smile that reminded him of his beloved wife, Georgina. 'Splendid, splendid, you are quite the young lady.' He turned to Kate with a request. 'Would you mind leaving us for a while? I would love some time alone with Rosie, if, of course, she agrees? '

'Of course father, I know how long you have waited for this moment. Is that all right Rosie? I will arrange for Nora to bring a tray of tea and sandwiches later.'

Rosie nodded eagerly. 'That will be lovely mamma. I would love to talk to grandfather,' grinned Rosie, taking hold of Howard's hand.

Kate silently closed the sitting room door, then dwelt momentarily outside in the knowledge that their relationship would be one of mutual love and respect. Satisfied, she returned to the East wing of 'Highclere House'.

'Sit here with me on the sofa Rosie,' said Howard indicating the empty seat. 'There must be many questions you want to ask me and I you.'

'There are a lot of things I wonder about grandfather, especially when mamma was young and what my grandmother was like?'

Rosie's curiosity was apparent to Howard and he became thoughtful. His mind wandered back to a time when his children were young and his devoted wife exuded an enthusiasm for life. His memories were happy ones and he was eager to share them with his granddaughter. 'Ah yes, my children...David, the eldest, I think you would consider, very good-looking,' he winked, unsure of the next words he should use to describe his personality. He scanned Rosie's face and decided she was old enough to understand his meaning...'he was, what you might call a ladies man!' he paused again, waiting for an adverse reaction or look of shock. He was surprised to encounter a young lady only too eager to embrace her family's history, no matter what skeletons may be unearthed. He continued unabashed. 'David had blonde hair and hazel eyes. He was very popular and an accomplished horseman, although inclined to be rather moody, which sometimes made him difficult to understand. He now owns a string of racehorses and is happily married to a girl he courted at Low Wood, Bella Somerton. Neither wanted children, so you and Beatrice remain my only grandchildren.

'Your mother, on the other hand, was a happy and cheerful girl. This made her very popular. Her hair was longer then, but she mostly wore it scooped into, what I understand is termed a 'chignon', under her riding hat. Her eyes were the deepest blue, just like yours in fact.' He became silent for a few moments, as a painful memory, which he found difficult to deal with, suddenly resurfaced. He looked earnestly at Rosie and, although there were many regrets, surrounding the implication of her birth, her presence here was proof that love had triumphed over fate. It was his opportunity to bring Rosie back into the fold and he intended to be honest with her from the onset. He took hold of her hand before continuing. 'Your mamma has been emotionally empty for a long while, her eyes lacked passion and she probably thought I hadn't noticed how sad she was. Now though, the old sparkle seems to have returned, which of course, Rosie my dear, is down to your reunion. In her younger days, Kate was, much to my frustration, rather head strong, but a very loving daughter nonetheless.

'My youngest, Alexander, was more studious and eager to learn. He was much more reserved and preferred to read, rather than ride!' he mused, remembering the hours his son spent in the library, together with Lizzie, as they poured over Dickens serialisation of 'The Old Curiosity Shop'. He was very proud that his son became a successful lawyer, although he now practised in America, much to his chagrin and disappointment. The last time Alexander paid the family a visit was several years ago.

He considered that Kate might have fared better had she concentrated more on academia, rather than men, but he loved their different personalities and allowed them to follow their own destinies. He felt safe in the knowledge that Kate would be chaperoned, which meant there would be little chance of any impropriety, but he later discovered his daughter to be very inventive. Her attempts to circumvent the system often succeeded and, apparently, David was also complicit with her subterfuge.

Rosie waited patiently for her grandfather to continue and squeezed his hand to remind him of her presence.

Jolted out of his reverie he took a moment to regain his composure. 'Now where was I? Ah yes, your grandmother! Georgina was a gentle, but very capable woman. She adored her children and devoted herself to them, but she also had a very good head for business and kept a tight rein on the household finances. I do believe the staff considered her a very fair employer, she even allowed personal possessions in their rooms. She did, however, insist on complete professionalism, especially on formal occasions. The only exception I remember was in relation to the budding friendship between Kate and Lizzie. Your grandmother was rather naïve in matters of the heart and struggled with conversations which concerned life's nuances, so she was most relieved when Kate adopted Lizzie as a friend and mentor, which was quite astounding in itself and contradictory to her own strict rule of servants not fraternizing with the family. Obviously, Lizzie took the pressure off Georgina, who had the propensity to dust things under the carpet, so to speak.

'I mentioned she loved her children dearly, which reminded me just how much Kate loved you from the moment you were born. I realised very soon after discovering I had a grandchild that this was the reason she could not give you up, no matter how much society might frown on her situation. It was then I determined to find you. I searched in every town and city, where I thought you might be, but eventually, I became too old to scour the country, much to my frustration.

'I know the past is the past Rosie but I do intend to make up for the lost years, so I hope you will be able to come and visit me when you can. Of course, I see Beatrice on a daily basis, but I will love you equally, even though I might not see you as often. I have thought about you every day since the moment I knew you were my granddaughter. I hope we can share good times ahead Rosie and maybe,' Howard grinned and tapped the side of his nose, 'maybe, we can even share secrets.'

Rosie was pleased with her grandfather's understanding of her birth and warmed to the elderly gentleman. 'I would like that grandfather, very much.'

'That's good Rosie, I am very pleased. Now, I do believe I can hear Nora's footsteps beating a path to my door. We shall take tea and then you can tell me all about yourself.'

Rosie surveyed the fields and hedgerows of a resplendent Oxford skyline and the surrounding hills from her bedroom window. At five-thirty, the sun was rising but she had already washed, excited at the prospect of visiting London zoo. Several dresses were strewn across her bed. She was still choosing, when a light tap at the door interrupted her. 'Rosie, are you awake, it's mamma?' Kate whispered, hoping not to disturb the rest of the household. She had been unable to sleep and had heard Rosie moving around as she passed her room.

Rosie bade her enter and encouraged her mother to help with the decision. 'I'm just deciding what to wear and I am not sure which dress would be suitable.'

Kate surveyed the array of dresses, any of which would suit the occasion. 'Well Rosie, the green one is awfully nice, but then the blue would bring out the colour of your eyes.'

Rosie agreed. 'Mmm, I think you are right, I'll wear the blue...Is Beatrice up yet?'

The corners of Kate's mouth lifted into a grin. 'I'm afraid not. Beatrice is not a poodle in the morning, more like a pug when it comes to rising from her bed. In fact, no one else is up, it's still very early. Why don't you put on your dressing gown and come down to the breakfast room. We could sit for a while and you can tell me your preferences, so that I can inform cook.'

Rosie eased into her slippers and pulled on her gown. 'That'ull be lovely mamma. I do want to get to know you, but don't want to make an enemy of Beatrice. I think she feels I am trying to get your attention and she will be pushed out.' Rosie offered, by way of explanation.

Kate smiled sympathetically 'Rosie, oh Rosie, you really mustn't worry about Beatrice. She will come round. I think she is a trifle jealous. She isn't used to sharing me with anyone, but I've no doubt that she will come to love you as much as I do.'

Rosie blushed. 'Do you really love me mamma, even though you still don't really know me?'

Kate, unsurprised at Rosie's intuitive response, replied positively. 'Of course I love you, you funny little girl. I have loved you from the moment you were born. It was because I loved you so much, that I got into such a fix. Everything was in place for an adoption, but I just couldn't go through with it. If your mam and Aunt Jayne hadn't come to my rescue, I think I would have run away, rather than allow the adoption to go ahead. Thankfully, your mam took the greatest care of you and looked after you as her own. I can never repay her, but I can try very hard to make it up to you both.' Kate took Rosie's hand. 'Come along let's find a nice comfortable chair and we can continue our conversation over an early morning tea.'

Rosie was content. She hadn't thought she could love two people quite so much. Of course, her mam would always be her mam...she would always come first, but, in time, she felt she could love her mamma almost as much. She followed Kate to the breakfast room in a high state of euphoria and optimism.

Kate poured out the tea, as Rosie settled herself into one of the comfortable chairs by the French doors. 'Would you like sugar Rosie?' asked Kate as she stirred in the milk.

'Oh yes please. Mam is always saying I have a sweet tooth and I do like muffins for breakfast,' smiled Rosie as she surveyed the elegant room, hoping to spy muffins on the buffet table. Unfortunately, the only item presently on the tabletop was a crisp, white linen cloth.

Kate passed a cup of tea to Rosie, whilst adding a welcome statement. 'Well, I am sure I can convince cook to magic a muffin especially for you.'

Rosie, suitably impressed, paused before commenting. 'I like it here mamma.' She looked thoughtfully out of the French doors, which led on to a large patio. 'Can I ask you something?'

'Rosie, you can ask me anything you like. I will always be here for you, no matter what problems or worries you might have.'

'Well...I did wonder why you didn't tell my father about me before you gave me to my mam.' Rosie placed her cup on the table, sat back and waited patiently for a reply to her rather evocative question.

Kate remained silent for a few moments, whilst gazing out across the lawn with a far away look in her eyes, until eventually, she turned to Rosie. 'You know Rosie, I have thought about why I didn't tell him many times over the years. I loved your father with all my heart, but it just wouldn't have worked for us. You see, we came from different backgrounds and I had to think of your future. My mother would have thrown me out and we would have found it very difficult to make ends meet. I wanted more than anything to be with him and him with me, such was our love for each other.

'When I told my mother I was pregnant, she was completely distraught. She concluded incorrectly that James was the father and, rightly or wrongly, I did not contradict her. I was very young Rosie and society frowns on unmarried mothers, so I had to go along with what mother wanted, either marry James, or put you up for adoption. Fortunately, luck was with me in the form of Aunt Jayne, who arranged for me to give birth in a private nursing home. Meantime, mother continued in her belief that I would eventually marry James.

'My father never knew of my pregnancy. As far as he was aware, I was only going away for a short holiday, to contemplate my forthcoming marriage to James. That didn't happen, of course, well not until I lost my mother and both of you. James and I eventually married, but I still loved your father very much. It was, I'm afraid, a marriage of convenience. I do regret not telling Robert, but the outcome would still have remained the same. Do you understand Rosie?'

Rosie fell silent as she absorbed the information. *It must have been a difficult decision. I suppose she wanted the best for me and probably made the right choice, even if it didn't go to plan.* She felt very sorry for her mamma and began to realise how hard it must have been, not knowing whether her baby was alive or dead. She was saddened and almost tearful. 'Oh mamma, I do understand, really I do. You were doing what you thought was best at the time. Your plan could have succeeded and maybe you and my father may have been reunited, but now we have a second chance. I do feel a closeness with you...I love you mamma...I do, but you know that me mam will always be me mam. I hope you don't feel hurt when I say that. I guess I am the lucky one with two mothers' to spoil me,' she said with a twinkle in her eye.

Mother and daughter embraced, then stood for a few moments, deep in their own thoughts. Kate broke the silence. 'I love you too Rosie and I understand why you consider Lizzie to be your mam. I hope you can love me too in the same way. I have such a lot of love to give and much to make up for our lost years.'

Rosie smiled and looked lovingly into the eyes of her birth mother. 'Oh yes mamma I will and I will come and see you often.'

Kate's eyes filled with tears. The love for her daughter was painfully apparent. 'I am so pleased Rosie. Everything will turn out all right. Now why don't you return to your room to get dressed before breakfast? Meantime, I'll go and see cook about those muffins.'

※

The fifty-mile train journey to London zoo flew by and they were soon in the queue to enter the enclosures.

ELUSIVE SHADOWS

Even Beatrice appeared excited, although she had still not engaged Rosie in conversation to the chagrin of Kate and James who were determined that the day would not be spoiled by their youngest daughter. Both girls were thrilled at the prospect of a ride on an elephant. Their anticipation grew until they were eventually seated on a gigantic beast. 'Listen girls, you have to sit really still up there. Hold on tight and we'll both be waiting here for you. The keeper informs me your elephant's name is Alice. The other one, Jumbo[19], is quite frisky, but he says Alice has a good temperament, so you will be safe with her. After lunch, we can visit the reptile house[20],' enthused James, who was pleased to see that Rosie was holding Beatrice's hand and had taken charge. She helped her on to the large animal first, before climbing up herself. They sat side by side some eight feet in the air and had a wonderful view of the entire zoo.

⁂

By the end of the day, the girls were quite weary and pleased to be seated in Aunt Jayne's comfortable sitting room, surrounded by cakes, sandwiches, lemonade and other delicious items. James organised the cases, delivered by coach from the station, while they were at the zoo.

---

19 London Zoo 1855. The Zoological Society's collection in Regent's Park had been open to the public since 1828. Among many exotic animals were two elephants, called Jumbo and Alice. The origin of the word *jumbo* (meaning 'very large' or 'over-sized'). The name was most likely derived from the Swahili word *jumbe* meaning 'chief'. The Zoo became famous for its rattlesnakes and giraffes. In 1849 there were nearly 170,000 visitors.

20 The world's first reptile house opened London Zoo in 1843.

Meanwhile, an exhausted Kate went for a long soak in the bath, which gave Aunt Jayne the opportunity to chat to the girls alone. 'Well girls, apparently, you've had a lovely day and the weather has been kind. Why don't you tell me all about it.'

Rosie was the first to offer a round up of the day's events. 'The best thing was the elephant ride. We were so high up, we could see all around the zoo. I've never ridden on an elephant before.'

Beatrice, obviously resentful once again, felt Rosie was trying to take centre stage and before Aunt Jayne could object, gave her own opinion. 'Well, it was all right Aunt Jayne, but I'm used to riding horses, so it wasn't so very different.'

A perceptive Aunt Jayne acknowledged the antagonistic attitude towards Rosie so deliberately brought her back into the conversation. 'Do you ride Rosie?'

Not to be outdone by her younger sibling Rosie embarked on an elaborate lie. 'Oh yes Aunt Jayne, I have ridden since I was nine. I don't have my own horse, but I ride with a school friend. She keeps her horses in the field next to our house, but I still thought the elephant ride was much more grand than riding a horse.' Rosie smiled and allowed herself another fairy cake, satisfied she had impressed her aunt.

Not long afterward, Kate called for the girls to take a bath and Aunt Jayne was left to decide what she could do to encourage Beatrice to accept that she had gained a half sister, not an enemy. An idea materialised, which she would present to Kate when the girls were in bed.

Everyone rose early the following morning to catch the train to Oxford. Aunt Jayne was pleased that they all appeared to have enjoyed their brief stay and that her suggestion to Kate was met with enthusiasm. She waved the family off and gently squeezed Kate's arm, as a look of understanding passed between them. 'Have a lovely time this week. I'll see you again soon.' She contemplated their leaving and mused, *I do hope everything will turn out all right.*

Two days before Rosie was due home, Kate suggested they all go for a ride and a picnic. Unusually, this idea was met with more enthusiasm by Beatrice than Rosie, who became subdued. 'Actually, mamma I don't have any riding clothes with me, so I wouldn't be able to come with you.'

Kate was not deterred. 'Oh, don't worry Rosie, I have some you can borrow. You are almost my size and I must have some boots you could wear somewhere. While I arrange a picnic, why don't you girls go round to the stables. Beatrice, you could show Rosie the horses and introduce her to Zaida. I think she would be most suitable. Ask Jamie to saddle up Sparks and Oscar and can you two manage to saddle your own horses?'

Beatrice nodded. 'Yes mamma, we can manage can't we Rosie?'

Rosie appeared less than confident and was now quite concerned, but deliberately put on a brave face. 'Of course, yes, I always saddle my own horse.'

'All right then, I'll leave you both to sort out the saddles. I assume you ride side-saddle Rosie? I haven't allowed Beatrice to ride astride her horse yet. I think she should wait until she is at least eighteen. There are a couple of Pellier[21] two pommel saddles in the tack room Beatrice.'

The two girls sauntered towards the stables and Beatrice questioned Rosie about her riding accomplishments. 'Have you entered any gymkhanas Rosie?'

Rosie became pensive and wondered how on earth she would carry on with this charade when she'd never ridden a horse before, not even a donkey. It can't be that difficult she decided. 'Oh, lots. We are always going to gymkhanas and I usually get first prize,' she said with confidence.

Beatrice was impressed. 'Oh...I've won a couple of firsts, but mamma won dozens when she was young. She rides astride her horse you know.'

Rosie was unsure what to say. Her mam didn't go horse riding and although she'd seen women riding side-saddle, she had never seen any woman sit astride a horse. Foolishly, she continued down a very dangerous path. 'Does she? My mam rides astride as well and she taught me.'

Beatrice was clearly surprised. 'Your mam allows you to ride astride? Mamma will not let you do that. It is dangerous for us girls, something to do with damaging ourselves.'

Rosie grinned, pleased that she had the upper hand over her sister. 'Well, I may not ride astride today, we'll see.'

The stable hand, Jack, had already groomed the horses so left Beatrice and Rosie with the two young fillies, Rafa and Zaida. Beatrice led Zaida out of the stable to introduce her to Rosie. 'Zaida is fifteen hands, so not much taller than

---

[21] In the 1830s, Jules Pellier invented a sidesaddle design with a second, lower pommel to the sidesaddle. In this design, still in use today, one pommel is nearly vertical, mounted approximately 10 degrees left of top dead center and curved gently to the right and up.

Rafa. Do you want to lead her around the manege, to get used to handling her?'

A fearful Rosie groaned inwardly. She had never been this close to a horse before and its shear size terrified her. Her heart beat faster as she took hold of the reins, but she continued with the pretence. 'Well she's not quite as tall as the horse I usually ride, but I expect we'll get along famously.'

Beatrice bemused, watched as Rosie tentatively led the horse around the manege. She frowned as she noticed that Rosie was holding the horse in a peculiar fashion, at arms length and looked uncertain what to do. She wondered if Rosie really could ride and decided to quiz her about other aspects of riding. An uncertain few minutes passed before Rosie returned to the stable and Beatrice began her interrogation. 'What sort of saddle do you have for riding Rosie?'

Rosie had to think on her feet. 'It's just the usual sort, brown leather with straps on.'

Surprised at her unusual description, Beatrice continued. 'I meant does it have one or two pommels?'

Now Rosie was completely out of her depth and guessing was becoming very difficult, but she remembered something her mamma had said earlier. 'Oh, two pommels of course,' she replied confidently.

Beatrice remained unconvinced, but continued placing a saddle on Rafa. Rosie stood with the saddle in one hand, trying to emulate her sister, but getting it right was proving difficult. She needed some assistance, without alerting Beatrice to her inexperience. 'Oh dear Beatrice, I think I might have sprained my thumb and putting the saddle on is quite difficult. Do you think you could help me?'

An alert Beatrice became even more suspicious, but helped Rosie secure the saddle nevertheless.

Just at that moment, Kate called to the girls to change into their riding clothes and soon the party were assembled ready to mount. To Rosie's relief, Kate employed the help of Jack, who gave the girls assistance to mount their horses. A much chastened and very worried Rosie sat side-saddle on Zaida. She felt sick and her heart was thumping. Her riding skirt was billowing around her horse and she didn't feel at all safe. She wasn't as high up as she had been on the elephant, but this saddle was neither comfortable, nor stable. This time, she had taken her bravado too far, but her mamma was smiling at her and asking everyone if they were ready. It was too late to back out now, as much as she would have wanted.

The horses walked slowly out of the yard, James up front, followed by Rosie and Beatrice, with Kate taking up the rear.

Kate called to Rosie. 'Rosie, darling, I think as you are not used to Zaida yet, we should take it slowly, until we approach the bottom field, further down the lane. We should not try any trotting or cantering just yet. Zaida has a lovely temperament, but sometimes suffers 'new rider' nerves; however, I am sure you will manage perfectly.'

Rosie hardly dared move, but managed somehow to turn her head to Kate. 'Yes, mamma, I think you are right. It's always best to allow a horse to get used to a new rider,' she said, tremulously quaking in her boots.

Zaida moved slowly at first, following Oscar along the lane. Rosie was becoming less nervous and she even began to enjoy the experience. The lane seemed endless, with little opportunity for any of the riders to trot, much to Rosie's relief. *If only we could continue like this,* she thought, but inevitably the peaceful interlude would end when they entered a field. Then, God forbid, everyone would want to trot or even gallop.

During their progress, Beatrice was formulating a plan to prove her theory that Rosie had never ridden before. Once they left the lanes, she intended, without being seen, to give Zaida a tap on her rump with her whip, just enough to set her off at a trot. Rosie's reaction would almost certainly determine her riding capabilities, one way or another.

The lane forked and they took a farm track down to a very narrow bridle path. On one side of the path was a five bar gate which led into a field. On the west side of the field, another bridle path snaked up to an area, which plateaued, before disappearing into a copse.

James dismounted and opened the gate for the others, before once again taking his place at the front. The horses walked along the path until they reached the plateau. Kate slowed Sparks to a stop, because of a minor problem with the bridle, which she adjusted while the others' continued. Beatrice saw this as her opportunity and gave Zaida a quick tap on her buttocks, which had the immediate desired effect. The surprised horse took off rather faster than Beatrice intended, bolting past James before disappearing into the copse. He called after the galloping horse, but his voice was lost on the wind.

Beatrice was aghast. This was not what she intended and she began to feel very guilty. She stared despairingly into the copse, hoping Rosie hadn't come to any harm and could indeed control the horse, but disturbingly, it didn't look hopeful.

James was the first to react and galloped after the fleeing horse with Kate in hot pursuit. *What on earth made her take off like that*, she thought. *Zaida is usually placid, she must have been spooked by something. Thank God Rosie is an experienced rider.*

That thought was instantly dispelled as the eerie sight of the riderless horse, outlined by the sun's rays filtering through the trees, came into view. Not far away, James was standing over the prone figure of Rosie. 'Oh my God James, is she all right?' Kate asked, her voice reduced to a whisper.

James reassured her. 'Well, I think, so, but she will be badly shaken.'

Unconvinced, Kate dismounted and ran towards her, icy cold fear stabbing at her heart. She knelt down by the motionless figure, immediately transported back to the day she had knelt by her mother at the bottom of the stairs at Low Wood Hall. *Oh God no, not Rosie, please don't let her die.* She gently lifted her daughter's head, which was face down in the undergrowth. She turned Rosie's face toward her. It was deathly white and a trickle of blood was oozing from a cut on her brow.

She appealed anxiously to James. 'I...I think she is unconscious. Ride back quickly and fetch Doctor Hamilton...I'm really scared.'

James mounted his horse and set off at a thunderous pace. He drew level with Beatrice on the way down to the lane and spoke urgently to her. 'Rosie has taken a fall. There is both chlorinated and fresh water, some gauze and bandages with the picnic box...take it up to your mother.'

'Yes, papa. Rosie will be all right won't she?' asked a distraught Beatrice.

'We hope so darling, we hope so. I am going to fetch the doctor now.'

'Yes papa, you go,' she paused, then unconsciously spoke her thoughts out loud. 'I didn't think the horse would bolt like that.'

James was stunned. 'What do you mean Beatrice? Did *you* see what spooked Zaida?'

Beatrice's voice trembled. 'Er...no...I...well, I just thought Rosie must have given the command to gallop.'

James knew his daughter was acting strangely, but had no time to dwell on the reason. Shaking his head, he dug his heels into Oscar and galloped off in the direction of Boar's Hill.

Beatrice rode to where her sister lay. She dismounted and carried the picnic box to Kate. 'I've brought water, gauze and bandages. How is she mamma?'

Kate glanced anxiously in Beatrice's direction. 'I...I don't know. When the doctor arrives it will be in his hands, but she needs to be kept warm, so let's cover her with our coats. Pass me the things you've brought.'

Kate poured a little chlorinated water onto some gauze and cleansed the cut on Rosie's brow. The stinging sensation caused Rosie to groan, so Kate stroked her head. 'Rosie, Rosie, can you hear me?'

Rosie's eyes opened sufficiently to encounter Kate's worried frown. In a barely audible voice she replied hesitantly. 'Yes, yes I can hear you, but my head hurts and I have some pain in my arm.'

Kate breathed a sigh of relief. 'Oh Rosie, don't move, keep very still, you may have sprained it. James has gone to fetch the doctor, they will be here soon. You will be back home in no time at all.'

Rosie was still shocked and bewildered but realised she had taken a fall. She began to register her surroundings. 'What happened mamma? Why did Zaida gallop off like that? I'm sorry, I didn't know what to do.'

Kate, surprised that Rosie was unaware of the reason for Zaida's behaviour answered her with a query of her own. 'I don't know. Didn't you give the command to gallop?'

Rosie, her consciousness rapidly returning, wondered if now was the time to come clean and admit her inexperience? 'Errm, no mamma. I...I really wouldn't know anything about commanding a horse to do anything.'

Kate was shocked. 'Rosie, are you telling me that you are not an experienced rider?'

Here comes the admission, she thought. 'Well, not exactly.'

Kate was dumbstruck. 'Not exactly...what does that mean Rosie?'

A contrite Rosie fumbled for the appropriate words. 'It means...it means, I haven't ridden a horse before. I'm sorry mamma.'

Kate was mortified. 'Surely...but I understood you were an experienced rider.'

Rosie needed her mother's compassion, not chastisement at that moment, so a change of strategy was needed. 'Mamma it's my fault.' But before she could continue milking the sympathy vote, reality reared its ugly head. The trees above appeared to sway and spin crazily, making her dizzy and her vision blurred. She cried out. 'Oh mamma, the pain in my arm is worse and I don't feel well.'

Kate reacted as a mother would. 'Never mind, darling, just lie still, the time for talking will be later. Would you like a drink of water?'

The pain in Rosie's arm was genuinely becoming severe, so much so that she conveyed her fear to Kate. 'Yes please mamma. Am I badly injured?'

Kate's concern increased because Rosie's face contorted in pain. 'Don't worry, you will be ok, when the doctor arrives. He will examine your arm and put you at ease.' She turned anxiously to Beatrice. 'Please hand me some fresh water Beatrice,' she ordered, then cradled Rosie's head in her arms, allowing her to take a few sips.

Beatrice stared at her sister. She had been right in her assumption, but should have voiced her suspicions to her mamma. Overcome with guilt, she prayed silently. *Please God, don't let Rosie die, I'll promise to try hard to like her and I'll never do anything like that again.*

※

After a thorough examination of Rosie's arm, Dr Hamilton confirmed their worst fears. 'I am afraid Rosie has a broken arm and will need to go to hospital.'

Kate raised her eyebrows in surprise. 'It's not just a sprain then? Oh gosh, it's a long way to the infirmary from here. How will we transport her?'

Dr Hamilton, spoke firmly but kindly. 'The hospital will undoubtedly confirm it is a break. Fortunately, I have a litter[22] in my trap, so with James's help, we can carry her gently down to the lane, but now I will administer some Laudanum. It will act as a sedative and relieve her pain and the application of a temporary splint will make her journey comfortable.'

Rosie, listening intently, already had misgivings. 'Mamma, I don't want to go to hospital. Can't I just go back home?'

Kate tried to calm her. 'Don't worry darling, I will travel with you. The doctor has given you something for the pain so all will be well.'

A subdued Beatrice was transfixed as she watched James and the doctor transport Rosie down the field and on to the trap. She pondered on the fact that people were only taken to hospital if they were seriously injured, but, ultimately,

---

22 A type of stretcher used in the 19th century

was more concerned about the trouble she would be in if Kate discovered the truth.

❦

Dr Hamilton arrived at the Radcliffe Infirmary and transferred Rosie to a private room, where a surgeon diagnosed a simple fracture. Thereafter, her radius bone was set and her arm placed in a sling. This came as such a relief after her agonizing ordeal. Another dose of Laudanum effectively kept the pain at bay, but she felt extremely woozy as a consequence. Eventually, the family were allowed to sit by her bedside.

A sorrowful Rosie rested her hand on Kate's arm. 'Will you stay with me mamma because I don't really want to be here? Can you let me mam know where I am?'

Kate, consciously aware of her responsibility dreaded what Lizzie and Robert would think of her, although her immediate concern was for her daughter. 'James has already sent a telegraph message to your mam and dad Rosie, but they won't be here until tomorrow afternoon. They will probably come down by train. I'll arrange a cab to bring them here immediately they arrive at the station. We will come and visit you while you are here and so will your mam and dad, so don't worry, you will be home in a few days to finish your recuperation.'

Rosie remained subdued. Did she want to return to 'Highclere', or would she prefer to be home in Lancashire? She wasn't sure.

Kate stayed at her daughter's bedside until she fell asleep.

❦

Beatrice was unusually quiet on the journey home and Kate felt extremely guilty. She imparted her thoughts to James. 'This is all my fault, I should have questioned Rosie's riding experience and ability more closely. I really didn't expect her to tell a fib[23]. Why would she do that?'

James raised his eyebrows. 'I don't know Kate, but it isn't your fault. There's no shame in being unable to ride, but you would have thought she would tell you the truth.'

Beatrice was eavesdropping on her parent's discussion. She was still unsure whether to admit to the truth, or keep quiet; after all, no one need know, so long as Rosie's memory of the incident remained foggy. Unfortunately, Kate continued to speculate and from that, Beatrice deduced they would soon find out about the part she played in Rosie's accident.

Kate, still searching for a cause and anxious for James' opinion, prompted. 'I still don't understand why Zaida took off like that. It was so sudden and I didn't hear anything that would spook her, did you?'

James tried to recall something Beatrice said after the event, but for the moment it eluded him. 'Well, no, I didn't hear a noise, or see a rabbit or anything run in front of Zaida,' he paused, noticing Beatrice's unusual lack of participation in the conversation. 'Darling, what's your opinion? You were closest to Rosie, did you see or hear anything? I remember you mentioning Zaida's behaviour, just before I left for Dr Hamilton's.'

Beatrice paled, but had enough acumen to throw her father off the scent. 'Errm...I don't remember now papa. It has been so awful and such a lot happened all at once.'

---

23 1560–70 - short for fibble-fable meaning nonsense

James observed Beatrice's reaction before continuing. 'Yes, of course, you are right, but if you do remember anything...anything at all, be sure to let me or mamma know. At the end of the day, the accident happened and no matter how many times we ask 'why', the fact remains that Rosie is in a hospital bed with a broken arm. We all need to be here for her when she returns.'

⁂

Howard Hemingway distraught at the news, became even more perplexed when Kate described the incident. He spent a long time trying to evaluate exactly what had happened and came up with a very disturbing conclusion. He hoped he was wrong, but his experience of life meant that his theory was, unfortunately, correct.

Chapter Eleven

Decisions and Consequences
May 1855

Lizzie admired the view of the valley, from outside number 9 Mile Ash Lane. She felt on top of the world, but pondered on how Ida would struggle up the very long hill with her shopping.

She knocked loudly on the white painted door and only moments passed before Ida appeared. 'Hello Lizzie, it's lovely ta see yer agen. My yer a sight fer sore eyes. Come in...come on in. It's abit nippy aht there terday. The wind blows the cobwebs off up here; mind, it's good fer drying the washing.'

Lizzie bent to kiss Ida on the cheek. 'It's lovely to see you again Ida and I bring good news.'

A cheerful smile lit up Ida's face as she showed Lizzie through to the living room, where a small fire burned invitingly. 'Sit yersen dahn Lizzie. Nah then, what's this abaht good news? A could do wi some a'that.'

'Oh Ida, it's Jimmy...he is well and has joined a Merchantman. Rosie and my cousin's son, John, bumped into him in Liverpool, when John was showing Rosie round his ship. He sends his love and says that when he returns from Australia, he will come and visit you.'

Ida's eyes misted over but her face radiated excitement. 'Oh my goodness. Fancy our Jimmy on a ship. A knew he could look after hissen. 'E 'ad ta afta bein beaten black and blue by 'is no good excuse fer a father. 'E's done pretty well annawl, God bless him and God bless you fer bringing me the best news.'

Lizzie reached for Ida's hand. 'I am so pleased for you Ida. Jimmy's a good boy...or should I say, man, because that's what he is Ida, all grown up and he has done you proud.'

Ida blushed, enjoying the compliment. 'How long will he be gone Lizzie? Australa's a long way. A often used ta wish his dad u'd da summat ta get hissen deported aht there, burree allus kept just within the law...more's the pity. Still, I mustn't dwell on the past. That's truly dead and buried and a cun look forward ta the future nah. All these months, 'ave wondered where Jimmy wah and whether 'e wah alright. He wah mi last thought before bed and the first in the mornin. Some days a'd imagine 'e wah walking up Mile Ash Lane and would knock on mi door any minit, then a came back ter earth, as a remembered 'e wun't know where a were living nah. A despaired of ever seein 'im agen.' As if on cue, another tear of joy escaped now she knew he was safe.

Lizzie grinned, pleased to see the delight on Ida's face. 'Well now you don't need to worry any longer. I think he will be back sometime in October or November. Apparently, he and John will be writing to Rosie about the voyage and posting it in Melbourne when they dock. I expect he might include a letter to you.'

'Oh, do you think so Lizzie? Am not much good at writing letters and a shun't think our Jimmy u'd be all that good either,' she laughed as she thought of her son struggling with the spelling.

Lizzie smiled encouragingly. 'I expect John will help him Ida and if his voyages bring him closer to England in the future, you will be able to write more regularly to each other.'

'Well yes, I am sure we will do our best. Now tell me, how is Rosie? She'll be fourteen soon and I'll bet she's growing into a lovely young woman.'

'Yes Ida, Rosie is growing up very quickly...almost too quickly, but she never forgets the time we spent in Narrow Marsh and misses Jimmy, despite her making new friends. I expect you will have made new friends too since you left Nottingham. Do you miss the Marsh Ida?'

A wistful Ida replied. 'A do and a don't. A miss having a gossip with Clara and Mabel, but there are a lot of bad memries 'ad rather forget. It i'nt quite the same here, although I have our Nancy next door but one. A don't see me sister Gertie, much though, even though shiz only in Wirksworth. Wi our Nancy unable to move very far from her own door, me visits ter Gertie get less and less. Yer see Lizzie, a don't much like travelling alone.' Ida gazed into the fire and a tinge of sadness crossed her face.

Lizzie interjected quickly. 'I tell you what Ida, I am going to Nottingham in a couple of days to see Clara. Why don't you come with me? Everyone would love to see you again,' suggested Lizzie, giving Ida an encouraging smile.

Ida perked up and considered Lizzie's unexpected offer. 'Well...I suppose there's noat stopping me. If yer sure...it would be nice to see me oad friends agen...Yes, I'll go...ooh am looking forward to it already.'

Lizzie, satisfied, drained the teacup of its contents and made another suggestion. 'If you aren't doing anything tomorrow Ida, we could take a cab over to Wirksworth and spend the day with Gertie. You can share your good news with her.'

Gorsey Bank, an area on the outskirts of Wirksworth enjoyed a thriving community. Gertie Fletcher, Ida's sister, lived with her husband, George, in a small cottage at the back of Providence Mill, where George worked. It had been the family home when the sisters' were small. All three shared a bedroom and conditions were cramped, but now the cottage was home to just Gertie and George, so there was more space. All the rooms appeared bright and airy.

Introductions were made, before Gertie joined Lizzie and Ida who had settled comfortably in the living room. Then, over a cup of tea, Ida shared her news with a delighted Gertie.

Ida's sister was a rotund, jovial woman whose face displayed a permanent smile. Ida mentioned that Gertie loved a party and when younger, revelled in organising family gatherings. She soon spotted another opportunity. 'I'll tell yer what Ida, when Jimmy comes 'omm, yer must all come round fer a gathrin. Bring our Nancy as well. We cun 'ave a rait old knees up. It's not often we all get tagether. By the way, d'ya know Flo Baker is ovver frum Nottinham. She's staying wi Elsie Trotter. She's bin there a week and they'll be travelling ter Nottinham tamorra.'

Ida's ears pricked up. 'Me 'n Lizzie's goan ta Nottingham ourselves termorra Gertie. A think al ger rahnd and see em later. D'ya think they'll want ter travel wi us?' asked Ida.

'Uh, well yer know Flo, she's allus up fer compny. Allus 'as a tale ter tell annawl. I should think they'd be glad to ga wi yer. A know Flo dun't like go-an be train. A remember when she wah travellin ter 'er sister Ada's in Charlesworth fer Christmas, she nodded off and finished up in Woolley Bridge. Spent Christmas Day in the church 'all 'elpin the vicar distribute Christmas dinner to the 'omeless. Ada 'ad ter send 'er 'usband ovver ter pick 'er up in cart, cus she threatened ter stay there. Took a real fancy ter the vicar. She eventually arrived on Boxing Day. Ada wah furious cus she'd got extra groceries in fer Christmas dinner,' explained Gertie as she threw back her head and laughed at the spectacle of Flo travelling in a cart.

The hilarity was infectious and they all enjoyed themselves as Gertie recounted more stories, complete with embellishments and mishaps that had occurred on Flo's many journeys. Time passed quickly and it was late afternoon before Lizzie and Ida left the cottage, with Gertie's laughter ringing in their ears.

Just a few yards away up the hill, stood the home of Elsie and Bill Trotter. Bill was at work, but Elsie and her friend, Flo, occupied two comfortable armchairs in front of the dying embers of a small fire. They were relaxing, after packing their cases for the journey to Nottingham. Both were 'catnapping', when a knock at the door interrupted their afternoon snooze. Elsie rose slowly and ambled to the front door, surprised to see her friend standing there with a stranger. 'Ee Flo, she called back to the sleeping figure, 'it's Ida Mitchell and...and...who's this Ida?'

Ida introduced Lizzie and they were welcomed into the small, sparsely furnished room, which Elsie referred to as the snug. She shook her friend awake, then put the kettle on for a reviving cup of tea. 'Ave yer bin visiting Gertie? She wah only saying yesterdee that she wah due a visit.'

Ida beamed. 'Yes, well I've had some really good news Elsie, me son, Jimmy's finally shown up. Lizzie's daughter, Rosie saw him boarding a ship. Turns out he's joined a Merchantman. Am that proud Elsie. 'E'll be coming ter see me when his ship returns. He's gone to Australa,' said Ida, her face aglow with pride.

Elsie was delighted for Ida, who had been her friend since they were children. 'I toad yer one day, yu'd see 'im agen. A knew 'e'd never set foot in Nottingham, but now yer living in Derby, yer cun bet y'ull be seeing 'im every time he's on leave. Speaking of Nottinham, me and Flo are goan termorra. I'm staying wi 'er fer a couple o' weeks. That's if we get there,' she said with a twinkle in her eye.

Ida grinned, recalling Gertie's story of Flo's mishap. 'A don't know if am speaking aht of turn Elsie, but Lizzie and me are also goan ter Nottinham termorra and wi wondered if yer wanted ter tag along?'

Flo's ears picked up. 'Well a don't know abaht Elsie, but I'd be glad ter. Can't stand trains at the best of times. A allus teck some knitting, ter teck me mind off it, all that bother wi tickets, seats, steam and folk pushing 'n shoving. A'd rather travel be cart.'

Elsie's eyebrows lifted in surprise. 'Travel be cart? A remember the last time yer tried that. It took yer brother-in-law and two other men fifteen minutes ter get yer up and settled. Gi me a train journey any day, I'm all forrit Ida. What time yer leaving?'

'Well, Lizzie has organised a coach ta teck us ta station, so we'll pick you two up around 9.30 if yer cun manage it. We'll be travling second class. Lizzie wanted ter ga first class, but a don't feel comfortable sittin wi the 'nobs' and any rode, they'd be frowning on Flo sitting there wi gret balls ov knittin wool.'

Elsie pursed her lips. 'It's a bit early Ida, although Bill's on an early termorra. 'E allus has use of the scullery sink first, but e'll be long gone be time me and Flo need ter wash, so we'll be ready an waiting wi our cases.'

'Well that's settled then. Don't ferget yer knitting Flo, we don't want yer being agitated all the way ter Nottingham,' Ida commented, as she rinsed her empty cup in the scullery sink and made to leave. 'I suppose we'd better be off Lizzie,' she said, as she put on her coat meaningfully. 'Tarra then, we'll see yer termorra.'

Flo and Elsie waved the two women off before Flo chuckled. 'That wah a bit ov luck Elsie, I din't fancy us chances mecking it ter Nottinham. Cud 'ave finished up in Woolley Bridge agen!'

Elsie frowned, pretending not to hear, before closing the door and pulling the bolt across.

Early the next morning, following the short coach journey from Wirksworth, Lizzie led the way on to the platform at Derby station. She purchased four second-class tickets. 'Come on you three, if we are quick, we might secure seats next to the windows.'

Ida, Florence and Elsie scurried along obediently and boarded the train, which, although it was a Monday, was fairly empty. They sat down in window seats opposite one another.

Florence settled immediately and pulled an old worn blue jumper, already unravelled to the chest, out of her bag. The sleeves were extraordinarily long, but still intact and would provide a huge amount of wool to be reworked. She handed Elsie an end and the pair were soon immersed in the job of forming a large ball.

Ten minutes passed before Florence cast a row of stitches on to an unevenly sized pair of needles. Elsie frowned, grimacing with curiosity. 'Wot yer goan to knit then Flo?'

Florence grinned broadly. 'Noat fancy, am knitting a scarf Elsie. A can't do oat else. Me sister, Ada in Charlesworth gev me the wool. She nicked it from imperfects box at Gnathole Mill where she wocks. A knitted a jumper from it fer our Walt's birthdy present last year, burree only wore it once. Ta be 'onest Elsie, after it wah washed, it wah dahn ta 'is knees and even though a cut a good six inches off, 'e weren't 'appy. Anyrode, it started unravling itsenn the first day 'e wore it at the facktreh. The manager said 'e wah a danger to hisenn and others. That it could get caught up in the lace machinery. The workers laughed their 'eads off, so when 'e got omm, e' chucked it in the bin. A got it aht, afta 'e'd gone ta bed. Well yer can't waste good wool can yer?'

Elsie nodded in agreement. 'Yer right there Flo. Anyrode, a scarf 'ull allus come in 'andy.'

Florence's demeanour changed abruptly. She was worried about Walter's visit to the magistrates on Friday. He'd been caught stealing a meat pie from the butchers waste bin. It was his first offence, but she thought he could possibly receive a sentence or worse. However, her amusing attempt to conceal her anxiety was commendable. 'Mmm...am not even sure 'e'll be around ta wear it, if them magistrates 'ave their way. Praps I should start lookin fer some black fabric.'

Elsie perplexed, chastised her. 'Thiz no need fer that sort o' talk Flo, 'e wont be hanged just fer that.'

Florence broke into a grin. 'A know that Elsie, it's not fer me yer daft sod, it's ta cut aht some arras ta sew on 'is scarf, so he cun wear it in gaol.'

The women laughed at Florence's dark sense of humour, then lapsed into silence, each with their own thoughts. Lizzie's memory catapulted her back in time to the Marsh and the camaraderie experienced there, which held the community together. She planned to ask Mabel Armstrong to reassure Florence, in the event that Walter had to spend time in goal.

The journey passed quickly and the women chatted amiably until the train trundled into Nottingham station.

Lizzie organised a coach and the four women were soon standing on Leenside. Florence and Elsie made their way to Foundry Yard and Lizzie knocked on the door of number 14 Knotted Alley.

Clara was vigorously ponching clothes in the large dolly tub, which took up most of the small scullery. On hearing the knock, she wiped her hands on her apron and hurried to open the door. 'Lizzie me duck come in and yo too Ida, 'ow lovely ter see yer agen. Sit yersenns dahn in the living room and al bring us a cuppa through.'

Lizzie and Ida removed their coats and hats and sat down. It was still quite cold for the time of year with just a watery sun peeking out from under the grey clouds. As ever, Clara had a roaring fire on the go, the flames licking over the coals and disappearing up the chimney. A large scuttle full of nutty slack[24] stood on the hearth for damping down if the fire became too fierce.

Clara bustled in carrying two cups, which she placed on a low table before retreating to bring in the third. 'Well Lizzie, am ready fer this. Am not as quick as a used ter be. 'Ave got the dolly tub in the scullery cos it's a biting wind aht there. Blows right up me skirt. Can't believe it's the start of summer. Washday seems to go on ferever, wi'out a moment ta put me feet up, but never mind me duck, it's lovely ter see yer agen. What yer bin up ta and yo too Ida, it's bin a while?'

---

24 Nutty slack - A cheap fuel consisting of slack (coal dust) and small lumps of coal (nuts)

Ida relayed her escapade to Gorsey Bank and the train journey to Nottingham with Flo and Elsie. It seemed strange returning to the Marsh. Many a time she had sat with Clara in front of the fire, catching up with the gossip. She hadn't ventured into Nottingham since leaving to live permanently near her sister, Nancy. 'Yer right Clara, it's bin nearly three months now since,' she paused, 'since the incident wi our Jimmy. A do miss 'im, but Lizzie brought me some good news. He joined a Merchantman yer know and sailed off to Australa wi a relative ov Lizzie's, 'er cousin's son, John. A suspect 'e'll 'ave a whale of a time. 'E were toad the news of 'is good fer nothin father and probbly won't be seen agen in Nottingham, but am 'opin 'he'll come ovver to Derbyshire to see us when 'e gets back.'

Clara pushed some stray hairs away from her face and tucked them into her mobcap[25]. She felt very comfortable sitting in front of the fire with two very special people. 'Am sure 'e will, Ida. Am glad 'is made summat of 'issen. Am not one ter speak ill of the dead, but 'es berra off wi'out 'is dad knocking seven bells aht on 'im. The only bells 'e'll be 'earing is them on that 'ere ship calling 'im ter ga abaht 'is duties, which 'ell be only too glad to carry aht.'

Ida studied the floor. Thoughts of that dreadful day flooded back. Now, she had something to look forward to, despite the fact that she was a widow, her health had improved and she was much happier. Seeing her Jimmy again, would be the icing on the cake. ''E will Clara, oh yes, 'e certainly will. Jimmy wah never afraid of 'ard work.'

---

25 A mobcap is a round, gathered or pleated cloth (usually linen) bonnet consisting of a caul to cover the hair, often worn by women performing chores in the 19th century.

She pointedly turned to Lizzie and added. 'Whoever marries our Jimmy, ull be a lucky gel indeed.'

Lizzie agreed. 'Yes Ida, they certainly will be. Rosie is writing to him and they are as close as ever. You never know, there might be a wedding in a couple of years.'

Clara and Ida nodded, but weren't too sure, now Rosie was, as they believed, 'hob nobbing'[26] with the upper classes.

Lizzie was comforted in the knowledge that Clara had recovered well, despite her slowing up a little. She took hold of Clara's hand. 'How's the family Clara?'

'They're all well Lizzie, thank the Lord. Arthur 'ull be omm around sixish. Said 'e'd try and finish 'is shift early. Our David and his wife said they'd pop in when Tillie and Alice come ovver Sunday aftanoon. They're all looking forward to 'avin a get tergether. A said we cud 'ave a bit of a do...noat too posh, some nice potted meat sandwiches, pork pie, barm cake...oh yes and a slab of Madeira.' Clara chuckled at the memory of the first slab of Madeira she'd bought when they'd celebrated the return of Lizzie's memory. 'Da'ya remember Lizzie when the two on us sat right here, drinking tea and eating a slice of Madeira spread thick wi butta? Seems a lifetime ago.'

'Oh, yes, Clara. It does seem a long while ago now, but I'll never forget the days I spent here. They were among the happiest I'd known, despite the circumstances and

---

26 In its earliest appearances as a verb meaning to drink, 'hobnob' was two separate words ('to hob or nob' or 'to hob and nob'). In the 1820s, people began using a combined form of 'hob' and 'nob', 'hob-nob' or 'hobnob'. That is also when 'hobnob' acquired the meaning it has today—to associate familiarly, to be on familiar terms, and so on.

I wouldn't change a thing. Do you know it is my brother, Robert's birthday today? Rosie and I made him a card...I cannot believe he is thirty two...where do the years go? Do you remember helping me to make birthday cards for Rosie? We spent hours at the kitchen table cutting up coloured paper and scrunching[27] it together to form flowers. You made a special 'pop-up' card for her fifth birthday Clara. She liked it so much, she kept it on the mantle-piece for a week! She still keeps all her cards in a box.'

Clara laughed appreciatively and smoothed down her apron, losing herself momentarily in the memory of Lizzie and Rosie's time in the Marsh, which had brightened her days. *It's funny how circumstances can change so quickly.* She shook her head and looked up to see the same old Lizzie gracing her living room, just as if she'd never been away and despite her change in fortunes, she would always be her Lizzie, the unassuming young girl found on the towpath all those years ago.

The following morning, Lizzie rose early, intending to take a walk by the river. Such a lot had happened in her life since she was found by Arthur and David, nearly fourteen years ago and she wanted to be alone to reminisce.

Unfortunately, her plans were short-lived, as she stepped on to Leenside. She glanced down the road and noticed a group of boys calling names and throwing stones at a solitary figure crouched down on the walkway. Drawing closer, she thought she recognised the victim. 'Tommy,

---

[27] 1815–25 Scrunching - perhaps expressive variant of 'crunch'.

Tommy, is that you?' addressing the man whose face was pressed against the wall.

Her demeanour changed as she turned to admonish the guilty group. The effect was instantaneous, the victimisation ending abruptly, but before she could speak, one of the boys stepped forward with a warning. 'Look missus, yer should stay clear on him. 'E's funny in the 'ead yer know. A bit simple. 'E's known rahnd these parts, but we ent seen 'im fer a while. 'E's bin locked up in the asylum[28],' volunteered a skinny, pimply youth, quickly followed by another; the smaller boy wearing torn trousers and a dirty jumper. ''E's right missus. We think 'e escaped and 'e's nicked summat aht the bins from the bakery,' he said, with an air of importance.

Lizzie was appalled, but as she took in Tommy's dirty clothes, she noticed a half eaten, but decidedly mouldy loaf at his feet.

The commotion caught the attention of the baker, who came out of his shop. 'What's going on here?' he barked, surveying the group of boys standing in the roadway.

Quick as a flash and eager to ingratiate himself, in the event of a reward, the older boy responded enthusiastically. 'That man there is a thief. We saw 'im stealing the loaf aht of yer bins rahnd the side of yer shop. Shall a go fer a peeler mester?' asked the boy.

Before anyone could continue, Lizzie brushed the group aside and intervened. 'Excuse me, Mr Braithwaite, isn't it?'

The baker looked Lizzie up and down, which confirmed she was not local to the area. 'Yes, that's right. Have we met before?'

---

[28] The first county asylum was opened in 1812 in Sneinton, Nottinghamshire and by 1841 a further thirteen had been added

Lizzie presented her most enlightened smile. 'On a few occasions actually. I used to live with Clara Milligan, until I moved away. I am presently in Nottingham on a visit. I remember Clara buying some of your delicious Madeira cake several years ago and I frequently placed the bakery order for Mrs Rachael Phillips of St James' Street, when I worked for her as a tutor.'

Mr Braithwaite softened, flattered that a lady of obvious breeding should speak so highly of his prized Madeira. 'Oh why thank you ma'am. I do remember now. Do you know the gentleman in question?' he asked, perplexed that she could possibly be associated with the man crouching on the cobbles.

Lizzie flashed another persuasive smile. 'I do know Tommy, he was entrusted to my care many years ago, after his mother died. He has been a patient at the asylum for several years and is completely harmless. However, I am yet to discover what he is doing here, which is more of a worry than anything else.'

The baker's demeanour changed completely, the assertiveness gone. 'Well yes, of course. The loaf of bread is inconsequential in the context of the wellbeing of this poor gentleman.' He turned to the group of boys and used his authority to dismiss them. 'You boys, move on and don't bother this gentleman again,' he ordered, nodding at Tommy apologetically.

The boys reluctantly made off down the street, kicking loose stones on their way and muttering obscenities under their breath, disappointed that there hadn't been any reward.

To make amends for his outburst, Mr Braithwaite went inside his shop and returned with a generous portion of Madeira cake, which Tommy accepted.

Lizzie took control. 'I will take Tommy to Clara's. He will enjoy the cake with a nice cup of tea and later...well we will see.' She smiled, but was still worried and her troubled brow emphasised her concern.

Tommy, now on his feet, looked a sorry sight. He was unshaven and his clothes were dirty. Lizzie realised the situation would need careful handling. 'Well now, Tommy. What are you doing down the Marsh?' she asked, her face breaking into a smile as she looked to Tommy for an explanation.

Tommy removed his cap. 'Hello Lizzie. I wah on me way ter see yo and Clara. I 'eard yo were coming dahn.'

Lizzie was astounded. Tommy had obviously just walked out of the asylum and made his way to the Marsh. She wondered how long he had been missing and whether anyone had noticed his disappearance. The main thing was not to panic him. 'How are you Tommy and how did you know I would be here?'

Tommy grinned widely. 'Am all right Lizzie, thanks ter yo. David let me know yer wah coming. 'E came ter see me last week and toad me Clara 'ad received word that yu'd be dahn. A know yer don't allus 'ave time ter come and visit me, so a thought I'd supprise yer and 'ere a am.'

Tommy's explanation did not alleviate her overall concern. She wondered if he had permission to visit, which seemed unlikely. The usual practice was for a family member to collect a patient and sign a responsibility waiver for the period of the patient's absence. If Tommy had just walked out, it was probable that the police would be looking for him. The doctors would be worried for his safety. Therefore, the proposal to take him to Clara's seemed logical. Later she would visit the asylum herself. 'Well it's lovely to see you Tommy. Shall we go and see Clara? That cake looks tempting and a nice cup of tea is in order too.'

A surprised Clara opened the door, her mouth agape. *What on earth was Tommy doing here?* Lizzie offered a partial explanation. 'I found Tommy on Leenside Clara. He's come to visit us.'

Clara, askance, rolled her eyes. 'Come in then and sit yersenn dahn Tommy. Don't stand on ceremony lad. Did yer decide to come ovver this morning then?'

Tommy removed his cap and sat on the sofa, warming his hands by the fire. 'No, Clara...a started off last night. A din't tell nobody, cus a din't want ter bother 'em. A just walked aht the gate when the visitors left. No one said oat, but then a cun't find me way in the dark, so a slept in one of them caves. A an't 'ad noat ter eat or drink since yesterdee aftanoon. Then this mornin a fount 'alf a loaf in the baker's bin, but a crowd o' lads started calling me names. That's when Lizzie came along and sorted it aht.'

Clara shook her head, totally mystified. 'Well me duck. Meck yersenn at 'omm and I'll sort aht summat ta eat and a mug 'o tea. 'owd that suit yer?'

Tommy grinned and held up the cake. 'Baker gev us a slab of Madeira. Would yer like a piece? Thiz enuff 'ere fer all on us.'

Clara took the cake and signalled Lizzie to follow her, leaving Ida to occupy Tommy.

'What da ya think Lizzie? Them in charge must 'ave noticed 'e's not in 'is room. Yer don't think 'e'll be in trouble da yer?' asked a worried Clara.

'No...I shouldn't think so Clara. The best thing would be to let him stay while I visit the asylum, explain the situation to the matron and tell her I will bring him back personally later today.'

Clara nodded. 'Yer right me duck. That sahnds like a plan. Meanwhile, I'll get this cake buttered. Would yer put the keckle on fer a cuppa Lizzie?'

༺♥༻

Tommy spent the rest of the morning with Clara, enjoying himself. This gave Lizzie the opportunity to slip away to the asylum, after making a visit to the police station to inform them of Tommy's whereabouts. The matron was most helpful and just as Lizzie thought, explained that it was usual for a family member to collect and return a patient who wished to be allowed a short period away. They were concerned at Tommy's sudden disappearance, as he had never attempted to leave in his whole ten years as a resident. The police were informed as soon as the wardens discovered he was not in his room. Their preliminary search yesterday evening had to be resumed at first light. The Marsh was the first area investigated, as they were unaware that Tommy had turned up on Leenside, after seeking the relative safety of a cave for the night. Clara Milligan's home was high on their list of 'possibles', but Lizzie's visit had saved them the bother. Now the loose ends had been tied, she could return Tommy after tea and without repercussions.

Lizzie let herself into number 14 and heard peels of laughter emanating from the sitting room. She waited behind the kitchen door and smiled at their conversation. This impromptu visit would lift their spirits. Tommy turned round as Lizzie entered. 'Where yer bin Lizzie? A wah just telling Clara abaht the time a met David on Leenside and he made a joke about me shopping bag being full of fresh air.'

Lizzie remembered and a tear formed in the corner of her eye. She collected herself. 'I've just been to the asylum to make arrangements for your return. The matron said you could stay here for tea but then we should make steps early this evening. Is that all right Tommy?'

Tommy's face crumpled. He had enjoyed the company of the three women. 'Do a 'ave ter ga back Lizzie? A like it there, but a like it 'ere better. Couldn't a stay 'ere wi yo Clara?'

Clara was non-plussed as she racked her brain for a suitable excuse. She knew Tommy would not be allowed to stay. His medication[29] was a consideration and she was too old to take on the responsibility. She looked to Lizzie for inspiration. 'A don't think 'e's allowed, is he Lizzie? The girls come back some weekends, so we don't really have the room.'

Lizzie had been expecting such a request and already had an answer. 'Clara's right Tommy. Much as she would like you to stay, it's just not practical, but I bet if you asked, she could pay you a visit next time David goes. What do you think Clara?'

Clara breathed a sigh of relief. 'Aye well, a could visit yer Tommy, now and again when our David goes. Not every week, but praps once a month.'

Tommy's face broke into a wide grin. 'Aw thanks Clara. A could ask the Matron to bring yer a cup of tea and...and a slice of cake. It'ud not be Madeira, but the cook mecks Victoria sponge fer us as a treat.'

---

[29] Sedative drugs such as laudanum (tincture of opium) could only be given orally. Many of the technical difficulties, which had faced those experimenting with blood transfusion were removed after 1853 by the invention of the hypodermic syringe, with its hollow pointed needle. Credit for the evolution of this universally useful appliance is usually given to Doctor Alexander Wood (born 1817), who was appointed Secretary of the Royal College of Physicians of Edinburgh in 1850

ELUSIVE SHADOWS

Lizzie remembered to buy some marshmallows[30] on her way back. It would finish the day on a high, eating toasted marshmallows around the fire. Days were often remembered for simple pleasures in life, like today with friends enjoying being together. Lizzie appreciated the big part these three people had played in her life at the Marsh. She wondered how many more such days they would share.

※

On the Friday following Tommy's visit, Lizzie rose early in a second attempt to take a walk by the river. She quietly closed the front door, only to be confronted by a telegram boy wielding a message form. Anxiously Lizzie opened the single sheet, before absently giving the boy three pennies as a tip. She quickly scanned the message - 'Come soon. Rosie broken arm. Robert informed. No cause to worry. Love Kate'. Lizzie stared at the message in disbelief. *How on earth could she have broken her arm?* but there was no time for recriminations so she hurried to the station to book a ticket on the afternoon train. It was still early when she returned to 14 Knotted Alley. Clara and Ida noticed the worried look on her face as she entered the parlour. Clara pulled out a chair. 'Come on me duck, sit yersenn dahn 'ere. Whatever's the matter?'

'Oh Clara, it's Rosie. There's been an accident. I received a telegram earlier, so went straight to the station to book a seat on the 4 p.m. train to Oxford.'

Clara, aghast questioned Lizzie solemnly. 'What kind of an accident? 'as she 'ad a fall?'

---

30 Until the mid 1800s, marshmallow candy was made using the sap of the Marsh-Mallow plant.

'I'm not sure Clara. The telegram was brief, but Kate said there's no cause to worry. However, I don't think she would have sent a telegram unless she did have concerns. I am so sorry Clara, but it looks as if I will have to cut my visit short.' Lizzie apologised.

Clara put her arms around Lizzie's shoulders. 'Never mind abaht that me duck. The main thing is to get yersenn dahn ter Oxford ter be wi Rosie. Poor gel wants her mam at a time like this. A know she's wi her other mam, but you are 'er proper mam Lizzie and sometimes, no-one else 'ull do. Nah then...did yer 'ave oat to eat before yer left?' asked Clara, filling up the kettle and greasing the frying pan in preparation for a hearty breakfast.

Lizzie had already eaten a slice of toast and did not have much of an appetite, but allowed Clara her need to fuss. 'Just a rasher of bacon and some fresh bread would be lovely Clara.'

Clara was delighted to be looking after Lizzie. It had been a long time since she had that privilege. 'Right me duck, it'ull be ready before yer can say 'Jack Robinson'[31]... whoever he was.'

༺༻

The train journey to Oxford seemed inordinately long and Lizzie was exhausted by the time the train finally drew to a

---

[31] 'Jack Robinson' is a name present in a common figure of speech used to indicate a period of time, typically in a sarcastic manner. The normal usage is, 'something is done faster than you can say Jack Robinson' or otherwise 'before you can say Jack Robinson.' The phrase can be traced back to the 1700s. Supposedly, an English gentleman of the early 19th century named Jack Robinson was a person who changed his mind. A person had to be quick to catch him in a decision.

halt. Kate and James were on the platform and, surprisingly, Robert was with them. *He must have managed to catch an earlier train*, thought Lizzie absently.

Robert helped Lizzie down from the carriage, picked up her case and escorted her to a waiting coach. 'Don't worry Lizzie, I have already seen Rosie and, apart from a broken arm, she is in good spirits.'

Lizzie breathed a sigh of relief. 'Oh, thank goodness Robert. How on earth did she break her arm?'

Kate placed her hand on Lizzie's arm. 'It was all my fault Lizzie. Rosie fell off a horse,' she explained guiltily.

Kate's account of the accident brought a gasp of incredulity from Lizzie. 'Fell off a horse?...but Rosie cannot ride. What was she doing on a horse?' asked Lizzie.

Kate, ashamed, continued to explain. 'Oh Lizzie, I am so sorry, Rosie told me she was an experienced rider and I believed her. We gave her one of our more gentle horses, Zaida. Everything was fine, until, unfortunately, something spooked the horse and she bolted. Rosie was thrown to the ground and broke her arm. James rode to fetch Dr Hamilton, who quickly transported her to hospital.' She paused, scanning Lizzie's face for some kind of understanding. 'Do you forgive me Lizzie? I realise I should have questioned her more rigorously, but she was so convincing.'

Lizzie remained quiet for a few moments, while she assimilated the information, before replying. 'Well Kate... maybe you should have questioned her more closely, if you were at all suspicious...but, Rosie does have the ability to fool anyone into believing what she says is true...even when that is not the case, so I do sympathise,' she said, remembering the many occasions, Rosie had fibbed her way out of a difficult situation.

Robert stepped in. 'Lizzie knows she can be very persuasive, as I can confirm. This time, however, she has paid for her manipulation and is probably feeling very sorry for herself.'

'I think so too Robert. Can we go and visit her now?' asked Lizzie, anxious to see her daughter as soon as possible.

'Yes, of course, Lizzie. She has been asking for you.' Kate smiled weakly, unsure that Lizzie had forgiven her totally.

On arrival at the Infirmary, they made their way to the private room occupied by Rosie. Lizzie's eyes rested on the pale face of her daughter as she lay back on the pillow. Rosie opened her eyes immediately she felt the presence of someone by her bed. 'Oh mam...it's you...I am so glad to see you. You aren't cross are you?' she asked tentatively.

Lizzie frowned and pursed her lips, ambivalent about her feelings. 'No Rosie, I'm not cross, but I have been very worried and wonder why you told your mamma that you *could* ride a horse.'

Rosie knew Lizzie was not pleased, even though she sympathised. It would take all her persuasive powers to escape this predicament. 'Well mam, I think Aunt Jayne suggested to mamma that we go for a picnic and that we ride to our destination. I didn't want to spoil their plans, so I just went along with them,' she argued, hoping her explanation was sufficient to encourage her into believing it was the only option.

Lizzie, however, remained unconvinced. 'I see...and you didn't think to tell your mamma that you had never ridden a horse in your life...knowing how risky it would be to attempt such an ambitious exercise?'

Rosie realised she was treading on dangerous territory and further embellishments were required. 'Well...you see... it all started with the elephant ride. I thought that was easy enough, so riding a horse couldn't be that difficult...and... and it was going swimmingly, until suddenly Zaida bolted and I couldn't control her.' Rosie shrugged her shoulders and raised her eyebrows in an attempt to illustrate that the fault was not with herself, but lay clearly with the horse.

Four pairs of eyes focussed on her. They were totally lost for words and Lizzie totally exasperated, Robert and James conceded defeat, but Kate had an inexplicable desire to applaud her daughter for her audacity. Thankfully, further conversation was curtailed, as Dr Hamilton walked briskly into the room, carrying a set of hospital notes. He addressed Robert. 'Good afternoon...Mr Cameron isn't it?'

Robert stepped forward to shake Dr Hamilton's hand. 'Yes, I am Rosie's father and thank you so much for taking such good care of my daughter.'

Dr Hamilton winked at Rosie. 'Oh that's not been difficult Mr Cameron, Rosie is an excellent patient.'

'We are glad to hear it doctor. When will she be allowed home?'

The doctor consulted his notes. 'Well now, I think we need to keep her in another few days for observation, but if all is well, she should be fit enough to travel home on Wednesday.'

'Oh that is good news. We will make arrangements for her to return to Littleborough. Don't worry darling, we will ensure you are comfortable and cosseted for the next few weeks. You will soon be feeling your old self again,' said a very relieved Robert.

Kate was surprised at Robert's announcement. She had hoped Rosie would convalesce in Oxford, but remained quiet in anticipation of Rosie's preference.

Rosie noted Kate's gloomy demeanour and her response was not what Kate wanted to hear. 'Ok daddy, will you and mam come to fetch me?'

'Of course, Rosie,' interjected Lizzie. 'We are hoping to stay with Kate until Wednesday...if she agrees, so we will be on hand to collect you.'

Kate nodded positively, although, saddened by Rosie's decision. 'Of course Lizzie, we would be delighted to have you stay, but don't you think the journey to Littleborough will be too taxing for Rosie?' she asked hopefully.

Rosie, who had remained non-committal as she sized up the situation, interjected. 'It is a long way, but my mam has always looked after me when I've been ill and you have Beatrice to look after...it wouldn't be fair to have to nurse me as well. Don't worry mamma, as soon as I am fit, I will come to stay with you again,' she paused, then added, 'perhaps you could teach me to ride,' smiled Rosie generously.

Kate could not disguise the disappointment in her voice as she tried to keep her emotions in check. 'Of course, Rosie. I quite understand and yes...I would love to teach you to ride, only this time, we have to start with a much smaller horse and only round the manege.' Kate said with resignation, hiding the feelings of rejection, which tugged at her heart.

There was a lull in the conversation, before Dr Hamilton returned to advise that his patient needed to rest. Lizzie comforted her daughter, after the others had left. 'Try and rest Rosie. We love you and will see you tomorrow.'

A wistful Kate gave Rosie a cheery wave before leaving the ward, but once outside, approached Lizzie. 'I wonder Lizzie, if you would consider persuading Rosie to stay with us for a little while, even if only until Sunday? I feel so responsible for her accident and desperately want to make it up to her,' Kate pleaded.

Lizzie realised from Kate's tone, that she would like the opportunity to take care of her daughter herself, especially as she felt partly responsible for her accident. However, Lizzie knew Rosie could be very stubborn and wondered what she could do to persuade her otherwise. 'I do understand your feelings Kate and will do my best to talk Rosie into staying, but I fear she is very strong willed and there might be nothing I can do to change her mind.'

Still Kate clung on to a glimmer of hope and tried to capitalise on the situation. 'Oh would you really Lizzie. I should be so grateful and it would give you the opportunity to return to Nottingham to spend time with Clara.'

Lizzie deliberated over the suggestion and the position in which she found herself. 'Mmm...I would have liked to spend more time with Clara. She has arranged a gathering of the family this Sunday and she was very disappointed I had to leave so suddenly. Perhaps when we visit Rosie tomorrow, I could have some time alone with her and see what I can do.'

Lizzie sounded optimistic so Kate steamed ahead. 'Yes that's a good idea Lizzie, I am sure you will manage to persuade her, after all, it is only five days. Oh, I am so looking forward to taking care of her. We need the chance to bond properly. Thank you so much.' Kate's mood lifted, certain Lizzie would succeed.

However, Lizzie wasn't too sure. She remained tight-lipped, powerless to dampen Kate's high expectations.

※

The following morning the four visited Rosie at the Infirmary with Lizzie spending time alone at her bedside.

Rosie was so pleased to see her mother and glad they had a few minutes together before being joined by Kate,

Robert and James. 'Mam, I have been thinking since yesterday about whether I should stay with mamma for a few days. She seemed quite upset when I suggested I go back to Littleborough on Wednesday, but I don't want to upset you and daddy...what should I do?'

Lizzie sighed with relief that she had not had to broach the subject and spoke encouragingly. 'Rosie...oh Rosie, we just want whatever you are happy with. Naturally, we will miss you, as I have always taken on the role of nursemaid when you have been ill, but these are difficult circumstances. Your mamma feels totally responsible for your accident and is desperate to make amends, so I think it would be a wonderful gesture if you agreed to stay with her.'

'You do?...ok, I will stay until Sunday, but would you come and fetch me, I don't really want to travel by train alone,' announced Rosie with concern.

'Of course, darling. We will come down early on Sunday morning and travel back after lunch. How will that suit?'

Rosie relaxed onto her pillow, satisfied with her mother's suggestion. 'Yes mam, I'd like that.'

'Well Rosie, shall I fetch the others, they are very anxious to see you?'

Rosie became pensive. 'I do want to see them, but there is something I want to tell you about the accident, that is bothering me.'

Lizzie frowned anxiously. 'Oh, I see, what is it Rosie?'

Rosie glanced at the slightly opened door and lowered her voice to a whisper. 'Well...after I was thrown and lay on the ground, my head was spinning and I could not remember anything, but now some memories of the incident have returned. I know I should not have told mamma that I could ride, but really mam, I was doing quite well. We had been walking the horses for several miles and I even began to enjoy it, then, suddenly, my horse bolted and I am not sure why. Mamma had stopped to adjust the bridle on her horse and it happened before she could remount...James had ridden a short distance ahead, while Beatrice and I had stopped to wait for mamma...that's when Zaida suddenly took off at a gallop right out of the blue. I didn't give her any commands to make her bolt like that and there wasn't anything around that would have startled her...so, mam, I am wondering whether Beatrice might have had anything to do with her sudden unusual behaviour.' Rosie became silent, not wanting to believe her sister would have risked causing an accident, but had to face up to the possibility. 'You see mam...Beatrice doesn't like me very much. She thinks I am taking all the attention away from her. What do you think mam?'

Lizzie was perplexed. 'Oh Rosie, I am sure Beatrice would never do such a thing. Even if she is a little jealous, I don't think she would deliberately put you in danger. Have you voiced your concerns with your mamma?'

'No mam...I've only told you. I think mamma would be really cross, as she has had to tell Beatrice off a couple of times for being grumpy. Beatrice also told me that mamma did not really want me here and only felt sorry for me, but I know that isn't true.'

Lizzie was shocked. 'Oh...I see. Well it certainly isn't true! although, I think you should try and put it behind you Rosie. She is younger than you and appears to be jealous of you and her mamma forming a relationship. I am sure she will have regretted her actions...if indeed she had anything to do with the horse bolting...when she saw the consequences. Why don't you give her the benefit of the doubt and see if you can win her over. You have a wonderful way of talking people round and I am sure Beatrice would love to have you as a sister when she gets to know you.'

CHAPTER TWELVE

Dilemmas
May/June 1855

Rosie's return to Oxford did not go to plan. Her relationship with her half sister deteriorated rapidly, as Beatrice conveniently forgot the prayer and promise offered to God, when she thought Rosie might be seriously injured. Friction manifested itself whenever they were alone, despite Rosie's 'olive branches'. Kate spent more time with Rosie, ensuring she was comfortable. Washing and dressing was one challenge amongst many, for which she needed assistance. Beatrice, on the other hand, did nothing to help her sister and deliberately went out of her way to ensure Rosie was kept waiting when she needed help.

The family planned to spend one day at the Harcourt Arboretum, but Beatrice had other ideas. She planned on diverting her mamma's attention from Rosie to herself. It called for desperate measures. She sneaked out of bed at five, to avoid the housekeeper, Mrs Pearson and Emily Bates, the cook. They would not be in the kitchen until five thirty. This gave her sufficient time to carry out her plan. She descended the stairs quietly and made her way to the kitchen.

Unfortunately for Beatrice, Gladys Pearson's medicine cabinet keys were kept safely on a key ring, attached to a belt around her waist. However, there was one medicine in the cook's cupboard...the ubiquitous cod liver oil, which wasn't locked away. It was kept with the herbs, spices and other condiments. Beatrice was given a spoonful once a day, although she hated it and protested loudly if it wasn't instantly followed by a 'Barley Sugar'.

Once in the kitchen, Beatrice gingerly opened the cupboard and instantly felt nauseous as she spied the large brown bottle. It glared back at her menacingly, but, after a moment's hesitation, she whipped it into her dressing gown pocket before retreating silently to her bedroom.

Kate maintained a strict 'no sweets' policy, unless it was a special occasion, preferring to offer Beatrice fruit instead. Howard Hemingway, however, was also partial to a 'Barley Sugar' and frequently indulged his granddaughter. Their secret hoard was hidden at the back of the shelf, which ran the full length above the clothes rail in the old toy cupboard. This cupboard now doubled as a wardrobe for Beatrice's vast amount of clothes. The retrieval of the all-important jar necessitated Beatrice to stand on a chair.

Now she had a self-imposed dilemma; just how much of the ghastly liquid would she need to take before the inevitable happened. A full fifteen minutes passed as she stared fixatedly at the bottle. Initially, she hoped a small slug might do the trick, but after some deliberation, she decided that only a good deal more would produce the desired effect. A moment's indecision followed, before she took a deep breath, held her nose and swallowed half the bottle. Three 'Barley Sugars' later convinced her that her daring plan would be worth it. She hid the bottle and its remaining contents, along with the jar of 'Barley Sugars', at the back of the cupboard. After removing her dressing gown, she lay on her bed and waited for the repulsive liquid to take effect. She sucked another 'Barley Sugar' vigorously, but the awful taste remained.

It wasn't long before she began to feel really sick and called out to her mamma. It was now barely six o'clock and Kate was still asleep, but Emily and the kitchen maid were already busily preparing breakfast and the picnic basket for the family's intended outing.

Beatrice's calls resonated along the corridors to the kitchen level two floors below. The plaintive sounds alerted Emily. She wiped her hands on her apron and hurried to Beatrice's bedroom. As she entered, her eyes focused on the obviously sick child, who was moaning and holding her tummy. 'What on earth is the matter Miss Beatrice? You don't look too well.'

At this point, Beatrice felt very sorry for herself and wondered if she had taken her plan too far. Supposing she became really ill and had to go to hospital? She groaned aloud. The pains in her stomach were intensifying and the need to be sick was fast overwhelming her. 'Please fetch mamma, I really do not feel well,' croaked Beatrice, still agonising on her self inflicted predicament.

Emily disappeared along the landing before knocking urgently on Kate's door. 'Madam, are you awake? Beatrice isn't well and is calling for you.'

Drowsily, Kate, slowly opened her eyes and noted the urgency in Emily's voice. She shook James awake, before grabbing her dressing gown and hurrying after the cook to her daughter's room. 'Darling what on earth is wrong? You don't look very well at all,' said Kate, as she stroked her daughter's forehead.

'I don't feel well mamma. I feel quite sick and have a headache,' moaned Beatrice.

'Oh dear, whatever could it be?' asked Kate apprehensively, before instructing Emily to contact Dr Hamilton.

Rosie was still in bed but on hearing the commotion, eased into her slippers and proceeded to the landing where she encountered what can only be described as 'organised pandemonium'. The front door slammed as Emily, galvanised into action, went in search of Albert, the driver, who immediately set off in the trap to fetch Dr Hamilton. James joined Kate and they tried to calm their daughter, although a glass of water seemed woefully inadequate in the circumstances.

Beatrice spent most of the next hour in the bathroom, vomiting violently. Her plan had developed into a monster, over which she'd relinquished control. Kate was more than concerned, so while they awaited the doctor's arrival, made the decision that Rosie would visit the Arboretum with James instead. Rosie was disappointed but Beatrice was inwardly ecstatic and queasily celebrated her success.

※

The Harcourt Arboretum, located six miles south of Oxford, near the village of Nuneham Courtenay, comprised some one hundred and fifty acres and proved an unexpected delight for Rosie. James ensured they both enjoyed the day, despite the absence of Kate and Beatrice.

He was full of interesting information, which gave Rosie an insight into the artist, William Sawrey Gilpin. It was he who laid out the pinetum,[32] which formed the core of the

---

32 An arboretum specializing in growing conifers

arboretum. She was entranced by the splendour of the Giant Redwoods and Monkey-Puzzle trees, planted twenty years previously. A ten-acre English woodland, carpeted with Bluebells in the spring, provided the backdrop to its most exciting feature; the exotic Peacocks, which inhabited the grounds.

They picnicked on a tartan rug amidst the splendid manicured lawns of Nuneham House, sipping fresh lemonade and eating blueberry muffins.

A flash of iridescent blue green caught Rosie's eye, a Peacock feather half hidden in a grass verge. 'Oh look James, it's beautiful! Can I take it with me?'

James grinned at Rosie's enthusiasm and noted the definitive similarity to Kate. They were alike in so many ways. 'Of course, Rosie, there's nothing stopping you. Peacocks shed their tail feathers, but you were very lucky to have spotted it. Go and collect it and place it carefully in the bottom of the picnic box for our return journey. Your mamma told me about your own special box, why don't you keep it in there?'

Rosie admired the feather, delighted with her find. 'Actually, I think I will give it to mamma, as she has missed being with us today. Do you think she will like it?'

'Well, that's a very generous thought Rosie, she will be delighted and I am sure she will treasure it.' A thoughtful James pondered on why his daughter seemed opposed to befriending Rosie, who he found charming, thoughtful and considerate. He determined to speak with her on their return to get to the bottom of this unnecessary and upsetting feud.

Back at 'Highclere House', Beatrice remained tucked up in bed, in-between visits to the bathroom. Dr Hamilton, mystified as to the cause of the sudden bilious attack, assured Kate that it would probably only last a short while. He ruled out any infection and concluded that it was something she had eaten. A relieved Kate thanked him for his quick response and recommendations, bed rest and small sips of water, taken frequently during the next twenty-four hours. Beatrice had succeeded in gaining the whole of her mamma's attention, but she was annoyed with how she felt physically and how she had to spend her day.

※

James and Rosie returned home weary but happy in the early evening. James was pleased to learn that his daughter's health was not a cause for concern and had considerably improved. He was, however, disappointed that her disagreeable mood had not changed.

Kate provided a welcome cup of tea in the sitting room. 'Well you two, how was your visit?'

Rosie was bubbling with excitement, despite the fact that she was obviously worn out. 'It was wonderful mamma, we picnicked on the lawn of the big house and I found this beautiful Peacock feather, which I want you to have.' Rosie proudly handed Kate the feather. 'Do you like it mamma?'

Kate's eyes misted as she accepted the feather. 'Oh Rosie, it is lovely. I will keep it on my dressing table and treasure it always.'

Rosie, pleased with Kate's reaction, felt she should pay Beatrice a visit. After all, she had missed out on a memorable day.

Beatrice, however, had other ideas; she feigned sleep when Rosie entered her room, which caused Rosie to reconsider her intention of recounting her experience. Instead, she silently closed the door, leaving a deflated Beatrice to consider whether her scheming had been as successful as she'd hoped.

※

The next two days were relatively trouble free and equilibrium was restored. Beatrice was not in the mood for any more devious planning. She did, however, make it abundantly clear to Rosie, that the fact they were half sisters, did not necessarily mean they would automatically become friends. Rosie was undeterred, but reflected on the statement and wondered whether it was at all possible to change Beatrice's mind. She knew it would be an uphill struggle, so she sought her grandfather's opinion, who always gave sound advice. 'Don't worry Rosie,' he said, 'situations arise and most of the time work out.'

What a wise man her grandfather was, she thought and found comfort in his words. Howard, however, secretly harboured many concerns and actively considered at what stage he should intervene.

※

Lizzie's time with Clara and her family was wonderfully fulfilling, although occasionally her thoughts drifted. Had Rosie managed to win the affections of her half sister at long last? She knew it was important that she bonded with Kate and, so far, it appeared to be going really well. The only fly in the ointment was Beatrice's apparent irrational dislike of

Rosie. Kate was obviously astute enough to see that a natural jealousy existed, as Beatrice would not readily share her mamma with a relative stranger. It would inevitably manifest itself in some form of rebellious behaviour.

⁂

After Rosie returned home, life became more settled, until a welcome letter from Marcus arrived for Lizzie on the 10th June. The news was positive and cheered her immensely, although he would not be home before July at the earliest. His absence meant she had to cope alone with many important issues and she really missed him, both as a friend and lover. How she ached to have him hold her again, to feel the closeness, only shared by those truly in love. Her resolve had wavered over recent weeks, but she determined to stay strong in the intervening period until his return.

My Dearest Elizabeth,

I hope you and Rosie are both well. I am rather tired, having journeyed extensively. I've followed several lines of enquiry with regard to Belle and Jack and have met with mixed fortunes.

I finally made the long awaited meeting with Samuel Jacobs, the business associate, after he returned from New York. He remembers Belle and Jack extremely well. He recalled that they were definitely taken to the hospital in Philadelphia for medical checks, along with some other survivors. Apparently, Belle wrote thanking him for saving their lives and he wrote back to the address on her letter. However, after this initial correspondence, he did not hear from her again. I have been to that address, but the present occupiers informed me that she left some time ago. They did not have a forwarding address. I intend making further enquiries, which might indicate whether they are still in the area or not.

When we agreed that I undertake this journey to find my son, neither of us could have envisaged me being away for more than three months at the most. Unfortunately, this is only the beginning and it's likely that the search will be considerably longer! I am so sorry my darling, but, on a positive note, I do feel I am closer to achieving my goal.

Please write back and let me know what you would prefer me to do. Whatever you decide, I will agree. I do not want to place any pressure on you to cope alone.

I hope you had a wonderful time in Berriedale and are now safely home. I look forward to hearing all your news and hope there's been some developments in your search for Kate.

These past months have seemed interminably long and I hate us being apart, but as you emphasized, it was something I needed to do. It hasn't been fruitless, because I have already established they are alive.

I miss you so much my darling and can't wait to see you. I dreamt the other night that you were in my arms again. I could smell your perfume and feel your body pressed close to mine. You looked into my eyes as we softly kissed and those familiar feelings enveloped me. I moved my hands slowly over your body and you responded by thrusting your breasts and arching your back. I entered you and we became as one, sensually lost in a climatic embrace, which seemed to last an eternity...then I awoke and you were not beside me... the bed was cold and I felt very alone. If I could be granted one wish right now, it would be for you to be by my side...I love you so much Elizabeth and thank God that we were given a second chance to be together - I will always cherish the memory of the day you walked back into my life. Nothing could ever come close to the sense of total fulfilment I felt when you stood before me that day. I hope you are missing me and looking forward to my homecoming, when my dreams can once again become reality. Until you are safely in my arms my darling, I am like a lost soul, searching in a wilderness, unable to find the joy and total ecstasy you bring to me. I pray that the rest of the time will pass quickly and that I will be able to book a return passage very soon.

It will be your birthday in a few days and I am sorry that I will not be with you. I hope you like the handmade card. Father has a friend in Massachusetts, who buys greeting cards from a young lady by the name of Esther Howland. She specialises in handmade valentine cards and designs birthday cards. Father carries a small stock, so imagine my delight when I found one with a still-life painting of a vase of freesias. Remember the vase of those flowers on the table when we first dined together at the Adelphia Hotel in Liverpool? Anyway, I hope you have a wonderful time, however you plan to celebrate. Until we meet again my darling Elizabeth, keep looking up at the stars. My thoughts and love are with you always.

All my love to you and Rosie,
Marcus xxxxxx

Lizzie read his letter several times, before folding it carefully and placing it in her keeper box. She thoughtfully removed several sheets of paper from the bureau and began penning a reply. It became a lengthy missive, but contained all her news. She particularly emphasized her support for him to continue with his search, which she considered really important for his confidence and wellbeing. Over an hour passed before she'd finished. As she spilled droplets from her scent bottle on to the five sheets, a tear formed in her eye. Sealing them in the vellum envelope, ready for posting, became an emotional undertaking, as she contemplated more months apart, but later, as she sat alone in their bedroom, she made the decision to place her birthday celebrations on hold until his return.

Chapter Thirteen

Voyage of the 'Lightning' May-September 1855

Everything was stowed away aboard the Lightning ready for her voyage to Australia. Cargo hatches were battened down and all ropes and rigging secured. John sought out Jimmy who was catching a quick nap in his hammock below deck. He was pleased to find him alone. 'Well Jimmy, are you looking forward to your first trip to sea?' he enquired, as he leant against the rope locker door.

Jimmy eyed his shipmate, a wry grin on his face. 'It's exciting John that's for sure. I've never left these shores before and am looking forward to the adventure.'

'Good, good Jimmy. It's important to maintain a positive attitude. I'll give you some sound advice to ensure you survive the passage. Keep your head down, carry out your duties with vigilance and give the old man, Captain Forbes[33] respect, but realise that you might have to stand up to him. Don't let him bully you Jimmy, but don't be disrespectful, as

---

33 Captain James Nicol 'Bully' Forbes, born in Aberdeen in 1821. He was known as 'Bully' Forbes, as tough a man as ever hauled himself hand over hand across the rigging of the flying jib boom. Under the command of Captain Forbes, previously master of the Marco Polo, the '*Lightning*' made its first voyage to Australia in just 77 days, and on its return voyage made it in a record 64 days, a record which has never been broken by a sailing ship.

he's not averse to rationing out severe punishment.' John frowned slightly as he delivered his take on keeping oneself out of trouble, but he'd put the fear of God up Jimmy. Just what did he mean exactly? 'Bully me?' he questioned, as a vivid picture of his dad taking off his belt came into his mind.

John softened and he placed his hand on Jimmy's arm to placate him. 'There's no need to worry Jimmy. I'm just forewarning you. It's best you know the kind of man you are dealing with. Captain Forbes' reputation precedes him. His nickname is 'Bully' Forbes and with good reason. He was captain of the 'Marco Polo' before he took command of the Lightning and there are tales circulating about his strict regimes in order to achieve his objective of cutting the journey times to the limit. I've heard he intends to break all records with the 'Lightning'. Apparently, he padlocked the sheets and threatened the crew from the poop with a brace of levelled pistols on one ship. On the Marco Polo, the passengers became so frightened at how hard he was pushing the vessel that a deputation pleaded with him to shorten sail. Forbes refused and shouted *'This is a case of Hell or Melbourne'*. Let's hope for us Jimmy, it's Melbourne, as I don't fancy the alternative!'

Jimmy paled. 'And you say I shouldn't worry. He sounds more of a monster than me own dad.'

John grinned and cuffed Jimmy's head. 'Jimmy, Jimmy, now you know the kind of man he is, you will be equipped to handle him. I will look out for you and do my best to protect you. By the way, I noticed you signed on under the name of James Marsh. Was there a reason for that?'

Jimmy was guarded in his reply. 'Well, the thing is, me dad 'ad summat of a reputation where we lived and a din't want ta be associated wi 'im. Worrit alright...am not in trouble am a?'

The truth was that Jimmy still felt uneasy about his father's death and did not want his whereabouts known to the authorities, in case he was indeed a 'wanted' man.

John nodded sagely. 'No, of course not Jimmy. You won't be the first and I doubt you'll be the last. I understand your reasons and will keep it quiet.'

'Thanks, John, thanks a lot. I appreciate yer looking aht fer me. Do all the ratings know what a bastard Captain Forbes is?' questioned Jimmy.

'Well, not all, most know, especially the officers, but he seems to give them a bit more respect,' concluded John, almost embarrassed by this statement. 'Any rate, Jimmy, there will be a lot of exciting times ahead. We will be crossing the line in around twenty five to thirty days, when the whole of the crew celebrate in their own inimitable way, including the old man.' John encouraged in an attempt to lift his spirits.

Inevitably, Jimmy's curiosity was roused. 'That sounds good John. So how exactly do you celebrate?'

John tapped the side of his nose and laughed. 'As a 'first tripper', you aren't privy to that. Suffice to say it will be entertaining.'

Their conversation ended abruptly, due to the continuous ringing of the ships bell, indicating all hands on deck for the final briefing before the ship set sail.

※

The outward journey was fairly uneventful, the prevailing winds were such that the topgallant sails never had occasion to be furled during the entire passage, neither was there occasion to reef the topsails. This ensured Jimmy gained a gradual introduction into life at sea and with the help of John, managed to stay on the old man's good side.

Jimmy found time to write his experiences down in a letter to Rosie. His spelling was crude and his grammar left a lot to be desired, but he knew Rosie would make allowances and be really pleased he had taken time to write. He felt rather foolish and a little reticent writing his feelings down, but he did manage a form of endearment, the salutation and the valediction. He promised himself to tell her exactly how he felt when they met up again. He also wrote a letter to his mother, thanking her for protecting him during his childhood and promising to visit her as soon as he was able.

The Lightning made Cape Otway Light on the night of the 29th of July and Port Phillip Heads on the 30th. She anchored in Hobson's Bay, opposite Sandridge, three miles from Melbourne, on the 31st. There she remained for twenty days. Jimmy was able to 'post' his letters when Lightning's mails were delivered, by the chandler's cutter. Although it would be the Autumn before Rosie and his mam would receive them, by one of the fast Clipper ships.

During one of Jimmy and John's shore leaves in Melbourne, they encountered two young British nurses, as they made their way to one of the many dockside taverns. The girls, Lucinda and Helen, were visiting Helen's parents who had emigrated two years previously. Helen had remained in England to finish her nursing course and lodged with Lucinda's parents in Cambridge. The girls were due to sail for England the following day, so were making the most of their last day in Melbourne, having duped Helen's parents into believing they would be sightseeing and then attending a performance of Handel's Messiah, by the Royal Melbourne Philharmonic Choir and Orchestra.

John soon engaged the attractive pair in conversation with the predictable consequence that they spent the whole evening in their company. Lucinda instantly took a shine to Jimmy, who surprised himself by finding her equally attractive. He did not, however, intend to become too familiar with her. John, on the other hand, was quite happy at the pairing and flirted outrageously with Helen. The evening ended too soon for John and Helen and they parted with a lingering kiss and promises to meet up again when they were both back in England. Jimmy, however, made no such promises, but when Lucinda pulled him close to say goodbye, he presented only a token resistance to the slow, sensuous kiss she planted on his lips. John and Jimmy dawdled their way back to the dock, which allowed a hesitant Jimmy to voice his concerns. 'Can I ask you something John?'

John raised his eyebrows as Jimmy fidgeted. 'Of course, my merry seafaring friend, what's troubling you?'

Jimmy shamefaced, stammered his thoughts out loud. 'It's just...well...I shouldn't have kissed Lucinda...it was wrong and now I feel guilty. Should I tell Rosie?'

John laughed loudly. 'Don't be daft man. You only kissed her. You weren't intimate. Rosie must know that temptation will rear its head many more times before you meet up again. You aren't married...yet anyway. What's a man to do? You will be away at sea for months at a time, so it's hardly likely you will remain a virgin is it, if indeed you are?' John speculated.

Jimmy blushed. 'No...no, of course not, but Rosie and I are kinda goan steady and a intend to remain faithful ta her.'

John once again raised his brows. 'It's expected Jimmy. You are a red blooded male. There'd be something wrong if you didn't give in to your urges. Don't give it another thought,' he said as he swaggered along the quayside with his hands stuffed into his pockets. He was secretly surprised at Jimmy's puritanical attitude and was left wondering whether Rosie might still be a virgin...or, more surprisingly, Jimmy, who hadn't sounded convincing. However, Jimmy's next statement negated any thoughts of his friend's sexual status.

Jimmy did not want to appear wet behind the ears in front of John, so dismissed his questions as some kind of joke. 'You're right, of course, a just wanted to see what yer would say...ta see if yer intended to mention our little exploit ter Rosie.'

John slapped Jimmy lightly on the back. 'Your secret's safe with me Jimmy. Whatever happens during our voyage together, you can be sure it will remain between us. Come on, let's have one last drink in the Tavern. Tell you what, that Helen was eager. I think I would have been all right there if we'd had more time.' Laughing, John entered the Tavern, leaving Jimmy trailing behind, deep in thought about possible future encounters...he already had misgivings!

⁂

On the 20th of August, the mail and several passengers were embarked and the 'Lightning' made ready for sea. It was a warm balmy day, with a very light North-West breeze. The anchor was hove up and the 'Lightning' was taken in tow by the steam tug 'Washington' as far as the Heads.

During their outward voyage, John had been instrumental in persuading old Josh, a bosun of twenty five years, to take Jimmy under his wing and teach him the essential seamanship duties, which would prepare him for all eventualities. He was looking forward to an uneventful journey home. Jimmy was well liked by his fellow crew members and the close bond he had formed with Josh meant he had a mentor with vast life experience.

They logged two hundred and sixty eight miles by noon the following day, as they passed Swan Island Light and, on the afternoon of the 24th, they caught and passed a large ship 'Mermaid', which had sailed two days previously for Liverpool. They were making good time and it appeared that Captain Forbes would achieve a very fast passage. At Four Bells on the first night watch, the 'Lightning' passed the Auckland Islands, which meant they'd achieved an average of 19 knots, so far.

It wasn't to last, at eleven p.m. on the 28th, while under a heavy press of canvas, a violent squall from the South-West caught the ship and carried away the foretopmast studdingsail-boom, the foretop, foretopgallant, and foreroyal yards, blowing all the sails to pieces. Jimmy saw first hand how quickly conditions could deteriorate and became immersed in his baptism of fire. Josh, battling the squall, was thrown violently against the forward cargo hatch and suffered a deep gash to his leg. Fortunately, the quick action of the ship's carpenter, brought the bleeding under control, but his leg required heavy strapping and he was ordered below by Captain Forbes. Thereafter, the ship was obliged to go under easy canvas for four days until the yards and sails were replaced, the damage being quite extensive.

The days passed and despite adverse winds the 'Lightning' rounded Cape Horn, into the South Atlantic and up to the equator off the east coast of Brazil.

One evening as dusk descended, Jimmy remained below deck, whittling away at a piece of oak found in the hold when they were outward bound. He had been drawn to the wood, as it was large enough to construct a box. During the voyage from England, Jimmy, had studied Josh who, in no time at all, had fashioned a piece of driftwood into the shape of an ornate cross, which he now wore on a chain, a gift from his wife, who said It would bring him good luck.

Jimmy figured he should start with something a little less complicated. He knew Lizzie had a box in which she kept precious items, so he determined to devote his spare time to producing an equally impressive box for Rosie. The task was almost complete, but while he was concentrating on carving her name on the lid, he became aware of John standing at his shoulder.

'Hey Jimmy, you're making a really splendid job of that. Rosie will love it,' he said admiring the box's smooth, uncomplicated lines.

Jimmy smiled proudly. 'D'ya reckon? 'Ave been working on it since a seen old Josh carving his cross. A wah wondring where a could get some wax to preserve the wood. A wah using wax on the sail twine yesterdee, but the old man was watching me like a hawk and a don't want 'im accusing me of nicking oat.'

John grinned widely. 'I'll tell you what Jimmy, I'll ask Captain Forbes for a tin of bees wax if you like. He's not the devil incarnate, he can be quite human sometimes.'

Jimmy frowned. 'You might not think so, but we able seamen have a different view on him.'

'Maybe you are right. I suppose as an officer, I do have a different perspective,' he paused, before posing a more personal question to his shipmate. 'Is Rosie the one for you then Jimmy?' he asked curiously.

Jimmy eyed John with an air of confidence. 'No question baht that. Allus 'as bin, allus will be. Though a do wonder if she might meet some toff a can't compete wi, while I am off sailing the world. A sailor on a Merchantman in't exactly an ideal occupation if yer want ter seckle down is it? but I don't see I 'ave much choice. I'll not ga dahn the pit, nor slave in a hot faktreh. This pays more, much more and, hopefully, I'll meck enough ta provide ferra. Though it'ull be many years yet.' Jimmy returned to his carving in wistful concentration.

John didn't agree with Jimmy's sentiments and thought he should play the field before settling down. He had joined a Merchantman to travel the world and expected to encounter a few girls on the way. He didn't want to entertain marriage...not yet anyway, so decided to avail Jimmy of his insight. 'You know Jimmy, Rosie isn't the only girl out there. Don't you think you should look around and see what's on offer? What about when we docked in Port Melbourne, those two nurses we met, remember? I thought you were keen on the dark haired one, Lucinda?'

Jimmy shook his head. 'That's as maybe, but I'm 'ardly likely to bump inta 'er agen am I? You were the one who asked for their address in England.'

John nodded his head vigorously. 'That's not the point. Don't you see...you *were* interested, albeit for a short time, but you were attracted to her. Supposing we do bump into them again? It's possible, as they were travelling to England the following day to take up posts on a sailors' recuperation ship, moored at Greenwich. You never know,' joked John, 'we might come a cropper and finish up there. In fact, I have been thinking I might write to Helen and, if I am down that way, I'll suggest we meet.'

'Well, that's up to you, but leave me out of it. I have no intention of meeting up with her again, even if she was good looking,' stated Jimmy.

John was determined to goad his friend and wouldn't let it rest, as he was enjoying himself. 'Never say never, Jimmy. All I'm saying is, if you can be attracted to another woman, maybe Rosie isn't *the* one.'

Jimmy became irritated with John's attempts at shaking his belief. 'You're wrong...I might admire other women, but that doesn't mean I'm going to do anything about it.'

John backed off, not wishing to upset him too much. 'Maybe...I was only pointing out that it *is* possible. Of course, Rosie's a 'looker' and a nice girl...she'd probably be my type if we weren't related,' John joked.

Jimmy reacted scathingly to John's jibe. 'Well, you are related, so you've no chance. Anyrode, Rosie needs someone older to look after her and you are only seventeen.'

John took a step back. 'I wasn't suggesting that I was interested, Jimmy. It was just a bit of harmless banter. I think we've become good mates, since we've been together on this voyage. I don't want to lose a friend I can trust,' grinned John, leaning on the door-jamb of the small cabin.

Jimmy let the subject drop. He valued John's friendship. 'Don't worry John, as a said, it'll be many years yet before a can seckle down. I expect we'll 'ave many good times together on future voyages. 'Ave yer plans for yer next voyage?' asked Jimmy amiably.

John stroked his sparsely tufted newly grown beard. He hoped that his next voyage would be to Bilbao, as he already had designs on a position as third mate, providing he passed his ticket, whilst ashore. 'Maybe...maybe. I was thinking Jimmy, that if I got my second mate's ticket, so that I can sail as third, you might consider joining the same ship. What do you think of that?'

Jimmy's eyes lit up. 'D'ya reckon yer could get me a berth on your ship then? Anyway where the 'eck is Bilbao?'

John grinned at Jimmy's lack of geographic knowledge. 'It's close to the border with France...in the Bay of Biscay, Northern Spain and yes Jimmy, I could probably pull a few strings. I'd look forward to us having another adventure together,' said John and smiled as he left Jimmy whistling and carving the last few letters of *'Rosie Cameron'* on his precious box. No doubt about it, he had found a good and loyal friend in Jimmy.

On the 28th, they passed six miles east of Pernambuco. The sea had been fairly calm, with light North-East to North-North-East winds, however, despite the calm conditions, the bosun felt uneasy. Something wasn't quite right. He shook his head, as he back spliced a rope for the running rigging and reflected on other occasions his senses had proved correct.

Dusk fell on the 29th. The ink black sky formed a dramatic backdrop against which the silhouette of the 'Lightning' appeared as a masterpiece in oil on canvas. The peace was short-lived, as the bosun's intuition was proved correct. The 'glass'[34] dropped spectacularly as a solid black curtain of

---

34 Nautical term relating to a Barometer reading

a line squall loomed angrily to starboard. Vivid flashes of lightning zipped and zig-zagged across the sky, before burying themselves in the ocean troughs.

John went below deck to find Jimmy. 'Jimmy, better get ready, the squall is almost upon us. It will be brief, but we will need all hands.'

Jimmy was off duty, but the Bosun's warning shout was heard loud and clear – *'all hands on deck'*. The next moments were frantic as the crew hurried to their allotted stations. Jimmy was astounded at the sudden change. Huge waves buffeted the hull and the ship listed to port dangerously. Heavy rain lashed his face as he fought to remain upright, while several of the other young, inexperienced crew were slammed on to the wet deck and into the scuppers[35].

Suddenly the chilling cry of 'man over board' resounded in Jimmy's ears. The bosun had disappeared over the stern and was now helplessly struggling in the huge waves. Mesmerised by the ghastly scene, Jimmy stared incomprehensibly as Josh struggled valiantly. Without hesitation and thought for his own safety, Jimmy dived into the dark raging waters, but he hadn't cleared the ship and his leg clunked sickeningly against the rudder. The salty black environment enveloped him as he sunk beneath the waves. A million and one thoughts milled around in his head and, momentarily, he had no clue which way was up. His lungs filled and a strange rushing sound assaulted his ears.

Suddenly he was on the surface and he could see a handful of stars in the night sky but the waves showed no mercy. Frantically he scoured the surface for a sign of the

---

35 A scupper is an opening in the side walls of an open-air structure, for purposes of draining water. Ships have scuppers at deck level, to allow for ocean or rainwater drain off.

bosun. Twice he dived beneath the waves and the second time, in a brilliant lightning flash, he caught sight of something shining. Josh's chain, which held the small wooden cross, reflected in the flash sufficiently for Jimmy to locate the bosun some yards away. He swam doggedly toward him and grasped his leather jerkin. The pair surfaced briefly, plunged again, then resurfaced once more, but the bosun was gone, his lifeless eyes bored unseeing into Jimmy's soul as they drew level with his own. There was no hope, but Jimmy had the presence of mind to do his mentor one last service, he removed his cross and chain, still struggling to remain afloat himself. Exhausted and saddened, Jimmy released Josh. He said a prayer and promised to break the news to his wife. If he survived, he would return the chain to her personally.

Gasping for air, and already weak, he was shocked to see the Lightning's silhouette disappearing. Still clutching Josh's cross, he prayed silently again, as he felt his own life slipping away.

⁂

John, distraught aboard the 'Lightning' scanned the unforgiving waves in the forlorn hope of a sighting of Jimmy and Josh. He hadn't moved for the last ten minutes and had gripped the rails until his knuckles were white. He peered solemnly into the blackness for any signs of life, but in his heart he knew there was little chance of either surviving.

Captain Forbes issued a stark command. 'Come away John, there is nothing to be done. Even a strong swimmer would struggle in such conditions. It was a very brave thing that Marsh did, but we cannot turn around, we must press on, we are losing precious time,' Forbes stated matter of factly. Then catching the horrified look of the young officer, he softened the blow with a more humanistic statement. 'We will hold a service for both men. They will be sorely missed. I have not known the bosun for very long, but he was a good man. It is a sad day, John, a very sad day.'

The captain strode purposefully away, but disturbingly, his countenance betrayed the short-lived sympathy extended to his officer. It was replaced by a look of cold-blooded determination. The thought of his record beating crossing being threatened by two incompetent seafarers was inconceivable. The ship would now have to struggle on with two men down...'Thoughtless bastards,' he muttered, shaking his head.

John stood for a few minutes longer, reflecting on what might have been. He swore when he became master of a ship, he would not put some speed record before human life.

Jimmy had become a good friend, but sailing together in the future was now but a dream that lay in tatters. His thoughts turned to Rosie. How would she take the news? He knew she would be devastated. She would, of course, remain oblivious to the tragedy until Jimmy's next of kin, his mother, had been informed. He took one last look over the stern and noticed the sea had calmed. The only sign there had been a storm was some floating debris from a small fishing boat also caught by the squall. Pieces of wreckage littered the area and an eerie silence prevailed. The sea could be a very cruel and unforgiving place. *God rest all their Souls,* thought John.

Chapter Fourteen

Delayed
September 1855

Lizzie received a disturbing letter from Marcus on the 6th September. Riots[36] had broken out in Philadelphia while Marcus and his father had been lunching in the town.

'My Darling Elizabeth,

I hope you and Rosie are well and missing me, as I miss you. I am enclosing a birthday card for Rosie's fourteenth birthday, but will bring her present home with me. I expect she is growing up quickly and will be quite the young lady when I see her again. When I was in New York City, I bought a silk dress from Stewart's Marble Palace and had to employ the help of an assistant, as I was unsure of her size. I hope she likes it.

Unfortunately, my return has been further delayed. Father and I were in town on the 6th August, following

---

36 On August 6th of 1855, riots broke out in Philadelphia spawned out of an intense rivalry between the Democrats and the 'Know-Nothing' party. Rumors began spreading that the Catholics were interfering with the fair voting process and a street fight broke out. The riot grew in size and twenty-two people were killed. Many more people were injured in the riot than were killed and property was destroyed on a large scale.

a tip off regarding Belle's whereabouts. The lead was insubstantial at best, but I could not allow any information, no matter how flimsy, to be discarded. I was ecstatic when I knew they were both still alive and it gives me hope that I am even closer to finding them.

We were in an hotel in the town centre, when there was a huge commotion outside. It appears that a riot broke out, spawned out of an intense rivalry between the Democrats and the 'Know-Nothing Party'. There had been rumours that the Catholics were interfering with the fair voting process, which resulted in street fighting.

Father and I took cover in the kitchens, together with several other patrons. The front doors were quickly locked and bolted. We remained crammed inside a store cupboard for several hours as the riot grew in size. We could hear tremendous bangs, falling glass, shouting and screaming...there were two women with us who fainted because of the heat and I was concerned for my father, as he does have a heart condition. However, he remained relatively composed, citing his survival during the Belgium Revolution as the reason for his ability to remain calm!

Eventually, the noise abated and when we finally felt safe to venture out, we discovered that twenty-two people had been killed and many more injured. There was large-scale destruction of property, but luckily the hotel, which suffered superficial damage, was not specifically targeted. Thankfully we survived unscathed, but it could have been much worse, Elizabeth.

I am missing you so much. It is harder than I ever imagined possible. The days drag by and the nights are even longer...I cannot wait to hold you in my arms again...the only dream that keeps me sane. Without you, I would surely be lost.

Anyway, my darling, I hope you are missing me and are looking forward to the day when we are together again. I cannot let you know exactly when that will be, but I am comforted in the knowledge that we observe Perseus simultaneously every evening, which is when I feel closest to you. I hope you haven't forgotten how wonderful it is waking up together and making love as the sun rises, especially the times when we are alone in the house...forgive me for hoping you will be there alone when I return! I picture it often...you running across the lawn and me gathering you in my arms... then a soft, lingering kiss with no one around to interrupt the sheer pleasure of that first embrace, after such a long period apart. Wanting you...needing you and finally making love to you in our bed...the softness of your skin...our bodies entwined...the exquisite moment when I enter you and see the pleasure in your eyes as we both reach fulfilment.

I will hold on to these thoughts until they become reality...we must never be parted again. I love you so much Elizabeth. Keep safe for me my darling.

Yours forever...Marcus xxx

Lizzie re-read the letter several times, relieved that Marcus and his father had escaped the riots unharmed. She had been expecting him home at any time, but once again her hopes of a reunion were dashed. Marcus wrote such wonderful letters, which kept her spirits up, but it was now almost seven months since she waved goodbye on the quayside of the Liverpool docks, which seemed a lifetime ago. Tears of sadness rolled down her cheeks as she clutched the letter to her breast and spoke out loud. 'Please let him return home soon...please... I miss him so much it hurts.'

She sat at her bedroom window for several minutes, before eventually wiping her tears. She consoled herself with the fact that his homecoming would only be delayed a few months at the most.

Chapter Fifteen

Bad News
October 1855

'Read all about it...extraordinary performance of the clipper ship Lightning...record broken', shouted the news seller, as people queued up to buy their morning paper. For one crew member, the record was only a pyrrhic victory at best, but the captain and most of the crew, celebrated the occasion in style. They had achieved and recorded an unprecedented time of sixty-three days, an extraordinary feat of seamanship indeed!

John considered the unenviable, but unavoidable task, which lay ahead of him, as he boarded a train to Manchester. How would he deliver the devastating news of Jimmy's death to those that mattered?

He reached 'The Beeches', some hours later, but still hadn't decided on what he would say to Rosie. Hesitantly, he climbed the steps, focusing on the large oak door, but with little idea on how to soften the blow. Indeed, he was still recovering from the shock of Jimmy's death himself. He pulled on the rope and the bell resonated loudly. His mouth, already dry took on the texture of an arid desert, while his heart beat faster. The door swung open to reveal a surprised Lizzie.

'John...oh John how wonderful!' exclaimed Lizzie enthusiastically, until she observed John's crestfallen mien. Her stomach lurched in instant foreboding and icy fear gripped her heart. 'John, what on earth's wrong?' she shouted.

'Can I come inside Aunty Lizzie? I am afraid I bring bad news.'

Not a single word was exchanged as Lizzie ushered John to the study. She closed the door silently. 'Rosie is at Robert's, John, so we are alone. Please tell me what is wrong?' said Lizzie, as she clasped John's hand tightly.

'It...it's Jimmy, Aunty Lizzie,' said John, deliberately studying the shiny toecaps of his boots.

Lizzie groaned. 'Oh no...not Jimmy. Has he met with an accident John? Is he...is it bad?' she asked hardly able to disguise the trembling in her voice.

Tears welled in his eyes as he squeezed her hand. 'He's dead Aunty Lizzie...Jimmy drowned trying to save a fellow sailor.' He knew his words were woefully inadequate as he sought to break the news gently. *Did his voice sound harsh and without compassion?* Oh God, that's not what he wanted.

Lizzie was indeed shocked, but put her arms around John's shoulders. 'Oh no...how...how did it happen? You must be devastated.'

They held each other in silence, both struggling with their emotions as tears flowed freely.

John felt helplessly inadequate explained. 'It...it all happened so quickly Aunty. Jimmy was very close to Josh, the bosun. He sustained a badly gashed leg during a violent squall when we were off Brazil, long after Cape Horn was rounded without mishap. We were enjoying relatively light breezes and fairly calm seas, when suddenly, but not totally unexpectedly, as those latitudes are notorious, a 'Line Squall' appeared out of nowhere. It was all hands on deck, but the ferocity of the squall caused the ship to roll dangerously and Josh was washed overboard. Jimmy dived after him without hesitation. They didn't stand a chance because the captain wouldn't come about, in case she 'broached to'.' Then his voice broke, betraying the enormous sadness he felt.

Lizzie's thoughts turned immediately to Rosie. 'How on earth are we going to break this devastating news to Rosie? She has loved Jimmy since they first met in the Marsh and he has watched over her since they were very young. I am sure they would have married one day. Can we tell her together John?' Lizzie pleaded. 'I need your support.'

'Of course, Aunty Lizzie, it is the least I can do,' offered John.

They lapsed into silence again, alone with their thoughts, when John remembered something. He produced a carved box from his bag and held it up for Lizzie to see. 'Jimmy made this for Rosie. He put all his spare time into ensuring it would be worthy of her. He finished it before the squall and he was so proud of it. He wrote a message to her...it's inside.'

Lizzie opened the box and took out a single sheet of paper, on which was drawn a large heart, encircled by the words –

'Ta my beloved Rosie. This box is fer you ta keep all yaw preshus poseshuns. I hope yer like it. Yer cun start it off by keeping my heart safe inside, it ull allus belong ta you. My love ferever, yaw Jimmy xxx.'

It was too much to bear and silent tormented tears rolled down Lizzie's face, as she contemplated a future for Rosie without Jimmy by her side. But, no matter how they both felt, they must be strong for her. She folded the letter carefully and replaced it in the box now resting on the oak table.

Unexpectedly and for the second time that morning, the doorbell rang. Lizzie found the intrusion perplexing in the light of John's news, but rose to answer it. She could hear the unmistakable voices of Rosie and Harriett outside and her heart sank. *Be strong Lizzie,* she said to herself.

The girls laughed as they stepped inside the hall carrying several parcels. Robert, who had dropped them off before returning to the factory, had indulged them on a shopping trip for new outfits and they were excited. A vibrant Rosie couldn't wait to recount her experience. 'Oh mam, you should see the lovely new shoes daddy has bought us. Mine are red with a small heel and Harriett's blue, but hers are flat as she cannot have heels yet,' enthused Rosie, whilst noting somewhat haphazardly that her mother was not her usual cheery self.

Lizzie put her arm around her daughter and held Harriett's hand. 'Come through to the study girls, I have something to tell you,' she said, her heart thumping loudly. She knew this would be one of the most difficult tasks she would ever have to perform.

They made their way to the study and as Lizzie opened the door, John stood up. Rosie immediately flew to greet him, but failed to notice the sombre look on his face. So, she thought, there was nothing wrong after all, her mother was just keeping John's visit a surprise.

John hugged Rosie more tightly than usual. If he didn't release her, then he wouldn't have to begin his sad, dreadful news. A fatalistic sigh escaped his lips, but before he had chance to begin, Lizzie stepped in. 'Rosie darling, sit down and you too Harriett. I am afraid we have some rather bad news.'

Rosie glanced from one to the other and noted their serious looks. 'What is it mam, has there been an accident?' she asked anxiously.

Lizzie held Rosie's hand in her own. 'Yes Rosie...there has been an accident,' she paused. 'It...it's Jimmy—' Her voice tailed off as Rosie interrupted.

'Oh no, where is he? Is he badly hurt? When can we go and see him?' she stuttered, as an icy finger stabbed at her heart.

Lizzie whispered softly. 'Jimmy...Jimmy has died Rosie. He dived overboard to save a friend and both were lost at sea.'

A dreadful silence ensued. No one uttered a word, then Rosie shouted in disbelief. 'No...no...Jimmy can't be dead, he can't be. I would know if he were. You've got it wrong mam...Jimmy isn't dead,' she cried adamantly.

Oh God, thought Lizzie, *this is going to be harder than I imagined.*

John held Rosie's eyes with his own and emphasised the reality of the situation as compassionately as he could. 'Rosie, I am so very sorry, but I saw Jimmy and the bosun sink beneath the waves...they never re-surfaced...they never stood a chance.'

Rosie glared at John and with a strange calmness reiterated her previous statement. 'I'm telling you John, he is not dead. I don't feel it here,' she said and placed her hand on her heart. 'I received his letter just over a week ago telling me of his exploits...he can't be dead.'

Lizzie tried to ease her daughter's state of mind. 'Rosie... oh Rosie, no one could have survived in those seas. There was a sudden Line Squall and the bosun was swept overboard. Jimmy did not hesitate and dived in to save his friend. You have to believe what John is telling you. He was there Rosie, he saw it happen.'

John interjected, emphasizing the point. 'There was nothing anyone could do Rosie. Jimmy and the bosun were drawn under by the currents. I wished with all my heart it wasn't so, but Jimmy *is* dead. I am so *very* sorry Rosie. We became very close during the voyage and he was like a brother to me. I do feel his loss as much as anyone but I have to accept the truth of the matter.'

The room fell silent once more, then Lizzie rang the bell for Elspeth to bring some hot sweet tea, before pouring two large brandies for herself and John. When the tea arrived, she placed a small slug of the liquid into Rosie's cup. 'Drink this darling, it will help you feel calmer.'

Rosie accepted the drink. 'All right mam, but I won't give up on Jimmy. I just know he survived.'

No one spoke for several minutes, until Harriett, who had listened to every word, gave an opinion. 'Aunty Lizzie, I think Rosie is right...Jimmy is probably alive. Rosie knows everything about Jimmy and she wouldn't tell a lie.'

Rosie smiled sadly but only in gratitude of Harriett's recognition. 'You are right Harriett, I am not telling a lie. He will come back home, he will mam, you'll see. He'll walk straight in that door,' she said, pointing confidently.

Lizzie shook her head imperceptibly to warn John not to continue. She'd already decided that Rosie would have to come to terms with Jimmy's death gradually. Maybe that was best. It was probably too shocking for her to comprehend at the moment.

John determined to placate Rosie and picked up the wooden box. 'Rosie, Jimmy made this box especially for you. See, he has carved your name on the top. There's a message inside.'

Rosie held the box, admiring the craftsmanship with pride. She lifted the lid and her eyes scanned the words encircling the big red heart. A slow smile formed as she clutched the paper to her breast, then out loud she made a promise. 'Dear, dear Jimmy...I will keep your heart safe until you return home. I will keep all our precious memories and mementos inside.'

Lizzie and John were sad for Rosie, but they would not deny her belief, or commitment. Rosie clutched the box and left the room quietly. Hot salty tears tumbled to her breast, as she closed the door, but she remained resolute. 'Jimmy will come home one day and I will be waiting for him,' she murmured softly. She hurried to her bedroom where she placed the box on her dressing table, before collapsing tearfully on her bed.

Downstairs, Lizzie comforted Harriett. With a heavy heart, John opened the French doors to the garden and contemplated how Rosie would cope with Jimmy's loss.

CHAPTER SIXTEEN

Disbelief
October 1855

With serious misgivings, Lizzie approached the newly painted white front door of 9 Mile Ash Lane. Ida had obviously been sprucing the house up for Jimmy's eagerly awaited return.

Earlier that morning, Ida had re-read Jimmy's letter, received only last week. She felt uplifted by his words and soon he would be here, recounting adventures enjoyed in foreign lands...lands that she would only ever see through his eyes. No matter, Jimmy would paint a complete picture of his achievements and dreams fulfilled. They would stay firmly etched in her mind and comfort her whenever he was at sea.

She could hardly contain her excitement as she went to answer the knock on her door. It was a shock, therefore, to see a rather forlorn Lizzie standing on her front step. 'Why Lizzie, this is a surprise. I wah expecting our Jimmy any time, but like as not, 'es bin delayed. Come in... come on in.'

Lizzie stepped into the parlour, her eyes clearly showed the tinges of sadness she felt in her heart. Ida was advancing in years and Lizzie knew her news required careful handling, as the shock could have devastating consequences. 'Sit down Ida and let me make you a cup of tea. I'm sure you are ready for one, I know I am,' she said, taking Ida by the arm and settling her into an armchair.

Unfortunately, Ida had already noted Lizzie's increasing anxiety. 'Is everything all right Lizzie?' a nervous tremor evident in her voice.

'I'll make the tea and we'll talk.' Lizzie retreated to the kitchen. She placed the kettle on the hob, before adding two large spoonfuls of sugar into china cups. After what seemed an age, the kettle boiled, emitting curls of steam, which covered the small window. Lizzie carried the freshly brewed tea to the living room and placed the cups on the table, then sat close to Ida. She gently grasped her hand, which caused Ida to stare at her with fear in her eyes. 'What is it Lizzie, what's happened?'

Lizzie took a deep breath and as gently as she could recounted the sad tale to her friend. 'It's Jimmy, Ida...He met with an accident aboard the Lightning.'

Ida quickly interrupted. 'Oh no, poor Jimmy. Is it bad Lizzie? Won't he be able to come and see me?' she questioned, her manner mimicking a rabbit caught in a bright light.

'Oh Ida...I'm so very sorry, but Jimmy died. He...he dived into the sea to save a friend and, tragically, neither survived.'

Ida was clearly shocked. 'Our Jimmy...dead. He can't be Lizzie...I...I would know if he were. He's me son...I would know,' she said as she searched Lizzie's face, for a glimmer of hope.

It was Lizzie's turn to be shocked. Twice in twenty-four hours, the two people closest to Jimmy had denied his death. 'Ida, listen to me. I know this is a great shock to you, but his death was witnessed by several aboard the ship,' explained Lizzie.

In a dreamlike trance, Ida crumpled Jimmy's letter tightly in her hand and stumbled silently out the front door.

She shook her head in disbelief, as she squinted at the clouds scudding across the autumnal sky. Far away she could hear the sweet sound of birdsong and strangely, noticed the last of the hydrangeas were still showing a faint hint of blue. She stood transfixed as a neighbour hurried up the hill...on her arm, a basket laden with groceries. Ida's shoulders slumped, only to be brought back to reality with a jolt when a stray cat brushed past her skirt. The world was still turning... except...except Jimmy was newly absent from that world. It didn't make sense. She could feel his presence...he hadn't gone. He would come back to her...yes, she was positive he had survived. A mother would know. She didn't feel sad, in fact she didn't feel any sense of loss at all. She returned to the parlour, to encounter Lizzie standing tearfully by the dresser. Ida smiled faintly before sitting thoughtfully in her chair. 'Lizzie...I know you might not believe me, but I just know Jimmy will come home. Did anyone see his body? How do they know he didn't survive?'

Lizzie's unsaid acknowledgement of Ida's denial prompted a suggestion. 'Ida, would you come and stay with us for a while? It will do you good to have a change of scenery.'

Ida took in the confines of her small cottage. 'What if Jimmy comes home while I am away? He will wonder where I've gone.'

Lizzie searched for an answer. She remembered Ida's sister lived next door but one. 'I'll tell you what Ida. I will go round to Nancy's and inform her of our plans, then if Jimmy comes home, she can let him know. Will that be okay?'

Reluctantly, Ida agreed. 'All right Lizzie, but yer must ask Nancy to keep her eyes peeled and get 'er to promise she will look for him evry day and bang on the winda if she's sees him ga past. She neen't ger rahnd ter check me 'ouse, as 'ave noat ter pinch and anyrode, she can't ga aht by hersen, wi 'er arthritus playing up. Just ta meck doubly sure, would yer also pin a note to me door, in case he arrives late at night. It should tell im ter ga rahnd to Nancy's? Al leave a key under the mat. 'E'll know where it is cause I allus left 'im a key under the mat in the Marsh ter let 'imsenn in if a wah aht.'

'Of course, Ida. Now you pack a few things for a couple of weeks stay and I will go round to Nancy's. We can catch a cab to the station. I think there is a train to Manchester in a couple of hours.'

Lizzie was relieved that Ida had agreed to her plan and called round to see Nancy. She carefully constructed a note to Jimmy, before pinning it firmly to Ida's front door. By ten o'clock that evening, Ida and Lizzie had arrived back at 'The Beeches'. Cook served a hearty soup for the weary pair, although neither could muster up much of an appetite in the circumstances.

CHAPTER SEVENTEEN

The Dinner Party
November 1855

Seven months had passed since Rosie's accident, during which time, she visited her mamma twice more. She planned another visit before the Christmas Day festivities, when all the family would celebrate their very first Christmas together.

An opportunity arose, when Kate invited Lizzie, Rosie and Robert's family to join the Renwick's one weekend for Rosie's belated fourteenth birthday party. Rosie delayed the event, in the hope that Jimmy might return in October, but by December she reluctantly accepted that Jimmy might never return.

※

Jimmy was never far from her mind, but excited at the prospect of seeing her mamma again, she penned an acceptance on behalf of Lizzie and herself. She signed with a flourish and folded the letter carefully before sealing it in an envelope ready for posting. Wistful but satisfied, she gazed through the French doors and down the long drive, which snaked through immaculately manicured lawns to the magnificent wrought iron gates of the 'The Beeches'. Someone was approaching the gates, but from this distance, only the gender of the person could be ascertained; oddly, the figure did appear familiar. The man approached steadily, then a glimmer of recognition dawned. It was John Jamieson. His practised seafarer's eye had already spotted Rosie, when she stepped out to the patio, hence his cheery wave. He strode purposefully in her direction.

'John, what a lovely surprise. Are you still on leave?' she asked, excitedly.

John took this as his cue and swooped her into his arms, kissing her briefly on the cheek. 'Yes I am Rosie. My ship doesn't leave until Tuesday of next week, so I thought, what better than to pay my favourite cousin a visit.'

Rosie blushed but managed a response. 'I am so glad you did,' she smiled mischievously and linked her arm in his while steering him towards the French doors.

John, unused to entering 'The Beeches' in such an informal manner, suggested he use the front door.

Rosie laughed, amused at John's insistence on formality. 'Oh John, sometimes you sound so utterly stiff and starchy, as if you were a stranger. Come on through,' she said propelling him through the open doors.

'Now, do sit down and I will let mam know you are here. Would you like some tea?'

'Well Rosie, you are becoming quite the little hostess... thank you I will.' John gazed longingly at his cousin. He knew his feelings had become stronger towards her, since Jimmy's death. He also knew that her feelings were steadfast in that she still believed Jimmy would return one day. He watched her closely as she summoned Elspeth to bring tea, by pressing the servants bell located on the wall. He pondered if she would ever come to terms with the loss of Jimmy and move on. Would they ever be anything other than good friends?' he asked himself.

'John, what are you thinking? You seem in a world of your own.'

John replied cautiously. 'My thoughts were not focussed on anything in particular. I suppose I am just happy to be with you again.'

'I see,' Rosie smiled, unaware of the slight consternation in his voice. She was always happy to see John, but sometimes, she sensed there was something troubling him...something, which remained hidden. She dismissed these thoughts and exited the study, calling back to him. 'Wait here, while I find mam, she will be so pleased to see you again.'

Lizzie had just received Marcus's latest letter, which gave her positive news about his homecoming. He was expected home sometime after the middle of December. On re-reading his penultimate paragraph she was saddened that he appeared to have all but given up hope of finding Belle and Jack in Philadelphia.

> '…..I do not seem to be any nearer discovering their whereabouts and fear I may never find them. I am convinced, in the absence of any facts to the contrary, that they have returned home to Scotland and that is where I will continue my search. With this in mind, I thought we could perhaps take a holiday in Glasgow. I know Belle lived there for a short time and I could advertise in the local paper, although I am mindful that you did not have much luck in similar circumstances when attempting to find Kate. Campbell is a fairly common name in Scotland, but we may strike lucky…'

Despite his misgivings and mixed news, Lizzie knew she must support him and remain strong. With a deep sigh, she replaced the letter with the others in her keeper box. She smoothed down her dress, intending to seek out Rosie, who she knew was in the process of writing to her mamma, but, as she rose, there was a perfunctory knock on the door. An excited Rosie rushed in. 'Mam, John is still on leave and has come to visit us!'

'That's wonderful Rosie, perhaps he will be able to join us at the dinner party on Sunday, if he is still on shore leave?'

'That's a good idea mam,' she paused, suddenly noticing Lizzie's apparent distress. 'Are you all right mam, you look upset?'

Lizzie was determined not to spoil her daughter's excitement at John's unexpected arrival so assured her. 'It's nothing really Rosie, I am just missing Marcus. I know he will be home soon, but with everything that has happened recently, I feel his absence more than ever.'

'Oh mam, I'm so sorry, I should have realised. You are always so cheerful and supportive, sometimes I forget you need support too.' Rosie regretted her lack of tact and put a caring arm around Lizzie's shoulders.

'I am all right really. I just needed a moment of reflection. Come on, we mustn't keep our guest waiting.' She took Rosie by the hand and they descended the stairs together.

***

Alone in the study John's eyes alighted on a sealed envelope placed on a side table. He noticed it was addressed to Kate Renwick. Rosie must be making a real effort to become re-acquainted with her birth mother, something close to his own heart. He wished he had the opportunity to know his real father, but he had died when he was only two or three years old. His mother didn't even have a photo and never mentioned him, determined as she was to pass his stepfather, Oliver, off as his 'real' father. Indeed, Oliver *had* become a wonderful parent to him, especially when, with great sensitivity, he imparted the news that his real father had died. The only stipulation was that the disclosure must be kept a secret from his mother at all costs. He told John that his mother hated his father and refused to have his name mentioned. John kept his word and up until her death, she was unaware that he knew the truth. Sadly, in later years, his parents argued vociferously. He was sent to his room on numerous occasions, but their raised voices still carried up the stairs. He felt sorry for Oliver, but loved his mother nonetheless, despite her flamboyant and unpredictable personality. When Oliver died, he seemed suffocated by women, his mother and grandmother among them and often wished for the presence of a male figure.

Lost in his thoughts, he did not hear Elspeth enter with the tea and jumped as she placed the tray on the table. 'Here we are master John. I expect you'll enjoy a nice cup of tea, after your journey?'

'Oh thank you Elspeth, I do miss English tea aboard ship. It's not like yours and it just doesn't taste the same from a tin mug.'

Elspeth blushed at his compliment. 'Thank you master John. I think I hear the ladies coming, so I will leave you to enjoy your refreshment.'

The noisy chatter of both women, made John smile. He had just been mourning the loss of a father figure, but these two women were very close to his heart and their cheerful banter lifted his spirits.

Lizzie was very pleased to see him and chatted, while Rosie took charge of pouring the tea. She cut an over generous portion of cake for their guest, which amused Lizzie.

'I was just telling mam, that I have accepted mamma's invitation for us to join the family for a dinner party this weekend and, as you are here, I wonder if you would like to accompany us?' Rosie raised her eyebrows as she awaited John's response.

'I would love to Rosie, but are you sure your mamma wouldn't object?' he enquired, whilst hoping for a positive reply.

'Of course not! Mamma doesn't stand on ceremony, she loves having guests for dinner and one more won't make any difference. Anyway, I have been wanting to introduce you to that side of the family for ages.'

'In that case, how can I refuse', John joked, delighted at the prospect of spending an entire weekend in Rosie's company.

'That's settled then. I will reopen my letter and add a 'PS'.'

⁂

Lizzie, Rosie and John arrived at 'Highclere House' early on Friday evening. It was intended that Robert's family join them later that Sunday morning, so that they could relax after their journey and be in fine fettle for the celebratory dinner in the evening.

Kate allocated rooms on the first floor, but was suddenly called away, as her father was not feeling too well.

Her father's deteriorating physical health had been causing concern, but his mind, was as sharp as ever. After spending some time with him, Howard encouraged her to rejoin their guests, if she promised she would send Rosie over to see him later. That agreed, Kate went straight to her daughter's room.

Rosie was unpacking when Kate tapped lightly on her door. 'Rosie, it's mamma, may I come in?'

'Of course mamma, the door isn't locked.'

Kate entered the room and, bursting with pride, embraced her daughter. 'Oh Rosie, you look even more grown up than when I saw you last. You are quite the young lady. I noticed that when you arrived, your cousin John seemed very protective and insisted on carry your cases,' she paused, 'or is it something else I see when he looks at you?' teased Kate.

Rosie frowned, surprised at her mamma's thinly veiled innuendo. 'I am sure I don't know what you mean mamma. John and I are very good friends. He would be mortified at your assumption. He knows, Jimmy is my first and only love and what you see is concern, rather than romantic thoughts,' she asserted, adamantly, surprising herself with her grown up reply.

'Darling...don't be upset. I didn't mean to infer any impropriety, but you must have noticed the look in his eyes. I hate to disillusion you, but I think you will find he has more than friendship on his mind. Of course, with you being so young, you would need to seek your father's consent, before you could be seen 'walking out'. However, at present, your relationship will still be seen as cousins and friends, so it's not a problem really. I know where you grew up no one was chaperoned and Lizzie and Robert did turn a blind eye to your relationship with Jimmy, but only because you were best friends. You don't need to tell me you are still in love with him, even though you are only fourteen. I know how painful young love can be, but you are moving in different circles now, so once you have completed your education and are of marriageable age, you will be chaperoned, as a matter of course. We will also need to arrange your 'Season'[37] in London.'

Graphic images of her wayward years suddenly invaded Kate's own thoughts, as she remembered the many times she had invented ploys to meet with boys, unbeknown to her parents. Rosie, she imagined, would be just as devious, when reaching an age where she would attract many suitors. Quite shockingly, the thought occurred to her that, under certain circumstances, she might also turn a blind eye, but, God forbid that she became pregnant out of wedlock.[38] What is it they say, *as you sow, so shall you reap?*

Rosie reflected on her mamma's statement, before commenting. 'Why don't I see that look in John's eyes?' asked Rosie perplexed.

Kate sighed. She had seen the signs too many times in the past and was concerned at her daughter's lack of awareness. Her voice contained a hint of cynicism. 'Rosie, my love, you might not want to see it. You 'feel' your heart lies elsewhere. Sometimes, we are so blinded by love, that we desperately hang on to the dream.'

---

37 The social season or 'Season' has historically referred to the annual period when it is customary for members of a social elite of society to hold debutante balls, dinner parties and large charity events. It was also the appropriate time to be resident in the city rather than in the country, in order to attend such events.

38 More than a third of all pregnancies among British women in the 1850s were conceived outside of wedlock, according to estimates.

'It isn't a dream mamma. Jimmy *will* return one day...you will see. I cannot give my heart to another, while ever I am convinced Jimmy is still alive,' asserted Rosie.

'Oh Rosie, I know just how you feel. For years I longed to meet up with your father again...to rekindle what we had lost. Sometimes, the past is best left behind...sometimes, feelings, resurface, but...sadly...they only survive for one person and the other will have moved on.' Kate thought of Robert and smiled sadly.

Rosie squeezed her mother's arm sympathetically, then hesitated before asking. 'You *are* over daddy now, aren't you?'

Kate's melancholy dissipated, as she noted the concern in Rosie's voice. 'Of course, darling. We have moved on and James is a wonderful husband...it's just that sometimes one wonders what life might have been like, if things had turned out differently. One thing I never wonder about, is what life would have been like without you. That's one thing I will never regret and to be given a second chance at being a mother, is something I will always cherish. I just worry a little about your conviction that Jimmy will return one day. I cannot blame you for holding on to that thought, but don't dismiss a chance of future happiness with someone who obviously feels a great deal for you. My advice would be to let the future take care of itself and approach each situation with an open mind. If you let your barriers down a little, you may find you can move on. Will you promise me you will see what life has in store for you, by allowing others into your heart?' Kate appealed.

Rosie was silent for a few moments as she considered her mother's advice and request. She would, she thought, agree openly to her wishes, but in actuality, may not follow her advice. 'Okay, mamma, I promise to see what life brings, although I really do not think John has any thoughts in that direction.'

Kate was again surprised at the improvement in Rosie's vocabulary, which belied her age. She surmised it was due in no small part to the time spent with John and her intention of impressing him from the moment they first met. 'Thank you, Rosie. Now let's see what outfits you have brought for Sunday's dinner party. By the way, your grandfather would like you to visit him, but he isn't too well this evening, so it will probably be better if you see him tomorrow.'

The following morning Beatrice made an appearance, somewhat contrite, after the disastrous episode with the horses and latterly during the days Rosie spent recovering from her injury at 'Highclere'. Rosie was keen to show Beatrice the gains she had made, since she and Beatrice first rode together. By taking lessons, she had succeeded in becoming quite an accomplished rider. Not surprisingly, John was disappointed when Rosie made the suggestion that Beatrice join them for a ride and picnic. He had secretly hoped they would spend the morning alone together, before joining the rest of the family for afternoon tea.

Kate's spectacular array of food for the picnic included a few muffins for Rosie...still her favourite breakfast item! It wasn't long before the three were ready and after a cursory warning from Kate to take extra care, they left, determined to have an enjoyable ride despite the ominous, fast moving clouds, which promised a small chance of light rain later.

Rosie was surprised how quickly they reached the plateaued area where Zaida had bolted. They dismounted and she dismissed a sense of déjà vue, which fleetingly surfaced out of hand. She was totally confident in her ability to ride competently. The reason the horse bolted that day, still troubled her, but would Beatrice have deliberately caused the accident? She hoped not, but believed the truth would out one day.

John laid out a rug on a grassy mound and set down the picnic basket.

They were soon enjoying the peaceful surroundings and chatting amicably. John included Beatrice and readily engaged her in conversation. 'Well Beatrice, do you enjoy confiding in an older sister and sharing secrets?' John asked, eager to know what she thought of Rosie's sudden entrance into her life.

Beatrice glared resentfully in Rosie's direction before replying, which left John slightly bemused. She did not enjoy the dubious delight of gaining a sister, but decided to put on an act for John, who she liked immediately and wanted to keep on side. 'Oh I really enjoy Rosie's company. It is great fun being able to talk and swap ideas,' lied Beatrice convincingly, who for her age, was quite accomplished in the art of deception.

John, somewhat at a loss responded. 'I am so pleased, as I know Rosie is eager for you both to be friends.' John looked at Rosie for confirmation of his statement and she obliged, anxious to put their sisterly rift to one side.

'I have two siblings now and a few years ago, I didn't have any, so consider myself very lucky. Sisters can be a lot of fun. I am sure Beatrice and I will get on swimmingly, once we really get to know each other,' she paused and looked directly at Beatrice. 'I know you are only eleven, but I am sure as we get older, we will be confidantes as well as friends,' smiled Rosie, with sincerity.

Beatrice felt affronted by the fact that, in her opinion, Rosie was being condescending and attempted her own 'put down'. 'Actually, I *am* nearly twelve and have seen much more of the world than you Rosie, but now that we share the same mamma, I'm sure you will also be able to travel and, as I have heard mamma say, increase your knowledge and lose your Nottingham accent.'

John, clearly shocked and annoyed by Beatrice's outburst, quickly interjected with a 'put down' of his own. 'You are probably right Beatrice, but maybe as you get older, you'll develop something called 'tact and diplomacy', which means, you shouldn't always speak so forthrightly, in case you upset the other person. You are still quite young and inexperienced in such matters, but I am sure Rosie will forget your little outburst on this occasion.'

Beatrice's indignation showed clearly as her face reddened. Eager to make amends, however, she still tried to ingratiate herself. Unfortunately, she did not have the awareness to carry it off. 'Oh...sorry Rosie, I didn't mean anything by that, it's just that sometimes, you sound very different to everyone else around, ' stated Beatrice dispassionately.

Rosie did not rise to the bait, but changed the subject forthwith. 'Would anyone like a muffin? These have a surprise centre and are filled with lemon curd,' informed Rosie, determined the day would not be spoiled.

John, proud of the way Rosie dealt with Beatrice's disagreeable manner, smoothed the waters some more. 'I'd love one Rosie, what about you Beatrice? Oh, and if you pass me your glass, I will top it up with some lemonade.'

Beatrice soon realised John was Rosie's ally and one person she could not wrestle from her sister's influence.

She would wait for another opportunity to make Rosie's life uncomfortable.

※

Kate and Lizzie took the opportunity to catch up. They would not be interrupted for a good two hours at least, as everyone was engaged elsewhere. Kate was keen to hear about Marcus. 'Well Lizzie, what a long way we have come. Here am I married with a daughter...two daughters now! You with a daughter and, apparently, the most wonderful man on earth. Tell me, are you truly in love? Does the mere thought of him excite you?' asked a curious Kate.

Lizzie, still slightly embarrassed when discussing such matters with Kate, bravely attempted an honest, in-depth reply. 'I do love Marcus very much. I must admit that after Daniel and I parted, I thought I would never love anyone else in quite the same way and to a certain extent, I don't. The feeling I had for Daniel was the young, carefree love of a young girl. It was all new then with nothing to compare it with. The love I have for Marcus is still as intense, but deeper...do you know what I mean?' asked Lizzie, interested to see what Kate's take on 'love' was.

Kate, pleased that her friend could open up to her was equally informative. 'I don't see young 'love' in quite the same way as you. My love for Robert was all consuming, I could not think of anything else. The fact we parted, not because we fell out of love, but because of circumstances, meant my feelings for him did not diminish. I never loved James in that way. I married him, rather selfishly for security, but not love, definitely not love. I am very fond of him, but,' she paused; unsure whether it was wise to reveal all. However, she trusted her friend, so continued...'please don't utter a word of this to anyone...because I know you will be shocked...I am still in love with Robert...so there it is!' uttered a desperate Kate. An uncomfortable silence prevailed, as she waited to hear Lizzie's reaction. She searched her face for signs that she understood and would as always, be able to give her sound advice and a possible way out.

Lizzie was not expecting such a heartfelt declaration and, for what seemed an age, silently considered her reply. 'Kate, oh Kate, I am so sorry you feel that way. I don't want to break your heart, but I do believe Robert is in love with Amy. Perhaps not in the same way as he was with you, but he would never do anything to hurt her and I am certain he would not forsake her for you, no matter how he felt. Robert is very loyal, as you know,' reminded Lizzie, still disturbed at Kate's admission.

Kate fiddled with the fringe on a cushion, trying hard to control her emotions. 'I know Lizzie, I know. Robert is perfectly clear on his position. The thing is, I don't have any clue how to rid myself of these feelings, which are in danger of spiralling out of control. I play the dutiful wife, but when we make love, the face I see is Robert's. I don't dismiss it, as it helps to keep me sane. I yearn to hold him and make love to him every time I see him and my heart pounds when we stand close to one another. What can I do Lizzie. How can I resolve this?' asked a mournful Kate.

Llzzie was clearly shocked, but sympathised. 'Oh Kate, I am really at a loss. I do understand your dilemma, but sadly, you are probably not going to get your wish. Are you sure you are not just in love with the romantic ideal of rekindling an old love, which has probably gone forever?' questioned Lizzie, hopeful that Kate would realise she was hankering after a lost cause. Although, on the face of it, that did not appear to be the case.

'No...no Lizzie, I am quite sure, but realise it is something I will have to accept. I may need your support tomorrow when Robert, Amy and Harriett arrive. I am not good at hiding my feelings, so if I'm about to overstep the mark, please steer me away from any calamitous path I might foolishly embark on,' pleaded a desperate Kate.

Lizzie sighed, despairingly. 'All right Kate, I'll do my best.'

'Oh thank you Lizzie. I really do not know how I managed without you all these years, but am so glad we are best friends once again. I suppose I had better organise tea, as James will be home at 4 p.m. and John and the girls will be back from their picnic soon. Meanwhile, why don't you pop along and have a chat with father. He will be really pleased to see you again and I will send Rosie over when she returns.'

The family enjoyed a leisurely Sunday, awaiting the arrival of Amy, Robert and Harriett, all except John. He was hoping to spend some time alone with Rosie, but the opportunity hadn't arisen. However, he was looking forward to the dinner party, when he hoped to meet with more success.

Kate was on tenterhooks at the prospect of meeting Robert again. She wondered how her father would react, but her fears were unfounded, as Howard was very gracious and obviously grateful when, in his butler's absence, Robert assisted him in making the short trek to the East wing where the festivities were planned. Howard's own armchair was placed in the living room, so that he was comfortable. It also gave him a welcome vantage point where he could observe everyone.

Amy felt embarrassed when Robert introduced Kate, even though he had already spoken with her at length and assured her that his feelings for Kate were limited to just an 'agreeable fondness' as Rosie's mother.

Howard, ensconced in his comfortable chair, surveyed the unfolding scene. His attention was drawn to Kate. Her whole being positively glowed, as she chatted with Amy and Robert. It was patently obvious from her body language, that she still held feelings for her former lover. She was standing a little too close for comfort. He hoped no one else had noticed and instantly decided to have a heart to heart, when he could manoeuvre a moment alone with her. He realised Kate had married James for security, but hoped she was over Robert. Clearly that was not the case and he felt compassion for his daughter in her obvious dilemma.

※

After a convivial lunch everyone was happy to relax during the afternoon. It was unusually warm for the time of year and the guests made the most of the outdoor amenities. Beatrice and Harriett played shuttlecock and battledore.[39] Lizzie, Robert, Amy and Kate sat at the wrought iron garden table, situated in a sheltered position close to the tennis courts.

Howard stayed indoors making the most of the silence. He considered taking a snooze in preparation for the

---

39 Shuttlecock and Battledore or jeu de volant is an early game similar to that of modern badminton. The game is played by two people, with a shuttlecock and small rackets called battledores. Games with a shuttlecock are believed to have originated in ancient Greece, about 2,000 years ago.

evening's entertainment, but remained concerned, not only about Kate's problem, but also about his grand daughter's suspicious behaviour. He sensed trouble ahead but fervently hoped to find a solution. He reflected on the fact that Jayne Munroe was sadly absent and her sound advice could not be sought. She had decided to take a tour of Continental Europe with Aubrey, as a reward to herself for a job well done. Over recent years, Howard had mended the rift with Jayne and the couple were frequent visitors to 'Highclere'.

※

John finally managed to spend some time alone with Rosie in the garden and casually engaged her in conversation. 'I'm glad we came here Rosie. It gives us chance to talk. I wondered how you feel now, as it's only just over a month since I told you about,' he paused, choosing his words carefully 'about Jimmy's accident. The news will have been devastating to you and life without him must still be difficult?'

Rosie glanced at John as they walked through the rose arbour and on to the miniature lake, where a wooden bench was placed conveniently under a weeping willow. *John really is a very thoughtful person and I am very fond of him*, she mused. 'I don't know John. Some days I feel fine and realise that I have only thought about Jimmy a couple of times, but on others, his face swims in front of me the moment I open my eyes. It's silly but until very recently, I still believed he would return. I postponed my birthday celebrations in case he just turned up. Jimmy always 'turned up' most unexpectedly. Whenever I thought I would not see him for some time, there he would be, surprising me.' She became silent, remembering the day he came to see her at home, before *she* surprised *him* in Liverpool. That had been a wonderful day and also the last time she saw him. She still had trouble coming to terms with her loss.

John took hold of her hand, as they sat beneath the willow. 'My heart goes out to you Rosie, as I know how much you loved him and he you. Sometimes, I feel so powerless to help you, but sometimes, you smile and appear happy, which gladdens my heart. Are you happy now Rosie?' John asked, hoping for a positive reply.

Rosie looked at her friend and saw something she had not seen before in his eyes, a look that *Jimmy* reserved especially for her. Perhaps her mamma was right. Oh dear, she hoped not, because right now, she could not see him as anything other than a dear friend. What was it her mamma said...*'If you let your barriers down a little, you may find you can move on.'* She wondered whether her mamma was also right on that score. *Do I owe it to myself to try and put the past behind me? If I am honest, what are the chances of Jimmy surviving?...none, she thought, absolutely none! After all, if he was still alive, he would have found a way to let me know. Here is someone who clearly has feelings for you...why not give him a chance? although we are far too young to become serious.*

She had enjoyed a fairly innocent relationship with Jimmy and he never put any pressure on her to take things to the next level. In fact, it was she who encouraged Jimmy to kiss *her*. She resolved to try her best to encourage that kind of relationship with John, friends first, perhaps sweethearts later.

'I am as happy as I can be John and that is partly due to being reunited with my mamma, but partly due to you. You do raise my spirits when we meet and I love having you as a friend and confidante.'

'Really Rosie?' he paused. Encouraged by her reply, he decided to push the barriers further. 'Do you think you might come to like me as more than a friend over time?'

Rosie remained cautious. 'Well, I might. I cannot promise more, but we could see how we get on. You may, of course, meet someone else, when your ship docks in a faraway port, so you should really consider whether you want me as a special friend or not.'

John gazed lovingly into Rosie's eyes. 'I don't need any time to think Rosie. I have thought of nothing else for weeks, but I do respect your decision. I realise we are both very young and could not marry for years even if we wanted. I would like it if you would become my sweetheart, but purely on a platonic basis. Someone I could write to and visit when I am home on leave.'

Rosie agreed cautiously. 'Ok John. We do get on well together and it would be nice to correspond. You do understand though that friendship is all I want at the moment, but you never know what the future may hold.'

John was satisfied that romance was not out of the question, but he wished fervently that she would look at him the way he had seen her look at Jimmy. *Maybe in time*, he thought.

Everyone was gathered in the sitting room before dinner when Kate made an unexpected announcement. 'I have a wonderful surprise for you all. We have three more guests, whom I know you will be overjoyed to see again,' smiled Kate, pleased with her secret plan that had come to fruition. She stood aside to allow Georgina, Daniel and nine year old Victoria to enter the room.

Lizzie immediately embraced Georgina and Daniel, while Rosie took Victoria by the hand to join in a game of 'pin the tail on the donkey' with Beatrice and Harriett.

Lizzie was thrilled, it was indeed a lovely surprise. Without the chance encounter made by Daniel at the Goose Fair in Nottingham in 1846, there would not have been a reunion.

Howard and John were introduced to them for the first time. Drinks were dispensed and Howard, with prior knowledge of the extra guests, in collusion with Kate, made a speech. 'Welcome everyone! This is a day I never thought would happen. Over the years, I tried hard to find my granddaughter, but as I became older, my hopes faded. Luckily...' he paused to face Daniel, 'a chance encounter by Daniel Lorimer nearly ten years ago, started the ball rolling. Unfortunately, it has taken until this year, 1855, with unstinting help from Jayne Munroe, who is unfortunately unable to join us, to bring that search to a successful conclusion and we can all look forward to a wonderful future together. I am sure everyone here will play his or her role to ensure that we are never parted again. Please raise your glasses to drink to the future.'

Glasses chinked in a gesture of good will and happy times ahead, but for some, their future wellbeing would be in jeopardy before the end of the year.

※

James, by tradition, placed himself at the head of the table, with Kate to his left and Beatrice to his right. He trusted his wife implicitly, but was jealous of the obvious rapport between her and Robert. The table arrangements reflected his concern.

Howard deliberately seated himself at the opposite end, to enjoy the company of Harriett and Amy. Lizzie was relieved that Robert was placed opposite her with Rosie to his right. At least her daughter was between him and Kate, leaving less opportunity for her flirting. *She really cannot help herself,* she thought sadly. However, she trusted her brother to resist any advances, as any impropriety in that direction would have dire consequences for the whole family.

Conversation flowed easily, filled with reminiscences and bonhomie. Everyone celebrated his or her long awaited reunion with warmth and happiness. After dinner, the gaslights were turned down low and Rosie's big moment arrived. Fourteen candles[40] on the cake were lit for her to blow out and make a wish. There were cries of 'Happy Birthday' and Rosie managed to blow all the candles out in one go. Then she closed her eyes tight and wished with all her heart that Jimmy would return home soon and that the news of his death had all been a huge mistake. When she opened her eyes again, John was staring at her sadly, could he have guessed what she wished for?

⁂

The evening wore on with 'parlour' games in full swing. Howard derived immense pleasure from the antics

---

40 The birthday cake has been an integral part of the birthday celebrations in western European countries since the middle of the 19th century. The tradition of placing candles on birthday cake is attributed to early Greeks who used to place lit candles on cakes to make them glow like the moon. The combination of melody and lyrics in "Happy Birthday to You" first appeared in print in 1912, and probably existed even earlier.

employed in charades and considered 'blind man's buff' a total hoot. It wasn't until Kate volunteered to be the 'hunted' in a game of 'Sardines'[41] that he felt apprehensive. Lizzie felt less so, as she could not imagine Kate capable of orchestrating a situation where Robert would discover her hiding place first, unless they were in conclusion and that, she felt certain, would not be the case.

Kate moved swiftly to her chosen hideout in Beatrice's bedroom, on the top floor, which was converted from the old large nursery. She hid in the toy cupboard amidst a vast array of clothes, shoes and old board games piled on a shelf, then waited patiently to be discovered.

Downstairs, plans were afoot to cover the whole of the East and West wings of the large house. The 'hunters', including James, Beatrice, Harriett and Victoria were counting to fifty. Their decision to explore the West wing was based on the assumption that it had been a favourite hiding place of Kate's on previous occasions. John persuaded Rosie to search the kitchens, while Daniel and Georgina took the ground floor. Amy and Lizzie decided to search the bedrooms on the first floor, which fatalistically, left Robert to explore the two bedrooms on the top floor.

Howard, although determined to keep a watchful eye on proceedings, found his eyes slowly closing. The laughter and

---

41 Only one player hides and all the lights are out in the house. The other players go hunting individually. When a hunter finds the hiding place, that player gets into the hiding place, too. And so it goes. As each hunter finds the hiding place, the hunter joins the hunted until they are crowded - like sardines.

rhythmic counting had a soporific effect on the old gentleman and he drifted off in his favourite armchair.

A minimal number of gaslights along the corridors provided a modicum of illumination. They proceeded cautiously, feeling their way around the large house, but the younger girls were excited to be exploring in the dark. They held each other's hands, as they snaked along the corridors following James, in anticipation of discovering Kate's hiding place.

⁕

Kate still waited patiently for what seemed an age. Her eyes had adjusted to the dark and she was able to see in the dim light. Memories flooded her mind. She remembered the happy times when Beatrice was small and her toys cluttered the nursery. The old rocking horse had been demoted to the basement storage area below the kitchens, together with her prized dolls house and the only items left were stacked at eye level on the long low shelf. Kate noticed a large box with the name of the game, 'The Mansion of Happiness',[42] emblazoned on its side. It had been Beatrice's favourite. 'Highclere', she mused, had been a mansion of happiness. Well perhaps not total happiness, but she had enjoyed

---

42 *'The Mansion Of Happiness' was an instructive moral and entertaining amusement* in the form of a children's board game inspired by Christian morality, designed by George Fox, a children's author and game designer in England. W. & S. B. Ives published the game in the United States in Salem, Massachusetts on November 24, 1843. Players race round a sixty-six space spiral track, depicting virtues and vices, with their goal being 'The Mansion of Happiness' at track's end. Instructions upon virtue spaces advance players toward the goal while those upon vice spaces force them to retreat.

motherhood and, despite the black cloud of Rosie's disappearance hanging over her, there had been good times.

Financially, she wanted for nothing and they employed the services of a fairly large number of staff. The butler, Frederick Paterson, presided over a groom, a gamekeeper and the stable hand, Jack. In later years, Frederick was adopted by Howard as his personal butler, which suited James, who was quite happy managing his own personal needs.

The housekeeper, Gladys Pearson, was in overall charge of Emily Bates the cook, Nora the kitchen maid, and Florence the maid of all works. The services of a governess had been dispensed with when Beatrice was nine. In no uncertain terms she declared she was too old to have someone, other than her mother, tell her what she should and should not be doing. Kate had given in rather too readily to her daughter's demands by agreeing to raise Beatrice herself. While the household regimes were changing, Howard's physical health defeated him. His efforts to find Rosie had failed and Kate was often absent. She continued the search, but it was a decision she came to regret in one respect, as a lack of discipline meant Beatrice was left to her own devices.

Kate, preoccupied in her reverie, failed to hear footsteps approaching and was quite shocked when the door slowly opened to reveal a hesitant Robert, who, unaccustomed to the dark, peered gingerly into the recesses of the cupboard.

Kate composed herself before grabbing him gently by the arm. 'Oh Robert it's you. Come in quickly, or we will be seen,' whispered Kate urgently, but ecstatic that he was the first to find her, unlike Robert, who felt distinctly uncomfortable in the confined surroundings.

Kate took the opportunity to move closer. Her heart beat faster and Robert sensed her scented breath, like a butterfly fluttering its wings erotically over his face and neck. He stepped back, in a gesture of self-preservation, but found a row of dresses and coat hangers prevented him moving to a safe distance. It was no good, he thought, he would have to wait here with her until someone else joined them. He hoped it wouldn't be Amy. *What would she think?*

His face was close to Kate's and the smell of her perfume invaded his nostrils, evoking memories of the exciting times spent together at the cottage. This wasn't supposed to happen. His resistance wavered as she whispered softly to him. 'Robert, please listen to me, you have to know that I have tried very hard to move on and put my feelings to one side, but it isn't working. Please don't be angry. I don't know what to do, as every time I see you, I want us to make love.'

Robert sighed as his defenses were pushed to the limit. He needed to get out of there, before he was tempted into something he would regret. Unfortunately, the brief chance to cut short their encounter evaporated the second he felt the softness of Kate's lips on his own. He felt powerless to resist and after a moment's hesitation responded with equal passion. He pulled her close, feeling the fullness of her breasts, heaving as her breathing increased. Neither spoke, but both knew there was no going back from this, not now, not ever.

༺༻

Moments later, a second 'hunter' ventured into the room. Luckily it was Lizzie and not Amy, who was curious that Robert had not returned to the first floor landing for some time. He must have discovered Kate's hiding place!

The room, insufficiently lit by a primitive gas-lamp, appeared empty at first, but an astute Lizzie noticed that a door on the cupboard at the far end of the room was slightly ajar. She crept stealthily towards the door and very slowly prised it open. The couple inside immediately sprang apart and, although unseen by Lizzie, looked very guilty.

Kate was the first to break the silence and somehow managed to stop her voice faltering. 'Come in Lizzie, I'll move along so that you can have some space,' she said with a confidence she did not feel.

Robert breathed a sigh of relief, as Lizzie did not appear to have noticed that they had suddenly broken off from an intimate embrace. No one spoke, but each entertained thoughts of their own. Kate was shaking, but deliriously happy. Robert, enjoyed the brief encounter, but was consumed with guilt and Lizzie remained decidedly apprehensive. She hoped that they had shown some restraint and not succumbed to any misplaced emotions. Unfortunately, she was not convinced that Robert would maintain his distance.

Half an hour passed before everyone else joined Kate in the toy cupboard and another person became the 'hunted'.

※

It was a very special occasion, so the younger girls had been allowed to stay up quite late. Each took a turn to be the 'hunted' and Victoria was the last to hide. It was nearly ten o'clock so she was under strict instructions to stay in the East wing and could only hide in one of the seven bedrooms. At the tender age of nine, Victoria was not very inventive so decided to hide in a place previously used, the toy cupboard. Because she was a little under four foot, she was able to climb on to the long shelf above the clothes rails via a chair and crouch down behind a row of boxes. What she did not consider was that anyone entering the room would immediately spot the open cupboard door and the telltale chair.

Ten minutes elapsed, before she became bored and slightly uncomfortable. It was also scary crouching in the dark, so she decided to climb back down. This manoeuvre proved more difficult than she anticipated; with the consequence that she knocked several items off the shelf. Most clattered noisily to the floor.

At that particular moment, Kate entered the room and quickly realised Victoria had chosen the same hiding place as herself, several hours earlier. She grinned and carefully opened the door, to reveal a relieved Victoria, not in the least bit phased to be found. 'Hello Aunty Kate, come on in,' she said, her voice full of enthusiasm.

'Hello Victoria, are you enjoying the game?'

Victoria hesitated momentarily, but explained. 'Well it was all right, but I have been here a very long time. One good thing, my mamma has allowed me to stay up late, but I think I will have to go to bed shortly, when everyone finds my hiding place. I do wish I could stay up a little longer.'

Kate remembered a time when she would try anything to avoid going to bed, so decided a little collusion was necessary. 'I tell you what, if I move the chair outside of the cupboard and pull both doors together, we may not be seen by the next person who enters the room, that should prolong the time before you have to go to bed,' grinned a complicit Kate.

'That's a good idea Aunty, but it is very dark in here with the doors shut and I am a bit frightened.'

Kate hugged Victoria to reassure her. 'Don't worry, you are safe here. You can stand right near the doors, where the gaslight will shine in from the landing. I will shuffle further along,' said Kate, but as she moved, she stumbled over the contents of 'The Mansion of Happiness' game. She replaced the items but as she put the box on the shelf, her hand brushed against a rather large and intriguing bottle, which wasn't what she'd expected. On examination, she discovered the content to be cod liver oil. *What on earth is this doing in the toy cupboard?* she thought, *when it's usually kept in the kitchen.* Frowning, she slipped it into her pocket and resolved to unearth the mystery.

It was Beatrice who begged her mother to play another game, in an attempt to prolong her nighttime adventure before bedtime. 'Mamma, can we just have one game of 'Grandmother's Trunk'?'[43] she pleaded.

Kate had often used this ruse on her own parents, so laughingly agreed. 'All right Beatrice. Help your papa to place these chairs in a circle. I have something to attend to in the kitchen and will be back shortly.'

Kate took the bottle from her pocket and reinstated it in its rightful place in the kitchen cupboard. She was still intrigued as to why it was in her daughter's bedroom, as she

---

43 One of the oldest word games is 'Grandmother's Trunk,' where one guest begins: 'My Grandmother keeps (a word beginning with 'a') in her trunk.' The next player continues: 'My Grandmother keeps (the 'a' word) and (another with 'b') in her trunk,' and so on, the list growing as the sentence continues around, making it a memory as well as an alphabet game.

hated the stuff. *So* why was it there? She sat down on one of the kitchen chairs and cast her mind back. It dawned on her in a flash, 'Beatrice's illness'! Gladys was restocking and gave her a list of items for approval. It was then that Gladys mentioned that an almost full bottle of cod liver oil had vanished. It seemed a complete mystery. Gladys was inconsolable, as she was ultimately responsible for ensuring Beatrice took her daily spoonful. Kate dismissed the incident as being unimportant at the time, but now she put two and two together and came up with a most shocking theory. Only half of the mixture remained, which meant Beatrice must have taken the rest. The penny suddenly dropped. *Beatrice had deliberately made herself ill, but why would she do such a thing?* Unpalatable as the truth might be, she needed proof and quite fortuitously an opportunity had just presented itself to gauge Beatrice's reaction.

Kate entered the living room, where the game had just commenced and availed herself of an empty chair. She was just in time for the next word beginning with 'c', which she added to the end of the previous items, 'Cod liver oil!' she said looking directly at Beatrice, whose face reddened instantly. The truth was plain for Kate to see, only guilt would evoke such an obvious reaction from her daughter.

Shouts of 'argh…awful, I hate that stuff' were uttered by several of the group. Beatrice, however, was stunned into silence. She realized the game was up and that she would have a lot of explaining to do in the morning.

༺ཀ༻

After the girls were dispatched to bed, the grownups settled in the living room with a glass of wine. Rosie and John were next to retire, but not before he persuaded Rosie to rise at first light for an early morning ride.

Conversation flowed until near midnight, when Howard requested James escort him back to his rooms in the West wing. James was unable to resist the inducement of a glass of his father-in-law's special reserve cognac. Amy and Georgina also took their cue to leave at this juncture, citing travel as a reason for their weariness.

This left Lizzie, Robert, Kate and Daniel to reminisce. Kate was delighted the evening had been such a success. The only fly in the ointment was Beatrice's inexcusable behaviour, but she was determined that the incident would not ruin her evening. In consequence, she opened another bottle of wine and brought a plate of Emily's special shortbread from the kitchen.

Daniel was by now merry and slightly giddy. After consuming three large glasses of red wine, he settled comfortably in an armchair. He had been studying Lizzie intently for the last ten minutes and now felt compelled to bring up the past. 'It's been a long while since we were all together! Do you remember the times we spent in Glasgow during the long hot summer of '40?' he asked, looking directly at Lizzie.

Lizzie, somewhat taken aback, excused his forthright question, attributing it to the consumption of alcohol, of which they had all participated freely. 'Yes Daniel, I do remember very well. It's fifteen years ago now, but in some respects, it seems like only yesterday.'

Kate joined in. 'Fifteen years isn't really that long in the scheme of things, but such a lot has happened. I for one don't regret a thing. What do you say Robert?'

Robert shuffled uncomfortably in his seat and took another slug of wine. 'Er, well yes I suppose one cannot regret certain things and my daughter is one of those. We were all very young then and mistakes were made.' Robert's voice conveyed a hint of sadness, but he instantly made an effort to lighten the conversation. 'I wonder what Andrew, Derek and Finlay have done with their lives,' he speculated.

Daniel chuckled. 'Andrew and Derek would, I think, be married with children. Both seemed the sort to settle down, but Finlay, well I can imagine him joining the navy and having a girl in every port.'

The others nodded in agreement, while Kate asked another question. 'Don't any of you wonder what would have happened if we had all married our respective sweethearts? You Daniel, how do you think things would have turned out for you and Lizzie?' teased a slightly intoxicated Kate, intent on posing the same question to them all, so that she could elicit a favourable response from Robert.

Unfortunately, Lizzie was not amused. 'How can he answer that Kate, we have all moved on and, as far as I know, each and every one of us has a good marriage with children. The question is hypothetical and really has no bearing on our present situations.'

Kate was undeterred. 'Oh Lizzie, it's only a bit of fun. I know we have moved on, but it would be interesting to speculate wouldn't it?'

Daniel, however, was keen to take part in Kate's little game, so replied honestly. 'I think I have an answer to your question. We would have been very happy!' he paused, his brilliant blue eyes bored into Lizzie's, but he was indeed startled and disappointed when he received a look of unmistakable irritation from her. He continued cautiously thereafter and amended his take on the situation. 'Sadly it wasn't to be and I accept we cannot go back, but must look to the future.'

'That's very philosophical Daniel,' Kate observed, 'but I am not sure you believe it.'

Lizzie shot a pleading look at Daniel and he obliged by remaining silent, keeping his remaining deep thoughts to himself. She knew the conversation had gone too far so tried to nip any further confessions in the bud, before Kate implicated Robert. 'Kate, you are treading a very dangerous path. We are all a little merry and should probably turn in, or perhaps a strong black coffee is in order. We have had a wonderful evening, so let's not spoil it now. We have all moved on, let's leave it there.'

Robert, who had remained tight lipped throughout, finally spoke. 'I think Lizzie is right Kate. There is no point in dragging up the past, as she said, we have all moved on.'

A deflated Kate had no choice but to drop her inquisition, but she knew beyond doubt that only one person in the room believed Lizzie's summation...and that was Lizzie herself!

Chapter Eighteen

Marcus Returns December 1855

Lizzie was alone at 'The Beeches'. Elspeth was visiting her sister for the day and Rosie was shopping with Amy, Harriett and Robert at the Bazaar in Manchester. Included in the mail delivery that morning, was a letter from Clara containing exciting news. Tillie was to be married the following April. Another bearing a Scottish postmark was from Morag whose signature was instantly recognisable. She read enthusiastically:

Dear Lizzie,
　I hope you are all well. Angus and I are very happy and we have some really exciting news - I am pregnant again and expect the baby around the middle of July next year!
　The pregnancy has been fine so far - no morning sickness and I feel really well - fingers crossed. We are so glad to hear that Marcus will be home shortly, you must be really excited. We look forward to meeting him when you next visit, perhaps in the Spring.
　Our other news is somewhat puzzling and may even come as a shock. I sorted through Annabella's possessions recently, something I'd been putting off. Anyway, in her suitcase were several letters tied

together with ribbon. It looks as if they have been read quite often - and, as such, are almost illegible. The letters were to our mither from someone named Andrew C...just 'C'. I've no idea what his surname might be. It appears that she was having an affair but I don't think faither ever knew. Most surprisingly, it transpires that Annabella was the result of that affair, so she was, in fact, my half-sister - not that it makes any difference to me - I still loved her, despite her flamboyant and sometimes selfish ways, but I was quite shocked nevertheless! It appears that mither told her on her deathbed.

You remember she was ill with consumption for some time and, just before she died, she summoned us separately. I thought it was because she wanted to say a special goodbye to us both. That part was true, but she never told me about Andrew! She probably thought it would change things between Annabella and me, but it wouldn't have made any difference and I truly believe she did what she thought best. Anyway I don't suppose it will affect any of us, but thought you should know.

Give our love to Rosie. I understand John has been seeing her...do you think anything will come of it? They are, after all, second cousins, but somehow, it feels more distant now? Perhaps we will have something else to celebrate when we meet again.

With much love from your cousin Morag. Xxx

The penultimate sentence shocked Lizzie and made her think. It was barely two months since they received news of Jimmy's death, although Rosie appeared to be coming to terms with the fact that he wasn't coming home. John and her had become very close, especially so since the lovely time spent at Kate's celebrating her birthday. She noticed then that John harboured obvious feelings of a loving nature towards her, but was unsure whether Rosie felt the same. He sent several letters from ports, on short trips to the near continent, which were read avidly, but she couldn't tell what Rosie was thinking.

If her observations had any basis in fact, then the possibility of them becoming sweethearts or even marrying one day, was highly likely.

Lizzie secreted the letter in her 'keeper box' before deciding to take a walk around the gardens. The sun was shining brilliantly on this cold crisp day, which seemed a contradiction in itself and delightfully out of season. A thrush's distinct song could be heard from the large Chestnut tree as she crossed the lawn, before she paused at the old wooden bench to collect her thoughts. The letter from Morag was uppermost in her mind. She remembered vividly the shocking day Annabella drowned in the most dreadful of circumstances, but the strange antics of her cousin, prior to her death still troubled her. There wasn't any logical explanation for her behaviour, maybe she was jealous of Morag who had the love of both her parents, whereas, Annabella never knew her father. Perhaps that accounted for her actions. Her thoughts preoccupied her until she suddenly felt someone approaching. Before she could turn round, the familiar warm tones of Marcus's voice invaded her senses. 'Elizabeth darling, how are you?'

Lizzie was overjoyed as Marcus instantly swept her into his arms. 'Don't speak, my love, just kiss me,' whispered Marcus against her cheek.

Time stopped as they embraced lovingly. Marcus gazed longingly into her eyes. 'Elizabeth, I cannot believe we are together once more. I have dreamt of this moment for such a long time.' He smiled and his heart beat faster as her exquisite loveliness took his breath away. He kissed her softly and held her close.

Their love would not wait. He carried her into the house and up to their room, gently laying her on the bed. He undressed her slowly and deliberately; unable to believe this moment had arrived. His hands explored her breasts and their breathing became more urgent. She caressed his body in turn, feeling his arousal. He wanted her desperately, but took time with their lovemaking. His hands moved sensuously over her smooth, silky thighs to the top of her legs. He was conscious of her sudden intake of breath as his fingers explored the softness of her most intimate part. They could wait no longer. He entered her and they reached unimaginable pleasures, as they became one. After their lovemaking, they lay in each other's arms for some considerable time, enjoying the closeness longed for during their time apart.

Marcus reluctantly broke the silence. 'How I have missed you my darling, my life has been on hold, until this moment.'

'Mine too Marcus. At times I have felt inconceivably lonely, even though I was surrounded by my friends and family. I hope we will never be parted again, as I really do not think I could cope. It has been an eternity and I am still thinking that this is a dream.'

Marcus smiled. 'You aren't dreaming, I am here beside you and never intend to let you go. I cannot believe you were here alone, just as I hoped. Where is Rosie?'

'She is out shopping with Amy, Harriett and Robert and Elspeth is visiting her sister,' smiled Lizzie, now visibly relaxed, contented and safe in Marcus's arms.

They made love again before Marcus suggested mugs of hot chocolate, which they took to the comfortable sofa in the living room. It was then that Marcus remembered his portmanteau in the loggia. 'Forgive me a moment Elizabeth while I bring in my luggage. I have a special gift for you, a birthday present for Rosie and something for Harriett.

Lizzie excitedly unwrapped her gift from Marcus. It revealed a most elegant and fashionable Rosewood portable desk with brass inlaid lines and a beautiful flush fitting handle which spoke quality and exquisite craftsmanship. There were many compartments and a writing slope with two inkwells, a pen tray and a rising tray with a splendid lid. Plush velvet covered blocks divided the box into sections for stamps, nibs and squares of blotting paper. In addition, a removable mirror formed the back panel. This hid the trade label – *'N Starkey, Manufacturer of portable desks, dressing cases, medicine chests and ladies work boxes. 66 South Fourth Street, Philadelphia'.* 'Oh Marcus it's truly wonderful! I hope my handwriting skills are up to the task of complementing this magnificent desk.'

Marcus was pleased with her reaction. 'I am so glad you like it. I know how much you love to write to friends and relatives. The only person I hope you never have to write to again is me! Well, perhaps little notes, but not letters which take weeks to arrive.'

Lizzie laughed, the tiny lines at the corners of her eyes crinkled, lighting up her face. 'You are right, I lived to receive *your* letters, but prefer you here with me.'

Marcus studied her face closely, encouraged by the love he saw in her eyes and the warmth in her smile. 'You may have noticed that I haven't had the cartouche inscribed,' he paused to kneel at her feet before taking hold of her hand. 'That's because, Elizabeth Cameron, I am hoping your new initials will reflect the fact that you will shortly become my wife?'

Lizzie responded passionately. 'Oh Marcus, yes, yes I will. Let's set a date soon!

Marcus pulled her close and kissed her softly. 'What do you think to the 1st March 1856? It's a 'Leap' year and the 1st is a Saturday. We could marry in the village church and honeymoon at the Adelphi Hotel.'

Lizzie glowed with happiness and tears of joy formed in her eyes. 'That's perfect Marcus, just perfect.'

'If you agree, we'll announce our official engagement to the family on Christmas Day?'

Lizzie wanted to tell the world now, but Christmas Day, with the family gathered together, seemed the ideal moment. 'I agree! This year had its fair share of announcements, some, unfortunately were devastating for the family, but everyone will welcome our news. Until then it will remain our secret. There is so much I have to tell you that I found hard to write in my letters, but, tonight we can spend time catching up, after Rosie is in bed…speaking of Rosie, I think I just heard a coach drive up, the girls will be back from their shopping trip. You need to prepare yourself for an onslaught,' joked Lizzie, as she rose to open the door.

Marcus seated himself in his favourite armchair, which looked onto the garden from the French Doors. He loved the element of surprise.

Amy, Robert, Rosie and Harriett piled into the hall, weighed down by parcels of varying sizes. Robert, as astute as ever, spotted the portmanteau at the side of the hall dresser, but remained silent. He quickly surmised that Lizzie had a surprise for Rosie, who was too busy embracing her mother and telling her about their expedition to notice. Lizzie released her daughter's arms from around her neck and said 'I have a surprise for you Rosie. Come through to the sitting room, there is someone who wants to say 'hello'.'

Robert indicated to Amy that she should wait in the hall, as he felt this special moment belonged to his elder daughter.

Rosie wasn't expecting a visitor and John was not due to return until after Christmas and Jimmy...well, Jimmy just wasn't expected. That only left Marcus, but he wasn't due for another week. Intrigued, she followed Lizzie to the sitting room. She quickly scanned the 'empty' room. 'It's a joke mam, there's no one here,' she laughed, but a second later, the high backed chair positioned near the window swivelled round to reveal - 'Marcus!' she exclaimed and ran to embrace him.

'Rosie, it is so good to see you. My, you are all grown up, where has our little girl gone? Who is this lovely young lady?' he winked, as he gathered her into his arms.

'It's still me inside Marcus, but I am fourteen now, so yes, I have grown up.'

It wasn't long before Amy, Robert and Harriett joined them.

Robert shook Marcus's hand. 'It is good to see you again. You will never know how much Lizzie has missed you. I am so glad to welcome you home.'

Marcus reciprocated. 'It's good to be back Robert, but I do have some idea how my absence has affected everyone.' He moved to kiss Amy on the cheek. 'Amy, you are looking as lovely as ever. Can I get you both a drink? A small brandy Robert and perhaps some vintage Port for Amy, which I know you will enjoy.'

It was still early evening but as this was a special occasion, drinks were in order. 'Thanks Marcus that would be most welcome. The girls wear out the most determined of shoppers, even Amy. She was flagging quite early on, but as most women love to shop, what can one do?' He said mischievously as he engaged Amy's eyes good-humouredly.

'It's true Robert, we do love to shop,' she laughed, 'but as the girls have such energy they try everything they see. No doubt, there will be a fashion parade after tea.' Amy was pleased as 'Punch' that Marcus was home again, as it was sometimes difficult to support Lizzie and keep her positive, during his absence. She couldn't imagine Robert being away for half a year or more. She missed him dreadfully, even when he was only away on business for the weekend. During his tireless search for Kate she had felt his absence even more acutely, so was relieved that the search was finally over.

Marcus dispensed the drinks and mixed a 'special' for Rosie, a small sweet white wine topped with lemonade and lemonade with a dash of lime for Harriett.

Lizzie was patient and played the perfect hostess. She served Elspeth's homemade shortbread along with muffins for the girls, but secretly craved an evening alone with Marcus. Whenever the opportunity arose, they stood close to one another and touched hands, in anticipation of spending at least some of the night together in a passionate embrace.

Chapter Nineteen

Fernando de Noronah[44] *September-December 1855*

Jimmy felt the full force of a heavy salty wave as it swept across his face. He knew he must fight to stay alive and frantically scanned the maelstrom. Astoundingly, the mangled remains of a small wooden boat's hull was floating towards him. With a huge effort he caught hold of a shattered plank, totally astonished at his luck. Painfully he heaved himself aboard and lay there exhausted. Adjusting his salt encrusted eyes he located some gash rope and timber cresting another wave a short distance away, the sad remains of a fishing vessel, its sails and mast already lost beneath the waves. The next time they crested, he made a successful grab, securing the items alongside.

As suddenly as the squall hit, the sea calmed. He was alone, drifting in and out of consciousness, still clinging to his hastily fabricated makeshift wood and rope raft. Time seemed insignificant, but several hours had passed as he floated aimlessly across the wide expanse of ocean. His subconscious played tricks as thoughts of his family flashed

---

[44] *Fernando de Noronah* is an archipelago of 21 islands and islets in the Atlantic Ocean, 354 km (220 mi) offshore from the Brazilian coast. The area is a special municipality (*distrito estadual*) of the Brazilian state of Pernambuco.

into his mind through one endless night and into the following day. Would he ever see his mother again, or Rosie, sweet innocent Rosie, the girl he wanted to marry as soon as they were able? What if he died out here alone? No one would know of his plight, his angst or his fight for life. His body may never be found and it would be months before anyone could say for sure that he had perished. No, he would not allow it to happen. He needed to get a grip of himself. Should he sing to prevent losing consciousness? Yes, that's it, he would sing. What would he sing? He couldn't think of a single song. What did he sing at school? He couldn't remember. *Think Jimmy, think...* Then suddenly a tune popped into his head from nowhere and he began to sing out loud -

'What shall we do wi a drunken sailor,
What shall we do wi a drunken sailor,
What shall we do wi a drunken sailor,
Early in the morning?

Weigh heigh and up she rises
Weigh heigh and up she rises
Weigh heigh and up she rises
Early in the morning'

My God, he thought, *where did that come from?* Then he remembered it was old Josh who taught him the words. He knew he was hallucinating, but still imagined Josh drifting towards him. He called out, 'Josh, Josh, ovver here, come on, I'm ovver here.' Then the vision disappeared and slowly his eyes closed again. He felt comfortable in this twilight state, he could just sleep and sleep...when suddenly a wave swept spray across his face and his eyes opened wide. *Stay awake*

Jimmy, you must stay awake. Keep singing...what is the next verse? Oh yes...

'Chuck 'im in the long boat till he's sober...
Chuck 'im in the long-boat and make him bale her...'

What would he give to be in a long boat at this very moment? He continued singing for a while, but again shut his eyes. He imagined he was back home, walking along the street where he lived in Nottingham, with Rosie by his side. Only it wasn't the Rosie he knew. This Rosie was a grown woman and she was holding the hand of a small child, a girl with golden curls, who gazed up at her chuckling with delight. Who was she? Then the vision ended abruptly and he reluctantly acknowledged his plight once more. He tried in vain to recapture the moment, but it was too late, it was gone.

※

Much later, as the sun rose above the horizon, he tentatively opened one eye and observed his own salt encrusted and battered body, but wait, could that be land? Jimmy raised himself on his elbows and squinting, sighted a stretch of golden beach and not too distant. The waves seemed to caress the white sand, forming curious ridges. Jimmy steeled himself and paddled furiously, using a small piece of shattered planking, until the sparkling surf propelled him into the shallows. He dragged and crawled his way up the beach until, exhausted, he reached a safe location above the tide line and lay there for several hours. Grains of sand carried on the warm wind coursed over his bruised and sunburnt body, which caused pinpricks of blood to surface on his exposed skin.

Subconsciously, he became aware of voices and painfully raised his head to see the startled eyes of a young woman, which spoke volumes as to his dishevelled and distressed state. Her tangled dark hair fell forward over her face as she knelt at his side. Jimmy, trying hard to remain conscious, was bemused because she spoke to him in her native Portuguese, so he said nothing. His lack of response prompted her to instruct her companion, a younger girl, to fetch help, who immediately dropped the wood she was collecting and ran off. Then she offered Jimmy some water from a bottle flask, which he gulped down, until she indicated that small sips were better for him.

Although disoriented, Jimmy absently noticed the younger girl's footprints, which led to a clearing before disappearing into a small hut. It wasn't long before she returned with a rough blanket to place carefully over his body. Minutes later they were joined by two men. Their concerned chatter was also indistinguishable to Jimmy, so partly in fear and partly in prudent self-preservation, he decided on silence until their intentions became clear.

However, he need not have worried, their only intention was to lift Jimmy onto a makeshift stretcher. Unfortunately, their efforts caused a sharp pain to shoot up from his ankle to his knee and he winced in agony, before the men gently lowered him back onto the sand.

Their conversation left Jimmy in a state of bewilderment, but he no longer felt threatened, as he adjusted his position on the warm supporting sand. Unfortunately, he didn't have a clear indication of their intentions either, until one of the men returned with two sticks and some bandages for a splint, which he expertly positioned around Jimmy's leg. The pain became less intense as they carried the stretcher from the beach and into a primitive hut, before carefully lowering it to the fibrous matting floor.

One man attempted to communicate and pointed to his leg, but Jimmy was still having difficulty comprehending. In his best 'pigeon', he pointed out to sea and tried to explain his predicament. 'Ship...overboard...drifted here,' embellishing his limited vocabulary with humorous hand motions.

They watched his antics with raised eyebrows, until one man understood his meaning. 'You sailor?' he grinned and inexplicably began dancing the hornpipe.

A delighted Jimmy nodded. 'Yes, yes, sailor...ship...Merchantman.'

The group threw back their heads and laughed loudly, while the woman with the dark hair lifted her skirts and joined in the dancing. Jimmy looked on appreciatively, until his leg wound caused him to grimace in pain. The woman stopped dancing and tugged at the lead man's arm to alert him to Jimmy's plight. There was a short consultation and both men left the hut. The woman then pointed to herself and spoke her name. 'Renata, Chamo-me[45] Renata,' followed by 'Meu nome de irmãs é Delfina',[46] and smiling, she pointed to the young girl. Then quizzically cocking her head she encouraged Jimmy to respond.

Jimmy obliged. 'Me Jimmy', he said, returning her smile.

Renata smiled again, her beautiful brown eyes glinting mischievously. 'Prazer em conhecê-la,[47] Jimmy,' then 'meu nome irmãos é Demetrio,'[48] she said laughing.

---

45 Call me Renata
46 My sister's name is Delfina
47 Pleased to meet you.
48 My brother's name is Demetrio.

Jimmy was intrigued. He was drawn to this woman, with her thick dark hair, olive skin and fascinating eyes, despite his wound and the circumstances of their meeting.

The men had still not returned so Renata instructed Delfina to bring chimarrão,[49] which had a soporific effect on Jimmy.

After Delfina left, Renata sat next to him and held his hand. She began smoothing his brow, which Jimmy found strangely exciting. He had no idea where he was, but apart from the pain in his leg, he was unquestionably enjoying this unexpected sojourn. He tried to guess Renata's age, possibly twenty, he thought, older than himself...definitely, but my, she knew how to arouse a man. Jimmy found himself concentrating on the pain in his leg, to take his mind off the undeniable sexual feelings building inside him. Unfortunately, circumstances dictated his next response because the men returned with a distinguished looking man, wearing a light beige suit and carrying a large black bag. He couldn't be sure, therefore, if he was relieved or disappointed.

Renata introduced the man to Jimmy. 'Este é o médico, Jimmy.' Jimmy caught the word 'médico' so assumed he was a doctor. Again he attempted to explain his circumstances in decipherable fashion, but was surprised when the doctor addressed him in fluent English.

'Hello Jimmy, I am Doctor Berredo. This is an island in the archipelago of Fernando de Noronah. I am pleased to make your acquaintance,' he said, shaking Jimmy by the hand.

Jimmy responded. 'Oh, well, me name's Jimmy...Jimmy Mi...Marsh and am a sailor off the 'Lightning'...well a was,

---

[49] An infused drink made from dried yerba maté leaves.

until a dived ovvaboard ta save a friend, then I found missen cast adrift, but managed ta cling on ta a piece o' wreckage which is 'ow a came ta be on these shores.'

The doctor fought to conceal his mirth. He had never heard an accent quite like Jimmy's before, but he warmed to the brave young man who lay before him, obviously in extreme pain. He tried to reassure his patient. 'Well now Jimmy, I'd like to take a look at that leg of yours and see what we can do to fix it.'

Dr Berredo scrutinised Jimmy's leg. 'Mmm, the thing is Jimmy, I believe your leg is fractured and I don't have all the necessary equipment in my bag to set the leg straight, albeit the splint is doing a good job.' He removed a bottle from his bag and poured a small amount of the contents onto a spoon. 'Take this Jimmy, it will alleviate the pain, but you really need to be hospitalized. That's easier said than done, given our location, but you were lucky I happened to be on the island today. I call here once a month in case anyone requires my assistance. The best thing will be to take you back with me to Natal, where there is a very good clinic. See that schooner out in the bay? that's my transport around the islands. We leave for Natal this afternoon where you can recover and wait for another ship to take you back to England. How does that sound?' asked the doctor kindly.

Jimmy sighed with relief. 'I'm much obliged ta yer sir. 'Ow long da yer reckon it'ull be before a ship docks that'ull be mecking its way ter England, Dr Berredo?'

The doctor shrugged. 'I'm not too sure Jimmy, but we are only talking a few weeks, I'd wager. It's a busy port now that coffee is a popular commodity. It's exported around the world, so it's big business Jimmy. Brazil exports sugar, cotton, tobacco, cocoa, rubber, and maté, which I believe you have already tasted?' grinned Dr Berredo spotting the empty vessel. 'I see Renata *has* looked after you well.'

Jimmy winked secretively at Renata. 'Oh yes, am very grateful fer everyone's assistance.'

'Well now,' said Dr Berredo knowingly, 'I suggest you rest while I continue with my rounds. I'll leave you in good hands until I return.' In an instant he had disappeared through the makeshift door.

Demetrio and Ramirez took the doctor's lead and left Renata alone with Jimmy. He still felt slightly uncomfortable, as conversation was stilted without Dr Berredo to translate, but he need not have been concerned, as conversation was the last thing on Renata's mind. She poured him a second chimarrão, and added a drop of golden liquid from a small flask secreted in her pocket.

Jimmy felt very relaxed and comfortable, as Renata caressed his brow and traced her fingers lightly across his shoulders. Jimmy fought to control his urges as the stroking and massaging intensified. Without a word, Renata took his hand and placed it on her breast. Jimmy was surprised and for a second almost pulled his hand away, but she leaned forward and kissed him softly on the lips. Jimmy responded eagerly and audaciously contemplated moving his hand between her legs, but then immediately felt guilty as thoughts of Rosie invaded his mind. *What was he thinking?* Rosie would be heartbroken if she ever found out. He would tell her...yes, he would be honest and tell her of his little indiscretion...as soon as he saw her again. He would say he wasn't himself and could she possibly forgive him. At all costs, he needed to resist and remain faithful to Rosie. It was indeed fortuitous that moments later, the two men returned to the hut and Renata hastily fastened her blouse. A conversation in Portugese ensued, interspersed with the name 'Dr Berredo'.

The men lifted Jimmy on to a stretcher, which left him in no doubt that Dr Berredo was to leave earlier than expected. Thank God he had managed some restraint. It could have been a very awkward moment, as he wasn't even sure of the relationship between Renata and the two men.

His mind in turmoil, he had no time to dwell on what might have been, as the doctor appeared, instructing that Jimmy be taken to his small craft, moored at a rickety jetty, further along the beach.

Safely ensconced aboard, he again thanked the islanders for their kindness, with a special squeeze of Renata's hand for good luck. She reciprocated by removing a charm, hanging from a narrow piece of leather around her neck and placing it over Jimmy's head. 'Isto é para você Jimmy para mantê-lo seguro. Espero que voltaremos a encontrar novamente algum dia.'[50] Then kissed him lightly on the cheek, in farewell.

Dr Berredo, translated, which gave Jimmy the chance to reply. 'Thank you, thank you Renata. I will treasure it always and if I travel this way agen, well...yer never know...goodbye,' said Jimmy wistfully, recalling something John had said to him on the Lightning - *'so if you can be attracted to another woman, maybe Rosie isn't the one,'* which, at the time, he'd dismissed as ridiculous, but on the way over to the schooner, Jimmy's thoughts turned to Rosie. He loved her...he did... with all his heart. What was wrong with him? How had this stranger been able to rouse feelings in him after such a brief encounter?

---

[50] Jimmy this is for you to keep you safe. I hope we will meet again some day.

Both he and Rosie were virgins...as far as he knew. That was it, he decided, he just wished it *was* Rosie. He really needed to let her know the intensity of his feelings. Would it be wrong if they were to make love...did she want to? Just then, the pain, which had subsided following the first dose of the liquid draft the doctor called laudanum, began to return.

'Are you all right Jimmy?' Dr Berredo enquired, then added 'we are almost there and once aboard the schooner, I will give you some more laudanum.'

Jimmy was far from all right, in fact, at that particular moment, wished his leg could be chopped off. The pain was acute and radiated from his ankle to his knee. 'Will the pain continue after the bone is set?' he asked anxiously.

'No Jimmy, it will subside considerably, don't worry,' smiled Dr Berredo. 'Meanwhile, I will try to control the pain and make you more comfortable.'

Jimmy languished at the clinic for several weeks when news arrived of a ship that would take him to England. His slow recovery was due to some initial problems in straightening his leg prior to the plaster cast being applied. The makeshift splints and the rough crossing from Fernando de Noronha had not assisted his recovery either and, additionally, the doctors' had concerns regarding Jimmy's mental attitude. His reluctance to use crutches, which restricted his movements, did not help his convalescence. He was happier careering around in a wheelchair[51], despite warnings that

---

51 In 1783, John Dawson of Bath, England, invented a wheelchair named after the town of Bath. Dawson designed a chair with two large wheels and one small one.

he should master walking with crutches to improve his mobility. However, Jimmy was unconcerned. He would, he said be back on his feet, on his return to England, although he had, at present, no idea where he would go to recuperate, or when that would be.

Dr Berredo visited Jimmy very early on the day before he was to embark on a fast schooner to England. The doctor had good news for his patient. 'Good morning Jimmy. How are you today?' he said, smiling and shaking Jimmy by the hand.

Jimmy shuffled up the bed into a sitting position. 'All right, Dr Berredo. At least as well as ta be expected. The clinic doctor is still a bit worried about me progress, burras a toad 'im, me improvement will come when a get 'omm ta England. Although, am not too sure, where 'omm 'ull be. I don't want ter worry me mam, nor me girlfriend, Rosie. As yet, they don't know what's 'appened ter me. Ferrawl they know, am still on the ship. I've 'ad alot of time ter think Dr Berredo and it might be berra all round if they remain ignorant abaht me whereabouts, 'til 'ave recovered.'

Dr Berredo looked puzzled. 'Why, Jimmy, surely you want them informed? After all, the 'Lightning' will have docked in Liverpool by now and you won't arrive for a while yet. Their first priority will have been to inform your relatives of your apparent demise. That shouldn't have taken long, as excellent communication exists nowadays.'

Jimmy considered Dr Barredo's statement, but did not alert him to the fact that the authorities would be unable to inform his mam, as he had given them a false name. 'Al think abaht it, but a might be able ter tell 'em missen soon,' shrugged Jimmy, as ever hopeful of a speedy recovery in England.

'Well it's your decision, but I have some good news about your convalescence. I was speaking to a colleague of mine by telegraph and mentioned how you came to be here, with particular reference to how you dived in to the sea to save a friend. He was very impressed and suggested making contact with the 'Seamen's Hospital Society'. That's a Christian organisation, which would arrange for you to recuperate aboard the hospital ship, the 'Dreadnought', presently anchored at Greenwich Reach. You would be well looked after Jimmy and, when fully recovered, they will give you money and clothing to help you begin again.'

Jimmy pondered the information. 'Greenwich Reach? I've heard of that before, but a can't remember where. Sounds ok, but, as soon as am fit, I will be signing on another ship,' Jimmy declared with certainty.

Dr Berredo was silent for a few moments, before commenting sympathetically. 'Jimmy, you may not be able to sign on again. That depends very much on your progress, because at present, you lack the determination to get out of that chair and on to your feet. You need to start walking with crutches to strengthen the muscles in your good leg. Muscles weaken very quickly during times of inactivity. You may have an aversion to the crutches because they slow you down, but perhaps it is something more complex?'

Jimmy looked puzzled, but remained silent as Dr Berredo continued his summation. 'If I didn't know what a determined young man you were, I'd say, for whatever reason, you do not seem in the right frame of mind to meet the challenge. You suffered from a fever on arrival, but thankfully that passed. You need to become mobile again and that means with crutches. So what's wrong Jimmy? Is there something else bothering you?'

Jimmy lowered his eyelids and looked sheepishly at Dr Berredo. 'I...it's just...' Jimmy stammered.

'It's just what Jimmy?' encouraged Dr Berredo. 'Don't be embarrassed. I've heard all sorts of reasons from men who need to recover their motivation.'

Jimmy pursed his lips before continuing. 'It's just that... am scared ov failure Dr Berredo. When a first came 'ere, a did try out the crutches. A wanted the toilet and tha were no one arahnd, so a hobbled off dahn the corridor, but somehow, the crutch went from under me and a finished up on the floor. No one came fer ages and finally a young nurse appeared...she had to clear up the mess...yer know...a cudn't meck it. It wah undignified, a din't want ter risk it agen,' muttered Jimmy, colouring up in embarrassment.

Dr Berredo gave a wry smile. 'Oh Jimmy, Jimmy, the nurse wouldn't have seen it that way. It's her job. She wouldn't have given it a second thought. They have dealt with far worse, I can assure you.'

Dr Berredo breathed a huge sigh of relief. 'Well, at least it's not psychological. We have been worried that you may have had a psychological problem that was preventing you walking. Sometimes this kind of accident can have a devastating effect on the mind and some patients never walk again. The tragic thing is, it *is* all in their mind, but they cannot accept that and believe it is physical. Thank God, this is not the case. Now Jimmy show me what you can do,' ordered Dr Berredo.

Jimmy shuffled to the edge of the bed and placing a crutch under each arm, stood up gingerly. With encouragement from Dr Berredo, he manoeuvred across the ward. 'Bravo, Jimmy, bravo,' shouted the doctor as Jimmy exited the ward.

The *Dreadnought* housed 400 convalescing patients. Jimmy occupied a hammock on the main deck, which had easy access via the companionway to the weather deck. Originally, he was given the choice of the surgical ward on the middle deck, with substantial beds, or a hammock, but despite the difficulty of actually getting in and out of the hammock, the main deck gave ease of access to other areas of the ship. Consequently, Jimmy used this to his advantage and moved around freely. He would sit out on the promenade deck, weather permitting whenever he chose.

This ship was hugely different to the 'Lightning'. The stark white bareness of the bulkheads and the lack of rigging seemed extremely odd, but the positive aspect was a clear, broad promenade, for those well enough to enjoy it. Large and lofty skylights framed the upper deck, which also enjoyed enlarged portholes. In addition, by 1855, all heads and bathrooms had been moved forward on all three decks, which dramatically improved hygiene and, possibly, the 'atmosphere' too. The staff were professional and the wards kept meticulously clean. On the lower decks were ten rows of beds, in a fore and aft configuration, occupied by men at different stages of recovery. All beds had a brown coverlet, above which was a board marked with the patient's name, his diet and time and date of admission.

Quite a deviation from the 'Lightning' thought Jimmy as he moved gingerly along the main deck to his hammock, cursing the 'dam' crutches under his breath. Some of the other patients were sitting up smoking pipes or reading and others dozed languidly. Convalescing, he mused, affected everyone in differing ways. He wondered how long *he* would have to stay and hoped it wouldn't be too long. At least it would give him chance to become a whole man again… worthy of Rosie's love. Rosie…what should he do about

Rosie? Should he get word to her that he was here? What if John had already delivered the news of his untimely death? He hoped fervently he hadn't, but even so, a million thoughts still milled around inside his head. Fortunately, he was lulled to sleep that first night by the gentle rocking, familiar creaking and splashing sounds associated with shipboard life.

England was experiencing warmer weather than usual for the end of November, so, the next day, Jimmy rose early and managed to reach the promenade via the companionway, before making himself comfortable on a deckchair. Sunrise came and he relaxed for almost an hour, enjoying the quiet solitude and the light soporific offshore breeze. Later, the wind strengthened and Jimmy became more alert, sitting up to take in his surroundings. No large expanse of ocean, just a wide river, edged by large buildings and smoking chimneys. He concentrated his thoughts and decided to write to Rosie and his mother. Unfortunately, he had neither a pen nor paper, but as soon as the opportunity presented itself, he would ask one of the nurses to obtain the items. He didn't have to wait long. Two young nurses approached, walking the promenade, obviously taking in the fresh air, before going on duty.

The taller of the two glanced at Jimmy as they neared. She grinned and nudged her friend, alerting her of the new arrival. 'He's quite cute[52] isn't he?' whispered Helen.

Lucinda glanced briefly at Jimmy. 'Can't really tell. Just like all the others, his face is hidden by a beard.'

---

52 *Cute (first recorded 1731-first used in relation to female/male 1838)*

To their surprise, the conversation was interrupted by Jimmy, who waved them over. 'Hello there, can yer help me?' smiled Jimmy.

Helen sauntered over, leaving Lucinda leaning over the Bulwark rail. 'What is it sir?' she asked of the familiar looking patient.

Jimmy's mouth fell open abruptly and he nearly fell off his chair, but recovered, swiftly. He pulled his coat higher around his neck because he'd immediately realised he had met this woman before, in Australia. It was Helen, one of the British nurses John had taken a shine to, which meant Lucinda was probably the other young woman leaning over the rail. He hoped Helen hadn't recognised him but, if she asked, he would give her a false name. 'I wonder if yer could get me a pen and some paper. I need ter write a letter to me mam?' he asked quietly.

Helen became curious. 'Of course sir,' she paused, peering closer at Jimmy's face. 'Have we met before?'

Jimmy groaned inwardly, but was quick with his reply. 'No...no I don't think so. I would have remembered such a pretty face.'

Helen blushed. 'What is your name, sir?' she asked, coyly.

'Me name?...oh well, me name's David.' He blushed and wished he had not engaged with her so readily.

'Well...David, that's a nice name, but doesn't ring any bells. I suppose I must be mistaken, but I will bring you the pen and paper, I just have time to fetch them before I start my duties,' said Helen with an agreeable smile, before signalling to Lucinda that they should return to their quarters.

Jimmy watched the girls disappear down the companionway, as he asked himself why he didn't want to be recognised. Did it matter? He wasn't sure, but felt he didn't need any more complications in his life; that much he did know.

There wasn't an alternative, other than to keep up the pretence and hope to pull it off. He had a lot to think about and didn't need any distractions. The best idea would be to concentrate on his recovery and plan his reunion with Rosie.

Several minutes elapsed before Helen returned with the pen, paper and a small bottle of ink. She was obviously in a hurry so spoke only briefly. 'Here you are David. I hope there is enough paper and, oh, I've included two envelopes.'

Helen handed over the items with a smile before walking back to the companionway. 'Thanks...thanks alot. What do I owe you?' shouted Jimmy, as she disappeared from view.

Helen popped her head back around the door. 'Nothing... it's okay. I don't do much writing these days. Anyway, I have to start my rota now, but I hope to see you later. By the way, I don't often get the chance to come up here, as I am mostly on the lower medical deck, but sometimes we are needed elsewhere.'

Jimmy heaved a sigh of relief, he had got away with it. Now he felt more relaxed and able to focus his mind on the task in hand. This would only be the second letter he had written to his mam, the first being full of his exploits. He would try not to worry her but was unsure what to say about his condition. He knew his spelling left a lot to be desired, but he persevered anyway.

Dear mam, Hope yer well. The pasage 'ome was not as plesant as the outward one. The thing is, there wah a kinda storm mam and a met wi a sort of axident. A dont no if yer aldredy ad news from me friend John. Anyrode yu'll be pleased ter no am safe. At the minit am on a ospital ship on the tems. A broke me leg divin ovver bord tring ter save me mate and got washd up on an iland. Ter cut a long story short a finished up ere. A expect ter be here a bit yet but ope ter see yer in a month or so. Am luckin forwood ter seein yer agen mam. Av reely mist yer. Anyrode teck care. Yaw lovin son Jimmy xxx

Jimmy read the letter through twice, quite pleased with how it turned out, but knew that some words were probably spelt differently and that some commas were missing, but, overall, she would get the gist. He folded the paper in half and pushed it into one of the envelopes on which he printed the address. He hoped he had remembered it correctly, before he smoothed out another sheet. The second letter would be even harder to write, but write it he must.

Me darlin Rosie, I ope yer ar well. Be now yer will probly here of the acident ave ad. I expect John as let yer no. The thing is yer musnt wurry abowt me cos am all rite. Well, not exacly all rite, buram gerrin there. A miss yer so much Rosie, my butiful Rosie. A thort abowt yer evry day a wa away from yer. Ad da enythin nar ter hold yer in me arms and feel yer soft skin agen mine. A feel sad we not tergever rite this minit. Am on a ospital ship darn south ter convaless a think thats the rite word forrit. Pleas excuse me spelin and me writin as ave not ed much chance ter practis. But Rosie even tho am no gud at writin, wot a am gud at is luving yo Rosie. Mor nah than eva befor. Me hart akes fer yer and a ope yer still feel the same as me. Anyrode it mite be sum time befor wi cun be tergever agen my love. Yud not reconise me rite nar, wot we me groin a beerd. Not shor yud like it it tickls like mad. Wunt be no gud fer yer soft skin Rosie...ah ah...ad like ter gi it a try. Well thats enuff fer nah me love cos a wont ter cach the post. Am goin ter gi the to leters ter sum one ter post. Av writ one ter me mam as well. A will rite agen soon ma luvly girl. Teck care ov yersenn. Love ferever Rosie yaws Jimmy xxxxxxxxxxxxx

Jimmy re-read the letter to Rosie several times. The first time he crumpled it in his hand and was about to throw it away, embarrassed by what he had written, then he had second thoughts. She would be so worried, he had to bite the bullet and let her know he was okay and make it plain how he felt about her. They would be apart for much longer than he envisaged and he didn't want any other potential suitor muscling in, so he carefully smoothed and folded the single sheet and placed it in the envelope. Just as he was getting up to go back to the main deck, an older nurse ambled by. Would she post them for him? He could only ask. 'Errm...nurse, could yer help me?' Jimmy asked hopefully.

'Well now young man and what can I do for you?' she enquired, pausing to put a small bottle into her pocket. 'Is it a drink you'll be wanting? because we aren't allowed to give you any alcohol.'

Jimmy grinned. 'No...no I don't need a drink. I just wondered how I get letters posted?'

'Letters? You want me to post some letters for you? Give them here and I'll make sure they go when one of the staff gets leave of absence. I can't guarantee it will be today, but maybe in a couple of days' time. A friend of mine is going to visit her sick mother and she's been given special dispensation. I am sure she would post them for you,' she smiled taking the letters and placing them in her pocket.

Jimmy grinned. 'Thanks alot, am very grateful ter yer.'

A relieved Jimmy considered he had accomplished a task he never thought he would manage. Letters were the only way he could let his mam and Rosie know he was all right. It was out of the question that he use official channels, as he could still be a 'wanted' man. Satisfied that he had undertaken an arduous task without serious risk of discovery, he spent the rest of the morning thinking lascivious thoughts of the girl he knew he would marry one day.

༺༻

The next week flew by swiftly as Jimmy became more confident and familiar in his surroundings. The staff were a friendly bunch and he soon learned the routine.

The following Tuesday he saw the older nurse, who he now knew as Maud, walking unsteadily towards him on the promenade deck. If he didn't know better, he would think she had been drinking.

She gave him a cheery wave before sitting on the deck chair next to him. Jimmy studied her closely. Maud was a rotund woman of indeterminable age, with a ruddy complexion and untidy hair scraped up into a bun. Her nurses hat perched precariously on top of her head, held there by two hatpins. She had kindly eyes, but her skin was leathery and her nose slightly crooked. Jimmy thought she must be at least fifty. She looked uncomfortable because wrinkled folds of skin were straining to escape from the starched collar of her uniform and the whole ensemble seemed an immediate threat to the top button. Jimmy stifled a sudden urge to laugh but distracted himself by enquiring about the letters she had promised to post. Her reply lacked any semblance of understanding. 'What letters are them?' she asked blankly.

Jimmy felt uneasy. 'The letters I gave you to post the other week,' emphasised Jimmy with a sinking feeling.

Maud conveyed an air of uncertainty and peered closely at Jimmy. Suddenly, a cloud lifted and her memory returned. 'Ah...yes...those letters... well, I gave them to me friend and...and she said she would post them...yes that's right...she said as soon as she could find a post box, she'd be sure to put them in.' She finished with a flourish by folding her hands on her lap, completely satisfied with her explanation.

Jimmy frowned, he wasn't confident with the tale, so persevered. 'When did yer friend leave the ship?' he asked.

The nurse presented Jimmy with a crooked smile, revealing a set of yellowing teeth. 'Er..let me see...oh yes, it would be a week as Friday last. She got dispensation to see her sick mother.'

Jimmy felt relieved, as Maud clearly remembered the date, or appeared to at least. In actual fact, he didn't really have a clue what 'a week as Friday last' meant. 'Oh well, thanks fer that. A suppose the letters ull be received any day nah then?'

Maud smiled. 'Ooh aye yes, I expect so. The post office are quite efficient I understand.'

Jimmy then fell silent and looked across the river to the far bank. He was wondering what Rosie would make of his letter writing, until he was rudely jolted out of his reverie when Maud stood up abruptly to mutter goodbye, before making her way unsteadily to the companionway, where she looked back at Jimmy, guiltily. His letters were 'burning a hole' in her pocket! Unforgivably but significantly, another week would pass before they would be posted.

A week later, Jimmy was still awaiting word from his mother and Rosie. His mood cast shadows over his demeanour and he spent less time on the promenade deck. He took to lounging in his hammock for long periods of the day and mulled over possible reasons why they'd not responded. Unfortunately, the consequence of his inactivity would undermine the healing process.

Three days of heavy rainfall followed until the sun made an unexpected appearance. It streamed through the portholes and bathed the deck in a spectacular orange glow. Jimmy woke early, to a scene that immediately lifted his spirits. For once he dressed eagerly and took a walk on the promenade. The warm rays and the fresh offshore breeze reinforced his determination to mend his body and mind and re-establish his relationship with Rosie. He leant over the ships rail, his eyes drawn to a flock of seagulls haggling over some fish heads, dumped in the river by local fishermen. The birds squawked in a determined mêlée, fighting over the eyeless, bony remains...eager to take the merest tiny morsel on offer in order to survive, in stark contrast to Jimmy, who had allowed life to pass him by whilst cooped up aboard the hulk. He contemplated his present dilemma, that the longer he remained, the longer it would take him to become whole again and be reunited with Rosie and his mam.

He was considering his position, when he sensed the presence of someone standing close to him, near the bulkhead. Jimmy turned rapidly to see Lucinda's engaging smile. Somewhat startled and surprised, he automatically returned her greeting, but instantly regretted his temporary lapse. Without his overcoat and with his jacket collar laying flat, his face was exposed. Jimmy blushed, it was obviously too late to disguise himself and consequently just stared inadequately at the young woman. Lucinda moved closer, recognising him, despite his beard. 'Jimmy...Jimmy Marsh... it is you isn't it?'

Jimmy, blushed and lowered his eyes, unsure whether to lie his way out of the situation, until inevitably, Helen joined Lucinda. Unbeknown to Jimmy, she'd already queried 'David's' true identity. She'd been unable to find a convalescent of that name, so continued scouring the patient list, until her eyes fixed excitedly on the name of 'James Marsh'. She'd immediately sought Lucinda to break the good news, as both women had hoped to cross paths again with the two men they spent time with in Melbourne. Now, that opportunity had materialised for one of them, with Lucinda keeping a watchful eye out for Jimmy on the promenade deck on her duty days. Frustratingly, she was unable to visit the wards to which she was not assigned and disappointingly, she had not seen him and had begun to wonder if he had been discharged, until their present fortuitous meeting.

The girls giggled at his discomfiture, so there was little point Jimmy denying his identity. 'Er...yes...yer right. I am Jimmy Marsh.' His voice remained flat as he struggled to find an adequate response to the situation in which he found himself.

Helen winked at Lucinda triumphantly. 'I told you so!' Then addressed Jimmy. 'Why on earth did you tell me your name was David?' she paused, 'you weren't trying to hide your identity from me were you?' laughed Helen playfully.

A contrite Jimmy fumbled with his jacket lapel and racked his brain for a suitable explanation. 'I...er...no, of course not...'

An awkward silence ensued as Lucinda's darkly attractive eyes bored into his head. He needed to address their concerns and miraculously he conjured up a plausible excuse. He addressed Helen. 'I weren't sure if I did recognise you when you kindly brought me the pen and paper and would 'ave felt foolish, if I 'ad been mistaken,' offered Jimmy, pleased with the confidence displayed in his voice.

Unfortunately, he wasn't as convincing as he thought, but Lucinda immediately came to his rescue. She realised his dilemma and didn't want to embarrass him needlessly. 'Yes...I see...that's understandable. It's happened to me before,' smiled Lucinda, lowering her lashes with demure deference.

A grateful Jimmy acknowledged the olive branch by unintentionally overegging his reply. 'Has it?...oh I am glad! I only saw *you* from a distance, but now I do remember your warm smile which lights up your eyes...and...your lovely long brown hair.' Jimmy was hardly able to believe he had complimented Lucinda with such gusto. *What was he thinking? He had just decided the path he would take to secure his future, now someone from his not too distant past had made an unwelcome, or was it welcome appearance?*

Lucinda's cheeks glowed with appreciation. 'Thank you, Jimmy. I am glad you remembered.'

At this point, Helen sensed Lucinda might relish being alone with Jimmy, so made a suitable excuse. She strolled off down the companionway, leaving them to become reacquainted.

Lucinda broke the ice. 'What happened to your leg Jimmy? Did you break it?'

Jimmy grinned. 'Aye, yes, I did break it, but am determined to walk unaided as soon as am able. Don't want to stay on this ship a minute more than a 'ave ter.'

Disappointed with his last statement, Lucinda took Jimmy by the arm. 'Shall we sit down for a while. I still have half an hour before I am back on duty.'

Jimmy accepted the invitation and supported by Lucinda gravitated to a small table and two chairs placed against a bulkhead. 'Would you like a cup of tea Jimmy? It will only take a minute. The steward always has the kettle on the boil and I'll take one with you,' Lucinda informed brightly.

'If yer like and it's not too much trouble.' He watched as her retreating figure hurried along the promenade deck. *She's an attractive gel, with a curvy figure*, he thought absently.

Not long after, she returned and placed two cups on the table along with a tantalising treat. 'I managed to persuade the purser to let me have a piece of sponge cake. Would you like some?' she said, cutting the cake and offering half to Jimmy.

'Thanks...me mam allus made sponge cake on a Sunday as a treat,' reminisced Jimmy...*that seemed an awful long while ago* now *and he wondered how long it would be before he would have the opportunity to sit down to tea with his mam again.*

Lucinda interrupted his thoughts. 'Tell me how you came to break your leg Jimmy?'

Jimmy brushed his hand down his plaster. 'Well, the ship wah caught in a bad storm and it wah all 'ands on deck. Me mate, the bosun, lost his footing and fell ovver board. Wi'out thinking, I jumped in after him, but sadly, a cun't save 'im. The sea wah rough and it wah all ovver in seconds. I managed ter cling ta a piece of drift wood and eventually got washed up on a beach on an island near Brazil.'

Lucinda was wide eyed, as she listened intently to Jimmy's story. 'Gosh, Jimmy, it is terrible that your friend didn't survive, but lucky that you did.'

Jimmy grinned sheepishly. 'Well some 'ud say a wah stupid, not brave, but there wasn't time to think about it.'

'Oh Jimmy, well I think you are really brave. What happened to you on the island and how did you arrive here on this hospital ship?' asked Lucinda with enthusiasm.

'There 'appened to be a doctor on the island...Dr Berredo,' said Jimmy, conveniently omitting to include the pleasurable time he spent with Renata. 'He took me ovver by boat to a hospital on the mainland, then arranged for me to board a ship bound for England...and here I am.'

'Yes...here you are', smiled Lucinda encouragingly.

An awkward silence developed, as they lost themselves in their own memories. Lucinda remembered the time spent with Jimmy in Australia and her wish to see him again. Jimmy recalled the period spent on Fernando de Noronah with Renata and the guilt he felt, also his efforts to contact Rosie and his mother. Eventually, he stood up and walked over to the ships rail. Lucinda followed and placed her hand on his arm. 'Have I upset you Jimmy, by encouraging you to relive those awful memories? If so, I am very sorry,' said Lucinda, because she fervently hoped to see him again.

Jimmy remained thoughtful as he observed Lucinda, whose eyes had lost their sparkle. It was obvious to him that she had read more into the lingering kiss in Melbourne. His thoughts were in turmoil. He loved Rosie, but what if she never contacted him again? What if she had found someone else during his long period of absence? Overall, it wasn't looking too good, he had no home, no job and no prospects, hardly a ringing endorsement on which to base a marriage proposal. Should he turn down an attractive woman who sought out his company, in preference to a possible empty dream?

He suddenly became aware that Lucinda was speaking to him. 'Jimmy...Jimmy', she squeezed his arm gently, 'I have to go on duty now. Could we meet tomorrow at the same time? You could use a friend while you are convalescing...I could be that friend Jimmy, if you will let me,' encouraged Lucinda.

Jimmy felt obliged to agree to her suggestion, but after they parted he looked out over the river and deliberated on the alternative path he could tread with Rosie, which would determine his future...

Chapter Twenty

Untold Joy...
December 1855

It was Christmas Eve morning and the family were spending the day together. On Christmas Day, Lizzie and Marcus planned to announce their engagement. A joyous and buoyant Lizzie was clipping sprigs of holly for the vase on the hall table, when a coach drew up unexpectedly in front of 'The Beeches'. The watery sun glistened on John Jamieson's uniform as he stepped down from the carriage. He immediately caught sight of Lizzie and went to greet her.

Lizzie smiled, put down her basket and embraced her nephew. 'John, how wonderful to see you. You obviously received my letter and birthday cards? I am so pleased you're here, because I thought you would be delayed until Saturday. Did you have a pleasant journey?' she asked the handsome young man whom she held in high regard.

'Yes Aunty Lizzie, thanks very much for the cards, although I have postponed my celebrations in anticipation of a wonderful Christmas with all of you.'

'Come through. Rosie will be delighted to see you and Marcus is looking forward to meeting you, although they weren't expecting you until the end of the month. It will be a wonderful surprise for them.'

Lizzie approached the open study door, but was careful to stop short of the entrance, while Elspeth relieved John of his cap and bags.

Rosie and Marcus were seated be any nearer discovering in the drawing room enjoying each others' company. They chatted animatedly, remembering other unforgettable moments shared on Christmas Eve. Tomorrow, the house would welcome more guests for the festivities. Ida had taken the opportunity to return to Derbyshire to spend Christmas with her sister. Amy, Robert and Harriett would be arriving early and would be joined later by Howard, Kate, James and Beatrice. Daniel, Georgina and Victoria were expected later that afternoon in time for a special tea and an evening's entertainment of singing around the piano. A fitting tribute to their first Christmas together since Kate's reunion with the family.

Lizzie was determined that her surprise would ensure maximum impact, so she delayed John's entrance until Rosie and Marcus finished their conversation.

Rosie had her back to the French doors, while Marcus lounged in his favourite leather chair, facing the garden. 'I'm really happy Rosie and I hope you are. I expect we would be happier still if the two people missing from our lives were here to share this special time with us on this perfect day.' Marcus grinned wryly. The thought that his son was still missing troubled him greatly, but he was still prepared to enjoy this momentous occasion unconditionally.

'I am happy Marcus. I have the best parents and you, of course, my very special friend. I've been reunited with my mother and gained another sister,' she paused as she remembered Jimmy, her eyes brimming with tears. 'It's over two months since Jimmy's accident, but John helped me come to terms with the tragedy. It's still painful and

I have dark days, but I know Jimmy would not want me to grieve. He always accepted what life dealt him and I must do the same.'

Lizzie listened cautiously with John by her side and seemed encouraged by Rosie's pragmatism in light of Jimmy's terrible accident.

John had courted Rosie on several occasions since he'd told her the sad news and his feelings had grown from friendship to those of a more intimate nature. He was, however, acutely aware of their solid relationship and realised Rosie still harboured a remote possibility that Jimmy might have survived. He wondered if he could ever be anything more than a friend to her, but fervently believed he could be given the opportunity.

Marcus held Rosie's hand. 'I am so pleased you have found a good friend to help you through this difficult time. I am really looking forward to meeting him. Your mam told me how devoted he is to you since Jimmy...since Jimmy's accident.'

Rosie, grateful that Marcus was so understanding, replied. 'Yes...he is, but Jimmy was my first love. I will never forget him. John has told me that life must go on...and he has been very kind and considerate...but for now, we remain friends.'

Marcus's brows were furrowed in thought when he decided to change the subject. 'John has the same name as my son, Jack. Did you know, that John is another form of Jack?' asked Marcus with interest.

The eavesdroppers exchanged surprised glances, both seemingly unaware of that particular snippet of information. They were still waiting for the right moment to make their entrance, so Lizzie indicated they remain silent by placing a finger to her lips.

Rosie shook her head. 'No...no I didn't know that,' she said repeating the name...Jack...Mmm, it will be my pet name for him. In fact, I shall call him that when we next meet up and surprise him with my knowledge. I feel sure he won't know. I am looking forward to seeing him of course, but he is not due home until the end of the month.'

Lizzie and John grinned conspiratorially until she could bear it no longer. Making her entrance, she announced. 'Marcus...Rosie, I have a lovely surprise for you and stepped back to allow her guest to enter the room.

Rosie, delighted at John's unexpected arrival rushed over to him. 'Hello Jack, how wonderful to see you again,' she teased.

A pre-warned John shook his head in mock surprise. Rosie's eccentric humour was always intriguing and certainly playful. 'You too Rosie, but you seem to have forgotten my name in the short time since we last met.'

Rosie did not explain, but winked at Marcus, who was quizzically observing the visitor.

Lizzie finally made the introductions. 'Marcus, this is my cousin Annabella's son, John.'

Marcus was stunned. He stared incomprehensibly at the young uniformed officer, until the silence became palpable. He tried desperately to assimilate his thoughts...*surely it wasn't possible!...My God the likeness was uncanny!* In a flash of realisation, the truth became abundantly clear...'Annabella...Belle!...John...Jack! My God, it all makes sense now,' he whispered, struggling to acknowledge what was incontestable.

Lizzie looked to John for an explanation, but he appeared mystified by Marcus's behaviour. It was then she saw the indescribable joyous expression on Marcus's face...there was undeniable shock, but his eyes, which had filled with tears, exuded incredible happiness.

John ignoring the somewhat strange atmosphere, smiled warmly and held out his hand in a gesture of friendship. Instantaneously, a shocked Marcus struggled shakily to his feet. He gripped the arm of the chair to steady himself, as a feeling of pure pleasure invaded his whole being. Astoundingly, after all these years, he still recognised his son, Jack Benard! With an overwhelming sense of fulfilment, he strode forward purposefully to shake his hand...

Epilogue

'Two will meet untimely deaths, but the re-acquaintance of the other two will bring untold joy...'

'By 1855 most passenger ships on the New York/Liverpool route were commandeered for the Crimean war effort, with few available for the Atlantic run.

On a cold crisp February morning of that year, a passenger ship, the 'New World', docks at the port of Liverpool. *Oliver Jamison's family, Annabella (Belle Van Der Duim) and John (Jack Benard Van Der Duim)* disembark, before joining the paddle steamer, the 'Princess Royal', for their onward journey to Glasgow. *Marcus Van Der Duim (Annabella's actual husband)* strides purposefully towards the ticket office, intent on booking a cabin for the return sailing to New York. They cross paths, totally oblivious of the others' existence, like elusive shadows manifested in the weak rays of a watery winter sun.'

Lightning Source UK Ltd.
Milton Keynes UK
UKHW012336200819
348297UK00001B/14/P